Terrors Unimagined

An anthology of the Supernatural
and Horrific that oozes past the
boundaries of your imagination.

Edited by Karen T. Newman

Copyright © 2018 Left Hand Publishers, LLC
1417 Sadler Road #245
Fernandina Beach, FL 32034
All rights reserved.
ISBN: 978-1-949241-02-0

https://LeftHandPublishers.com
Twitter.com/LeftHandPublish
Facebook.com/LeftHandPublishers
editor@LeftHandPublishers.com
Cover design by Paul K. Metheney

ACKNOWLEDGMENTS

Special thanks go out to Karen T. Newman, and her company, Newmanuscripts.net, for her tireless efforts in editing, formatting, and compilation. Many kudos to Paul K. Metheney and his company, Metheney Consulting, for invaluable assistance with our cover design and marketing.

Recognition should also go out to our friends and families who tolerated our working hours during the creation of this publication. None of this could have been possible without the creative imaginations and perseverance of the wonderful writers who submitted works to this anthology.

To the readers who purchased this volume, thank you.

Left Hand Publishers Books

Terrors Unimagined
YouTube - https://youtu.be/ow4XfWt2q7w

Drawing from the Well by Rachel A. Bollinger
LHP Web Site - https://bit.ly/2LqIzER
Amazon - https://amzn.to/2th8WGE
Goodreads - https://bit.ly/2M8h57h

A World Unimagined
YouTube - https://youtu.be/2IO3rl0N_q8
LHP Web Site - https://bit.ly/2IG7Dea
Amazon - https://amzn.to/2yvJ4vS
Goodreads - https://bit.ly/2K7b6zj

Beautiful Lies, Painful Truths Vol. I
Amazon - http://amzn.to/2reSyIe
YouTube - https://youtu.be/4m1BR6BIBTM
The Reviews on YouTube - https://youtu.be/tTtdf0LQC7Q
LHP's Web Site - http://bit.ly/2FHXzw9
The Reviews on LHP - http://bit.ly/2FHhMlN
Goodreads - http://bit.ly/2BobVCi

Realities Perceived
Amazon- http://amzn.to/2Dbe1ny
YouTube - https://youtu.be/3SLjzDd9o3Y
LHP's Web Site - http://bit.ly/2Do87SE
Goodreads - http://bit.ly/

Beautiful Lies, Painful Truths Vol. II
Amazon - http://amzn.to/2ngBq0i
YouTube - https://youtu.be/i8dAMSAbkAM
LHP's Web Site - http://bit.ly/2Dxu9n8
Goodreads: http://bit.ly/2slkBpP

The Demon's Angel by Maya Shah
Amazon - http://amzn.to/2EVjj7V
YouTube - https://youtu.be/FZuvbiGjMcU
Maya Shah's Web Site - http://mayashahbooks.com/
LHP's Web Site - http://bit.ly/2DuXieD
Goodreads - http://bit.ly/2son5E2

CONTENTS

Writer's Block
by Brit Jones, United States

I lived. Alone. Every day that I walked into my quicksand apartment, I sank a little lower. I usually made it to the bed. I hadn't changed the sheets in weeks and they stank of sweat and tears. Mostly I put on the same clothes I had on the day before, if I had bothered to take them off the night before. He had left in September and it was winter now, so I didn't smell so bad. He called me a slob, a hack, a loser, and other things before he finally left. I don't miss him. Much.

At the beginning of each month I got my royalty check. I paid the rent. Then I spent the rest on booze, cigarettes, saltines, and cheese. I ``slept late. When I got up, the typewriter snarled at me from the corner. It wanted to play. I would go out into the street looking for I don't know what. People assumed I was homeless. A bum that never asks for money.

I won a fucking Pulitzer, you assholes, I would think. *I was famous for five minutes.*

It was on one of my outings that I saw the first one. He was leaning just outside of an alley next to the bank, wearing a long grey trench coat and a fedora reading a newspaper. People were walking by without noticing—in this city eccentricities are more the norm than not. He didn't seem to have a face, shadowed by the brim of the fedora. Just what looked like swirling shadows where a face should be. He appeared to be watching me over the top of the newspaper. How I came to that assumption I don't know, but I was convinced.

Never one to turn down a confrontation, I started walking toward him to ask what the hell he was looking at.

As I crossed the street he folded the paper and walked down the alley. I followed but when I got to the alley, it was deserted. There was a

1

chain-link fence at the other end. Unless he was hiding in one of the overflowing dumpsters or had wings, he had disappeared into thin air. I stood for a moment, confused, then decided it was my persistent paranoia and my eyes playing tricks on me. Dismissing the whole affair, I went into the corner store across the alley from the bank. I bought two bottles of Mad Dog and headed for home.

*

My phone rang. The caller ID informed me it was my editor. One of her sporadic, increasingly hopeless calls. I decided to take it.

"What do you want, Maya?"

"The first hundred pages of your next masterpiece," she said. "It's been two years. People in the industry are actually speculating that you died."

"I think we'd all be better off if I had."

"Oh, a sad John Kennedy Toole refrain. Classic."

"That motherfucker could write, even if it took a suicide and eleven years to get published."

"Your book. Seriously. I need pages."

"I'm still diagramming. It's going to be long."

"You've been spooling out that shit for the last year. I've been giving you a lot of rope. If you don't do something tangible soon, you'll have enough to hang yourself."

"It's not like spinning wool. Do your worst, Maya. I don't give a shit anymore."

Her tone changed.

"Well, if you make money, it means I make money. I have good news."

"Thrill me," I said.

"The New York University Press is re-issuing your novel. And they paid through the nose for the rights. You can expect a fatter check every month. You can move your tastes up from that turpentine you drink. Speaking of, are you drunk yet?"

"I was working hard on getting there when your call interrupted me."

"Well, try working hard on your next book. As much as I hate to admit it, you're a genius. Quit letting it go to waste."

"I'll get back to you," I said and hung up.

*

That night I was woke up. There was a persistent tapping on my window. This soaked through my already saturated head as being highly unusual, as I live on the second floor of my apartment building. I dragged my bleary self up and out of bed. Stumbling to the window I almost stumbled right through it. I cracked the blinds and looked out into the street.

There were two of them. Standing under the street lamp across the street. In their trench coats and fedoras they were identical. Just as I was watching them, it was obvious that they were watching me. I raised the blinds and cranked open the window.

"What the fuck do you want?" I yelled.

One of them lifted his head and waved at me. He didn't have a face. Then the two of them turned and walked down the street and out of sight.

I'm a paranoid person. I come by it naturally. Everybody in my family is paranoid. Mostly they're paranoid that one of the other family members is going to kill them. It's not as unlikely as one might think.

I called Maya.

"Hello?" she asked sleepily.

"Are you having me followed? Watched?" I asked angrily.

"Oh Christ, it's you. Do you know what time it is?"

"I don't have a clock."

"Of course, you don't. For your information, it's almost four in the morning."

"You didn't answer my question."

She sighed.

"No, I'm not having you followed or watched. Why would I do such a thing when you never leave a two-block radius from your apartment?"

"Somebody is. I saw one of them this afternoon and two just now outside my window. One of them actually *waved* at me."

She sighed again.

"Somebody's having nightmares. Are you sure you drank enough to completely pass out?"

"Don't fuck with me, Maya. Somebody's watching me."

"Swing by my office tomorrow and I'll have a tinfoil hat waiting for you."

"I said don't fuck with me."

"I don't know, okay? Neither I, nor anyone in my firm, have you under surveillance. If you're that freaked out about it, call the damn police."

"The cops won't do anything. You know that."

"Yeah, sure. While I've got you, and you sound vaguely coherent, I have news," she said. "I was going to wait until tomorrow but, hell, it is tomorrow. Your book's being optioned for a movie. You could become a very wealthy man in a few weeks."

"Terrific. More publicity."

She laughed.

"More? You're completely under the radar. You fired your publicist over a year ago because you wanted to be left alone. Remember?"

"I remember. And it's worked out great so far."

I heard her yawn.

"Look, call me when it's really tomorrow and I'll fill you in on the details. While I try and go back to sleep, you sit by your window, keep an eye out for your spooks, and try to sober up. I'm serious. This is big."

She hung up.

*

It was a gala event. I wore my rumpled suit which hadn't been laundered since the last time I wore it to one of these things. Two years ago now. There were NYU Press people there, Hollywood types, various sycophants and wannabes who I wondered let in and, of course, four or five of my new friends scattered through the crowd.

There was also an open bar. That's where I chose to spend time before my speech. Most of the people there didn't recognize me, for which I was thankful.

That didn't stop one of the wannabes from cornering me.

Maya saved me. She was elegantly dressed. I knew she was forty-seven but somehow didn't look a day over thirty. Her usually impeccably styled blonde bob was slightly out of place.

"There you are! I should have known you'd be as close to the booze as possible. Can I borrow him, young man?"

The wannabe wasting my time scurried off.

"Well, I can see you're capable of cleaning up, if not so well," Maya said.

I caught the bartender's eye. I dropped a hundred-dollar bill in the tip jar and said, "Whiskey, neat, a double. And keep them coming."

Maya laughed her scintillating laugh.

"Are you trying to pick him up?"

"If I were twenty-five years younger I might," I said.

He set a whiskey on the bar. I slammed it. It made my eyes water.

Maya said, "And here's me thinking you were already drunk."

"I am. I hold it well. I'm trying to get plowed enough to get up in front of all these douche bags and puke on the podium."

"Do your worst? Wasn't that what you told me to do? You can't ruin this. There are contracts being drawn up. You could walk up to one of these NYU people or one of the Hollywood producers and piss on their shoes. They might get mad. They might punch you in the face. But they still wouldn't call things off."

"I assume I'm going to have to sign these contracts."

She laughed again. Heads turned.

"Of course, you jackass."

"What if I refuse?"

"I'll forge your signature and make sure I have witnesses to swear that it was you."

"Bitch."

"Asshole."

I had downed a couple of whiskeys by this point and was starting to feel better than I had in weeks. One of my trench coat and fedora entourage was leaning against a decorative pillar.

I said to Maya, "I want you look over your left shoulder at the pillar and tell me what you see. There's no need to be discrete."

She looked.

"I see people milling around. I see a pillar."

"No guy in a trench coat and a fedora? A guy without a face?"

"You need to slow down on the booze, cowboy. That shit won't play in Peoria."

I snorted.

"Like I give a shit."

"Look, just try for one night. One solitary night. Don't embarrass yourself or me. Once it's over you'll be able to drink yourself to death in wealth and peace. Just put me down in the will. I want whatever's left after they put you in the ground. You're on in thirty—it would mean a lot if you could walk up to the podium unaided."

She walked away. The person in the trench coat nodded at me and disappeared into the crowd. I heard Maya's scintillating laugh from somewhere in the room.

*

I made it up to the podium without help, but just barely. I hadn't prepared anything.

"I can't believe I used to enjoy shit like this," I said.

There was laughter.

"When I sit down and write, something I haven't done in a couple of years, I just write. I let go. I wrote *The Glass Fountain* in about two weeks, on an old school typewriter and didn't pause to fix mistakes, grammatical errors, shit like that. I let Maya and her people fix all that."

More laughter and scattered applause.

"Maya's firm was the first publishing house I sent the manuscript to. Thank God they bought it. I had no idea about the shit storm that would erupt around it, culminating so far in nights like this."

Scattered laughter.

"The question on everybody's mind seems to be when will my next novel be ready for publication. I have no idea. I haven't started writing anything yet. For the first six months after I won the Pulitzer, I sat at my typewriter and stared at a blank page. Day after day. *The Glass Fountain* pretty much wrote itself. I had the idea and two weeks later it was finished. The reason there's no follow-up is: I don't have a clue what to write. I don't have any ideas. That may be because I try my hardest at staying drunk in my every waking moment."

Scattered laughter.

"I'm serious. And while I'm being serious, somebody, probably in this room, is having me watched. Men in trench coats and fedoras who have shadows for faces. There are at least five here tonight. It pisses me off and I want it to stop. Now."

Dead silence.

Maya appeared by the podium and shoved me aside. I almost fell down the steps.

"A big round of applause for the man who may be this generation's greatest American novelist!" she said. "There will be no formal Q&A, but you can find him, probably at the bar, and ask him questions. Beneath that gruff demeanor beats the black heart of a true asshole. Have a wonderful evening!"

I got a standing ovation.

What is wrong with these people? I asked myself.

*

I was stumbling home on foot when I finally met one of my new friends. I hate cabs and refused a ride from Maya, mostly to prove some kind of point. I wanted to walk off some of the whiskey so I could start again at home. As I passed an alley entrance, a feminine voice called my name. At first I thought I was hearing things—it had happened before. But then she called again. And then a third time.

"If this is some kind of setup, I don't have any money, credit cards, or jewelry. The only thing worth jacking is my life."

"No setup, honey. We just have something important to tell you. Or, should I say, a proposition"

Unwisely, perhaps, I decided to see who this person or persons was. I walked down into the dimly lit alley.

There was a woman there, dressed in a 1920s style flapper dress and a broad-rimmed, sequined hat. She smelled like scorched skin and perspiration. It didn't surprise me that she didn't have a face.

"That was quite a performance you put on back there," she said.

"Who the hell are you people—or things—and what the hell do you want from me?"

"You're a writer, aren't you?"

"Once upon a time," I said.

"Silly rabbit. We want you to write a book."

"I don't work on commission. In fact, I don't work at all. I'm done. I'm about to have more money than I can spend. Why can't everyone let me drink myself to death in peace?"

"This is a very special book. We'll bring you outlines. You just have to weave them into brilliant prose."

"Not interested."

"Would it change your mind if I told you that you don't have a choice? We can be very persuasive."

"Still not interested."

"Well, silly rabbit, you really don't have a choice. One of us will bring you the first outline tomorrow. There is a condition. When it's finished, you'll only sell one copy of the manuscript. To us."

"Like hell," I said. "If I bust my balls writing another novel, I want it to at least go to my editor. Get her off my back for a little while. It won't matter. I doubt I can write anything publishable anymore."

"No, no, no, little bunny. One copy. To us. You'll be well compensated."

"Well compensated? Jesus, lady. I just became a very rich man."

She laughed.

"There are different kinds of compensation. Who knows? We might even let you keep your soul."

I was about to shout at her. Physically attack her. I wasn't getting through and I was much too angry to be afraid of her. But I didn't get a chance to do anything. Her head twisted on her neck to an unnatural angle.

"We'll be in t ... t ... t ..."

She burst into flames. Like she'd been hit by napalm. In what seemed like an instant, she was a burning heap on the ground.

I ran all the way home.

*

Nothing happened the next morning. I sat around smoking cigarettes until about noon when I ran out of booze. It was easy to believe that what I saw, what I was seeing, had something to do with my heroic consumption of alcohol. But I doubted that.

I waited until the shakes and nausea got so bad I was sure I was about to die before I put on my bathrobe and slippers. Judging from the pedestrian traffic on the street, I wasn't the strangest looking person on it. At a break in traffic, I scurried across the intersection and into the corner store.

The proprietor knew me. Unavoidable I had to be his most frequent customer. He was a Vietnam vet, about twenty years older than me, and was missing his right arm. I couldn't tell if he actually liked me or not. For all I knew, he thought I was another piece of street flotsam passing through.

"Looking dashing today," he said.

"Go to hell. I've had a shitty week."

"Tell me," he said. "What has four legs, three arms, and one liver?"

"Who's got the liver?"

"It's gotta be you. One that's not going to last much longer."

"While we're on the topic, I need two fifths of Jack and two liters of MD 20/20. And a carton of Lucky Strikes. The coffin nails without filters."

He whistled.

"Tall order, even for you," he said. "Holing up for the rest of the week?"

"Yeah. Better make that three fifths of Jack."

"You're gonna need to eat something, all that booze."

"I ate last night, which is one more night than I usually eat in a week."

"Suit yourself," he said as he bagged my stuff.

I gave him an appraising look.

"Can I ask you something, well, a little discreet?"

"Fuck you, queer."

"No! Not like that! I have a problem I need dealing with."

"Drugs? Muscle? I gave that game up when I lost my arm."

I had always thought he'd lost it in Vietnam.

"I'm being followed. Watched. I don't know why or who they are, but they've been dogging me for a week or so. I'm hoping to find someone who can hire some bone breakers to send a message "

"If almost anyone else walked in here and asked me that, I'd shove the sawed-off pool cue behind the counter up their ass. But I know you're not police and, for some reason, I like you. Or at least feel sorry for you. How many are we talking about?"

"Five or six men I know of, and I think a woman, although I watched her spontaneously combust in front of me last night."

He said, "We'll just leave that last part out. Yeah, I know some kneecappers, but for that kind of juice, it ain't gonna be cheap."

"Money's no object. Whatever they want, I'll pay. They can rip me off. I don't care. I just want them gone."

"Where can my friends find these creeps?" he asked.

"There are usually at least two outside my apartment building every night."

"Two's enough. The guys I know will disappear them and find out where the others are holed up. Nothing to it if the money's right."

"Believe me, money's no object,"

"To look at you I'd say you're a fucking liar. But I know you've got money coming from somewhere, so I'll make the connection. And, by the way, and obviously, if you're fucking around, they'll never find your body."

"The fuckers I'm talking about will."

I was in such a good mood I let him buy me a sandwich.

*

When I got back to my apartment, there was a manila envelope somebody had slid under the door. It wasn't a tough guess who.

"Oh, for Christ sake!" I yelled, almost dropping my supplies.

It was just a common manila envelope. Unmarked. Unblemished. No telling what was inside. A bill. A subpoena. A fan letter. Something from Maya.

I knew it was none of those things.

I stepped over it and took my things to the kitchen. The plan I concocted involved eating my sandwich and drinking one of the bottles of Mad Dog before I concocted another plan, which may or may not involve the envelope.

I ate my sandwich, drank the Mad Dog, and went back to sleep.

*

Three days passed. Three envelopes. Cheese and crackers. Lucky Strikes. Lots and lots of booze.

I ignored the envelopes. Let them lay on the floor where they ended up. The third night the game changed.

I woke up in the dark. I didn't keep a clock so I had no idea what time it was, which generally suited me fine. This particular dark seemed a little darker than dark. It was like someone had put aluminum foil over the windows. I knew there was someone there because they were smoking a cigarette. I couldn't bring myself to be afraid.

"Mind if I light up, too?" I asked without waiting for an answer. I found my pack and lighter and lit the cigarette. In the dim flame I could tell it was the woman from the other night. The one I had watched explode into flames. I groaned.

"For crying out loud, lady, what now? And didn't I see you explode the other night?"

"You've been a very naughty little bunny," she said. "You haven't even started your homework. It would be a mistake to flunk out of this class. And there's the matter of those nasty men you sent around. Not smart. I hope they didn't have families."

That got my attention.

"What are you talking about? What did you do to them?"

"We ate them."

"You what! You fucking ate them! What the fuck, lady?"

She had me by the balls. I was suddenly terrified.

9

"Close enough to make no difference. What's a body but a sack of meat anyway? There's more edible fare. Less messy."

"What are you talking about?"

"Keep on ignoring us and you'll find out."

Suddenly she was on top of me, straddling me. She ripped my shirt open and lightly dragged razor sharp fingernails down my chest.

"You don't seem to get it, little man. This whole burned-out author shtick may fly with your agent or your public or whoever else, but it doesn't mean shit to us."

I don't scare easily. I was terrified.

"It's not a shtick. I don't know where you freaks call home, but this is the really real world."

She started carving into my chest with her nails. It hurt like hell and I cried like a baby to try and get her to stop. She finally did. There was blood soaking into the sheets.

"You know what you have to do, little bunny. Best get to work. You're falling behind. We'll speak again soon."

I managed to croak, "Just don't burn down the fucking building when you leave."

When I turned on the light, she was gone.

I staggered to the bathroom, poured some whiskey on my chest, and howled in pain. When I looked at myself in the mirror I saw she had carved "get to work" into my flesh.

*

I finally washed the sheets. I threw in some clothes for good measure. Hanged for a penny, hanged for a pound. The blood stains didn't come out of the sheets but at least they were finally clean. It relieved me that it was the middle of the night and no one was in the apartment building laundry room—I would certainly have been fingered as a murderer.

When I got back to my apartment, I made the bed and tidied up the joint. There must have been a racket when I dumped all my empties into the recycle dumpster, but nobody said anything. Once I was done, the place looked entirely different. Like someone other than a squatter lived there.

I went to the door, picked up the envelopes, and opened them. The first page of each had a numeral on it. One, two, three. After shuffling them into order, I poured myself a tumbler of whiskey, laid down on the bed, and started to read.

It was brilliant. The bones of the story they wanted me to write were exquisite. Disturbing as hell. Fetishistic. But utterly brilliant. The further I got, the more excited I became.

When I came to the end of the third outline, it cut off so abruptly I was startled. I read the whole thing again and possibilities began to swirl through my head. Phrases. Sentences. Entire paragraphs. All my hesitation had evaporated without my even realizing it.

I rushed to the typewriter with the outline, sat down, and started to type. The typewriter made a clacking noise and froze. The ribbon was completely dried out. I cursed and whacked it on the side, feeling foolish a moment later. I don't know why I expected anything else.

There was still plenty of whiskey.

Dawn was creeping over the horizon when I passed out.

*

That afternoon, after shaking out the cobwebs with a hot shower, a shave, and a couple of belts, I got dressed and went out into the city. Not a single one of the dozen or so antique stores or junk shops I hit had ribbon for a manual typewriter. I gave up and at the last one bought an electric typewriter, and the two ribbons it came with, right at closing time.

When I got home, I carried my old typewriter to the dumpster and deposited it. Then I set up the electric one. Fortified by a tumbler of whiskey, I placed the outlines next to the typewriter, scanned the first page, and started to type.

It just clicked. I was riding the crest of a big, beautiful wave. When the tumbler was irritatingly empty, I got up, knocking the tumbler aside so I could drink straight from the bottle.

I wrote all night. I forgot about the outlines and let the story carry me away. The wave crashed and rolled back some time after the sun came up. I was seeing double. After powering down the typewriter, I staggered to the bed and fell down, unconscious before my head hit the pillow. I had written a hundred pages.

*

When I woke up, it was late afternoon. I brushed my teeth, ate some cheese and crackers, and cracked another bottle of whiskey. It was all irritatingly mundane. Once I got back to the typewriter, it started to flow again, and I knocked out another forty pages in a couple of hours. At some point, somebody slid a manila envelope through the crack under the door, but I didn't notice when it happened. I took a breather, looked over at the door, and saw it. There was another outline inside, labeled with the numeral four. Considering the manuscript, I was pretty sure I was deep into outline two. After examining outline four, I was pleased to see that I was, more or less, still on the track that the outlines dictated. But I didn't care. At less than a hundred and fifty pages, it had become my baby. My manuscript.

I called Maya.

"Almost one hundred and fifty pages!" I said.

She literally squealed.

Sounding breathless, she said, "When can I see them?"

"Give me an hour to find a copy shop, then send someone around. It's good, Maya. Really good."

"You loveable son of a bitch! You just made my week. Maybe my year."

"An hour. You'll have the pages before the sun goes down."

*

When I woke up, I was being dragged by the ankles through some kind of cave, my head bumping on the irregular floor. There was light, but I couldn't tell where it was coming from. I managed to look up to see who was dragging me, but I already had a pretty good idea as to who it was. I saw the backs of two trench coats. I was profoundly frightened.

We eventually reached some sort of wide cavern. I was dragged to my feet by hard hands. They took up position behind me, preventing any half-baked ideas of running before they could form. The woman, the thing, stood in front of me.

"You just can't help being naughty, can you, silly rabbit?" she said. She sounded hard and serious. Very serious.

"Jesus! You can't really expect me to keep quiet about this. It blows my last book out of the water."

"Not part of the deal, boyo. I told you, in no uncertain terms, what is expected of you. You've experienced the carrot in your enthusiasm for the writing, haven't you? Now, I'm afraid, it's time for the stick."

Suddenly she was right in front of me. I hadn't seen her move. I felt a coldness on my chest and looked down. Her hand was, somehow, inside me. Something, my heart maybe, started feeling compressed. Then the pain hit. It was unimaginable. I tried to scream, but didn't have any breath.

"This is only the tiniest part of what we can do to you, if you keep deliberately fucking up. Or even accidentally. Our patience is at an end," the woman hissed. "If you want to feel this, and worse, forever, you'll start behaving yourself."

She squeezed harder. I wished I could pass out.

"I doubt a man like you believes in the soul," she said. "But, for lack of a better term, you better believe it's what I have a hold of in there. I could rip it out. You think this hurts? Imagine worse. Forever. Now get back to work."

The pain peaked as she ripped her hand out. I finally passed out. When I woke up, I was in my bed.

*

Now I write. As slowly as possible without raising their ire. I drink to pass out every day, which is the only way I can get any sleep. I'm deep into outline eleven, and every day a new outline shows up. There's no sign that the work is nearing completion. Yet. I threw my cell phone out the window, severing connection with Maya and the rest of the world. No one has come around to check on me so far.

My masterpiece. I'm terrified of what will happen when I finish it.

***

The Librarian's Apprentice
by Cedric Tan, Philippines

"You want to plagiarize Shakespeare?" the Librarian said, though it was less of a question and more of a statement. His elbows were rested on his desk and his chin upon his interlocked fingers. Narrow eyes peered through half-moon spectacles, accusingly, at the guest standing in front of him.

"No, of course not," the guest protested, hands in the air as if a thief caught in the act. "Only the names. The names!" He wore a black mask, a plain one with a long sharp nose, with white plumes on either side of his face giving him the impression of a haggard bird. Other than that, he wore a plain ensemble: black cloak, nondescript boots.

"Only the names? You're taking *many* names."

"Well, maybe a *few* ..."

"When people read your stories, they will know," the Librarian pointed out. "Othello. Macbeth. Hamlet. It's too obvious."

"They will see it as an homage," the guest insisted. "It's nothing like Shakespeare, anyway. I am writing a comedy."

"You didn't read enough Shakespeare. William wrote comedies too."

"Not comedies like mine." He was inordinately confident, this one.

The Librarian rubbed at his temples in exasperation. "Yes, well. An homage, then. I'm clearly not stopping you."

"Ah. Thank you very much!"

The guest adjusted his mask and jollily skipped away for the shelf dedicated to Shakespeare, humming a worry-free tune.

Today is a busy day, the Librarian mused, looking over the top of his spectacles. A decade or two ago, he would have been lucky to welcome a fraction of the crowd that occupied the library that day. More hands than ever were on the books, taking them down from the shelves, opening, flipping, slamming them shut. He allowed himself a smile for the gusto with which people were attacking the shelves. Up the spiral staircases they went, down the hallways and corridors, the arrays of stories and ideas occupying the spaces with admirable organization in some wings, and remarkable chaos in every other.

From the Librarian's desk, one could see two enormous windows set on opposite walls. Daylight perpetually shone through one window, while a starry night and a golden moon was always the view out the other. It was a well-lit place: perfect for him, and perfect for the guests.

He looked up toward the Hall of the Animal Kingdom. A young girl, no more than eight years old, hopped down the grand staircase with a thin book under her arm. *Her first story*, he thought. She found an empty table and lay the book upon it, opening it to the first page with reverence. *It's about horses*, the Librarian reflected. *Ponies. She's going to write a story about ponies.* That made him smile.

A chill crept down his back, a cold that emanated from somewhere near his nape and crawled toward the tips of his fingers and toes, despite there being no change in the temperature. With a practiced movement, he leapt over his desk and strode toward the huge double doors set in the wall, brushing some imaginary dust off the shoulder of his sharp beige suit, combing his fingers through his gray hair. He stopped a few strides away from the doors, and just in time. They opened with a bang, and in walked the Lady in Black, looking so proud and important that it was a wonder a trumpet fanfare did not accompany her entry.

A young woman in a wheat-colored vest over a stained white frock followed the Lady in Black like an afterthought.

"My Lady." The Librarian bowed low; a grand, sweeping gesture. "To what do I owe this unexpected pleasure?"

"Hello, Gene," the Lady in Black said. "How's the library today?"

"It's well."

"Seems a little crowded."

"There *are* more than usual," Gene admitted.

"Well, let's consider that a good thing. We haven't had this many people taking an interest in the arts since the Renaissance. Anyway, this is perfect. Do you need a hand down here? Because I have a favor to ask you."

"A favor of me, Your Morbidness? I shall do my best to oblige."

"Very well. Aisling, come here." The Lady jerked with her head, and the young woman edged forward, eyes downcast. The Librarian inspected her. *A mousy little one.* Fiery red hair fell in messy tresses over a freckled face. Her eyes were like dull gemstones and were focused on the floor, but as she approached Gene, they lifted to take in the wondrous sight of the library. It was hard to say how old she was—maybe seventeen, or eighteen? She was a skinny thing, with knobby legs and an uncertainty to her walk.

"Aisling, meet the Librarian, Gene." The Lady in Black nudged her forward. "Gene, this is Aisling. She died just a few moments ago."

The girl gave the Lady in Black a look of mild irritation. "Thanks for the reminder," she muttered.

"However, there's been some commotion over at the Afterlife, and things must be sorted out before I can collect a few more souls. Aisling's death was very untimely."

"A ... commotion, my Lady?"

"Yes. I think the Angels are on strike. Or was it the Valkyries? I'm not quite sure, I should be checking on that now. So, regarding Aisling. I thought maybe she could stay here for some time. Can you look after her, maybe even put her to good use? Let her work here for a while, you know. Show her the ropes. An extra pair of hands won't hurt."

"Ah," Gene nodded. "Of course, Your Grimness. I will apprentice her most dutifully."

"Excellent. She's all yours." The Lady in Black brought out a pocket watch and examined it, clicking her tongue. "Now if you'll excuse me, I have some business to attend to. There's a suicide in India, someone in Scotland's about to choke on a fish, and unless the mess in the Afterlife is fixed, none of that will matter. Farewell, you two."

She exited the room with a flourish. Gene swept into another bow as she left; the chill disappeared. *Ah. I will never get used to that.*

He turned to the red-haired girl. Aisling.

"Hello, there," he said, smiling.

"Hello."

"How did you die?"

She chuckled. "I got hit by an automobile, crossing the road."

"I'm so sorry."

A shrug. "It hurt, but only for a while. I died before it became too terrible."

"Well, I'm sure it wasn't your fault."

The girl walked passed him and looked up the stretch of the library, far above her. They were at the base of a massive atrium with emerald-green tiles underfoot, and floor upon floor of bookshelf-lined levels rose above them in innumerable tiers. There was no ceiling to be seen. "Actually," she mused, "it was, in a way. I crossed the street without looking."

"Why is that?"

"I was busy reading a book." She grinned sheepishly. "It's too bad. I was near the end. I suppose I'll never get to finish it now."

*

Before the accident, Aisling lived a decidedly normal life, much of it composed of her studies at the university, turning away suitors, whistling popular tunes and strolling. She discovered the library of her college a few weeks after her studies began. The first time she borrowed a book and went strolling with it was also her last. When the automobile struck her, the complete collection of *Perrault's Fairy Tales* dropped out of her hands and clattered on the cobblestones stained by her blood.

She'd thought it a cruel joke when the Lady in Black told her she was going to spend some more time in another library while the details of her death were sorted out, pardon the inconvenience.

"Aisling," Gene called. "This young man wants to write a story about the city of Pompeii. Would you kindly assist him?"

"Right away."

The guest was a short and stocky man, but how old he was, it was hard to say. He wore a solid red mask with wide cheeks and a sardonic grin. "Follow me, then, sir." She started up the stairs, and the guest quietly followed.

Her job was very simple: Assist the guests.

"They are here to research, to be inspired," Gene had explained during the first day, leading her around with wide, self-important strides. "To gather ideas, facts and opinions. Drawing from history and memory. Through these books, art is made. Literature is born. You and I are going to help the world's artists do this. No more and no less."

"Sounds like an important job," Aisling chuckled. "*All* the artists?"

"Yes, Aisling. All of them."

"Even the bad ones?"

"Regrettably, but yes. Remember, no denying the people what they need, and no tampering with the library books. Simple rules. Understand?"

"Yes, sir."

"No 'sir.' That makes me feel old. Just Gene."

"But you *are* old."

"Then respect your elder's request. Just Gene."

"Yes, Gene."

He offered her a kindly smile before replacing it with another serious look. "Aisling, we follow the rules of nature here. Is that understood? We do not defy the laws of nature. You and I are dead—"

"Thank you, you've only reminded me a hundred times ..."

"—and that's why we're librarians here. We are not artists. *They* are the artists. I don't want to find you suddenly making your own revisions to a book, just because you disagree with it. Is that clear?"

Aisling nodded. "Yes."

That got another smile out of Gene. "Very well. Let's continue with the tour."

Now, despite the library's size, its layout was quite intuitive, and Aisling caught on assisting the guests quite quickly. For this one drafting a novel about Pompeii, Aisling only needed a moment to recall their destination, leading him up ladders, staircases, and bridges that connected one floor to another, until they finally reached a floor with racks of scrolls on the walls. "Ancient History of Western Europe," Aisling announced. "I'm sure you'll find Pompeii around here somewhere."

The masked guest turned toward Aisling and nodded in thanks before scouring the shelves and racks to begin writing his story; before long, his quill was scratching away. Returning by way of the Hall of the Greek Pantheon—a section where statues of Olympians towered over marble bookshelves—she hopped daintily onto the bannister and slid down the railing until she landed back at the bottom of the atrium, in front of the Librarian's desk.

"How big is it?" she asked.

Gene was busy using a woodblock to stamp his seal on some books and did not look up. "How big is what?"

"This. The library."

"Very big."

"How big?"

"Well, what is the extent of human history and imagination, Aisling?"

"Hmmm ... well, I'd have to argue that it would be near infinite."

"Then there's your answer." He glanced up. "And it's getting bigger every day."

"Do you ever get bored here?"

"Aisling, we have already discussed the particulars of your work and responsibilities in the library. I've shown you your resting quarters. Are these questions urgent?"

"No."

"In that case, I'm a little occupied at the moment, if you don't mind."

She shrugged and strode off. "I'm sorry. I was just making polite conversation."

"There's nothing polite about your interruptions. Go find someone to assist."

"Hmph."

Wandering the library, one could easily get lost if one didn't mind where they were going, and Aisling was very quick to learn this. A huge amphitheater dazzled her as she passed it by, the backdrop of the stage a giant shelf for the dramas, new and old. It was next to a corridor where a galleon had crashed through the wall and left there, the bow of the ship a makeshift shelf for books dedicated to the voyages of the greats. Up and down Aising went, passing by artists scouring the shelves for inspiration for an early magnum opus.

For a dead girl, her walk was quite lively. In her irritation at Gene, she did not realize how far she had gone until she noticed the dimness of her surroundings. The labyrinth of shelves through which she traversed now towered over her, so tall and imposing that she had to crane her neck backwards just to spy the tops.

"And getting bigger every day," she murmured. "This is a terrible profession." She let her back lean against one of the shelves and slid herself down until she sat on the floor. A loud sigh escaped her. "Better to have just died properly, eh?"

At first she'd thought that this wing—whichever it was—was completely deserted. It wasn't until she heard shuffling footsteps that she realized she was not alone. She peeked around the shelf to find a crooked old figure in front of the books. He had one of the leather-bound volumes open in his hand and was reading it intently, his mouth opening and closing in quiet murmurs. The old man wore threadbare but dapper clothes—slacks, a velvet vest, a cotton suit. There was no mask on his face unlike most of the other guests. She could see his wrinkled prune of a face clearly, his wispy white piebald hair, his cyan eyes.

Aisling stood up, composed herself, and put on a dignified appearance. "Good day to you, sir," she announced. "Please let me know if there's anything I can help you with."

He turned toward her and smiled a friendly grin, the kind that instantly reminded one of their grandfather, or maybe their favorite teacher. "I am all right, my lady. I've found exactly what I need." He turned his book toward her in a small gesture. Aisling stepped forward uncertainly, and the old man grinned again. The letters on the yellowing pages were faded, but written in a fine penmanship. She took it in her hands and glanced through some random sentences.

"*The rifle felt right in my hands; the steel cold, but sure,*" she read with her eyes. "*With a practiced breath, I eyed the deer in the glade, turning the barrel toward its neck. A sure kill.*" She looked up. "Sir, what story is this?"

He only nodded. She understood.

"You were a hunter?"

"I was many things, in my youth."

She flipped to a random page and continued silently, "*I held the raven-haired woman in my arms,*" she read, silently. "*The thought of all the forbidden things we were about to do rushed through my head. But I could not turn away, not now ... My hands were fumbling with the laces of her dress, her fingers on my belt buckle ..."*

Aisling stifled an awkward giggle. *Okay, I think that's private.* She flipped to another page.

"I held my newborn son in my arms, and in a moment of euphoria I realized that everything was going to be perfect. As I embraced him, this treasure of mine, I made quiet promises for him, for the world I would build for him. My love, my son ... And little did I know that they would be taken from me ..."

She looked up. The old man's smile was forlorn. "Little did you know?"

"Little did I know. Such was the story."

She handed him back the book.

"You're writing a biography, aren't you?"

"That's quite a word for a glorified journal. But yes ... aye, a biography it is."

"That's why you need this book. It's your life."

"It is a small portion of my life." He nodded at the rest of the bookshelf. "The rest of it is here somewhere. My work, my dreams, my family ..."

"Family ..." Aisling stopped short, but feeling bold, continued, "I had a family once, too, you know. I suppose I could also write a story with them, but ..."

He chuckled. "Couldn't you? We're all storytellers here."

Aisling stared down the row of immense bookshelves and wondered.

*

Sometime later, Aisling was in another corner of the library, claiming a desk. She had a paper and quill and ink and was writing. Stacked before her were several books. She occasionally glanced up at the titles embossed on their spines.

*

"Were you able to assist a lot of artists today, Aisling?" Gene asked, pouring her a steaming cup of tea. The fragrance of some unfamiliar, exotic flower wafted over her.

"A few," she answered.

"How was it?"

"Could have been worse. I think I nearly led a playwright to a Bach story when he was looking for Chopin, but we sorted that out very quickly."

"Very good." They took sips of their tea, the better to fill in the gaps of silence between them. The table at which they sat overlooked a chamber where the bleached skeleton of a massive dragon lay, surrounded by lanterns of every color. The dragon's rib cage was wide enough for several guests to pass under; masked and unmasked men and women alike leafed through their chosen volumes, some resting against the dragon's claws, others leaning against the vertebrae of its tail. "The artists here do seem to appreciate the assistance you provide for them. Thank you for your diligence."

"There's an awful lot of them, aren't there? And it seems like a great deal of them are new to their craft."

"Yes. Well, you heard the Lady. The most we've had since the Renaissance."

"How long have you been here, Gene?"

"Long enough that I've forgotten my true name," the Librarian laughed.

"Gene is not ...?"

"It's something the Masters gave me. I could not remember if it was the Lady in Black, or perhaps one of the others. Well, it no longer matters. I do not feel the passage of time within these halls. So, as old as I may be, I do not feel my age."

"Did you have a life outside the library?"

"I did. I no longer remember it as well."

"Did you have a wife?" Now Aisling leaned forward in earnest. "A family?"

"I do not remember."

"A house? How about a single childhood memory? Come on, try!"

A resigned sigh escaped from lips turned up in wistfulness. "If I could not even remember my own name, how could I remember all of that?"

She stared into the swirl of tea in her cup and took a thoughtful sip. "I don't want to wind up like you."

Gene looked as if Aisling had slapped him across the face. She bit her lip regretfully, and considered apologizing for the comment.

"You would rather continue with the journey of your death, wouldn't you?" he asked, the gentle smile returning to his face. "Don't worry, Aisling. This apprenticeship of yours is nothing more than a brief detour. The Lady will be back for you in no time. Meanwhile, though ... thank you."

"What for?"

"For doing your job well. You help the guests who need you, the world is seeing more art than ever before, and ..." He raised his teacup, as if in a toast, "You haven't broken a single rule. I like that."

Aisling remembered the paper she'd been scribbling on earlier, a horrible wave of guilt washing over her. She hid her face with her teacup and laughed the comment off. They sipped away the rest of their time in relative silence—a silence broken only by the guests walking to and fro, taking down the books from the shelves surrounding the dragon's skeleton. The sound of ideas giving birth to new ideas stormed the library from top to bottom, and yet the tempest was no louder than a whisper.

*

They finished their tea and Gene gave her leave to continue her work as she pleased. Once she was sure that he was preoccupied with his work at the front desk, she slipped up the Wing of Chinese Philosophy, danced her way past some guests, and then found the spot where she'd left her parchment and paper. She continued writing.

Occasionally Aisling would scurry over to some other corner of the massive library, searching for just the piece of material she needed. Usually, she encountered no problem. Even when she found herself misplaced within the vast collections, she was getting familiar with the pronounced landmarks: the giant standing globe made of stained glass; the enormous tree that grew through four floors, the hollows of its trunk being used as spaces for books; the spherical room suspended above an indoor lake, housing a mural depicting every religion's version of the world's creation. Other times, a masked guest would stop and request her for assistance, when the writer's block was simply too difficult to overcome.

She was grateful that Gene at least didn't hound her after her first few days. She could snatch enough time to write away at her own pace, in quiet corners far from him.

You haven't broken a single rule. I like that. Aisling struggled to keep his words out of her head. It made her hesitate.

Occasionally she'd remember the automobile. The accident would come back to her in an uncomfortable rush: the noise, the pain, and then the Lady in Black coming to take her away. But she pushed it aside, and steadily her book, her creation, came together. The slowness of it made the finished product she had in mind all the more desirable.

*

Back when she was alive, Aisling could never name the feeling she got whenever she watched dawn break. But shades of that nameless emotion tugged at her now, as she found herself putting the finishing touches on her book. Her quill scratched furiously, with purpose. She leaned so close over her writing desk that her nose hovered mere inches away from the page. There was no smile on her face; no, she would not allow it, not just yet.

A title, thought Aisling. *What I need is a title.*

"Aisling?"

In her surprise, she nearly spilled her ink pot all over the pages. She turned around to find the Librarian standing behind her. She had not paid attention to the footsteps signaling his approach, dismissing it as another of the taciturn guests. Gene was holding a familiar-looking black book in his hands.

"Oh, uh ... hello, Gene," Aisling stammered.

"I brought you a present," Gene said, offering her the biggest grin she'd seen from him yet. "This was the book you were reading the day you died. *Perrault's Fairy Tales*, right? I found you the original edition by Charles himself."

"Yes. Right. Thank you."

"What is that you're hiding?"

Suspicious of the bound pages Aisling was trying to keep behind her back, Gene strode forward. Aisling stepped away, held the book protectively to her chest in response. A range of expressions flickered across the Librarian's face—surprised, confused, and then upset. "What is that?" he demanded.

"Nothing."

"I can see your name written across the front. That's not a book I am familiar with. Did you ... did you *write* it?"

Aisling's silence was the only answer he needed. Gene let out one of his exasperated sighs, rubbing his temple with his palm. "Aisling, I thought we had an understanding. Art is for the *living*."

"I just wanted to tell a story."

"This was not why you were brought here."

She held the book tighter to her chest. "Everyone has a story to tell, right?"

He gestured with a sweep of his arm. "The ones you left behind? Your family and friends, back in the real world? They are the ones responsible for telling those stories. Not us. You and I and the rest ... we're just memories now. Hand me the book."

"But it's mine."

"Your duty, Aisling. Listen to me, now."

"Please."

"The book."

"No."

"*Aisling! The book!*"

"*NO!*"

He reached, but she was quicker. She slipped by under his arm and ran. She leaped over a desk, dashed out of the room, and ran down the rugged hallway. Along the way, she elbowed aside a guest wearing a green, owl-like mask so hard that he stumbled into the nearest shelf; somewhere in New York, a promising young playwright completely forgot about the next line in his newest drama.

Aisling slid down the bannister, landed in another wing, and desperately dashed down the hall. In her haste, she accidentally slammed into the writing desk of a blue-masked guest, sending his pages flying; a man in Florence suddenly lost all train of thought on his tale about Saint Joseph's final week.

When she arrived at the base of the library's atrium, right in front of the Librarian's desk, her heart sank to see that Gene was waiting for her, breathing as easily as if he had been there the whole time.

"You shouldn't have done that," he murmured. "Aisling, your time—*our* time—is up. You forget. We're here to inspire others to create, not to create ourselves."

"Gene, I'll never ask for anything ever again," she pleaded. "Just let me have this. Please."

"I said no. Don't test me."

"Please!"

The double doors opened with a bang. Both turned to see the Lady in Black stride in, light and smoke streaming from behind her, an emphatic smile on her lips. Gene turned about and swept into a low bow immediately; Aisling stayed where she was, clutching her book to her chest, apparently still unwilling to let go.

A few moments passed by in silence while the Lady in Black looked from the girl to Gene and back. Finally, she spoke: "You should read it, you know."

Gene glanced up, uncertain. "I'm sorry, Your Deathliness?"

"You should read it." Her smile was a little perplexing; her eyes on Aisling's book. "You might find that it may be worth saving after all."

Then she turned to the young woman, who looked ready to start running again. "It's all right, Aisling," she said in a soothing voice. "The hiccup in the Afterlife has been corrected, and I've come to fetch you. Though, not for the reason you think. You see, there's a reason you're still so determined to write ..."

"A reason?"

The Lady nodded. "I made a mistake. This ... happens once in a while, I'm embarrassed to admit. Rarely, yes, but it does happen. I beg your forgiveness."

"What reason?"

"You're not dead, Aisling."

"I'm not?"

Gene was just as confused. "So, her body ...?"

"You were mostly dead. Your body was broken, you'd lost blood, and by all means, you were fading into the darkness. That's why I came to get you. But maybe I was a little excited. A part of you was still fighting. You were as close to dead as humanly possible without actually being dead, but still ..."

"But still, I'm alive?"

The Lady nodded. "You are. I've apologized to the other Masters for my mistake, but now I've come to take you back. There will be a lot of pain when you return to your body, but at least that says you'll still have a life."

There was a pause that reminded Aisling of a heartbeat. "Thank you. Now?"

"Now. Your friends and family and the doctors have been trying to bring you back and they've almost given up. Come on. Best not to keep them waiting."

Aisling glanced up the library's atrium. All around them, cloaked figures wearing masks—a few bare faces among them—continued to scour the shelves. None of them were paying any attention to her. Not even one dropped their book, nor even paused, to look down on her and the Lady in Black. *It will continue, then. With or without me.*

She took a hesitant step toward Gene, whose face was once again exceedingly difficult to read.

"Thank you for the lessons," she said. She held out her book to him. After a brief pause, he took the book with his right hand, and with his left, handed her the black one he'd been holding. Aisling accepted the trade and murmured, "Am I going to remember any of this, when I'm back?"

"No."

Aisling froze. For many more moments, she only stared at her feet. She and Gene stood that way, facing each other but not looking. Finally, the Lady in Black brought out her pocket watch and cleared her throat, the first sign of impatience that Gene did not dare aggravate.

"*I'll* remember," he said.

"You will?"

"Yes. I'll remember for the both of us. Now you should go. Just through the door. The Lady will follow; she'll guide you back. Don't worry. Goodbye, Aisling."

"Okay. Umm ... bye." She took a breath and walked out into the bright light in the doorway, embracing the leather-bound *Perrault's Fairy Tales* against her heart.

Gene asked, "A mistake, my Lady? The truth?"

She shrugged. "I said, it's rare. But you know how humans are. You used to be one of them." She nodded toward the book in his hand. "The story of a girl whose life is narrated by her dead self. Not an uncommon concept. Universal themes, snappy prose, and a wonderful ending. It's a good story, rest assured."

"I'll make time for it."

"Are you bored yet, Gene? Have you thought about giving all this up yet? I can think of a few mortals who'd gladly take over the job."

"I appreciate the thoughtfulness, My Lady. But not yet. I'll let you know when I've had enough."

"See? You're drawing out your own ending yourself."

"I beg your pardon?"

"Nothing. When you're ready to join us in the Afterlife, just say the word."

She smiled at him one more time and turned to the doors. She made her egress with the same flourish she always made her entrance, her coat sweeping out like smoke behind her. The enormous double doors slowly swung closed as she left, a low rumble echoing up the atrium, until they finally shut behind her with a resounding boom.

✱✱✱

Soul Dew
by Keith Gouveia, United States

Mor'vor stepped out of the woods and stood at the edge of the clearing.

If she can't grant me eternal life, I'll cut out her black heart and offer it to someone who can, he thought as he stared at the quaint cottage, then wondered if he had taken a wrong path. He had expected to find the trees decayed and wilted, the ground ashen, and the sun blocked out by an unholy darkness, but instead, the witch's abode looked the part of any other farmhouse he had passed on his journey. Creeping ivory reached up the stone walls of the farmhouse draped in thatch. Three crooked steps led to the arched wooden door, and a ribbon of smoke wafted from the chimney. A welcoming light burned in the front window, it almost looked inviting.

Almost, he thought as he fixated his gaze to the wound on his right arm. Its edges didn't run deep so the pain was easily overcome, but the wound burned with humiliation and doubt. He had known the day would come when his body would be too feeble to keep up with his skills, but to have that young, brazen ruffian foresee his strike, parry, and counter-strike, that was too much for the seasoned warrior to comprehend.

He would have taken my head from its perch, had he not been so overzealous, Mor'vor thought, recalling the duel.

Labeled a world-renowned swordsman, Mor'vor was accustomed to the random challenges. Every man, woman, and child of Cruor sought to claim his title. Exhaling through his nose with a heavy sigh, he steeled his nerves and stepped out of the woods, toward the cottage.

A gentle breeze kissed his cheek, the scent of evergreens filling his nostrils. He breathed in the aroma to enjoy its purity. He had slain countless, hopeful adversaries and these moments of peace, where the air did not carry the metallic, salty scent of blood, were few and far between.

He took the steps one at a time and reached the door, then held his balled fist level with his gaze and stopped before knocking. The wrinkled, purplish hue of his once mighty hands caused his stomach to clench. Seeing the swift instruments of death now ravaged by time disgusted him.

A shadow of their former selves, he thought, *just as I.*

"Please," a voice, ancient and calloused, came from the other side of the door, "enter."

She knows I'm here without my knocking. Perhaps the stories are true. Mor'vor took the wrought iron handle in hand and entered. Stagnant air choked his lungs. The putrid smell of rotten meat saturated the air, forcing him to cover his mouth. The cottage itself was a modest dwelling. A single room divided into living quarters, off to the right, a pile of straw haphazardly covered by a single, sweat-stained bed sheet. A large wooden table rested in the center of the room with bowls of various sizes scattered across its surface, partially eaten food and grime clung to the dishes, adding to the myriad of smells. Over to the far left sat a single red-clothed chair by the fireplace where an unattended, large, black pot filled the hearth with a bubbling crude threatened to spill over its rim.

"What is it you seek?"

Mor'vor jumped forward and spun on his heel. His aging heart skipped a beat by the unexpected startle. "Where did you come from?" he asked, not understanding how she could have flanked him. Had his senses dulled to the point that a mere woman could sneak up on him?

The woman's sun-kissed skin looked much like his leather tunic, cracked and wrinkled. Long, matted white hair framed her face. He stared into her dead eyes. On the edges of the irises he could tell they were once as blue as the ocean. She smiled, exposing yellowed teeth and blackened gums; the teeth housed inside ground to uneven nubs.

"Do I know you?" she asked in return.

"My name is Mor'vor Von Asten."

"Ah," the woman said, stretching the word and stepping toward him. "The blade master."

"I see my reputation precedes me, even way out here in these vast woods."

Her gaze traveled over him. "For a hardened warrior, I expected bigger."

"And I expected a wart on the tip of a crook nose."

The witch cackled; her eyes pushed closed by her bulbous cheeks.

"I didn't come to play the part of a fool," he said, silencing her laughter.

"No, I suppose you didn't. Why then?"

"I feel the weakness of age consuming me, deteriorating my skills. The skills I have spent a lifetime honing."

"I see," she interrupted. "It would be a shame to lose them to the ages."

"Then you can help? Can you prolong my life? Perhaps grant me immortality so I may never have to lay down my arms."

She stroked her chin in contemplation. "It is in my power to make your skills everlasting."

"Excellent. What do you need from me? Gold? A lock of hair? Blood? I would give anything."

"My dear, what I require in return is your soul. And I don't need your permission to take it."

"How dare you?" He reached for his sword to unsheathe it, but his arm suddenly dropped to his side, too heavy to hold up, as the witch's right hand shot upward.

"*Per vestri animus, vestri vires ero notus,*" the witch chanted and Mor'vor felt an icy touch permeate at his core.

His stomach squeezed itself into a ball as his shoulders curled in. "What's happening to me?" he asked as a vibrant blue light with sparkles of white seeped from his pores. Like a running river, the light snaked its way closer to the witch and pooled in the palm of her hand. Each breath was a struggle to take as his strength ebbed. As more light poured forth, he collapsed to his knees and the last thing he saw was the light take on the shape of a teardrop.

*

"I hope I'm not too late."

Benan Dewloren, armed with his trusted weapon, hurried through the cobblestone alley between the apothecary and the blacksmith's forge. The thick fog blanketing the ground gave way to his rapidly falling feet. He imagined himself running on clouds as puffs of white swirled upward. Word had traveled fast that Cruor's greatest swordsman was on his way to Fogsmoor in search of worthy challengers.

Though still a child, the significance of Winstrom's arrival was not lost on him. The desert town of Fogsmoor received few visitors due to the occasional sandstorms and the dry, harsh climate. The town's namesake fog rolled in from an oasis over the dunes, which the residents retrieved most of their water from. Superstitions and the density of the fog at the source prevented the townspeople from building closer to the lagoon. The people were poorer than the other towns and villages of Cruor, but that could all change if one of Fogsmoor's warriors could go toe to toe or even defeat Dexter Winstrom.

"I wonder if Orlach will be brave enough to challenge," he said as he came around the bend. He stepped out from the buildings in the hopes of catching a glimpse of Dexter Winstrom. Instead, he came face to face with Kandall and Trese.

"Watch where you're going," said Trese as Benan nearly collided into him.

"Well, if it isn't Benan the Great and his wooden spoon."

"Kandall," he muttered as he glared at the two boys. They were older and bigger than he, at one time Benan had looked up to them, but that was before they used him to make themselves look superior.

"Where are you off to in such a hurry?" Kandall asked.

"Didn't you hear? Dexter Winstrom is coming," Benan answered.

Kandall folded his arms in front of his chest. "And didn't you hear, he's already here?"

Oh no! I missed his entrance? "What? How?"

"It was a grand entrance. One worthy of a champion," Kandall said. "He was led in by warriors willing to lay their lives down for the chance to study under him."

"Yeah," Trese interjected, "even the horses wore armor."

"He smiled and waved, and even tossed gold coins into the air. The crowd loved him."

"See." Trese held up his share of the bounty. A single coin worth more than his mother brought in for a hard day's work.

I should have been there, he thought. "I meant to be there ... I tried."

"Perhaps if you weren't too busy mixing flour, you would have," said Trese.

"That's the price you pay for doing woman's work," Kandall added.

Benan gritted his teeth. With his father dead and buried, and he the man of the house, helping his mother in the bakery was his duty. "You take that back."

"Or what?" Kandall stepped up to him, nose to nose. "You're going to whack me with that pitiful excuse for a sword?" Kandall unsheathed his dagger and placed the point of the blade at Benan's chin.

Benan stood firm and met the bully's unblinking stare. Lips pursed, brow wrinkled, he prepared for his next move.

"Kandall, you're going too far," Trese whispered. "People are looking."

"Let them," he replied.

"Put it away," Trese demanded.

"Some warrior you are." Kandall withdrew his blade and sheathed it.

Benan refrained from releasing the breath he held, daring not to show the boy unnerved him.

"If you want to see Dexter, he's at the Olden Flask. Maybe you can learn a thing or two from him, but you'll always be a commoner to us. Let's go." Kandall shoved his shoulder into Benan as he walked away.

"Sorry," Trese whispered, and then followed Kandall's lead.

Benan uncurled his clenched fist and finally exhaled. He took a moment to steel his nerves and tried to push Kandall's harsh words from his mind. He fixated on his mother, the one constant in his life, then reminded himself he still had time to meet his hero. With a smile, he trotted off to the town's tavern.

The drunken revelry wafted out to the street from the tavern and Benan pushed his way through the swinging doors and looked around. It wasn't hard to pick his hero out from the other patrons. With his fiery red hair, Dexter Winstrom stood nearly a head's length taller than all others in the Olden Flask. Gold epaulets saddled his otherwise silver armor. His long, broad sword weighed down its sheath and scraped the floor, a two-handed weapon that commanded respect. With a barmaid on each arm, it was apparent Benan was not his only admirer. Wide-eyed and awe struck, he slowly approached.

"Are you lost, little boy?" asked a burly man, stepping in front of his path.

"This isn't a place for children," said another.

"Gentlemen," Dexter said, turning to see the commotion, "allow the boy to pass."

The large, bullish men stepped aside and Dexter stepped forward. His smile wide, teeth bright, his eyes the deepest blue. Even Benan, at the age of thirteen, could understand why the ladies swooned.

The smile on Dexter's face faded. "Have you come to challenge me with that stick?"

Laughter filled the air. The two large men beside Dexter grabbed hold of their bellies as they reverberated.

Benan fought the urge to run away and said, "I just wanted to meet you, sir."

"Well, my time is better served facing worthy opponents and pleasuring the women." Dexter lowered his right fist and Benan winced. When a blow failed to strike him, Benan opened his eyes. The fist uncurled and revealed two gold coins. "Run along. This is no place for a child."

Child? Tears pooled at the base of his eyes, but he pursed his lips and fought them back. "Thank you," he said, swiping the coins from Dexter's hand.

The tavern's doors slammed against the walls and the crowd jumped. Benan spun around, pocketing the coins as he did. He smiled at the sight of a true warrior. Orlach!

Orlach filled the doorway with his broad shoulders, his bald head nearly scraping the top of the doorframe as he stepped inside. He wore a simple, iron-studded leather tunic and leggings with his double-headed axe mounted to his back. The patrons closest to him scurried away, some squeezing by him and leaving all together, fearful at the possibility of a bar fight between the two titans.

"Winstrom, I hereby challenge you. Do you accept?"

Dexter turned back, hefted his mug of ale and threw back its contents in one gulp. He slammed it back down and said, "The hour is late. And what kind of a gentleman would I be to turn my back on these lovely ladies? After all, they promised to teach me a move or two."

The bar whores giggled.

Is he a coward? Benan thought.

"You really shouldn't be in such a rush to die," Winstrom said. "Spend your last night with your family. Tell them you love them and apologize for being so weak."

A pale tint of red radiated in Orlach's throat and brightened as it crept upward to his cheeks. The sizable man exhaled through his nose and from where he stood, Benan could hear the *swoosh* of air.

"At dawn then." Orlach turned and left, leaving Dexter to laugh at his expense. The two bar maidens continued their giggling and when Dexter stopped, they too stopped.

When Dexter's eyes opened at the end of his fit, his gaze locked on Benan. "Still here, boy?"

"You shouldn't have provoked him. Orlach is not weak."

"So that's his name, Orlach. I'm not impressed."

"Perhaps tomorrow, you will be." With that, Benan bolted toward the door, shoving his shoulder into a stout patron partially blocking his path.

Tears welled, slipping away from the corners of his eyes as he ran home. The tall tales of Dexter Winstrom had left out the man's arrogance and Benan felt his admiration misplaced. His stomach in knots, breath caught in his throat, he shed the last tears for his faux hero.

As he ran past the blacksmith's shop, Benan paused. He looked up at the shop's sign hung above the door, a painting of two combatants locked in battle. He rolled the gold coins across his fingers, thinking of the fine blade they could afford him; one even Kandall would be envious of.

No, he thought, then shook the selfish thought out of his mind. He curled his fist around the coins. *With these, Mother wouldn't have to work so hard. Maybe she could even hire some help.* He took one last look at the shop's sign, then continued on his way.

By the time he reached home, Cruor's sun was setting and the pale red moon rising. The mixture of yellow and red in the sky cast a soft orange across the land and soon the sand at the town's border would be stained crimson.

"Mother," he said as he gently pushed the front door open, "I'm home." Since the bread cart was still outside, he was certain he would find her cleaning up the kitchen from the day's work, but the pots and bread pans were still piled in the basin.

Where is she? he wondered as a single loaf of bread lay waiting for him on the table.

He fought the urge to call out for her again and decided to go upstairs. As he ascended the rickety staircase, he skipped over the one board that creaked no matter where one's foot touched down. If his mother was up here, it meant only one thing, and he was not about to disturb her.

At the top of the stairs, their living quarters was a small open space with two wool mattresses on the base of the floor and two reading chairs by the fireplace around a bear skin rug. It was all they could afford, all they truly needed.

His mother moaned and rolled over in her bed.

Is she ... ? He walked carefully over to her bed, balancing his weight so not to creak the floorboards. As he stepped closer, he could see the sweat beading her brow. *Is it fever,* he wondered as he placed his palm on her forehead. *She's warm. Better let her be. Maybe it'll break after a good night's sleep.*

Benan returned to the kitchen, but before eating his dinner he brought the bread cart inside and tucked it against the far right wall of the kitchen, then washed the day's dishes. Once he took care of all his mother usually did, he filled a pitcher of water, then sat down to enjoy the meal his mother made for him, despite her sickness.

*

Unable to sleep due to the combination of his conflicted emotions and his mother's tossing and turning, Benan ventured out. If his mother were not feeling better by the morning, the gold coins given to him would have to go to the town herbalist, which Benan knew would only be a temporary solution. His mother worked herself to the breaking point. They needed more gold and there was one place he no longer felt guilty acquiring it from.

He was certain Dexter Winstrom would have secured one of the tavern's upstairs rooms for the night. The whores who clung to him would have seen to it. When he reached the Olden Flask, its patrons were drunkenly shuffling out and he was able to sneak inside undetected, the men too busy laughing, thrusting their swords into the air, telling adventurous tales to notice him.

With the stealth and grace of an assassin, Benan climbed the stairs, keeping to the shadows. At the landing, he peered down the narrow hallway and wondered which room would yield his desire.

I'll have to check them all, he thought and took his first step.

The floorboard suddenly creaked in protest and he froze in place. Realizing he was holding his breath, he exhaled and continued toward the first door. Gently, he pressed the iron latch and cracked the door open. Given the darkness of the room, he closed the door and turned around. He checked the room across the hall and found that one empty as well.

Chances are, they're all empty save for Dexter's. No one in Fogsmoor could afford such luxury.

He peered down the hallway and found a solitary door with light filtering into the hallway from underneath. *That has to be it*, he thought, then walked toward it.

Once at the door, he placed his ear to it and listened. No sound came from behind the oak wood. With his lip pinched between his teeth, he gently pressed the lever of the door handle and slowly opened it. He could feel the warmth of the orange glow upon his face from the dozen candles burning brightly throughout the room.

Inside, Dexter lay upon the bed in between the two whores, their arms thrown across his chiseled chest, the sheet barely covering their naked backs. Benan scanned the room and found the silver-plated armor resting against the wall. His gaze locked on the small, leather skinned pouch tied to the waist.

Steady now, he instructed himself as he stepped into the room on his tippy-toes. One shaky foot after the other, Benan made his way toward the armor. He slouched and placed one hand on the epaulet to steady the armor, while the other untied the cord. He pulled the cord through the stitching, separating it from the pouch.

As he stood, he tipped the bag out into his open palm.

What ... nothing?

He shook the pouch, but still nothing poured forth.

Did you hand it all out?

The thought of stealing his sword crossed his mind, but he doubted he could heft the mighty blade; the metal would surely drag across the floorboards and alert its owner. Then the woman closest to him pulled her arm from Dexter's chest and rolled over and the candlelight refracted off something that caught his eye. He let the pouch drop to the floor and stepped closer to the bed. There, at the base of Dexter's neck, a small pendant sparkled blue with fragments of white.

It's beautiful, he thought as he leaned in for a closer look. *It may not be gold, but I'm sure it would fetch a handsome price. Even if I can't sell it, Mother would love it.*

He lowered to his knees and fumbled through the harlot's dress knowing they often concealed small knives in the folds of their gowns to deal with the occasional ruffian or swindler.

Oh! He found the blade the hard way and his finger shot toward his mouth. As he sucked on the tip to stop the bleeding, his free hand removed the blade more carefully.

Confident the bleeding had stopped, he stood over the edge of the bed and leaned in. The moment he touched the teardrop-shaped pendant, a shockwave pulsated through his arm. *Through my soul, my strength will be known.* The voice echoed in his mind, leaving a pins-and-needle sensation in its wake. *What was that?* He looked around the room, but there was no one else. Too afraid to pull away and drop the pendant, he stood there motionless until the feeling passed.

Thinking his nerves were getting the best of him, he shrugged his shoulders and carried on. With the pendent resting in the palm of his hand and the cord pinched between his finger and thumb, he slid the knife's blade under the cord and quickly pulled up. The blade's sharp edge passed through the leather with ease. When he stepped back, the pendant came with him, Dexter's sleep undisturbed.

Perfect, he thought, placing the blade on the floor atop the gown. With his prize in hand, he tiptoed out of the room, into the hallway. Not feeling the need to close the door behind him, Benan left the establishment and returned home undetected.

As he lay in bed, he untied the knot in the pendant's cord and removed the small section he had cut. *It will still fit me*, he thought as he wrapped it around his neck, *but I'll have to replace the cord if I want to give it to Mother.* With a secure knot in place, he let the pendant fall upon his chest. A blue light flashed, and then subsided.

Strange, he thought before drifting off to sleep.

When morning came, Benan's first priority was his mother.

"How are you feeling?"

"Better," she said, "but the fever hasn't broke yet."

"No," he said, stepping to her bedside and placing his hand across her forehead. "You should probably stay in bed."

"How can I when there is so much to do?"

"I've got it under control," he said.

"Oh?"

"I'll show you. Wait here."

"Where are you going?" she asked as he darted downstairs.

The gold coins were on the table where he had left them. With one hand pressed against the table's edge, he slid the coins across the table with his other. He held the coins up. The morning's rays caught the gold and shimmered brilliantly. The sparkle was nearly blinding, but it filled him with joy.

She'll be so surprised.

He darted up the stairs taking them two at a time in his haste. "See," he said, holding them up for her to see as he approached.

"Is that..."

"It's gold, Mother." He placed the coins in her hand.

She sat up in bed and looked at him with wide eyes, her mouth agape. "How did you? Who did you —"

"I didn't steal them, Mother. Dexter Winstrom has come to town in search of a worthy challenger. He handed these out to a lucky few."

"Are you fibbing?" she asked with that quizzical look, the single raised eyebrow and crooked glance.

"No, Mother. I am not. Kandall and Trese also got some."

"I don't like those boys. They're a bad influence."

"Don't worry, they're not my friends."

"Good." She looked at the gold coins, bit down on them to check their authenticity, then said, "I suppose with these I can afford to skip a day."

"Yes, Mother. Better to concentrate on yourself than others right now."

"When did you become so wise?"

"So you'll stay here then?"

"Yes," she said, dragging the word.

"Is there anything I can get you?"

Her curious look still prominent, she said, "Why, are you leaving?"

"Orlach challenged Dexter. I want to be there."

"Oh my, what if —"

"I don't know, but I have to see it with my own eyes."

"All right, I suppose no matter what I say, you're going to go. Just promise me you'll stay out of the way."

"I promise."

"You be careful."

"I will, Mother."

She breathed in deeply through her nose. "All right. Go. I'll be fine."

"Thank you," he said, already making his way to the staircase.

Downstairs, Benan washed and dressed hastily, then grabbed his trusted weapon off the table on his way out. As the door closed behind him, he spun around to lock it.

"Why bother? Nothing worth stealing in there anyway."

Benan's teeth ground as he recognized Kandall's voice. He turned around slowly, the wooden spoon clutched tightly in his right hand.

"Why don't you leave that thing in the kitchen where it belongs?" Kandall asked.

"Yeah!" Trese followed.

"There's no time for this, Orlach has challenged Dexter."

Trese's jaw dropped and Kandall's eyes went wide at the news.

"What? You mean you didn't hear?" Benan could not resist the smile that stretched across his face.

"When is it happening?" Kendall asked.

"I imagine now," he said.

Kandall slapped Trese on the arm, then ran past Benan. Trese followed his lead.

"Do you even know where you're going?" Benan called after them.

"It would have to be in the town center. There's no other place worthy of such an epic battle," Kandall replied.

The fog at Benan's feet grew heavy. He turned around, toward the direction of the oasis, and saw the blanket of white rolling in. *What will this mean for the fight?* he wondered, then ran after Kandall and Trese.

As he ran through Fogsmoor, he saw not a soul and he prayed he was not too late. When he came onto the main road that traveled through the heart of town, he stopped and stared at the wall of people already gathered, all wanting to bear witness. He looked to the right, then the left for an opening, and noticed Kandall and Trese pushing their way through. He darted in their direction and quickly followed on their heels, taking advantage of the displaced townspeople who were too busy griping about the two arrogant boys who had disturbed them to notice him sneak past.

Benan slipped by the last body and came upon the vast open space where blood would soon be shed, but whose fate had yet to determine. There, in the center, Orlach waited, a patient giant standing steadfast against a tidal wave of rage. The morning's sun glistened off his bare chest, and shimmered off the steel of his axe. His sculpted muscles, defined like chiseled marble, rippled with each anticipating breath.

Dexter's insults still rang in Benan's ears and he knew it was the same for the proud warrior before him.

"Where's Dexter," Trese asked.

"He has yet to show," answered someone from the crowd.

"Cowardice, I tell you. Orlach's calls have gone unanswered," another townsman said.

"Perhaps he was taken in his sleep," Kandall said.

"No," a man interjected, "his whores came out and said otherwise."

"Aye," another said, "men have been sent in to drag his worthless carcass out here. No matter who wins, we have much riding on this."

"It will be a battle all in Cruor will sing praises of. And all the land shall know and recognize Fogsmoor as a place of champions."

The sound of arguing and tables tipping over wafted from the tavern. Then, the armor clad Dexter stumbled through the swinging doors and fell upon the cobblestone. The crowd laughed at his expense.

"Please ... my pendant. It has to be in there somewhere. Give me more time to find it."

"This battle is about brawn and steel, not trinkets. The time to fight is now," Orlach said, taking a step closer.

One of the men charged with retrieving Dexter from his hiding place tossed the warrior's large sword to the ground beside him. The weight of it displaced the thin layer of fog as it clanged against the stone. Dexter eyed the crowd. The admiration received the day earlier replaced with contempt. He pleaded with his tear-filled eyes, "My pendant. Please."

Benan clutched his ill-gotten gains under the fabric of his shirt, his heart heavy with guilt.

"On your feet, knave, or do you require a moment to kiss your loved ones goodbye?" Orlach teased.

Dexter grabbed his sword by the grip, just below the guard, and stood. "You shall have no honor in this victory."

"We shall see what victory brings," Orlach replied, then charged with his axe overhead.

Dexter smiled and with the aid of his left hand pressed against the diamond-shaped tip, he deflected the arcing blade of the axe before it could gain more strength from gravity than he could handle. The metal sang. Sparks erupted.

Orlach pulled back in preparation of another blow.

Is he toying with Orlach? Benan wondered as the combatants regained their footing.

Dexter swung his massive blade around and Orlach dipped the head of his axe to block it, then planted his mighty boot into Dexter's midsection. Caught off balance, Dexter fell to his backside and quickly scurried back, the smile no longer present on his handsome face.

The crowd roared with bloodlust as Dexter took a defensive stance.

"Come at me, brute," Dexter said, and Orlach charged.

Dexter's smile returned as he raised his sword and brought it down, his eyes wide and anxious to see blood.

With both hands on his axe, Orlach pushed his weapon forward and deflected the blow, but Dexter quickly recovered and thrust his sword. Orlach leaned his hips to the right and the blade grazed his abdomen, a small stream of blood jettisoned from the wound. In retaliation, Orlach brought his closed fist down upon Dexter's brow as if it were a hammer. The arrogant swordsman dropped to his knees under its weight. A trickle of blood ran down the edge of his nose and passed his lips.

"Die!" Orlach commanded as he raised his axe above his head.

Benan's instincts told him this was a mistake, and he watched with unblinking eyes as Dexter rammed the pommel of his sword into Orlach's unguarded midsection. The behemoth of a man stumbled backward, hunched over. Dexter stood and threw his right leg out, catching Orlach square across the chin. As Orlach's back straightened, the axe head lifted in the air. With his eyes still locked on his opponent, Orlach brought the axe down. Dexter's sword raised up to meet it. Metal clanged. The sword faltered under the weight and the axe slammed into Dexter's armor, denting it.

With a look of panic in his eyes, Dexter's head tilted down to inspect the armor and Orlach capitalized. His left fist hurled into Dexter's jaw. The blow rocked Dexter's head sending a small stream of blood to the sand.

The crowd cheered and chanted, "Kill him, kill him, kill him."

Dexter drooled blood and righted his posture. Orlach stepped in for the killing blow, but as the axe's head was lifted over his right shoulder, Dexter ran his blade across Orlach's tree-trunk legs. The giant screamed but remained upright. As Dexter stood, the blade of the mighty axe circled around and cleaved Dexter's head from its perch.

Silence befell the crowd as blood erupted in a geyser and the fiery mane of Dexter tumbled away from his body. With his axe in one hand, Orlach limped over to the severed appendage, grabbed it by the red hair, and hoisted it to the heavens for all to see.

The crowd's roar was deafening, their cheers carrying on the wind.

Benan turned away from the scene and made his way through the crowd. *It's my fault*, he thought as he clutched the pendant under his shirt. *Through my soul, my strength will be known.* The words replayed in his mind. *Is it possible?*

Benan knew it to be no easy task to sever Dexter's head, given his armor, the precise angle needed to be calculated. However, he could not shake the suspicion that had Dexter still wore the pendant in battle, Orlach would have fallen at his hands. And for that, Dexter's blood was on his hands. *But then again—*

"Hey, spoon boy, where are you going?"

"Leave me be, Kandall. I am not in the mood."

"Aren't you going to share in the celebration?" Trese asked.

"Not much to celebrate," he replied.

A hand upon his shoulder tried to force him around, but instinctively his left hand shot toward it, grabbed hold of the index finger and pushed it back. The sound of bone cracking echoed in his ear as he willfully removed the unwanted gesture.

Kandall cried and Trese pulled his arm back, and then launched a fist. Benan swatted the hand downward with the aid of his spoon. The skin on the back of Trese's hand split and Trese's tears joined Kandall's.

Benan stepped away from the boys, putting several feet between them. The courage swelling in his heart surprised even him. He found an uncanny confidence in his moves, one not known to him before placing the pendant around his neck.

Kandall pursed his lips and flared his nostrils. "You'll pay for that." The boy ran headlong at him.

An image of him slamming the palm of his hand directly into Kandall's nose flashed in Benan's mind. Knowing it would be a deathblow, Benan ignored the impulse and spun on his heels, then extended his left foot, tripping his would-be assailant. Kandall fell face first to the ground.

"Aargh," Trese roared his battle cry as he swung his dagger.

Benan ducked and slammed the head of his wooden spoon into the side of Trese's knee. The boy buckled under the blow and Benan reeled the spoon back in an upward arc. The blow caught the boy under the chin and took him off his feet.

The sound of gravel rustling underfoot alerted him to Kandall's next move. He spun around in time to see a dagger thrust forward. With reflexes he didn't know he had, he pivoted his right elbow, bringing it down and brought the spoon's head slamming into Kandall's wrist. Thrown off target, the attack missed Benan and before Kandall could recover, the wooden spoon was planted in his midsection. He keeled over. Benan took advantage and drove his trusted weapon into the back of Kandall's skull. The boy fell to the ground where he remained unconscious.

Benan turned toward Trese and said, "I suggest you stay down."

Trese looked up at him, tears streaking through the sand covering his cheeks. "How did you —?"

"I do not wish to fight with you anymore. But should you continue to torment me, I will be forced to bury your dagger in your gullet." Benan knelt down and placed his hand upon Trese's chin. He lifted his head out of the fog and stared deep into the boy's hazel eyes. His own aggression stared back at him, reflected in the pupils.

Trese nodded in understanding.

"Make sure you relay that message to Kandall when he awakes."

"I will."

Benan stepped away from the fallen boy, his gaze fixated on his trembling hand. *Am I afraid*, he wondered. *Or does my hand call for blood?*

As Benan walked the streets home, he couldn't help but wonder if the arrogance Dexter Winstrom had showed him was his own or stemmed from the pendant. *Mother would not be proud of my actions*, he thought as he lifted the pendant out from beneath his shirt.

Through my soul, my strength will be known. The voice echoed upon his caress.

"I don't know who you are, but there may come a time when your strength is needed. This day is not it," he said, tugging on the cord and pulling it free from around his neck.

Should Kandall and Trese bully me again, I shall deal with them with my own strength. My own skill. He pocketed the pendant and returned home, knowing when his mother looked upon him it would be as her baby boy as she so often called him, and not a hardened warrior.

***

The Devil's Fingers

by Clark Roberts, United States

"'Twas the Devil's fingers that stole that girl from the community."

"Why do you say it like that? 'Twas?"

"'Twas how my grandpappy said it," I answered. We'd just broken through the shin-tangle of the boreal forest which consisted of cluttered small pines, fallen pines, and rotted pines. We stepped out onto a lightly grassed sand dune. Below us Lake Superior, the cold bitch, was lapping the shoreline. I smiled, turning the flashlight beam on my companion, Dena, an old high school flame of mine. "You know how ridiculous you look wearing a winter coat in June?"

"First of all, it's not a coat; it's called a winter jacket. Secondly, I'm a Miami girl now, and the Keweenaw beaches aren't exactly hot when compared to South Beach."

"No," I said, shaking my head slowly as if surmising. "Probably not. Still looks like a coat from my angle."

Dena balled up a fist and slugged my shoulder, called me a dick, and then laughed. Not for the first time that night, I was struck nostalgic. She'd done that a lot when we were dating, laughingly punch me and proclaim me 'dick!'

"Come on," she whined. "How much farther? You promised me a ghost."

"I didn't *promise* anything. I said there was a real possibility we'd see Misty. The conditions are ripe for an appearance tonight."

"Well, you *did* say there is a lighthouse, one I never heard of despite growing up around here—and a bench! You said there was a bench where we could sit together to wait for her."

"There's a lighthouse," I said. "There's a bench. We can sit."

What I didn't tell her was that the lighthouse was really a ruin, a relic of the past. That structurally it had also served as someone's home, a brick house with a brick lighthouse on the shoreline side, or that those bricks had been charred by a fire years before I'd ever laid eyes on it. I didn't tell her the fire had collapsed the roof in and ate up most of the floor. Now, moss and small pines grew up through the floor's holes. Or that the lighthouse hadn't shone a beacon light within twenty years before either Dena or I, or Misty for that matter, had walked into our first day of grade school.

I didn't tell her she wasn't going to see Misty, because like my grandpappy had spoken of Lake Superior, not only is she a cold bitch, she also never gives up her dead.

I motioned with the flashlight for Dena to follow. If the Devil's lighthouse had been south of us, the going would have been pretty fair as sand stretched to that direction for miles upon miles. But the Devil's lighthouse wasn't south of us, and I thought I should warn Dena.

Over my shoulder I said, "I know we're out of the woods, but we aren't *really* out of the woods just yet."

"What do you mean by that?"

"You'll see."

Soon, as I knew was the case, the easy stroll in the sand turned into a slow touch-and-go kind of ballet as we scuttled and scooted over a terraced shoreline of damp sandstone.

"What the heck is this so slippery for?"

"Here, easy does it," I said. I held out a hand to assist Dena down a particular large drop of sandstone, so perfectly rounded it might have been a stairstep molded by the earliest people's gods. I went on explaining, not without annoyance of having to address such a stupid question. "It's sandstone on a shoreline. It gets wet and then it naturally gets slick."

I didn't tell her we were already at Devil's Bay, or the science about it. I didn't tell her that we were only a stone's throw away from Devil's River. Over thousands and thousands of years, possibly hundreds of thousands of years, Devil's River and all of its tributaries, with all their twists, turns, and meanderings, had carved out the soil of this land. It was the very land she'd been raised on but knew and cared so little about. The river had deposited the sediment of red clay along this shoreline and, of course, at the bottom of the rip current where the mouth of Devil's River empties into the cold bitch that is Lake Superior. I didn't relay any of this to her because she wouldn't have found it interesting, at least not in the way Misty would have.

"Is it this difficult to walk around the lighthouse?"

"No. It gets sandier again."

That much was true, but I didn't tell her about the small rocks littering the sand, how the cold bitch that was Lake Superior let go of them sometimes, leaving them behind on the shoreline the way a child might discard a toy they've outgrown.

We shuffled onward in the direction of Devil's River.

"Why did I let you talk me into leaving the reunion for this?" Dena asked.

I said, "The party will just be starting to rock when we get back. It's not even ten yet. Besides, you want to see the lighthouse. You want to see a ghost. You want to sit on a bench—with me."

Dena twirled me around, throwing her arms over my shoulders. Suddenly we were kissing. When she drew back, she said, "That was nice. I liked it."

For me there had been no spark. All I could say was, "I can taste the strawberry from your lip gloss."

"Carry me," she suggested. She was smiling, her pristine teeth nearly glowing in the dark. "Be my knight and carry me."

I didn't carry her, but I did hold her hand the rest of the way as we maneuvered delicately over the uneven lakeside. We reached Devil's River. With no moon or stars visible from the shrouding clouds, the darkness was enveloping. I swiped the flashlight over the river. It was roaring hard from the violent storms that had passed through the previous days. I didn't let my light linger long at the mouth of the river, but I saw enough to know the rip current, the one my grandpappy referred to as the Devil's Fingers, was industrious tonight. As it dumped into Lake Superior, the river's water roiled and churned as it moved steadily out.

"We can't cross here," I said. Using my flashlight, I waved for Dena to follow me back into the woods where we had to push through brush and duck branches.

"There better be a bridge and it better be sturdy," Dena griped from behind me. "I'm not balancing my way over on some fallen tree."

"There's a bridge," I said. I didn't tell her that I knew there was a bridge because I had been the one that built it. About every other spring, I hauled some lumber with my four-wheeler and replaced any board that had warped or rotted from the damp springs that inevitably followed the harsh winters of Michigan's upper peninsula. I wasn't meticulous with my upkeep, but I visited the Devil's lighthouse enough that it made my biannual efforts worthwhile.

Dena and I reached the bridge and crossed it. The wooden boards had soaked up a lot of water over the past forty-eight hours, so much that one particular board had warped and swollen too snug. The end had popped loose. I would have to be careful not to trip when I made my way back.

We once again maneuvered and bushwhacked through the woods. Just when I thought maybe I'd played a poor guide and had somehow veered us off course into the wrong direction, the shoreline once again opened up to us. Lake Superior is like that away from the main roads and tourist traps; her thick forests run deep as if protecting the secrets of her water's edge.

"This is it," I said in presentation. Dena stepped abreast of me. I glided the disc of light up the fire-scarred brick exterior of the lighthouse all the way to the top where mounted there was a deteriorating metal cage that must have housed the beacon light decades before.

"Oh my God!" she exclaimed. "It's so freaky!"

The square tower rising above us was surrounded by another, somewhat shorter, square and brick building. It only made sense. Whoever had been responsible for operating the lighthouse moons and moons ago hadn't trekked out here daily. No, this had been their home.

The glass of tall windows had been blown out from the fire, who knew when. I let Dena peek inside with the Maglite. The interior of the house had been modest at best with the layout of crumbling walls alluding to at most three small rooms.

"Have you ever, you know, crawled over and poked around in there?" Dena's eyes were wide with mystery, excitement.

"I have." I didn't tell her that in our ninth-grade year I'd actually tucked myself small and hidden behind one of those crumbling walls and waited for a man, a drifter of sorts, possibly the very devil himself, to fall asleep. Or that when that devil of a man finally was sound asleep, I stealthily approached him with my jackknife out and the blade opened, the very jackknife my grandpappy had given to me as a Christmas gift when I was seven. I didn't tell her what it was like to slit a throat. How, with a deadly sharp blade, the skin just opens up as if it was naturally perforated or how the blood starts to bubble, rush, and wash out with increased pressure. I didn't point and say *I killed a man in there once, right there, right where you're looking, on a night as dark as this. Just before the life slipped out of him, the whites of his eyes popped brilliant with fear.*

"I'm not going in there," Dena said, her face reproachful. "I don't want to disappoint you, but it's spooky here, like there's an energy in there or something. I really don't want to go in there."

"Nor do I," I said. "Come on, let's go sit and wait."

I took the flashlight back from Dena. By the hand I led her around the building to where the bench that I'd built and anchored into the beach was facing Lake Superior. We sat.

Dena asked, "You've never seen Misty's ghost out here, have you? I mean, nobody ever really found out what happened to her and you've been sitting on this secret for twenty-five years? I don't buy it. This was just some elaborate plan to get me away from the party, wasn't it?"

"Maybe."

I'd never told Dena the whole truth about Misty and me, how the two of us had grown up together close friends, a boy and a tomboy, how we'd played ball together, caught snakes together, explored the woods and shoreline, studied rocks together, and that miraculously Misty one summer was no longer a tomboy. She'd blossomed beautifully, with chestnut eyes, waves of full hair, and skin so perfectly unblemished that just holding her hand was like touching a shined and smoothed stone. A precious stone so beautiful it would be a crime to hide it away from the world.

Nature had won out and we'd fallen in love with each other. I didn't tell Dena that I was the only living soul that knew the answer to the mystery of what happened to Misty. That just two days after her disappearance I came out here to Devil's Bay to search for clues, because this place, this very spot I was now sitting at with Dena, had been mine and Misty's spot the summer after our freshman year.

I found a clue that day. Before I'd crawled into the lighthouse for inspection, I'd seen a man far out in Lake Superior either swimming or bathing. I remember feeling cheated because I truly believed no one else had known about this forgotten place except me, Misty, and my grandpappy. Once in the lighthouse, I discovered a canvas rucksack. It was the color of military green, grimed with dirt, and stuffed with nearly as grimy clothes. There were loose cigarettes and torn-out magazine pictures of grimy women doing grimy activities. At the bottom of that bag I'd discovered Misty's bathing suit.

Stained with blood.

I remember I was scared to goose bumps and wide eyes at first, terrified the drifter had returned from his bath and was watching me at that very moment and was going to overtake me. When that didn't happen, I set my mind on revenge. I made myself discreet. From the shadows I waited for the dirty bum to crawl in through the window. I watched him make his bed from a roll-out mat and his pillow from his rucksack. I watched him defile Misty's swimsuit. When he fell asleep, using my jackknife, I killed him.

"I'll bet our fellow alumni are starting to miss their homecoming queen," Dena spoke. "If there's no ghost, I guess there's really no reason for us to be out here. Or is there?" Her voice rose with the question hinting at the possibilities.

"Just a little longer," I said.

The breeze off the lake had turned cold and had ratcheted up to an actual wind. Dena no longer looked so ridiculous in her winter coat. It wasn't long before she was leaning into me for warmth. I wrapped my arm around her pinning her close to me. I found it amazing that this woman in her late thirties was so much like the eighteen-year-old girl I remembered her being. I shouldn't have been surprised, though, because I guess that's the way it is with most people, they find an activity in life they can put up with and they ride it out. For Dena, that said activity just happened to be cuddling up with the nearest handsome devil.

That hadn't been the way of Misty, though. Sometimes, even to this day, I flip through the pages of my freshman school yearbook. Looking at her picture through the lenses of an adult, it's easy to see why our small community mourned her disappearance. Her youthful beauty transcended desire and lust. It was the type of beauty that bubbled over the brim with happiness; it was a precious beauty, a beauty that promised to cleanse the soul of the man that ultimately won her heart. As an adult, would that have been me? I'll never know because I never got the chance, and she was never afforded the opportunity to offer all of her outer and inner beauty to the world.

This time when Dena moved in to kiss me, I had a surprise for her. She hadn't noticed that I'd picked up a stone, smooth and oval that fit perfectly into my palm. With my other hand I grabbed her chin tenderly. I tugged her mouth open ever so slightly. She paused. I imagine she was waiting for my tongue to tease out and play onto her lip gloss. Instead, I gave her the stone and I was not tender.

I crammed it down, forcing it deep until my hand was swallowed in her mouth past the wrist. With my other hand, I pinched her nostrils shut. Dena's eyes bulged.

I did not tell her that I hated everything about her, or that I'd desired to kill her the night I'd lost my virginity to her because in her eyes there had been nothing special about it as I hadn't been her first, or second, or third.

Instead, I said something to let her know just how insignificant she really was. I put my lips close to her ear and whispered, "You would have never been homecoming queen if Misty had been alive."

Only now did Dena begin to struggle, and so I rocked my weight, pitching both of us off the bench to the ground. To her credit, she fought maddeningly, kicking and thrashing. Death can be a long time coming. In the end, however, my will for her to die was stronger than her will to live.

With the deed done, I dislodged the stone from her throat and chucked it as far out into the greatest lake of the Greats as I could. I stripped off all clothes from the both of us. I dragged her lifeless body by limp wrists over the sand and waded out into Lake Superior. The water was bone-chillingly cold. The wind of yet another promised northwestern storm was kicking, and the water passing by me had begun to swell into humps. Soon the waves would grow to a height above my head and begin absolutely assaulting the shoreline.

With cautious steps, I inched my way deeper over the hand-sized rocks loitering at the surf's bottom. Those rocks, worn smooth from the current of time, shifted with each wave and draw of water, some of them rolling over my bare feet like bones. I angled off towards the mouth of Devil's River with the knowledge that the earlier storm had transformed it turgid.

When the painful bite of rocks with each step had been replaced by sand, I was nearly shoulder deep. I felt the first steady pull of the Devil's Fingers. The rip current was powerful this night, stronger than an Olympic swimmer. I swung Dena's body in a massive arc beneath the surface. I held firm for a time, relishing the feeling of the rhythm of the Devil's Fingers through her dangling body. Precariously, I leaned out farther, and sand began to wash out beneath the balls of my feet. The largest wave yet rolled over me. The next lifted me, tossing me haphazardly, and I was set down in the rip current where the bottom was untouchable. I could only trust that the Devil's icy hands had latched onto Dena or risk myself being captured as well.

With all my might, I kicked my legs in unison, arched my spine, and thrust backwards. I released the dead weight I had been holding.

The body seemed to roll away and out from me ... and out ... and out ... and out, a wayward flag caught in a gale.

I swam parallel to the shore a short distance to break free of the rip current. I did not panic, but nor did I waste any time. The Devil of Superior has many hands, and one of them had drawn from the dark depths. I could feel its fingers tickling my bare skin, icing my veins.

Once free from the rip current, I let the now crashing waves carry me shoreward.

Back on land, I first gathered Dena's clothes making sure not to miss a single item. Then I gathered mine and tucked the tangled ball under an arm.

"For you, Misty," I whispered. "For you."

I looked out over the angry expanse of Lake Superior hoping to hear my love answer back. But all that could be heard was the wind howling and the wall of rain rushing at me that I would never be able to beat no matter how much I hustled.

Next was a massive squeal of rusted metal grating on rusted metal. To this day, I have a recurring dream in which I'm haunted by that sound. Only in my dream I'm not at the Devil's Lighthouse, but the Gates of Hell, and they swing open. Inviting.

Like a bullet from a rifle, the beacon light shone down on me. It did not emit a blinding light but an orangish hue, the color of a dying fire's embers come to life with a breath. It was dull but powerful in a cosmic way. I was pinned to the spot, and when the first drops of rain fell upon me, they sizzled against my skin and steam rose.

I could make out a shadowy figure up there standing just to the side of the light. Impossible, I knew, as the lighthouse stairs had been laid to waste, but no more impossible than the hellish light that would immolate me in a matter of minutes.

The beacon light clicked off. Now two eyes glowed cinder red. They did not shine down on me, but I felt them bore into my soul just the same. The shadowy figure nodded, as if pleased, and when it did, there were two protrusions just above the eyes curving to points that breathed aglow as well.

A clap of thunder, a flash of lightning, and the figure was gone.

Fine, I thought. I've done right by my lover. I have no more worries, no more concerns.

Lake Superior— she's a cold, cold bitch, and harbors a demon. She never gives up her dead.

Naked, dripping, and cold, I followed the beam of the flashlight back to my car.

*

Two days later, three police cruisers wheeled into the drive of my humble home. It was inevitable really, seeing that I was the last one seen in Dena's company as we exited the reunion party. I imagine a boyfriend worried about her failure to board the flight home to Miami. Phone calls were made, followed by questions being asked of my former schoolmates, followed by all fingers pointing at me.

I obliged with the chief and the two deputies he'd towed with him. I even agreed to a ride in the back of the chief's car.

My story? Yes, Chief Pastewick, Dena and I did leave the reunion early. I took her back to a spot along the shoreline where we used get our groove on. Didn't I know a storm was coming? Well, yes, of course, I did. Shucks, Chief, I'm just a middle-aged man who saw an opportunity to rekindle an old flame. No, we never did get our groove on, the storm was on us too quickly. Sure, she was upset with me. I mean, I don't know if you ever knew Dena, but she could get pissed off something fierce. Despite being sopping wet, she wanted to go back to the reunion. For some reason on the ride back to the bar she started yelling at me about a love tryst from way back in high school. Who knows, maybe it was the alcohol in her system. She was pretty drunk. I left her out front in the rain. Yes, with hindsight I can see she would have been vulnerable. But to be completely honest, I was embarrassed by the whole situation. I sped away before I saw her enter. Where was our spot? Do you know of the Devil's Lighthouse? Okay, I'll draw you a map.

I was taken to a holding cell while the chief and his two deputies went out to search the Devil's Lighthouse.

Hours later—and I do mean hours—the deputies returned. No chief. I was released. The deputies claimed Pastewick had wandered into the woods in search of clues, and he never returned.

I wonder, though.

Imagine.

Imagine with me.

The chief and his deputies are searching for clues, kicking stones, turning rocks, digging in sand. The deputies are ordered to search the abandoned lighthouse. There truly is a power of seismic proportions in that lighthouse. I felt it shake my soul when I killed the drifter and probably the drifter had been influenced by it when he killed Misty. Imagine then the state of mind of the deputies as they enter one of Hell's portals, good men, upstanding men of the community, but their thoughts are already razzled, swirling, and hell-bent on finding the evidence to take me down, some scumbag living within the community they have vowed to protect. Their minds are vulnerable; their emotions able to be coerced. There is no evidence to be unearthed, but they yearn for some type of justice to take place, even if it's a deflected justice. They are presented with a vision so consuming they have to take action. Chief Pastewick, a known philanderer of the community, plowing their wives, or maybe their daughters, or maybe their sons.

In their state of mind, what might the deputies have done?

Admittedly, it's just a theory, but still, only the deputies returned. Nobody has caught neither scent nor sight of the chief's tail since. Once more I ask you to contemplate. What might the deputies have done?

With only circumstantial evidence against me, and the chief of police officially scrawled down in a report as a missing person's case, it appeared the demon in our community was still roaming scot-free. For I had been in a cell when the chief vanished.

On certain nights I'm still drawn to the Devil's Lighthouse, the fledgling moth to a millennium's old flame. I hope to see those cinder eyes and the glow of horns. I yearn for the Devil's fingers to flick the beacon light to full power and burn me down this time.

It's what I deserve. It's what I desire.

TERRORS UNIMAGINED

***

One Night in the Roach Motel

by Seth Peterson, United States

Carl Kellham needed sleep. It was three in the morning, and he was trapped on Highway 60—the most boring road in all of Florida—on the way back from a funeral in St. Petersburg. From Clearwater to Vero Beach, there was nothing to look at. On either side was flat, brown pasture, laidback palm trees, and a drowsy cow once every twenty miles. In the dark, there was even less to see. Clouds fogged out the stars and dimmed the light of the full moon.

Carl turned the volume down on the radio. The alternative rock station that had played for the last two and a half hours started to repeat, and Carl didn't think his eyes would let him listen to "Dig" a third time.

He flexed his right hand. It always stiffened when he was anxious. Even after Carl had the cast removed, the bones had never properly healed. His middle and ring finger were slightly bent, the knuckles lightly purpled. They cracked with the movement, aching with a dull pain.

Carl bounced his leg up and down; he slapped his face, trying to stay awake. If he didn't find a place to stop soon, he'd fall asleep at the wheel. He looked out the window, praying for some sign of life. Then he saw it, about a thousand feet ahead on the left—a light, beaming through the darkness.

Carl drove closer and saw the light came from the roof of an old motel. The tan paint was chipped, as if the building itself was molting; the wood underneath was a termite buffet. Dust clouded the windows and a severely rusted black metal arrow sign read "Welcome to the Roach Motel." What mattered to Carl more were the letters, barely attached, below. They read "vacancy," but to Carl they spelled relief. He pulled into the sand and gravel parking lot, got out of his car, and trudged through the motel's front door, ringing the bell overhead.

Inside, the lobby was dim. A fan spun dangerously loose on the moldy ceiling, pushing stale air in its wake. A mirror hung on the wall to the right of the front entrance, the same height as Carl, stained by water splotches and covered in dust, so much so, Carl could barely see himself. A check-in desk sat on the left. It was made of laminated wood, painted tan, with rose and orchid floral designs carved into the base. A pot of dead lilies decorated the top left of the desk and a rusted bell sat on the far right. In the middle was a guest sign-in ledger, the pencil-etched names and check-in dates fading into the browning paper. Behind the desk an old radio, made of varnished oak with black plastic dials, played softly through static—*we all have something that digs at us*. A piano—another victim of termite gluttony—sat behind moth-eaten couches in the waiting area. Old sheet music rested on its stand, the inked notes barely visible. Beyond the waiting area, a dark hallway led to the various rooms.

Carl scanned the lobby for an employee, but all he found was a cockroach crawling over the top of the desk. He ignored it and rang the bell.

"Hello?"

"Hello there," a voice answered. Carl thought it came from down the hall; he edged his way over there. "Name's Jasper. How can I help you?"

"I know it's late," Carl said. "But could I get a room?"

"Sure you can. Just take a look down here and I'll help you out."

Carl started down the hallway with the cockroach following close behind. He stopped at a red door. It was paneled with daffodils and at the top was the number one.

"Hello?" Carl said again. "Are you in here?"

"Why don't you have a look inside?"

We all have something that digs at us.

Carl opened the door with a creak and stepped in. He felt like he went back in time. A tall window, covered by red velvet curtains patterned with carnations, loomed ahead of him. A four-poster bed, perfectly made, covered by a blue blanket also patterned with carnations, sat to his left. To his right stood several old bookcases stacked to the ceiling. The leather bound tomes looked like they hadn't been touched in a while; dust gathered under some; spider webs covered others. In between the bookcases, another red door, paneled with daffodils and marked with the number two, led to an adjoining room. In the corner sat an old wooden desk, books strewn about on top like a ten-car pile-up.

Carl wanted to leave, but froze when he saw what sat at the desk. His right hand stiffened. She—was it a she?—had wisps of silver hair floating above her wrinkled, otherwise bald head, as if they were underwater. She wore a blue, silk nightgown patterned with tulips. Her skin was a pasty gray-green, pocked with liver spots. Her bony arms moved back and forth. Carl heard the faint scribbles of pen on paper. It was all too familiar.

"Lacy," he breathed. He had just come from her funeral.

We all have something that digs at us.

The creature's head whipped around. In a flash she was two inches away from Carl, her acrid breath crinkling his nose hairs. Her face was even more hideous than the rest of her. It had the same pasty, gray-green skin, but there was no nose, only slits, sniffing back and forth over Carl's body, and no ears, only holes. Black lipstick colored her lips. Her mouth opened to reveal rows and rows of serrated teeth. Her tongue would've put Gene Simmons to shame, but her glasses scared Carl the most— small, rounded, with a crack in the right lens shaped like a thunderbolt, just like Lacy's, yet she had no eyes.

We all have something that digs at us.

She closed the door softly, thrumming her long fingernails, painted black, against the wall with a *clickety-clack*. "Someone's in my room," she hissed, her voice barely above a whisper. "I can smell you. I can hear your heartbeat." She licked her lips. "I can taste your fear."

Carl tried his best not to shiver, not to breathe. The door he came in was only a few feet away, but Carl didn't move, couldn't move. The creature blocked him from that door. Anything sudden would be the end of him. He'd have to find another way out. His gaze drifted toward the adjoining room door. Slowly, very slowly, Carl crept along the wall toward the bed. He crouched and crawled under it, but as he did, his foot hit a creaky floorboard. Quicker than he could blink, the creature's hand darted for Carl's foot. It missed, hitting the floor with a *crack*. It walked forward on its fingers under the bed, inches away from Carl's leg, feeling for his flesh, drumming on the floor with a *clickety-clack*.

Carl focused on the fingers' movements, trying to avoid them. After an agonizing few minutes, they disappeared, and Carl heard the squeak of the mattress springs. The creature was right on top of him.

"I know you're down there," she said, her voice muffled by the sheets and blanket. "Why have you come to rob me?"

Carl heard the faint scratching of her long fingernails on the pillow. He turned to crawl out the other side, but stopped when he saw her head inch down in front of him. If she'd had eyes, she'd be staring right at him.

"Is it for my books?" The creature lifted her head back up. Carl crawled out toward the window. "I know they're valuable, but only to me."

Carl shrouded himself in the curtains with a *swoosh*. The creature leapt off the bed and threw them open, bathing the dark room in moonlight. Carl curled up into a ball, trying to make himself smaller.

"Have you come to kill me?" the creature growled. "Why? Because you think I'm ugly?" She grabbed the curtains and ripped them down, the curtain rod crashing to the floor. Carl snuck around the creature toward the bookcases, measuring each footfall carefully, so as not to make a sound.

"I'm not ugly!" the creature continued. "I'm beautiful, the most beautiful woman in the world!" She scraped the glass and wailed. "Why would you want to steal from someone as pretty as me?"

As Carl approached the bookcases, his heartbeat quickened. The door was just in front of him. On the lintel, the cockroach following Carl emerged from a crack in the wall, its antennae moving back and forth like a ground controller at an airport.

"You're almost out," Jasper's voice said.

The creature turned its head toward the sound. She screamed, planting herself right in front of Carl. Carl stopped short, holding his breath.

"Perhaps you've come to save me." She extended her hand, touching his face. "But you can't. No one can save me." Carl expected her hand to be cold, lifeless, but it wasn't. It was ... warm, affectionate, like reuniting with a loved one after years apart. "There you are."

The creature grabbed Carl and shoved him into the door, her fingernails digging into his shoulder. Carl cried out in pain. He flexed his right hand and balled it into a fist, aiming a punch at the creature's jaw, but she caught it. Slowly she squeezed, breaking one knuckle, then two, then three, crushing Carl's hand and forcing his arm back. The creature's head wound its way toward Carl's ear.

"We all have something that digs at us," she whispered. Then "AAAAAHHHHH!" The screech was like the squeal of brakes slammed hard on a car. Carl's brain rang with the echo. He shrugged his shoulder to nurse his ear. As he faltered, his left hand found the knob of the adjoining room door and turned it. Carl fell through and kicked the door shut. The cockroach scurried behind him.

Where the first room was large and fully furnished, this room was small and empty. The only furniture was a twin bed, covered in hydrangea patterned sheets, and a faux wood dresser, both cut in half. Ripped lace curtains adorned by chrysanthemums hung down from a tiny window. The walls were painted a stark white and the floor, like the dresser, was faux wood. A single light bulb hung down from the ceiling, illuminating the room in a harsh yellow light. To the right stood a red door, paneled with daffodils, leading back to the hallway.

Carl had no time to register these new surroundings, rolling away just in time to avoid the stab of a silver knife. The knife stabbed again. Carl dodged it and crawled toward the bed, wincing from the pain in his hand, but another knife beat him to it, slashing apart the already broken frame. Carl doubled back, hoping to hide behind the curtains, but the knives were too fast, rending the curtains and curtain rod in two. Carl half crawled, half ran on all fours, scrambling for a hiding place.

"There's no place to hide here, Carl Kellham," the knives sneered—no, not the knives. Carl saw an arm attached to them, covered by black cotton fabric. The arm led up to a shoulder, which led to a head, and a face, and that face ... that face. It was covered in the same black cotton fabric as the rest of it, almost like a full body ski mask. The eyes, nose, and mouth were shadows and moved independently from the fabric, like someone or something else was underneath. When it spoke, its speech was muffled. "Thieves get cleaved."

"I'm not a thief," Carl said, standing. "I don't know what you're talking about." Carl looked behind him. He saw two loose two-by-fours, the nails still in them, laying in the open by the broken dresser. He backed away toward them.

The creature stalked forward. "My knives say different." It flicked its wrists. "They're hungry, see?" With a *shink*, one knife became three on each hand. "I have to feed them. I have to feed them right now."

Carl backed up until he heard the *clank* of wood underfoot. He tried to pick up the plank with his right hand, but the pain was too great. He used his left instead, cradling the other by his side.

"Eat this," Carl said. He swung the wood, nail side out, toward the creature's face, but the swing was awkward in his off hand and the smiling creature parried it easily. It counterattacked with its own left-handed slash. Carl sidestepped and brought the plank up to shield his face. Metal met board, the plank broke in two, and Carl slipped to the ground. The creature pounced, but Carl rolled out of the way, grabbing the other two-by-four. He swung it toward the creature's head, stabbing it where its ears would've been. The creature turned, more in annoyance than pain. It looked like it was wearing a large wooden earring. Carl didn't stick around to laugh. He got to his feet and sprinted for the door.

"Oh no, you don't," the creature said. It pulled the board out of its face and threw it, the corner hitting Carl in the small of his back. Carl collapsed, struggling to breathe, the door knob just out of reach.

"So, so close." Jasper's voice returned. Carl wanted to scream at it and to smash the cockroach sitting on the doorknob. They both seemed to taunt him, but Carl forgot about them when he felt a soft touch on his leg. Carl looked back and saw the creature dragging him away from the door. He flung his free leg wildly at the creature, forcing it to let go. Now on his back, he crawled in reverse toward the door, but the creature jumped on top of him, its knives centimeters from his face. Carl grabbed the creature's wrists with both hands and pushed, crying out as the pain in his re-broken right hand flared.

"C'mon, Carl." The creature strained with the effort. "Don't fight so much. Accept your punishment. Don't worry, it'll only hurt a little bit."

"What punishment? What are you talking about? What is this place?"

The creature smiled again. "It's the price of an unlocked door."

We all have something that digs at us.

Carl's eyes widened. He grit his teeth and, with the last of his strength, kicked the creature in the stomach. It loosened its grip long enough for Carl to get away. The cockroach, seeing Carl coming, skittered through the crack in the doorway, just as Carl's hand found the knob. Without looking back, he opened the door and slammed it behind him, bounding into the hallway.

Carl sprinted for the lobby. Once there, he made for the front door, but when he pushed against it, it wouldn't budge. He pushed again and still the door wouldn't open.

"C'mon, c'mon," Carl fumed. The pain in his right hand was torture. "Open! Open, you stupid door!"

"Amazing what a locked door can do, isn't it?" Jasper's voice said.

Carl wheeled in circles, searching for the voice's source. "I've had enough of your games, Jasper!" He kicked the door for good measure. "Where are you?"

"Right in front of you."

Carl turned toward the desk and found himself face to face with the cockroach that had followed him the whole time. It flexed its mandibles back and forth, almost like it was laughing.

"Hello, Carl," the cockroach said.

Carl blinked furiously. "I must be dreaming."

"I promise you, you're not."

"Then I'm—this is—you're really a—you're Jasper?"

"You betcha."

"Then what is all this? Why is this happening to me?"

Jasper chittered. "Oh, come on, Carl. On some level, you must know."

Carl looked at the floor, then the door, and the dusty windows. He massaged his right hand, his mind drifting. He heard the distant sound of ambulance sirens; the *clickety-clack* of a hospital gurney coming down the stairs, being wheeled over asphalt; the *thump-thump-thumping* of flesh against metal; the cracking and breaking of bone; the cries of agony, both physical and emotional. Carl dropped to his knees, cradling his right hand, his face awash with tears.

"We all have something that digs at us, Carl," Jasper said. "We try to bury it as deep as we can, but like a zombie back from the dead, it inevitably thrusts its hand above the dirt, hungry for our brains. You felt it when you broke your hand the first time. You felt it at her funeral. You feel it right now."

"I don't understand."

"Look in the mirror, Carl."

Carl obeyed. The water splotches and dust parted, and Carl saw a room, much like the first one he entered, bathed in a blue hue. Carl's view looked out from the bed. He could see the vague shadow of a single bookcase and a small desk and a door to the right. Instead of a haggard monster, a young girl, about eleven, sat on the bed reading. She wore a blue, silk nightgown patterned in tulips. She had long, thick, brown hair and green eyes behind a pair of small, rounded glasses with a crack in the right lens shaped like a thunderbolt. She turned from her book and looked back at Carl, her eyes lighting up in recognition. She tapped the glass.

"Daddy," she mouthed.

"Lacy," Carl said. He crawled over to the mirror and placed his hand on hers, tears flowing freely now. "Don't worry, sweetie. Daddy's here. Daddy will—" Lacy touched her ear and shook her head. Carl turned to Jasper. "What's wrong? Why can't she hear me?"

"Did you live in a safe neighborhood, Carl?"

"What? What does that have to do with—? Don't worry, Lacy. Daddy will get you out." Lacy tapped on the glass and smiled.

"Did you live in a safe neighborhood?"

"It was the best I could afford." Carl pushed on the glass.

"And to afford it, you had to work nights, right?"

"The night shift paid the most." Carl kicked the glass. It didn't budge. He kicked it again, but still nothing. Lacy looked worried.

"Before you'd leave for work, I'm sure you had a routine, right?"

"Yes."

"You'd pick Lacy up after school?"

"Yes."

"You'd make her dinner?"

"Yes."

"You'd tuck her in?"

"Yes."

"You'd lock the door when you'd leave?"

Carl rammed his shoulder into the mirror. It still wouldn't budge. He punched it. Lacy flinched. "Yes, goddamnit!" Carl snapped. "What does that have to do with anything? And why won't this damn mirror break?"

Jasper sidled up next to Carl. "You did this every day, right? Every single day like clockwork?"

Carl grabbed the pot of dead lilies and hurled it at the mirror. Lacy ducked out of reflex, but it was still no good. The pot of lilies broke against the glass, scattering dirt and dead plant across the floor. The mirror remained unscathed.

"Yes," Carl said.

Jasper returned to the top of the desk. "But one night you didn't, right? One night you forgot, even though you'd done it a thousand times before."

Carl turned toward Jasper, then back to the mirror. His right hand felt like it was on fire. On the other side of the mirror, the doorknob turned, and the door opened. A tall, slender figure slinked through, brandishing a knife that shined bright silver through the haze of blue.

He was dressed in a black ski mask.

Lacy pounded on the mirror with both fists, looking from the intruder back to Carl. "Daddy!" she silently screamed. "Daddy, help me! Get me out of here!"

The intruder stalked toward Lacy, knife held high. Carl ran to the mirror. He pressed his head against Lacy's. "Baby, just hold on. Daddy will think of something."

Carl pulled on the mirror. He ran his fingers along the back, looking for a switch. He tried kicking and punching the mirror again. He rapped the glass barehanded—*whump, whump, whump*—the pain in his right hand felt like it would kill him, but Carl didn't care nor did it seem to matter; the mirror remained intact. The intruder kept coming.

Carl fell to his knees, out of ideas, crying. Lacy tapped the glass. "Don't give up, Daddy. Please, don't give up." She smiled at him. Then, her expression changed to horror as she was pulled back by her hair.

"Lacy!" Carl screamed.

But the intruder was on top of her, one hand around her throat, the other clutching the knife. Lacy kicked him in the chest, freeing herself from his grasp. Enraged, the intruder stabbed down onto the bed, but Lacy rolled out of the way. She tried to get off the bed and go for the door, but the intruder grabbed her and pulled her back toward his knife. He stabbed at her again, but she caught his arm, locking the two of them in a fateful tug of war.

Carl sat by, completely helpless. He flailed his arms and called Lacy's name. What else could he do? Carl looked around the room. Hadn't he tried everything? He already threw the lily pot. He couldn't throw the radio or the piano or the couches in the waiting area. What else was there? His fists and feet hadn't worked. The check-in ledger wouldn't work. What else was there? Carl turned toward the front desk and saw the customer service bell.

On the other side of the mirror, Lacy was losing the tug of war. Her face strained with the effort. Sweat moistened her forehead. She shoved with all her might. But it was no use. The intruder was stronger than she was. Gravity worked against her. Each push brought the knife lower and lower, until the point was just above her chest.

Carl sprang for the bell. He raised it high above his head, ready to throw, the weight of it killing his right hand, but then it happened: Lacy's strength gave out. The knife plunged deep into her chest, spewing blood all over her nightgown. She gasped for air, choking. Her eyes rolled back. The intruder took the knife out and stabbed Lacy again.

"Lacy, no!" Carl's face tightened, his fist clenched around the bell. The pain, the rage, Carl put it all into his throw. He launched the bell at the mirror and, with a crash, the glass broke. Carl leaped through the threshold, ready to take revenge on the masked intruder, but he wasn't there, neither was the room as he had seen it. There was no bookcase, no bed, no desk, no door, no window, no curtains. Just a cold, empty place with rotted floors stained white. In the center was Lacy's body: broken, covered in cuts and a sea of red.

Carl ran to his daughter and held her in his arms, sobbing. He remembered a different sea of red from that fateful night, red and blue. It had come from the five police cars and the ambulance parked outside his apartment, number twelve. A crowd had gathered behind the yellow "Do Not Cross" line as Carl pulled up. He had gotten out of his car, curious as to the commotion. His downstairs neighbor, a sweet, elderly woman, had seen him and rushed to embrace him, crying onto his shoulder. Then he had seen why. He had seen the gurney come down the stairs, a pasty gray-green cover over the body.

"Any sign of forced entry?" the detective had asked.

"No," one of the officers had answered. "The door was unlocked."

And Carl had lost it. He had shoved his neighbor away and paced the parking lot, fuming. His daughter had been murdered, the murderer had escaped, and Carl could do only one thing—punch his car. Punch it for the rage he felt at the intruder; punch it for the rage he felt at himself; punch it until something broke. That something had been his right hand. Only then had he stopped, but his pain hadn't. It had overflowed, became tears, as it did now, with his daughter's body held tight against him.

But then her eyes opened.

Carl felt elated, smiling through his tears, until he saw her scowl.

"You have let me down," Lacy said, her voice ghostly.

"Yes, yes, I have. I did. I am a terrible father, a terrible man. I'm sorry, Lacy, so sorry. Please, please, can you ever forgive me?"

"I will make you hurt."

Lacy grabbed his forehead, digging her thumbnail into Carl's brain. He screamed and she pushed harder and harder until there was nothing left of Carl Kellham, nothing but an empty shell.

Afterward Lacy disappeared, but Carl remained with Jasper on his shoulder. One night in the Roach Motel became one thousand and every night Carl and Jasper would sit in the empty room behind the mirror and sing the same chorus over and over and over again:

We all have something that digs at us.

***

Norn

by Ailish Sinclair, United Kingdom

I am Norn. I am debt from the past. I am future. I am that which ought to be. And now, I am human.

Nine tall stones. For a time they are all that exist. For me. Just the nine. They start to spin and spin until they blur into one.

I'm dizzy. I'm warm. I'm safe. And then I'm not.

Everything has aligned correctly and I'm here. In the tower, the monument, looking from one window to another in the distance. My position swaps and I am looking back at the dark tower on the hillside from the other window. I turn my head in an attempt to see the room but there's not time, because now I'm standing directly on the earth. In the place that truly matters. And the stones are gone.

No moonlight. No starlight. I feel the depth of dark in the place. It is like a physical being, a character in the story that has been woven. It's not so bad it can't be corrected. I am here before the atrocities. I know it.

It's dark with cold damp in the air. Winter in Scotland. There's mud. Soft and deep, my human feet sink in with every step. Newly formed muscles soon tire of this mud walking. I have to find my way home. I see houses in front, windows lit with electricity. They look warm. Kind places. They're not where I'm going. They're not what I chose.

Straight on. Walk straight on. This was easier to understand when I was in the warm. I studied the ancient maps. And the facts, all the facts, so many names and dates and words and practices. So I know to go downwards, towards the village, and not to the right. Down, down. And over a fence, and oh! I feel the weakness of flesh! The fence cuts and rips through clothing and into skin as it wobbles around under my feet. I remember the fact: barbs, to keep animals in and people out.

There are two more fences and then I am there. Here. It's definitely it. The right house. Was once a school. Then a home to pigs. Now, is it the place I'll call home?

The window is open. Only a crack, to allow a white electric cable to enter, but I pull it wider and heave myself up onto the outer stone sill and then step through and perch on the white painted inner ledge. I survey the room. All being well, it should be my room. I should be young, a minor, a teenager, unburdened with employment or worldly concerns. I should have a plethora of free time with which to accomplish my mission.

I look down. Purple floor covering, coming away at the edges. Thin wooden bed. Plastic shelf. I jump down onto the floor when I see that. I want to touch plastic, to feel what it's like. It's hard. It's smooth. I touch the walls too and they're sticky as if with pollen or juices from the large purple flowers that are depicted there. And smelly. I detect strong chemical residue. Strange.

"Skye!"

The fact that the word is shouted with great ferocity is nothing to me. It's not my real name. Which is a protection of a sort.

The small woman who has just burst into the room is exhibiting fury. She called me by name so the anger is not because she knows there's a stranger, an interloper, a traveller, in her home.

"What have you been doing?" she shrieks. "What a mess you're in! Your best trousers?"

It is my clothing to which she refers, the mud and the rips. I try out a smile which enrages her further. And seemingly I am to be allowed no food. I'm to wash and go to bed. Beside the plastic shelf and the toxic walls. I walk through the narrow hallway to the tiny bathroom. All laid out just as I thought it would be: bath, toilet with cistern, that's fascinating, and sink.

There's running water, it's warm, and there's soap, it's functional, so I am soon clean. Back in the bedroom I locate nightwear in a stiff wooden drawer. I climb into the bed which is lumpy. Full of bumps. Halfway through the night the mattress slips through the wire mesh base with a jolt. Which is good. Because I had fallen into a deep sleep. I now have time to plan.

Will tomorrow be school? Or will it be church? Either way, I know who I'm to look for and what I have to say. I chant the two names. I rehearse the speeches in my mind. I whisper them into the dark. And then I sit up onto the painted wooden ledge of the window and look back up the hill. To the tower. To the place where the stones once stood. To the place where they will again.

66

*

At some point I must have lain down on the bed again because I'm just waking up. To daylight and total silence. I tiptoe across the floor to the door and open it carefully, in keeping with the silence. There's no one here. It's just the house and me. Which is perfect. I can explore! I can learn! I can acclimatise!

I turn left, take three steps and I'm in the kitchen. I see my name. My human name. On a piece of paper! It's so strange to be holding paper in my hands. It's real and white and solid. It conveys information.

SKYE! We have gone without you. You were fast asleep. We would like tomato rice and vegetables in white sauce for dinner.

Where have they gone? Church. It must be church if they've all gone together. Well, I have to go too, but as I am already late, I will have a look round first.

Refrigerator. Dirty inside. Odd-looking vegetables and bright orange cheese. Cooker, three rings, rusty, showing the passage of time. I love that. Wooden cupboards, painted with toxic paint. I love those too. Wooden table, wobbly. I walk through the rest of the house. Big room with chairs and a big brown boxy television. Books. Lamps. And that's about it. The two other bedrooms have beds, a desk, drawer units, and clothes hanging spaces.

But I must dress for church. Back in my room, the smallest, I find various black clothes. I put some on and hope they're right. Trousers, tight. Top, baggy. It's cold though, it's winter. I find a thin coat with a zip and fake fur round the hood. It seems insufficient but there is no other. The window is still open with the white cable coming through. It's the only window in the house that is like this. I checked. It's also the only window in the house that faces the tower and the empty space in the field below.

Outside it's bright but the dark is still there, behind it all. I walk up the hill leading from the house to the street and immediately see the church. Not where it said on the map, but some inaccuracies are to be expected when journeying through time. It's big and wide with a pointed roof. No spire or ornate architecture. I open the door and am faced with the truth of how dark things are.

Sunlight streams through a large window onto the altar space. But there is no altar. Only tables and counters and animal innards. Red everywhere! Blood! Hearts! Livers! Bodily fluids. Seeping. Dripping. Desecration! I scream and people appear.

"What you doing here?" asks an overweight man in a white apron with a smear of blood across it.

"That's Skye, that is, from across the road." A younger man, similarly attired. He points at his head and raises his eyebrows.

The older man nods. "What you looking for, dearie? You lost?"

"Church," I say. It's the only word that comes out. Are those only animal innards being dragged across sacred places? Or am I in danger of the mission ending before it has begun?

"Let me show you then," says the man, leading the way back to the door, stepping outside and pointing the way down the street. "You go right to the end of Main Street here, and you can't miss it. This, here, is the pie factory."

I look up at it. I'm sure it's a church.

"Repurposed," says the man as if I'd asked out loud and goes back inside his repurposed church to continue his activities.

I walk fast. Away from that. Past shop. Post Office. Another shop. Then I see the church. But it's all locked up. Both doors. I see another church, farther on down. I feel tricked. How can one small village have so many churches? But then it was/is a sacred place. That's why there were two stone circles. Maybe it's why there's three churches?

The third one, the biggest, with a steeple, is open. There's not many people in it but I sneak in and sit at the back. Faces turn toward me, eyes stare and look away again. The preacher, minister as he will be called here, continues to talk from the pulpit. Things are more as I thought they would be now. I feel myself calming down.

But not all is as expected. The preacher is not an old man. He's youngish with long hair and dressed in a colourful baggy top and blue jeans. Actual jeans. I love those. I don't seem to own any of those. Here in this place. I suspect the small woman does not allow them. Where is she anyway? Where are any of them? Not that I would recognise the others.

I read the words from the hymn book and sing along with everyone. The minister stops us. He mimics us and says we are droning on and that that's no way to worship God. Everyone laughs. It's good that that can happen here. I take it as a very good sign. Maybe the different minister is a good sign too.

At the end of the service he stands by the door and shakes everyone's hand as they're leaving. I hang back till last.

"Skye," he says, taking my hand and holding it. "How are you today?"

"Hungry," I answer at once, aware of the hollow feeling in my belly. He frowns and I move on, jumping straight to the mission. "Do you know anything about the destroyed stone circle? The one that was up by the monument?"

"Yes," he says, still looking perturbed, still holding my hand. "To the Church's shame, it was smashed up and used in the foundations of The Manse." He grimaces. "My house. Two hundred years ago, I think."

"I'm doing a project on it," I tell him.

He nods. "I have some papers about it at home. You'll have to come by and have a look at them. Have you visited the remains of the other circle? The white quartz one?"

"No!" This is news. They were both completely destroyed. According to my information.

"Would you like to?" he says, a smile forming on his face.

"Yes!" How amazing, how utterly amazing to see, maybe to touch if it's not protected by glass or fences, how wonderfully and totally fantastic this is going to be.

"It's a little hard to find," he says, thinking. "You go on ahead, up the Kilmore road and then take the turn towards Kilbeg. I'll meet you up there in the first layby. Maybe do something about that hungry problem too."

The streets are empty. Just like they were earlier. Where is everybody? Is it so bad here that they all just stay inside most of the time? Scuttling out to find food now and again?

It's sunny but sort of grey sunny. I don't think pollution was a great problem at this date but history misses much. Clearly. I walk past the graveyard, purportedly the site of an earlier church, and down a steep hill, The Brae. I cross the road and begin the ascent up the Kilmore road. It's quite a long way. I walk past large sheds. There's a bad smell coming from them. On and on I go. Green grass at the sides. Grey road under my feet. A car zooms past. Sounds its horn.

I take the narrow Kilbeg road. It's really hilly here. Maps didn't show that. Up I go, body weak from lack of food. The first layby, or widening in the road, is some distance up the road but I eventually find it. So is this near the circle? I stand up on the verge and stare around at the fields, all barren and bare, winter fields. I don't see it. How much is left? I feel excitement growing in my belly, at least there's something there.

He arrives. It's awkward that I don't know his name. Unless he is the Reverend Hunter and maybe just his age was wrong. I should have looked outside the church. There might have been a sign or a plaque or something. With that name. I have two important names emblazoned across my soul. Reverend Hunter is one of them.

He climbs out of his old-looking car, smiles, and goes round to the back—the boot I think that's called. He removes a beautiful woven picnic hamper. I've seen them in paintings. And a tartan blanket to sit on. My excitement and my hunger grow.

"Ready?" he says. "It's just a short walk."

We go up the side of a field and then I see them. Two shiny white stones! They're enormous. I find myself running towards them, desperate to see them closer and better and, oh, to touch with physical hands! They're just sitting here, at the edge of a field, no protection, no recognition of their power. My hands can do them no harm. And what good are they doing? They've fallen. They are not properly positioned. But they're still here. "They're still here!" I press my palms onto their cold surface. Again and again. All over. I want to sit on the lower one, the flatter one. But would that be sacrilegious? Probably not in a place that turns churches into pie factories and stone circles into foundations. But in a bigger reality?

"The Rocking Stones of Auchnacloich," says the minister, catching up, laying down his basket and blanket, pushing some of his long hair out of his eyes. "I'm glad you like them, Skye."

"I had no idea they were here," I say, accepting and then devouring a white bread and orange cheese sandwich. What is it with these people and orange cheese? It has to be dyed this colour, it cannot be natural. But it's good. So good. To eat food. To feel energy return to my limbs.

The minister, name unknown, talks on about some other white stones that could have been taken from here. They're situated in walls and nearby gardens.

"So this circle would be easy to restore?" I suggest.

He shrugs. "Who would want to, though?"

"Other villages have done it." I hope that's still true. They were circles where the stones had been taken by farmers, just for practical purposes, no smashing, no hate.

"Yes," he says. "But this place? No one will put in that sort of effort unless it's to make money."

Really? No one? He could be right. But I have to try. The worst has not yet happened here. Having the stones back should cast a protection that will avert it. Having the stones back will return this place to light. That's the mission that I'm on.

"You could speak to the farmer," says the minister.

"It's really the other stones that need putting back. The ones near the tower."

He laughs. "Need? Well, you could speak to that farmer. He might be willing to mark the place with something. Though I think that's in a field that's used for crops. Here, Skye, have a cake."

The cake is a small purple cylinder. Chocolate cake encased in foil. It has a swirl of icing through it. Buttery. Nice.

"You're so pretty," he says, and reaches out, putting some of my hair back behind my ear. So, that's how it is. In this story. It's something that's ongoing. I can tell. But he doesn't try anything else. Other than to give me lemonade. And thin slices of fried potato. Crisps, he calls them.

I ask him about the other church, the pie factory. He talks about deconsecration, how he doesn't approve, how wrong it is, how it leaves the place open to evil. There's two churches like that here and two sites where others have stood.

I make my own way home after that. He can't be seen driving me back into the village. Uphill and downhill. I probably burn off the entirety of energy I've just eaten and I'm still hungry when I reach the school/piggery/house. But things are not good there.

"Skye, is that Skye?" The shout comes as soon as I open the door and step inside. Was I supposed to knock? I don't think so. Not as I live here. She doesn't give me time to ask. I'm not sure what I would tell her anyway. "We came home and no food prepared!" she shrieks. "Just wandered off on a whim, did you? Well, you're going to make it now. Into the kitchen with you! Now! Do you hear me?"

I suspect much of the village can hear her. Maybe this is why they live down a lane.

She goes on. "While you live in our house and eat our food you will pull your weight and contribute to this family!"

"Don't I go to school?" I say, because don't I? Maybe not.

"What's that got to do with anything?"

"Well, I'm a child ..." This was past the time of child labour, surely that's right?

"That's enough of your cheek! You get that food made and be quiet. Your sister needs to study."

So I'm shut away in the kitchen. With raw ingredients. Shame. I would have quite liked to meet the sister. Or the father. Are they as cold and cruel as the small woman? I don't know. The more pertinent lack of knowledge right at this moment is culinary. I have no historical cooking skills.

Rice. I find it and try to follow the written instructions on the pack. It burns. Right through the pan. Vegetables. I wash and chop them and put them on a plate. She comes through and it's not good. They are going to get takeaway. I am sent to my room. So, second night, no dinner. I am so hungry it feels like my body is eating itself from the inside out.

I wait. The weakness that hunger keeps bringing will not help the mission. I will have to obtain sustenance. There's the minister. But that might have a high price. There was a fast food place. On the hill, The Brae. Maybe it is open now? I'll need money. There is none in this room. Not one single little coin.

I can smell their takeaway. It is spicy and aromatic. Garlic. Onions. Curry. They are busy with it in the room with the chairs. The door is closed. I tiptoe through the house and into the sister's bedroom. There's coins and notes in her drawer. I take them. All. I don't know how much things cost.

Pockets full, I retrace my tiptoes to my bedroom and out the window I go.

*

The chip shop is lit up, all golden in the gloom of hungry winter. There's a crowd of teenagers sitting at a table in there. They go quiet and stare as I go in. I look at the prices and laugh. I can afford the whole menu! I order chips and a coke. Sugar. Fat. Energy.

"Skye Gilmartin's gracing us with her presence!" says one of the boys from the table. Now that I look at them properly, they're all boys.

"Yes," I say. "I am." I take my chips and go and sit at the table with them.

This surprises them. There's a pause before they move along the bench to let me in and they all stare again, wide-eyed, as if this is an unprecedented occurrence.

I actually don't care. They can stare all they like. The chips are wondrous, all hot and filling and salty. At this moment, they are the greatest food on Earth.

The first boy to recover the shock of my presence says, "You been sucking the vicar's cock, Skye?"

"No, I've been eating his cheese sandwiches." It's just the truth but they fall about as if it's the funniest thing they've ever heard.

"So you here to eat our cheese sandwiches?" says the only boy who seems to talk.

"No, I'm here to eat chips."

"Classic," says one of them, a skinny boy with squint eyes. "Oh that's classic, Aeron, that is."

"Aeron," I say, looking at the boy who speaks the most. "Aeron Duncan." Can it be?

"At's my name, dinna wear it oot," he says, smiling widely.

"You're beautiful," I say because he is. He has deep brown eyes with thick eyelashes. Perfect teeth and skin, unlike his companions. Dark curly hair. How can someone so aesthetically pleasing go on to do the things he did, or more correctly, that he will do? Hopefully things that will be prevented.

He smiles as if to make some quip but then doesn't know what to say. I'm not doing the banter properly. I know that. And I've finished my chips. And I need to think. And be out of his presence. So I just get up and leave. I step out into the street-lit darkness. But it's not that simple.

"Somewhere you need to be Skye?" He's followed me. Just him. Not the others.

"Yes," I say.

"Want some company?"

"No."

"Well, I'm walking this way too."

And I wonder. There are many ways to change events. This, our walking together up the straight main street, is already a small change. This would never have happened before. The main street, with its slight upwards trajectory, buildings looming in on either side, is like some sort of dark road into hell. It doesn't feel so bad with him by my side, and how strange is that? He's different, like this, on his own, but can he really be that different?

"Are we going to your house?" he asks.

"No. I'm in too much trouble there already. Burnt the supper."

"You serious?" he asks, looking at me, trying to make eye contact. "You got some sorta Cinderella story going on there?"

"It's not their fault," I say. "I'm different from them. They know it, so ..."

"So they treat you like crap."

"Basically." I can't tell him that they sense I wasn't here before. They detect an intrusion, they just can't see where it is, but the hate comes naturally and they need to express it.

"If we're going far, I'll nip into my house and get stuff. Good stuff," he adds as if this makes some sort of difference to me. Interesting. Even more interesting is the fact he lives right behind the pie factory. Possibly on deconsecrated ground.

We walk over a tarred driveway and through a grand front door. I wonder at myself, being led like this. But then who knows where changes will be made? "S'alright," he says. "My stepdad's nae hame." So Aeron Duncan is an interloper too, at least to one person in this house.

"Aeron, is that you?" A woman's voice. Slurred.

"Just in to get something," he yells, then whispering to me, "Wait here, I'll just be a sec."

He's up the stairs before she says, "Have you got someone with you?" and lights come on. "A girl," she says as if in amazement. "Come through to the kitchen, sweetheart, let me get a look at you."

I follow her. I can get a look at another kitchen.

We're in a big square room, much more equipped than the one in the school/piggery. There's a great big oven thing, looks like it runs on wood, and an early microwave, and two sinks. There are also smaller brightly coloured things: a toaster, a blender, something else big and square, I don't know what it is.

"I love the colours," I say.

"Oh, so do I! My husband thinks I'm crazy but I don't see anything wrong in a bit of brightness. So, where you off to with Aeron, pretty girl?" she asks, squinting at me in the bright light of the kitchen.

"A walk."

"Then you'll need hot chocolate." And she gets out a pan. And milk. Say what you like about the ignorance and intolerance of the people of this era. With the exception of "my family," they're all really keen to feed me. She puts chocolate powder in a flask while the milk heats.

"You know you shouldn't cook when you've been drinking." Aeron is back with his beautiful hair and big bright eyes. "Remember last time?"

"I'm not cooking. It's just hot chocolate for you and your little friend."

"Mum," he says, cross.

"It'll only take a minute. See? Here, it's hot enough." She puts the milk in the flask, closes it and shakes. "Put that in your backpack," she says to Aeron and he does. And we go. Back out under the dark street lights, past the dark end of the lane to the piggery, and on up the high street as it is at this end of the village.

"High is better than main," he says as we walk on up and round the corner, the monument coming into view. "We going up there, Skye?"

"Yes." Well, why not?

He gets a torch out of his bag, a big one, it's like a car headlight.

"We don't need it," I say. "The moon is full."

"You're right weird, Skye, you know 'at?"

"Oh aye, I know 'at."

He laughs. Perhaps at what I said, perhaps at how I said it. We walk on up the road, past the graveyard and sit on the steps below the pointy monument. This means we went past the site of the stone circle. I don't know if I want to tell him about that yet. The sky is clear and the moon bright, it would be easy to find if I wanted.

"Picnic time!" He takes out the hot chocolate and some biscuits and a small flat tin. I reach for the biscuits. "Not yet," he says. "You wait. It'll be better."

I want to laugh. In fact, I do. The contents of the tin reveal that we're going to smoke a joint. Cannabis? Marijuana? I think it's called grass or dope here in this time. It's harmless. Relatively. I think. He lights it with a lighter and his face glows golden orange in the moonlight for a second. He breathes it in. He breathes it out. He leans back against the barred door of the tower.

"You done it before, Skye?"

I shake my head.

"Here, this'll be easier. Breathe it in from me. A blowback." He grins, teeth white under the moon.

And his mouth is on mine. Blowing strange tasting smoke into mine. I take it. I swallow it down more than breathe it. And I cough. It's funny. He finds it funny, but then so do I. And he was wrong. I soon discover that inhaling straight out of the joint is far easier. I tell him this.

"Yeah," he admits.

"So you just wanted to kiss me?" This seems unlikely in the extreme.

"Yeah."

Maybe this will change everything, this kissing, this breathing, this touching, this moment of warm closeness. This lying on the ground and looking at the stars. Now that's amazing. They're amazing. We're amazing. And the chocolatey-ness of the biscuits. That's beyond good. So sweet. I'm so hungry. I eat more than half the packet. More than my fair share. He doesn't mind. He finds it funny.

Laughter doesn't stop the night getting cold around us.

"I'm going across the fields," I tell him. "They might see me if I go in the front door."

"I'll come with you." And he does. Over all the barbed wire and right up to the wall of the piggery. But he shouldn't come closer. I know that. I tell him that. He tells me the house used to be his auntie's house. He tells me she ran a hair cutting business in the room I now have and that clouds of hairspray used to waft out the window and door. Sticky walls explained.

"I'll see you tomorrow, Skye," he says, as he disappears into the night. "On the bus."

I haul myself over the wall. I feel weak and strong all at once. Wobbly like so many things in this place. But able. Then there's the hoist in the window, the always open window. Onto the ledge and into ... the flames of anger.

"It's her! She's here!" Shouty woman. Summoning the others.

Oh well. I'll get to see them. I want to see them. There they are. At the bedroom door. Staring in. The man and the girl.

"Where have you been?"

I don't want to say so I say, "For a walk."

"Look at the state of you! Look at the state of her, Albert!"

The state of me is looked at.

"Did you steal your sister's money?" Still only the shouty woman speaks.

"Yes," I say, reaching into my pocket to get it and holding it out to the girl. "I was starving and I didn't know how much food would cost. I didn't use much of it."

The girl steps forward and takes it. She doesn't speak. She doesn't smile. She doesn't express any emotion at all.

"Why were you hungry, Skye?" asks the man, which is strange. Was he not here for the takeaway dinner eating? Does he not know about my burnt offerings?

"I'd had no food."

He frowns. "Why?"

The shouty woman speaks very loudly. "Oh well, you know her, she could have had something but she didn't bother. Anyway, better get ready for bed, school tomorrow!"

So I go to bed and I sleep really well, and when I wake, it is snowing. I lie there and watch the snowflakes sail past my face. It is snowing in my room. At first I wonder if it's a hallucination, an effect leftover from last night's joint, but I reach out an arm into the icy wind and icy specks hit it. This can't be right. Can this be right?

I pull on clean black clothes. They highlight the white flakes that land on them. Snow has built up beside the door, just a fingertip's depth. I walk through to the kitchen, it's warm, it's cosy, and I tell the shouty woman about the snow.

"Oh Skye," she says. "I suppose when you have a house everything in it will work perfectly."

I look at her. I don't understand.

"You know that window has to be open for the heating system to run! The house has to be kept warm for the rest of us."

Ah. The whole house except for my room. Because I'm different. "Gotcha," I say and walk back to my room. There's a canvas bag with books in it, a frayed hole in the corner. I guess that's for school. I take it and go to the front door.

"What are you doing?" It's the sister. Her clothes are different from mine too. Newer. Blue and white, smart skirt and shirt and blazer.

"What time do we go?" I ask.

'Not for another half hour.' She sneers. It twists her face into something ugly that it wasn't before.

She walks away. I stay there. It is warmer than the snow room. I get fed up. I'm leaving early. I'll go and see Aeron and his nice drunk mum. That was better than here.

*

Aeron is sitting on the wall by his house smoking a cigarette. He smiles when he sees me. And that makes me want to cry. Nobody smiles when they see me. Not in this time and reality. And of all people, he does. This boy who has to be stopped, this boy who will commit atrocities. He holds out the cigarette and I take it, inhaling like the night before. I don't cough this time and I feel the small relaxation the drug brings.

"You're not like I thought at all," he says, watching me smoke. "It's almost like you weren't properly there before and now you've arrived." Of all the people who should be able to see this, only he does. "And it's not going to be the same," he adds, jumping down off the wall. "Nobody's going to touch you now. You're with me." I am.

We walk down the road together to where others are already congregating at the bus stop.

"Oh aye, fits this?" says one of the boys. "Nae her!"

Aeron moves fast. He grabs the boy's arm, twisting it so the sleeve rides up and then he holds his cigarette, almost burnt down to the filter, to the boy's wrist. Not touching, but almost.

"Aeron! Dinna! I didna mean onything!"

"Okay then." The boy's arm is dropped. Aeron is smiling again. "Anybody else got anything to say?"

Nobody else has anything to say. Well. I think maybe some of the girls do. But they only think it at the bus stop. Once we're on the bus they gather together and giggle, but we go upstairs. We don't stay in sight or sound of them. Which is good.

"What classes you got today?" asks Aeron as we sit in the front seat.

I'm about to say I don't know, when I realise I do. The story is there for me too. "Nothing I want to do," I say. "Chemistry, biology, physics, maths. History." All outmoded and outdated. The history teacher thinks Norns are mythological goddesses! But all I say to Aeron is, "All rubbish."

"Too brainy for the brainy classes," says Aeron, laughing. "What do you want to do today, then?"

It's such an odd question. What do I want to do? Me? I always just do what I'm told. Before. Now. Anywhere. Anytime. So what do I want to do?

"Look at trees."

"Trees?"

"Really big trees."

"Well, that's easy. Unless you're worried about getting caught bunking."

I'm not worried. Why would I be? My time here is limited. And there's no way back. School will not further my mission. But it will sap my energy. Trees won't. I'm pretty sure about that.

So we get off the bus and walk round the back of the building and then run straight into the woods. Where there are trees. Lots and lots of pine trees. I like the smell. The cold of the snow and the warm pointed tops of the branches that show pine cones. It's nice. Like I think Christmas would be.

The wood has many trees. We dive in among them whenever we see anyone coming. We kiss among the trees. We touch each other's bodies. In the piney, twiggy dark. Through clothes. By a giant redwood a thought grows.

"We should go up to the place where the stone circle was tonight," I say to him.

"Where's that then?"

"Near the monument."

"It's a date, Skye."

*

I'm confident they won't know I bunked. Aeron says it takes ages for the school to write a letter about an unexplained absence and then we can fake a signature. But I won't be here by then. But for now? I step into the piggery.

"Ah good, you're here." This is the only time I can remember that she's not been angry to see me. "Come through, come through."

Through to the kitchen we go and she flourishes an arm in the direction of the table. There's one plate on it. A big oval dish with some small bits of food: a two-centimeter cube of cheese, a two-centimeter cube of meat, a tiny tomato, one raw floret of broccoli, and one shiny roasted salted peanut.

"No one is going to say I don't feed you enough again! There you go! Every food group is represented there! Eat it and then you can make dinner for the rest of us."

I don't eat it. I wait till she goes out of the room and then I tip the food onto the floor and stamp on it. The cheese and meat squish easily into the cream-coloured kitchen rug. The tomato leaves a satisfying red splotch while the broccoli just sits there. I don't know where the peanut went.

I go into my room.

I go out the window.

I go into the darkening evening. Over wall. Over fence. Over field and fence, fence, fence.

He's already there. Sitting on the monument steps. He has more Kit Kat biscuits and blow as he calls it. Both good. Both so very good.

"So what we doing here Skye? Where's this circle place?"

I lean back against the door of the tower, bars hard on my back.

"I'll show you," I say, holding out my hand to him.

We walk down the hill a small way. His hand is warm in mine. The moon is newly risen. I think I can see the glitter of white quartz in the soil in places where the snow has melted.

"Here in the mud?" he asks as we stop.

"Here in the mud."

"So what did they use to do here?" he asks.

"The same thing we're going to do."

"And that's ...?"

"An act of love."

I see his smile through the dark. I feel his excitement. I feel my own.

"Just as well I took this then, isn't it?" He pulls a blanket from the back pack. We laugh as we spread it over the hard ground. I think we would be nervous if it weren't for the drug.

We lie down on the ground. There's kissing and touching. "Did you know this was going to happen?" I ask when he produces a sheath.

"Always live in hope, Skye," he tells me and I find that very funny.

"Live in hope," I repeat as he puts the condom on.

Oh. Not how I thought. There's some pain but it's okay. Close and warm here in the dark and cold. A human woman's first blood on the earth. And over so very quickly.

We wrap the blanket 'round us as we lie there, all cuddled. It's so good. I feel so relaxed. I'm not sure I've ever been relaxed before. I feel different, changed. I feel human now, fully and completely, capable of love and joy and peace and calm and happiness. And fear. I can feel all the vulnerability and weakness of being human. But of course, I'm not. "It was nice of you to bring a condom—" I start to tell him.

"I bought twelve."

And that's so funny too, but I have to tell him this. "You didn't need to. I won't be here for long."

"What d'ya mean?"

"I won't exist for much longer. Here, like this."

"That's the blow talking. Know what else I've got?" And he holds up a shiny key.

"Mum's on the village committee," he explains. "Has a key to the monument. Wanna go inside?"

I do. I want to be there again, like I was on my first day of being in this form. First night of the change. Then it was a glance at what was to come, a flash, lighted and brief. Now it's hard and cold and dark. He unlocks the padlock, drops the chain to the ground. I feel the noise and vibration jangle right through me, my human senses heightened in the aftermath of sex.

Aeron has a torch with him again, a small one, and he shines it on the stone steps as we ascend. Aeron is a man of many lights. We come to a bird skeleton, picked clean and spread out on a stair. Not a good omen. We come to a window in the inner wall and round and up we go. There are more dead birds on the upstairs floor. Feathery ones. Juicy ones.

"Don't look at them," says Aeron.

So I raise my head. I look up at the inside of the tower. Rough brickwork rises round and round into deep unseeable darkness.

"You can see for miles in the daytime," he tells me from by the windows as I climb up onto the inner bannister that's around the stairs.

I am Norn. I can fly. And it's time.

I hear the warning in his voice as I hold my arms out like wings. I hear his panic as I fall forward to take flight. And then his scream as I descend, as my body bashes and breaks on the stone steps. I see his fate. I understand now. They will say he murdered me. When they examine the body I left behind, they will say he raped me too. My last human heartbeat swells and hurts for him.

I see it all. The Reverend will have the stones put back, rebuilt, in my memory. As if he's a good man. The family I lived with will pretend to be sad. As if they're good people.

Only Aeron will know the lie. Only Aeron will suffer for it. Together, we are the sacrifice that brings the stones back.

I am Norn. A debt repaid. A future changed. And all is as it ought to be.

***

The Burden Unknown
by Timothy Vincent, United States

Leonard Paxon was angry. Well, Leonard Paxon was nearly always angry. But this time he had cause. Someone was trying to kill him.

Paxon was not terribly surprised that someone would want him dead; his had been an aggressive and sometimes bloody climb to the top of the economic food chain. No, what bothered Paxon wasn't so much his listing, as which assassin answered the call. "The Hand of Passing"—a rough English translation—was disturbingly efficient when it came to killing. Paxon considered it incredibly bad luck on his part.

"We consider this a credible threat, Mr. Paxon." This was from the taller of the two agents on the video screen of Paxon's desktop. He was dressed like the other in an overcoat and hat, but was clearly second. Lanky and dark, he didn't bother to hide his frustration with Paxon's attitude.

"I'm sure you do," said Paxon.

The agents had been cooling their heels in a private room off the lobby for about fifteen minutes. Just the thought of feds on his property made Paxon nervous. The lobby would be as far as they got.

"We recommend you let us secure your person and premises," added the other.

What was his name, thought Paxon. *Spencer?* He was older than the other, and harder to read.

"I appreciate your concern, gentlemen," said Paxon. "But I'll handle this on my own."

The tall, dark agent frowned.

"Good day, agents," said Paxon, flipping off the video camera.

Paxon watched from another screen as the two agents left the building. He drummed his fat fingers absentmindedly along his desk, frowned, and barked once more into the air, "Hector."

Hector arrived shortly. His chief of security was tall, wiry, obsessively fit, and taciturn by default. It was a quality Paxon admired and distrusted, in part because he could never stop talking.

"Mr. Paxon."

Paxon rested his chubby hands on his belly, a posture he often used to show his disdain or annoyance. Paxon was a big man with big appetites, and he liked people to realize he met those appetites, often and well. Only two things were small about Leonard Paxon: his eyes, which sat like a pig's in rolls of fat; and his patience with failure.

"Hector, I've discovered something about myself," said Paxon.

Hector offered no response.

"I've discovered I like things to go my way," continued Paxon, a hint of iron coming into his speech. "And when they don't, I'm very unhappy."

Hector continued to stand quietly, waiting.

"Do you know why I'm unhappy today?" asked Paxon.

"Because your name is now on the Death Market List," answered Hector.

"Because my name is now on the Death Market List." Paxon rolled forward in his chair. "How the hell did that happen?"

Hector ignored the question. "I've ordered all staff, except level one, home for the duration of the Listing," he said. "That means anyone left in the building has been personally approved by me. All commercial and public entrances to the building have been sealed. You'll have to do your business from the bunker computer for the time being."

"Not convenient," said Paxon, glaring at Hector as if this were his fault. "Or practical. I have business to attend to, Hector. Face-to-face business."

"You'll remain here in the underground facilities," insisted Hector. "Everything has been prepared well in advance; you'll lack for no comfort or need. Our firewalls are as secure as any, if you have to communicate."

But not foolproof, thought Paxon. *I noticed you're careful enough not to make that claim, Hector.*

Paxon sighed. He was about to become a nonentity in the business world; that or the feds and hackers would have a field day with his most confidential information.

"So, I get to live like some animal in a burrow," he said. "I suppose you think that a holiday? Do you know how much money I stand to lose?"

And he would, too. There were certain things one did not do on the computer: face-to-face dealings were an integral part of any successful business, more so now than ever. By living underground until the attempt had passed, Paxon was reduced to using only secondhand and online communication. That was unacceptable.

"Hector, did you consider that my sudden listing has nothing to do with my actual death?"

Hector raised one eyebrow.

"Maybe," continued Paxon pedantically, "this is just an elaborate distraction, something to upset my day-to-day activities, something to do with business."

Hector shrugged. "You've been around a long time. Whatever the motivation, the listing is real and so is the respondent. The Hand will not settle for mere distraction."

Paxon slumped back in his chair. There *had* been an incident, in Shanghai, but it was so long ago it couldn't possibly relate to this. What was that girl's name? It didn't matter. She was a no one, and no one connected him to her. He had been careful to cover his tracks. No, this wasn't about that. This had the stink of business about it.

"Hector, I want to know facts. What do you have for me? Who is it behind this? Who is trying to have me killed?"

The briefest of frowns crossed Hector's face. This hesitation, more than anything else, even more than seeing his name actually listed in the Death Market, unsettled Paxon.

"I don't know," answered Hector flatly.

Paxon stared at his chief of security, caught in a rare moment with nothing to say.

"The Death Market is the most secure site next to the Federal Information Chamber," explained Hector.

"And we know how secure the feds can be," said Paxon, finding his tongue again. "Maybe I should have thought about that before I took you on."

The reference was intended to sting, and Paxon regretted it almost as soon as he said it. Hector had applied to the agency—and been rejected. But pushing Hector now was not only dangerous, it was stupid.

"Sorry," he mumbled.

Hector acknowledged the rare event with a shrug.

"Could you at least tell me about this ass who took the assignment? What is this ... Hand? And why would he want to kill me for a lousy hundred grand?"

"The fee is up to half a million," said Hector. "And no, I can't tell you about The Hand. No one can."

Hector turned then and left without being dismissed.

Maybe his skin wasn't so thick, after all, thought Paxon.

*

Kong Xiao Wei sat under the pavilion in the palatial gardens of his estate. He was watching his niece pour the tea and his nephew, Ziyang, try to hide his impatience. With deliberate, graceful movements, Ling held the sleeve of her robe with one hand and poured with the other. *It was a pleasure to watch Ling perform the tea ceremony*, thought Kong. It was a pleasure to watch Ling do anything. He let the briefest of smiles pass his lips.

"Uncle," said Ziyang, trying to draw his attention.

Kong ignored Ziyang as Ling offered him the small porcelain cup of tea on a tray. Kong carefully picked up the cup along the rim with his thumb and forefinger and used his little finger to brace the bottom.

Ling waited as he took his first slow sip. When it was evident he found the tea to his satisfaction, she poured her uncle another cup and then one for Ziyang. Finished, she sat with her legs folded beneath her, her small hands clasped in her lap and eyes to the floor.

Only then did Kong turn to Ziyang.

"Uncle, there is news."

Kong sipped his tea, watched a butterfly flit behind Ziyang's head.

"Ling," he said quietly. "Would you care for some tea?"

"No, thank you, Uncle," she said, her voice soft and rich.

Inwardly, Kong sighed and finally gave Ziyang his full attention. "What is your news?"

"Paxon is now on the Death List. Paxon Industry is in a vulnerable position. Now is the time to act."

Kong considered the butterfly again. "Now is not the time."

"But Uncle, if we don't act, someone surely will. We can utilize our influence to move some of Paxon's holdings and capital in our direction while he is inhibited by the listing. We ..."

"Now is not the time," repeated Kong, this time with finality.

There was a slight pause while Ziyang composed himself. When his nephew was ready to listen, Kong continued. "When I decide the time is right, you will move those holdings and capital you speak of in our direction. But not before I say so. We will not be seen to take advantage of our competitor's misfortune."

"As you wish, Uncle," said Ziyang carefully. "I only hope there is time."

Kong looked to his nephew, waited for his eyes to meet his own.

"I understand," said Ziyang. "We wait."

"And watch."

"And watch."

"Return to the business center and make your plans," said Kong, dismissing his nephew. "If Paxon survives this trial, he will need an ally,

84

one who did not take advantage of his troubles. If he does not survive, then we must be prepared to negotiate the turbulent waters of whatever and whoever takes his place."

Ziyang rose, bowed to his uncle, and said farewell to Ling.

Ling poured Kong another cup of tea. Kong waited until he was sure Ziyang was outside the garden and by consequence the soundproof zone he had erected around the pavilion.

"Ziyang has a good head for business," observed Kong. Ling did not respond, which pleased Kong on many levels. "Our plans remain unchanged?"

As if given permission, Ling raised her eyes to meet her uncle's. "Everything is in place."

"You are certain the contact knows his role?"

Ling turned her head as if considering the question. "He said as much when last contacted. Now, he is beyond safe communication. Paxon's chief of security has sent all but level one employees and their families home and has sealed the building. All communications are being closely monitored."

"When did we last speak with the contact?" asked Kong.

"Six months ago, when you first suspected the time for Paxon's listing was drawing close." The admiration Ling had for this fact was obvious in her expression and tone. "I arranged at that time for our representative to shop in the same market as his wife."

"Which representative?"

"Mae."

He nodded his approval. "Go on."

"The contact's wife invited Mae home for dinner. Mae reminded him of his duty when they had a private moment together."

"Good. And did he seem receptive?"

"Mae believed so."

"Then we are, as the Americans say, on the clock."

"What should I do about the contact's family?" asked Ling.

"Do they have any idea who they are working for?"

"No. All communication was through Mae."

"It is important that those who serve us loyally know we are loyal as well," answered Kong. "Follow through with our agreement."

Ling poured herself a cup of tea. They sat for a time in silence.

"Uncle?" she asked carefully.

"Yes?"

"Why Paxon? Are you not happy in retirement?"

Kong sighed. "It is a long story. Suffice it to say, long ago Mr. Paxon took something from me, something I held very dear."

Ling blushed. The thought of her uncle losing to anyone filled her with an almost unbearable anger. "Let me do this, Uncle. I am ready."

"It is mine to do, little one," said Kong. "We all own our past, and the burdens that come with it."

He rose. "Compose yourself. It is time to continue your training."

Ling rose, found a hidden panel in the wooden pavilion and turned the isolation measures to full. Now they were as invisible to the outside world as they were silent. Ling removed her traditional robes to reveal a form-fitting, one-piece exercise suit. Kong watched Ling stretch, again admiring her grace and confidence. *Yes*, he thought, *she is the one*. Ling possessed talents and resources at levels Ziyang did not. In this, she was more like her uncle than anyone in the family. She would make a fine successor.

*

Justin Monroe came home, tossed a stack of student papers on his coffee table, and made himself a drink. He finished the drink in one long pull and then reclined on his couch. He was not a drinker by habit, but today was special. He glanced at the papers, an anachronism in the virtual world of education but one he insisted his students follow. He decided to grade them tomorrow. The students would wait.

He had responded.

Even now, he couldn't believe the moment had arrived.

He sat up, checked his window-wall to make sure it was shuttered and secured, then pressed his thumb on the coffee table corner and activated his private computer. The glass tabletop darkened and a blinking cursor requested his password. An illuminated keyboard filled the bottom half of the glass. Monroe typed in the appropriate response and watched the tabletop flicker again to a dark metallic blue screen. Unprompted, Monroe again pressed his thumb on the right-hand corner of the coffee table. If he didn't do this, all files on the computer would be automatically erased at the next command. He waited for his firewalls to boot up and then pulled up the Net. He leaned back on the couch, the desktop automatically adjusting its angle to meet his new line of vision, and took a sip of his drink.

And there it was, just to right of the listing for Leonard Paxon—now three hundred thousand for verified termination in thirty days—the name Monroe had been waiting to see for some time now: *The Hand of Passing*.

Next to The Hand's listing was an icon that offered a detailed listing of the subject's rank and more infamous kills. Monroe knew all the stats by heart. The Hand was listed as the fifth ranked assassin, behind the Demonetization Corporation, X/iX, the Black Widow, and O.2. Like others, Monroe knew that listing was misleading. The Hand could be first with little effort. Demonetization was a conglomerate network of assassins trained and employed by heads of states from various governments. To many, including Monroe, they didn't really belong on the List. Their stats, like their kills, were sloppy, suspicious, and lacked any of the finesse that marked a true professional. So, too, were the notorious Men of the Mountain who ranked seventh. Neither group was a true representation of the Death Market's professionals.

The same could not be said for X/iX.

X/iX was every bit the individual, an iconoclastic in both personality and method. He was currently serving time on the prison planet Madagascar for the assassination of Konrad Millet, CEO of the former Nillon Corporation. X/iX had left Millet's head on a spike outside his mansion. Millet's face had been painted up like a clown. Though Monroe respected X/iX's abilities, he thought the assassin lacked the necessary grace that separated the true professional from the journeyman.

For Monroe, the true artists on the list started with numbers three and four: the Black Widow and O.2. The Widow was a figure of legend and hadn't registered a hit for years. Many believed she was in retirement or dead. That she was still ranked in the top five was a testimony to her volume and quality of early work. O.2, on the other hand, was a relative newcomer, but like the Widow, generally respected by his or her peers. O.2's climb up the rankings had been marked by a series of pragmatic and business-like hits that appeared to be driven solely by commercial interests. O.2 did not work the personal vendetta, and didn't come cheap. Though deadly efficient, some thought O.2 lacked a certain flare that often associated with some of the other Death Market's assassins, like the Widow and Poetic Justice, a lower-ranked assassin that specialized in killing with a sword.

But of all the names near the top there was one that Monroe respected most, and in some ways feared. Number five: The Hand.

Despite the nature of the work, The Hand possessed an iconic, if infamous, persona, a holdover of a particularly dark Romanticism that never seemed to die in the public mind. The Hand's successes were distinguished both by their difficulty and their tangential sense of nobility. Poison, close-range hand weapons, and bare hands were the tools of his or her craft. That the assassin was proficient with the latter was established when he literally beat the heavyweight boxer, Hans Richter, to death. Forensic evidence determined that it was one person who supplied the beating, and that Richter had apparently been free to defend himself. Richter had been a notorious rake and suspected murderer. He was found not guilty by way of a mistrial for the death of his fifth wife. No one was upset to see him suffer, and The Hand's reputation grew. Death List pundits began to note that the many of The Hand's victims were themselves notorious, often escaping justice on some technicality or abuse of power. Others, they hinted, may be carrying secret crimes. The Hand became a celebrity of sorts. Some called him The Hand of Justice.

Monroe poured himself another drink. It had been some time since The Hand's last official kill. He worried that the assassin had retired, or died. But then came the Paxon listing, and suddenly The Hand was in the game again. The pundits were already speculating as to Paxon's hidden culpabilities, and how long it would be before The Hand made him pay for them.

Monroe suspected the matter was personal for The Hand. It had that kind of feel to it. He sipped his drink and rubbed a hand along his smooth, hairless chin. The chin, like the rest of Monroe, appeared soft, almost effeminate. His hands, however, told another story. They were heavy with calluses and muscles, muscles people outside of certain martial arts and Eastern yoga rarely develop. To hide this fact, he made it a point to attend yoga classes and to never shake hands. At school, his colleagues put the latter down to an affectation, but no one complained. He was liked and respected as a teacher by both the administration and students. He gave them no reasons to feel otherwise.

He scrolled the Death List to his own modest, albeit pseudonymous, listing. It gave him a mild thrill to see his hits listed on the same page with The Hand, Widow, and O.2, though no one would ever know that he, or anyone, was responsible. His listing was not like the others. His was a deception; an inside joke. He was a non-entity, overlooked by all the Market followers and the rest of the assassins. Only a few, select individuals were ever aware of the truth of his listing, and then only for a brief, special time. They died with his secret.

Monroe turned off the computer, rose from the couch. He put his glass down and went to the shuttered window. He ordered the view open and considered the panorama of blurring air shuttle traffic against the background of building lights. The night lights were so bright they paled the stars into oblivion.

The Hand had signed on for Leonard Paxon.

Monroe could not be happier.

*

"What kind of world do we live in?" asked Paxon of his chief of security. "I'm supposed to just sit around in a hole until some China-nutcase tries to kill me."

"We don't know the assassin is Chinese," Hector reminded him.

Paxon was growing more irritated by the day. The literal deadline was drawing close; there were less than ten days remaining in the Listing contract. *Of course*, thought Paxon, *they could just renew the damn thing or extend a new contract. It cost a great deal of money, but it had been known to happen before.*

Not that *Hector* thought it would come to that. He believed The Hand would act, and soon. Paxon tried to find some comfort in that fact.

"There are still ten days left," said Hector. "We need to be ready for every contingency."

Paxon glared at his security officer. "Leave me."

Alone, he stewed for a time, staring at his desk. The phone rang. It was his private, off-line phone. Those who knew the number were limited to a select few. He looked to the ID, and considered ignoring the caller. It wasn't that he disliked the person calling. On the contrary, he was one of the few people in the world Paxon believed understood him. But taking this particular phone call at this particular time was risky. This was business, and Paxson knew a ten-day window of unavailability because some asshole wanted to kill him was bad for business. But ignoring the call had its own risks.

He hit the connection button. "Bennie!"

"Hi, Leonard!" Benjamin Lerner's smiling cherubic face turned a moment later to curious concern. "Hey, I can't see you. Something wrong with your video?"

"Yeah, sorry about that, Bennie. Security measures."

"Yes. I heard about that," answered Lerner, sounding genuinely sympathetic. "It's one of the reasons I called. If there is anything I can do ..."

"Thanks, Bennie. That means a lot. But I've got everything covered here."

"I can't imagine what you must be going through."

"What's the other reason you called, Bennie? I'm kind of pressed for time these days."

"I know this is absolutely terrible timing, Leonard, and I don't want to be the bearer of bad news, but given the circumstances, I had to call."

"What is it, Bennie?"

"Well, you know that project we've been working on?"

Paxon felt his stomach roil. "Yeah?"

"Well, it's come due, partner."

Paxon cursed silently, grateful Lerner couldn't see his expression. The project Lerner represented was a sizable investment opportunity for Paxon Industries. But to close the deal, the parties involved had to meet face to face, had to literally sign on the dotted line the old-fashioned way, on paper and in front of witnesses. The protocol supposedly insured authenticity. The new business reality was a return to its roots: shady backroom deals made face to face with teams of lawyers and recording equipment, where a man or woman's word and signature meant the difference between a solid, protected enterprise and catastrophe. It was a reality that Paxon had exploited in the past, but today it was working against him.

Lerner looked truly miserable as he asked his next question. "Leonard, is there any way at all that you can meet them face to face? They want to sign now."

Before he could answer, Hector walked in the office. He was already shaking his head no.

Paxon knew Hector was monitoring his private lines during the crisis—Hector told him he would—but it was a bitter pill to see it so openly in effect. The sight of him now sent a troubling thought through his mind: *when the crisis was over, would he be able to get his private line back? And just how hard had it been for Hector to "start" monitoring his private lines anyway?* Maybe his so-called ultra-private lines weren't so private after all.

Paxon put that worry aside for another time, and turned back to Lerner.

"Sorry, Bennie," he said. "No can do. How about postponing the deal for just a short time? Eleven days?" Paxon looked to Hector. Hector considered, and then slowly nodded his approval.

"That's just it, Lenny. They want to close the deal now—yesterday as a matter of fact. We still have the right to counter, but it has to be in the next five days. You know the contract." Then Lerner lowered his voice, and delivered the final nail. "I think they have another offer. I think they know about your trouble and that's why they're playing hardball. They're playing for a better deal."

"Goddammit, Bennie! How can there be another offer? How did anyone find out? I certainly didn't leak it."

Lerner ducked his head as if avoiding a physical blow. "I assure you, it wasn't from me or my office. Frankly, Leonard, I think it's a bluff." He hesitated, searching the blank screen. "But can we afford to take the chance?"

Paxon was furious. Leak or not, Lerner might be right. His so-called partners were probably taking advantage of his dilemma. He certainly would. They must have been offered a better deal and wanted out of the contract. They had to know that Paxon couldn't respond in the open now, no matter how secure the setting. He was being played.

He was in a corner. He was going to have to crawl out from his protective shell and make the deal. He glared at Hector, who stood like a living wall of precaution. He drummed his fingers along the desk, frantically searching for an alternative.

"What about a proxy signing, Bennie?" he asked.

Lerner considered the question with some surprise. His expression became more hopeful, though still cautious.

"I suppose that could work," he said. "But who do you have in mind?"

Hector started to protest, but Paxon held a hand up to hold him off. "It would have to be you, of course, Bennie."

"I'm flattered, Leonard. Are you sure?"

Paxon turned to Hector, daring him to say no. After a time, Hector reluctantly nodded.

"I am," said Paxon with enthusiasm. "You contact the other party and make it happen, Bennie."

"I'll do my best." Lerner sounded a bit distracted.

Of course, thought Paxon, *he probably just realized he was about to walk into an assassination zone.*

"Get back me to later today, Bennie," said Paxon quickly, before the other could back out. "My security officer will arrange all the details."

"Okay, Leonard, I ..."

But Paxon had already disconnected.

"Now, you gloomy son of a bitch," said Paxon, turning to Hector. "You earn your money and make sure that little worm gets in and out of here with no problems. There's a nice bonus in it for you, if all goes well."

Hector's expression didn't change.

"Oh, relax" growled Paxon. "I'd bet your salary that our potential new business partner is behind the assassination attempt. They're quite capable of it, the dirty bastards. Kill me or kill the contract, either way they win. But the proxy will fix them. Go on now, make us tight."

*

Monroe considered his hand-drawn plans for Paxon Industries.

Though not a comprehensive picture of Hector's defense measures, he was fairly certain about what he would find. There remained, however, one gaping hole of vital information, one piece he couldn't fill in: the underground facilities, the inner sanctum, the holy of holies—Paxon's Bunker. It would remain a mystery until Monroe was inside.

Looking at the sketches of the facility gathered from various sources, Monroe recognized that Hector had designed a modern-day fortress. The structure was of reinforced concrete walls, and each room a virtual containment center, capable of isolating itself from the rest at a moment's notice. The building ran on redundant and autonomous internal power sources, and used intra- and inter-communication services. A highly trained and thoroughly vetted security staff patrolled each floor and was supported by a web of open and hidden security cameras. Monroe suspected a series of secret passages ran along many of the floors and these, too, would be monitored.

The Bunker, presumably underground, was likely a fully equipped panic room. Knowing Hector, the walls and entrance would be of the strongest possible construction. A military operation, given enough time and firepower, could eventually break down any door. But an assassin wouldn't have that time—even if they could somehow put their hands on the firepower and get into the building without alerting every fed in the city.

But Monroe was not really worried about getting in the outer building, or for that matter the ultra-secure Bunker. He was equally confident that The Hand would find a way in as well. No, he had only two concerns.

The first was the timing.

If he understood The Hand's tactics—and he had spent the last ten years making sure he did—then most likely the attempt would take place in two days, and in the evening. If Monroe was wrong on this count, then all his efforts were for naught. Well, almost naught. He had a contingency plan, of course, but it was hardly the desired outcome.

The second concern, more troubling for its very real personal implications, was how to get out of the building once events took their course.

It had become clear early on to Monroe that Hector had created more than just a secure facility. Paxon Industries was, in fact, a trap. Any thief or assassin who managed to enter the building risked being shut up in one of those deadly self-contained cell rooms if they raised an alarm. Hector was sure to trigger one, should he suspect anything out of the ordinary.

Monroe absentmindedly tapped the drawings with his finger. It all came down to Hector. What to do about Hector?

*

Kong, dressed in suit and tie, held the door open for his niece. Ling had passed her cousin in the hall on her way in, Ziyang's bearing and expression a careful mask of suppressed satisfaction. It was her turn for the news.

Kong indicated a chair across from his desk with a formal gesture.

"Paxon will be my last contract as The Hand of Passing. I am retiring on all levels. After this, you will take my place—if you wish it."

The offer, never openly spoken about before, now settled around Ling like a robe of appointment.

"I wish only to serve you," she said.

Kong nodded. The pride he felt for Ling was matched only by his regret; she would soon know what a burden this appointment was.

"From now on," he said, "you serve no one, except honor."

"I will follow the path that you have laid."

"Should something happen to Ziyang, you will assume control of the family business."

"Nothing will happen to Ziyang, Uncle. Not while I live."

Kong nodded. "When I am gone—"

"Uncle!"

Kong raised a hand to still her protest. "We cannot afford to comfort ourselves with false assessments, Ling. Our world will not allow it. I am not as young as I once was." He rose from his chair, walked to her side and took her hand. "But rest assured, I plan to enjoy a long and restful retirement."

"Uncle, let me come with you, to Paxson," said Ling. "It would be a fitting transition."

"No, this one I must do alone."

He wondered why he did not tell her, even now, about her mother, his sister. She deserved to know. But he couldn't bring himself to speak his failure aloud. He would do this last thing, and lift the burden he had carried alone for all these years.

Ling, sensing his distraction perhaps, pulled his hand to her cheek, her long black hair and hot tears running across the back of his hand like silk and heated oil. "You will not fail, Kong Xiao Wei. The Hand will never fail." Her tone brooked no argument in this matter.

Kong smiled. "Whatever the outcome," he continued, releasing her hand and stepping back, "I have taken steps that my identity will remain unknown. Ward yourself similarly."

Seeing he was finished, Ling rose from her seat and faced her uncle. Her demeanor had changed and now she looked him boldly in the eye.

"There are many things that remain for you to teach me, Uncle," she said. "I do not give you permission to die just yet."

*

"Bennie!"

Paxon's heavy jowls and tiny eyes peered down at Lerner from the giant flat-screen mounted prominently just inside the main entrance of Paxon Industries. Lerner and the Kolden lawyer, a Mr. Nathan Carter, had already passed through three security checks, including a full body scan just outside the main entrance. They had been cooling their heels in the front lobby for about ten minutes when Paxon finally made his appearance.

"I'm awfully sorry about this, Bennie," said Paxon. "I'm afraid there's just a slight change of plans."

Lerner and Carter exchanged glances. When he looked around, Lerner saw Fidel Hector walking their way. Behind Hector were two armed security guards. Looking around, Lerner noticed that the front desk clerk and every other staff member in the lobby were now openly bearing weapons.

"Mr. Lerner. Mr. Carter." said Hector, nodding to each. Carter looked to Lerner for an explanation, but Lerner could only return his expression of confusion and concern.

"You see," said Paxon, drawing both men's attention back to the screen, "it's all this Death Listing nonsense. I'm afraid I'm going to have to ask you both to submit to one more security measure. We're not going to meet in my office, as we discussed."

"But to officially witness the contract ..." started Carter.

"Oh, we'll all be in the same room," answered Paxon smoothly, his multiple chins bouncing up and down in assurance. "It's just I'll be behind a special, transparent wall. You'll be able to see me, and can watch me sign. Not really that much different at all, is it?"

"But, Leonard," worried Lerner, "will it hold up in court?"

Lerner glanced at Carter as he said this. From the lawyer's expression, Lerner suspected that Carter was thinking along the same lines. A technicality, however small, could give Kolden the excuse they needed to get out of the contract and pursue another bid. Carter's eyes were practically dancing with the possibilities.

"Don't worry, Mr. Carter," said Paxon, "my lawyers assure me that this is all very legal and binding. You can rest assure, I would never agree to it otherwise."

Carter's eyes carefully held no expression as he answered Paxon's image. "Doubtless they are right. You understand, however, I must note the change in protocol for the record—just in case there's a question later."

Paxon's expression darkened. "Of course."

He turned to his chief of security. "Okay, Hector. Bring them through."

"Mr. Lerner," said Hector, standing carefully a few feet away. "Would you please come with me? Mr. Carter, if you could wait here just a moment. This is for your protection as well as convenience."

"You have an interesting definition of convenience," noted Carter. He glanced meaningfully at Lerner. "Mr. Lerner, is this way you usually moderate contracts?"

Lerner looked from Hector to Carter. "No."

*

Kong stood in the shadows just outside the secret exit to Paxon Industries. His blackened body armor and hood made him just another shadow. There was nothing to indicate the exit hole nestled in the park grounds, half a mile away from Paxon Industries. Hector had built the underground tunnel himself and the trapdoor exit camouflaged beneath a foot of lawn. Only Paxon, Hector, and a few select security personnel supposedly knew of its existence. And Kong.

Kong checked his timepiece one last time and left his cover, stepping close to the trap entrance. A moment later, a small crack of light lined the ground as an earth-covered hatch swung open.

"Turn your light off," whispered Kong. The light was immediately extinguished.

"Everything's clear," said a voice from inside the darkness. "I disabled the surveillance along the tunnel."

"Good."

Somewhat more tentatively, the voice asked, "Do you require anything else?"

"No," said Kong. "Your wife and family will join you soon."

"My wife ... she said ... she wanted me to ask ... they will look for me later ... how ... how can I live?"

"You have not seen my face. You do not know my name. Even if they catch you later, you could only confirm what I want you to: The Hand was here. But they must find you first. I will make it look like you were lost in the explosion. Now, follow your instructions."

The man emerged from the darkness, and left without looking back.

Kong slipped inside the dark.

*

Bennie Lerner sat in the chair indicated for him. He was left alone with a stone-faced guard who kept his weapon drawn but not pointed directly at Lerner. The guard refused to answer any of his questions.

Hector wasn't long in returning. He dismissed the guard when he walked in, but made a point to show Lerner the gun in his hand.

"I hope this is all being recorded," said Lerner, letting his fuming anger spill out. "I have never in my life ..."

"It is not being recorded," interrupted Hector, laying the gun on his desk, but close at hand, and pointed at Lerner. "Not yet. I thought you might be more open if you thought we were off the record."

The two men considered each other for a time.

"Yes," said Hector, finally. "I know."

Lerner's expression slowly revolved from his usual cherubic naiveté to a face absent of all expression. When he spoke, it was in quiet, confident tones with little or no resemblance to the usually whining consultant chatter.

"What have you done with Mr. Carter?" he asked. "Just curious."

"He's now in the room with Paxon, separated by the safety partition, and signing the necessary papers in front of the necessary witnesses. You were not really needed for that, were you, Mr. Lerner?"

"No. But Carter will have the deal thrown out anyway, afterwards."

Hector nodded slowly. "Yes, that's likely. Afterwards."

Lerner looked around the room. "Are we really alone? No recordings?"

"Yes. Are you really Benjamin Lerner?"

"Of course," answered Lerner, sitting back in the chair. "And a dozen others. And no one," he added with a half-smile.

"Are you The Hand?"

Lerner snorted. "No. I'm afraid I'm not that prize, Hector."

"But you are here to kill Paxon," insisted Hector.

"No."

Hector blinked in surprise. "Carter?"

Lerner shook his head, a small smile of sympathy on his face. "No. He's just what he appears to be, a lawyer from Kolden Enterprises."

"Then why are you here?"

"I don't believe you are telling me the truth, Hector," said Lerner. He smiled and leaned forward in his chair until his elbows rested on his knees. "I think this is being recorded."

Hector's eyes narrowed.

"But it doesn't matter," continued Lerner. "These things will be taken care of, in time."

"You are not here for Paxon or Carter," said Hector, his hand inching toward the gun.

"No," repeated the other. "Not them."

Hector made a grab for the gun.

But even as he lifted it from the desk, he knew it was too late.

*

Kong reached the other end of the tunnel and a bare antechamber. He knew from the mole that a secret door was behind the antechamber, one that opened to Paxon's inner locked sanctum. Kong also knew that there was a hidden utility closet in the wall to his left. It was stocked with weapons, communication equipment, and a panic button that could call in reinforcements and the police if necessary. Kong looked closely along the wall and found the small chalk mark left by the mole. He left the closet closed; he had all the weapons he would need.

He stepped to the hidden inner sanctum door, marked by another piece of chalk, and tried the handle. It was unlocked. He gently pushed the door open, revealing a dark room. He stepped cautiously into the darkness, his night goggles adjusting to the lack of light.

Paxon was not there.

But someone else was.

The lights came on. The man leaned against the wall, his legs and arms crossed, his expression amused. He was dressed in a business suit, and looked like a lawyer.

"Hello," he said, standing up straight. "I assume you are The Hand."

Kong did not answer, but dropped a throwing star into the hidden palm of his hand.

"Paxon is behind that door," continued the other, pointing to his right. "He's all yours. You don't have to worry about the cameras or security—or Hector. I've taken care of all that."

"Who are you?" asked Kong.

The other smiled. "Oh, I'm like you, I have lots of names ... and none."

Another assassin, thought Kong. He studied the man more closely. "Are you here for Paxon?" he asked. "I didn't know there was another bid."

"No," said the other with a shake of his head. "I told you, help yourself. I assumed this was a personal matter. I don't imagine you need the money."

Kong nodded, shifting his feet ever so slightly to the right.

"I thought so," said the other, smiling as he looked to Kong's feet, then back to his masked head. He nodded to the door he'd indicated earlier. "I'll wait for you here. We should have enough time."

"Enough time?"

"For questions, conversation," shrugged the man. "For me to kill you."

"I see," said Kong slowly. "Why not just deal with that matter now?"

"I want you to have Paxon," said the other. "I understand personal matters. It was your sister, wasn't it?"

Kong considered the man before him.

The other shook his head, as if reading Kong's thoughts. "No tricks. My matter is personal too."

"Do I know you?"

"No."

"But it's personal?" asked Kong.

"Yes."

"I'll be back shortly."

"I'm sure you will."

*

Leonard Paxon was happy, as happy as he could be under the circumstances. The papers were signed. He was rich, again, and twice over. He rolled a cigar between his fat fingers, savoured the smell of the expensive leaf and closed his eyes in appreciation.

When he opened them again, it was to find a man dressed in black from head to toe standing beside him. Paxon dropped the cigar and reached for the panic button. The man knocked his hand away with a deceptively simple gesture. Then the stranger reached out and laid a finger against Paxon's fat neck.

"What the hell?" started Paxon.

He felt the finger press against his neck and his entire body convulsed in an iron-like cramp. He tried to scream, but his throat, like the rest of his body, was locked in pain. He looked desperately to the man beside him, strange whistling noises coming from his mouth and nose.

The figure in black cocked his head, watching Paxon's reactions carefully. After a time, he leaned close to Paxon and whispered in his ear. Something like recognition shone for a moment in Paxon's eyes.

The figure in black stepped behind Paxon, drew a blade from a pocket along his forearm, and slit Paxon's throat from ear to ear.

*

Kong cleaned and sheathed his knife. He pulled a small black bag from his utility belt and removed a thumb-sized camera. He took a few pictures of the lifeless Paxon and the office. Then he took out a piece of wire with thumb grips on either end, and removed Paxon's finger. He put the finger in a separate bag and stored this in his belt. He would arrange to have the photo and finger delivered to the proper people, insuring The Hand was given credit for the hit.

He checked his timepiece, and then considered what waited for him outside the door. He removed a small incendiary device from another hidden pocket, set the timer for fifteen minutes and armed it. He carefully removed another microchip, similar to the one he used on Paxon. He fit the chip in place on the velcro-tip of his fingered glove. He checked his weapons one last time.

Then he turned around and re-entered the first room.

*

Monroe was surprised to find himself apprehensive. It was a new sensation for him. He took a deep, calming breath and reviewed the room dimensions one more time. He had checked and rechecked the gun tucked in his belt behind his back, but hoped it wouldn't be necessary. Doubtless The Hand's body suit was bullet-proof in critical places, and if he fired a shot, it would take valuable time, time that he might not get back.

Still, he might need the gun in the end. He kept it tucked away.

Ideally, he would have his own body armor and a few selected weapons from his personal collection, but his entrance into Paxon Industries made that impossible. He did find an unexpected gift: Hector's surprisingly flexible and strong chest armor. Hector wouldn't need it anymore. Monroe now wore it under his suit and shirt; you never know what measure might make the difference.

He took his suit jacket off and stood in the center of the room. He hoped The Hand would allow him the time to explain. The explanation was important.

The door opened.

*

Kong stepped quietly through the doorway, and stopped.

"The deed is done, I take it," said the other.

Kong did not answer.

"You have your souvenirs?" asked the other.

Again, Kong did not answer. Instead, he took a slow step into the room. He watched the way the other carried himself, the way he shifted his feet ever so slightly to keep the proper spacing and angles between them. The man moved casually, almost without thinking, but his actions were precise and appropriate.

"I assume you left behind something to take care of the evidence," said the other. "Are we on the clock?"

"A little less than ten minutes," said Kong. That was a lie; the bomb wouldn't go off for another fifteen minutes. But the press of time might make the other rush.

The other frowned. "I was hoping for a longer chat—before we get down to business."

"Talk, if you must," said Kong.

"You don't wonder why I'm here?" asked the other.

"In our line of work," said Kong, "one gets to know the competition, even if only in name. You're not the Widow or O.2, and you are too competent to be one of the lower rankings. Are you a new listing?"

"Not exactly."

The other slid to the right half a step. Kong countered with a step to his left.

"There is a listing," said Kong, "that I have wondered about for some time. Contracts that are fulfilled but never collected. The listing is both correct and misleading, for it implies that more than one party may be responsible."

Without missing his place in the deadly dance, the other nodded with approval. "You've guessed." He sounded both delighted and a little disappointed.

"You are Unknown," answered Kong. "A catchall listing of those assassinations unclaimed by their contractors, but clearly of our kind. I've wondered about those kills. I was almost certain one of them was the assassin who went by the name of Mantis."

The other made a slight, careful bow. "Mantis was my third kill."

They continued their subtle dance of shifting positions as they talked, like two scorpions circling each other, looking for just the right moment to strike.

"Why the anonymity?" asked Kong. "If you don't draw the money, if you don't claim the kill, no one will know of your success."

"Some know, for a short time," answered the other, his eyes shining. "They die knowing the truth. That's enough."

The eyes lost their shine for a moment. The other began to paw the air slowly in front of him, shifting his arms to match Kong's position.

"But why?" asked Kong.

"I consider myself a necessary balance. Something to make you people fear too, at least for a little time."

"You are not a federal agent," said Kong. "And I know their private hired guns."

"No. I'm not with the law."

"You consider yourself an agent of justice?"

The other snorted. "Hardly. That's your domain."

Kong considered this for a moment. "I have offended you in some way."

"I'm not that invested in the subjects."

Kong frowned.

"I want the best," said the other. "I want to beat the best."

"Ah," said Kong. "I see. For the art. For the honor; though no one will ever know."

"They know. You'll know."

"I think I understand," said Kong. "It is, as you said, a personal matter."

"You understand."

The dance took on a different nuance, becoming more deliberate.

"You have taken precautions against discovery, dead or alive?" asked the other.

"Of course."

"Would you agree to temporarily dismantling any such devices? I would hate to win, only to lose. I promise to leave no trace of your body after this is over. You have my word on that."

Kong hesitated for just a moment and then pulled out a small wire that ran along his neckline.

"It is done. Will you do the same?"

"I do not carry a personal device of this nature," said the other. "I have no family or reputation to protect. If I fail, then the remains will show not one person but many, all of them with legitimate backgrounds. I will remain even in death a mystery, the unknown. But you can call me Monroe, if you like."

He stopped for a moment, held a hand up and slowly lifted the gun from his belt with the other, holding the butt with his thumb and finger. He set the gun on the floor and kicked it outside the door. He showed his empty hands to Kong. Kong nodded and quickly removed the blades along his forearms and legs. He tossed these to the corner.

"Thank you," said Monroe. "Better this way."

As he finished, he stepped forward, feinted a jab with his left hand and tried to find Kong's wrist with his right.

Kong shifted, blocked the reaching hand with a sweep of his left arm. At the same time, he flicked the hidden dart he had been holding in his right.

Monroe bent and turned his head, letting the dart fly by. He resumed his fighting position with a small frown of disapproval.

Kong launched a sweeping sidekick at Monroe's knee. The other sprang back. Their speeds were well-matched, and Kong's sweep only brushed the other's shin. Nevertheless, there was a rip now in Monroe's pants. Again, Monroe shook his head.

"The Hand cheats," he muttered, and sent a jab like a cobra strike at Kong's head. It connected, though Kong's mask took most of the blow. Monroe followed it with a straight kick to Kong's hip. Kong made a downward sweeping gesture with his right arm and twisted his hip. He stepped into his hip turn to try a spinning back kick of his own. But Monroe was already falling back out of range.

Both men took a small step back to gather themselves.

Closing again, Monroe sent more jabs at Kong's face. Normally this type of attack would not bother Kong, particularly with his face armor. But he sensed the power in Monroe's hands. They were deadly.

With a speed he had not shown before, Monroe followed a left jab up with a right-hand uppercut. Kong bobbed his head back to avoid the rising fist.

But the uppercut was a feint, as well. Monroe's real attack was a crushing leg sweep at Kong's exposed legs.

Kong continued to fall back, turning the bob into a backward half-somersault. He avoided the leg sweep this way, but landed on his back. He brought both of his legs up and kicked at the oncoming torso of the other. He sent Monroe crashing back against the wall, giving Kong time to stand again.

Monroe collected himself with a wry shake of his head. He stepped forward, and they circled once more.

Now Monroe's hands were open, like a wrestler. Kong shifted to a jujitsu stance. He had no desire to grapple with those hands. As he waited for an opening, he was distracted by an image of Ling's face as she accepted her inheritance. A strange paradoxical premonition gripped him and he felt a cold drop of sweat run down his back.

Monroe, sensing an opportunity, closed in. He caught Kong's right wrist in his left hand and pulled it across his spinning body. Kong felt his wrist break as those deadly hands unleashed their full power and the torque of his own momentum worked against him. He tried to correct, rolling with the toss.

He landed on his back, his left wrist still in the grip of the other. He saw a chopping hand rushing to his head.

And for the second time in as many seconds, time seemed to stand still for Kong.

He saw the purpose of the attack, knew it was aimed not for his head but his throat. He knew that the speed and weight of the blow might push his armor into his larynx, crushing or knocking the breath out of him. He knew, too, that to avoid this possibility he must forget the pain in his wrist. He must roll into the pain and make the deadly hand deflect off his chest armor.

But even as he saw the truth of that possibility, a higher awareness allowed Kong to see another opportunity, another way. The other's exposed ankle was just to the right of his outstretched hand. That hand carried the paralyzing microchip on its middle finger. A touch on the exposed skin and his opponent would fall to the same seizure that had incapacitated Paxon.

All this Kong saw and understood in a moment of a moment, an immediate, instinctive reaction: to attack or roll.

He reached for the ankle, even as he felt the crushing pain of the other's hand against his throat.

He felt the microchip activate as his head slammed against the floor. Another vision, this time of a distorted Ling pouring tea under the pagoda, passed through his fractured mind.

And then everything went dark.

He came to a moment later. His armor had proven enough, after all.

Monroe was still kneeling over him, drenched now in sweat, his hands shaking in paroxysm and pain, his face tortured and frozen.

Kong started to rise, then stopped in disbelief. He had heard legends of masters who could step outside their physical nature, operate solely on will or muscle memory. He had assumed they were only stories.

Somehow, Monroe was acting. His head twitched, and a small, impossible smile crossed his face. With a visible effort, he fell across Kong's chest, pinning him to the ground and driving the air out of Kong's body.

Kong continued to watch in horror as the other's eyes rolled upward, a string of saliva running down his chin to fall on Kong's mask plate. Somehow, those deadly hands found a will of their own. They ripped Kong's mask away and put two stone-like thumbs over Kong's incredulous eyes.

Too late, Kong tried to struggle.

With a sickening crunch Monroe's thumbs went down and in.

*

Spencer walked around the temporary perimeter set up outside Paxson Industries. To the naked eye the building remained whole, if unnaturally still. But Spencer knew the truth; the Paxson building was merely a shell of its former self. The inside was a hollow crater of burning metal and powdered concrete. He knew there would be no answers for him to find there. He left Taylor to the digging and canvassed the streets instead with a sense of futility and frustration.

Paxon was missing and presumed dead. Fidel Hector, his chief of security, also missing, was also presumed dead. God alone knew how many others were killed by the blast.

A small crowd had gathered outside the police barricades. Spencer considered the homeless man pulling at his beard, the young Chinese woman standing beside him, the middle-aged woman holding the baby. Were any of them responsible? Could he be looking at The Hand? Was it one of the street toughs standing in the shadows? Maybe it was the mousey-looking fellow, standing so wide-eyed and innocent with his hands in his pocket.

Which one of you isn't who you pretend to be? he thought.

He was interrupted by his partner. Taylor came to stand beside him. He also studied the wreckage with a grim expression.

"What have you learned?" asked Spencer.

"A local consultant, Benjamin Lerner, and a lawyer representing Kolden Enterprises, Nathan Carter, were scheduled to meet Paxon earlier this afternoon."

"Any connections to The Hand?"

Taylor shook his head again. "Looks like they picked the wrong time to go visiting Paxon. The Kolden lawyer made it out. We're questioning him now. Says he was separated from Lerner during the deal and just assumed he was still with Paxon. Forensics is still trying to sort through the mess down below, but it was a comprehensive incendiary event. DNA, hair samples, blood—it's likely all gone. A similar explosion took out the surveillance equipment. Very professional. We are checking to see if there is a remote backup somewhere, but we think everything was erased in the explosion."

"Paxon wouldn't use a remote bank," said Spencer. "He liked to keep a tight ship. Run the background on Lerner."

Taylor nodded.

"I think," said Taylor after a moment, and then he stopped, checking to see if Spencer cared to hear what he thought.

"Go on," said Spencer dryly.

"I think this whole thing is going to end up an unknown. The Hand—all the contract killers—they usually post as soon as they finish. No one's come to claim the contract yet."

Spencer looked again at the crowd. New people were coming in, and old ones were leaving. The homeless guy was gone, replaced by a man in a business suit. The Chinese girl and the wide-eyed innocent had left, as well.

Spencer frowned. "This is a crime scene. Paxson doesn't have rights on the grounds now. Get the drones here and take surveillance of the crowd."

Taylor nodded. "Paxon should have pulled us in," he said.

Spencer stood stone-faced. "He knew what he was doing. We've been trying to get inside his operation for a long time."

"Still," said Taylor, looking to the smoke now rising from the Paxson window.

"Still," agreed Spencer.

*

Ling stood behind the high-powered lens looking down from the apartment window at the Paxson compound. She had respected her uncle's wishes in this much, she did not follow him, nor would she interfere. But she would watch. That was her right now. The torch had been passed.

She made note of the two well-dressed men entering Paxson's. She wondered at the timing, and circumstances. Traffic had been non-existent around the building. She studied the men's faces as they stood briefly outside the entrance. When they were finally let through, she tried again to see her uncle at his ingress point. But the park was too dark, and the rabbit hole was hidden by trees. It was not too dark for her to see one of the men from earlier leave the Paxson building a short time later. Again, she wondered at the significance, if any.

She waited and watched.

Later still, she felt the smallest of tremors beneath her feet. The Paxson building was suddenly flooded in lights and even from her window a block away she could hear the alarms. Her knuckles grew white on the scope as she desperately searched the park and then turned back to compound.

What was left of Paxson's security started to run out of the front building, smoke erupting from the open doors as if it too wanted to flee.

In the confusion, Ling saw the other visitor from earlier stumble out, as well. He looked dazed and appeared to be hurt. His movements were awkward, as if he were learning to walk again. Her heart sank as she recognized the condition. She knew, though she could not say how, that her uncle had failed.

She quickly disassembled the scope and packed it in her carry bag. She didn't have time to return her equipment to her vehicle, so she stashed the bag in an alley dumpster, moving on quickly and joining the early crowd outside the police barricade.

She scanned the growing numbers of gawkers, fearing she was too late, that he had fled to the shadows.

But no, there he was, just on the edge of the crowd, his hands in his pocket. What made him risk the exposure, she wondered? Maybe he feared his condition would draw attention, maybe he was playing for time, maybe he took some perverse pleasure in seeing without being seen.

She averted her eyes as a detective joined the crowd and looked around.

Not long after that, when the detective's attention was elsewhere, the other finally moved. He still had a hitch to his step, but it was getting better. She could see that his hands were shaking. Large, red-stained hands.

She kept to the shadows, and followed.

***

The Tale of Days

by Bill Davidson, United Kingdom

It was a source of aggravation to Lawrence Juniper that, in the last weeks of his life, he could no longer read for more than ten minutes at a stretch. If there had been anybody in his big, old house to speak to, he would have told them that if he couldn't even read, he wished he could just get on with it and die.

There was nobody to tell, but he told them anyway.

He had spent this chilly autumn morning in his sunken leather wingback skimming one of his own books, *Museums and Social Change in the Twentieth Century*, but found himself disappointingly dull and pompous. He even attempted some fiction by the American author John Steinbeck, who came highly recommended, but his attention would slip over and again to Salisbury—and Kirsten.

He had managed to keep thoughts of Kirsten from his waking mind for more than half a century, but now it seemed she was there at every turn. Still young, still blonde, with her wide smile and breathy laugh. A natural academic, just like him. But, unlike him, looking nothing like one.

He didn't want to end his life dwelling over Kirsten Dean. Even after all these years, it hurt too much.

So, it was very nearly a relief when he heard the unusual sound of his doorbell. His front door was heavily stickered with signs discouraging doorstep sellers, so he feared no grinning salesman.

Groaning deeply, he levered himself onto his feet and stick, but by the time he had gained the hall, the bell had rung twice more and he was calling out that he was coming, for God's sake.

Reaching the heavy door, he glanced through the window to see a long, black car on the gravel. More surprisingly, a uniformed army corporal stood beside it, almost at attention. Frowning, he undid the lock.

Two men stood on his step. One looked like a youngish lawyer holding a slim file, a small man in a smartly cut suit, with short dark hair and dark eyes. The other was a sandy haired soldier in his forties. A major, no less.

It was the soldier who spoke. "Doctor Juniper?"

Lawrence nodded and pulled his baggy, old cardigan straighter, swept a shaky hand over his shiny head. "Well, this is unexpected."

Even as he said it, Lawrence thought that there was something almost familiar about these men, the soldier and the intense-eyed civilian; déjà vu maybe, a far-off echo that dissipated even as he reached for it.

"I'm Major McEwan, and this is Mr. O'Dwyer, of the Ministry of Defense. I wonder, can we have a moment of your time?"

Despising his unsteady feet, he shuffled to turn back. "I suppose you'll better come in, though I can't think why."

Tea declined, the three men sat in the book-strewn lounge and McEwan leaned forward, perhaps noticing how Lawrence angled his good ear towards him.

"This is a lovely house, Doctor. Have you lived in Scotland long?"

"Almost forty years."

"Alone in this huge pile?"

"Always. It suits me best."

O'Dwyer kept up his unnerving stare in silence as McEwan asked, "You once worked in the Salisbury Museum?"

Lawrence sat back, on guard now. Strange how, just when Salisbury had been on his mind, a soldier, of all things, should turn up asking about it. "Many years ago."

"And left under strange circumstances."

"I just left."

"A young woman went missing." He checked his notebook. "Kirsten Dean. June the first, 1964."

Lawrence sighed and put his veiny hands on his knees. Kirsten Dean. The name dropped so carelessly from the man's mouth.

He waved an irritable hand. "Nobody discovered what happened to Kirsten. She just disappeared."

"You were the main suspect."

Lawrence glared at the man. "I was never suspected of any ..." His eyes widened. "Has she been found?"

"No."

He dropped his head and tried to stop the trembling, but McEwan continued.

"You and Miss Dean were together the day she disappeared. Alone in your office."

"You make it sound improper! We shared a room, if you must know. She was my assistant."

"And your fiancé?"

The ring in the nappy black velvet box, even now lying in the back of a drawer.

Lawrence shook his head. "No."

"What were you doing that day?"

"Normal stuff. What is the Ministry of Defense doing, pestering an old man about this? I should throw the pair of you out."

"Please, Doctor. This is a defense matter."

"Cataloguing old documents is a defense matter? Bah! You probably think working in a museum is dull. Well, it isn't, but what we were doing that day, well, it was about as dull as it gets."

O'Dwyer spoke for the first time, something about him put Lawrence's teeth on edge, the background chime of déjà vu stronger. "What sort of documents?"

"How on earth can I be expected to remember that?"

He frowned, and, maybe because it was his last day with her, found himself recalling an old pine chest, Kirsten smiling as she handed him something from it.

"A museum is like in iceberg, Mr. O'Dwyer. Only a tiny amount of what's in there can be on display. And the job of cataloguing and storing ... sometimes things go wrong."

"So ..."

"So, we were housekeeping, really. Cataloguing old Cathedral documents that hadn't been properly recorded."

"And they were?"

"Nothing to speak of. Maintenance documents from the 1700s. Deadly dull stuff, I'm afraid."

"You and Miss Dean catalogued this?"

"Yes."

"And then ..."

"When we finished, I left. Our office opened onto a much larger workroom and there must have been six of my colleagues there, beavering away, including my manager—what was his name, now?"

"Cedric Sextant."

Lawrence stared, wondering how much this man knew. "That was it. The point is, my office led off the bigger workroom, do you see?"

"Yes, we've just come from there."

He could hear the surprise in his voice. "It must be five hundred miles away."

Then, "Look, what is all this about?"

McEwan said, "You left that day in quite a state. Went straight home, as in your mother's home, in Kent. The police had to fetch you."

It was Lawrence's turn to be silent.

"Meanwhile, Miss Dean disappeared, like smoke. She could not have left your office, or she would have been seen. She should have been there, but she wasn't."

Lawrence remembered standing beside her that day, her scent, the little noises she made when she was thinking, watching her write in the creamy ledger. The ring waiting in his pocket.

"When you came out of the room, before you ran off, you attacked a member of the staff."

Lawrence passed a hand across his face. "I don't recall, but I'm aware I did it. Young Owen, a thoroughly decent chap. It seems I struck him."

"You had to be dragged off. You struck Mr. Sextant too."

"Clearly, I wasn't in my right mind. I'm grateful they didn't press charges."

"Let's not pretend this was some small matter, Doctor. When the Police came for you ..."

"I know, I know! I'd had a total breakdown. Lost all my blasted hair, for comedy effect. It's ancient history."

McEwan leaned forward, his expression sympathetic. "We know about trauma in the military, Doctor, and I've seen total body hair loss. It followed a massive physical and psychological trauma."

"I'm sure."

"So, come on. All these years later, can't you, even now, tell us what happened?"

Lawrence pulled the grubby cardigan to rub his skinny, hairless forearms, and shook his shiny head.

O'Dwyer opened the file on his lap and came out with a large black-and-white photograph. "You may not have seen this."

Even as he was placing it on the coffee table, Lawrence was asking, "What is it?"

"You. And the rest of the staff of the museum."

"Kirsten?"

He didn't have to ask, because there she was, with a skinny, young Lawrence Juniper grinning like a fool as he leaned over her. Lawrence had no recollection of this being taken, but there they all were, a group of twelve, standing on a lawn in front of the leaded windows of King's House; the home of the museum.

His eyes flicked over the group, recognizing Sextant in his tweed jacket. And there was young Owen, smaller than he remembered, smiling at his side. His dark beard was fuller and hair longer than anyone else's, a bit of a beatnik.

But he really only wanted to look at himself and Kirsten. Those two were half turned towards each other as they smiled for the camera; an overly tall guy, skinny and improbably long necked, wearing his battered hounds tooth jacket and with thick, curly hair. In real life, it had been auburn.

She came no higher than his shoulder, but was still the glowing center of the group. Pale skin, straight white-blonde hair, and that smile. She hadn't taken her spectacles off for the photograph, and why should she?

He came back to his own image, surprised to feel tears pricking his eyes, his throat constricting. He didn't want to blub in front of these two strangers, but the wave of emotion almost undid him. Look at him, that overgrown, enthusiastic puppy of a man, fit and tanned from all that tennis he played. So conscious of the girl beside him, brim-full of hopes and expectations and without a clue of the hand life would deal him.

Lawrence felt scared for him, he was so damned vulnerable.

He had been poring over it for a long time, when O'Dwyer said, "You look quite different there, don't you?"

"So would you, if you'd been in this picture."

O'Dwyer laughed, seemingly genuinely amused, then leaned over and took the photograph, plucking it from Lawrence's hand.

McEwan seemed surprised at that, but said, "We'd like you to come back with us."

The cane dropped out of Lawrence's hand, hitting the floor with a slap. "To Salisbury? You can't be serious!"

"It really is very important, Dr. Juniper."

"Nonsense."

O'Dwyer leaned forward, and for the first time he smiled. An unpleasant, and weirdly familiar smile. "We insist."

"I'm dying, man! I can't undertake a journey ..."

"We have a jet on standby. A short drive at each end, a hop on a luxury plane. A stay in a top-end hotel, all paid."

Everything seemed to be sliding away from him. He twined his hands together and stared at a point between his feet, trying to control his dread at the thought of going there. Then he straightened as much as his back would allow.

"I'm not going and that's flat. What are you going to do about it? Arrest me?"

"If needed."

"Then you'll have to fight me, gentlemen. And, frankly, I can't see me surviving."

"Aren't you curious? Why we want you to come?"

He opened his mouth to say something, but nothing came out. It hadn't occurred to him to be curious. He simply didn't want to go anywhere near Salisbury.

"Why, then?"

O'Dwyer was bringing out more photographs, three of them, color this time.

"What do you make of these?"

Lawrence drew in a breath and froze, wanting to but unable to pull his eyes away. His insides were frozen also, as though someone had dumped ice water in there.

The images showed his old room, just as it was. He shook himself and looked away.

"Dr. Juniper?"

"Why are you showing me this?"

"Can you tell us what these are?"

Lawrence took some time answering. "Our office."

"Sorry, who's office?"

"Kirsten's and mine. I'm guessing the police took them, after what happened."

McEwan was leaning forward, suddenly excited. "You can date it so closely?"

Lawrence was still looking away. "That was my hounds tooth jacket, on the back of the chair. The Cathedral's chest was still on the table, the one we were working on."

"Can't you look?"

Lawrence stared at the man. "Don't you understand? Something happened to me, right then, right there, that destroyed me. Kirsten ..."

"Yes?"

Lawrence just shook his head. Over the years, a strange notion had taken him. That that room in 1964 had eaten her.

O'Dwyer crossed his legs and sat back. "I took those photographs myself."

"What are you talking about?"

"I took them. Yesterday."

"You're not making any sense."

"This is what your office looks like today."

Lawrence screwed his face up, trying to understand what the man was saying.

"You're claiming it has lain undisturbed ..."

"Not at all. The room has seen many uses since your day. Most lately, it was the server room, hard paneled walls and racks of IT stuff. I'm told you wouldn't recognize it."

Lawrence made himself look at photographs again, his eyes wide.

"Three days ago, all the computers went down. As you can imagine, the first thing they did was go into the server room. Only, it wasn't the server room." He leaned in and tapped the photograph. "It was this."

"Nonsense!"

McEwan. "It took us a few days to work out what we were looking at. We had no idea that it was the same room, but from a different time. Then, we had to estimate the date, track down someone still alive, from then."

"Who is that?"

"You. You have to come, Dr. Juniper. You're the only one left."

O'Dwyer. "It's a rift in time. If it can happen once, it can happen again. The entire world may be on the edge of its destruction."

Lawrence lurched unsteadily to his feet. "I need a drink."

Ten minutes later, Lawrence was studying the photographs, now with a whisky in his hand.

"This was my world, for five years after leaving uni. I was happy, there, once." Then, "I should be refusing to believe this."

"But?"

"Something inexplicable happened back then. Kirsten just ..." He clicked his fingers. "... winked out of existence."

It ate her.

"And as for me, perhaps I saw something so terrible that my mind broke. Or maybe I was attacked."

"You think that what happened to you is linked to this phenomenon?"

"Don't you?"

"I'd say it must be. So, will you come?"

"I don't think you understand yet." He tapped the photo, "I've not been within a hundred miles of Salisbury since the day I left. I'm terrified just looking at these."

"We're all terrified."

Lawrence was working hard to keep his breathing under control. "What can I do, that you can't?"

"We're not sure of anything. But it's possible you can go in there. In the room."

"You can't?"

McEwan spread his hands, then looked at them. "I'm thirty-five years old. Before I went in there, I used to pass for thirty. The scientists reckon I aged about a decade in twenty seconds."

"My God."

"I'm not meant to be in there. I knew it as soon as I stepped inside. Maybe you are."

"If not, I'll last about a millisecond."

"You can simply brush your fingertip over the threshold. Believe me, you'll know if it's okay."

Lawrence sipped his whisky and stared at the photographs. He was thinking, Kirsten had been there, right there, right then, and maybe she still was. He was also thinking, it nearly destroyed me, when I was young and strong.

"I'll have to pack, I suppose."

O'Dwyer pointed behind him and, when he turned, there was the corporal, holding his own valise.

"You're packed."

*

The journey took a shockingly short time, but was still exhausting. Still, there was no suggestion of rest and he was driven straight to the museum. When the car door was opened for him, he just sat there, staring

The King's House was and remained a truly beautiful building in which to house a museum, and itself had a long and fascinating history. Seeing it again took what little breath he had from him, and weakened his legs so that he had to be helped to his feet. The last time he had been here, so had Kirsten.

McEwan asked, "Do you need a wheelchair?"

He shook his head.

The entrances were guarded by armed soldiers, and he was led to the staff entrance, the one he had used daily for five years. The memories were coming so thick and fast that he found he needed the corporal at his elbow.

The door was opened by yet another soldier and as they walked down a short corridor, Lawrence hit by that unmistakable smell of chemicals and age. Then, before he was ready, he was entering the big workroom, the one his old office led off.

The workroom had changed, of course. Computer screens and fancy lighting everywhere, soldiers and scientists with strange equipment, and yet it was still essentially the same. The old oak door leading to his office looked exactly as it had except now there were two soldiers guarding it.

Lawrence looked around, recalling some of the faces who had worked here, men and women, friends. Cedric Sextant, self-important and bumptious; Owen, bearded and friendly; Mrs. Carr, always making tea.

McEwan spoke to one of the men by the door. "Okay, Sergeant."

Lawrence's heart was in his mouth as the soldier turned the handle and pulled the door open. Then he simply stood, stunned into silence.

McEwan put his hand on his arm and whispered. "Doctor?"

"It's one thing seeing a photograph. It's quite another being here."

"What do you think? Your impressions?"

"I think it's waiting."

"What for?"

"Me."

"Do you want to try maybe just the tip of your finger? Brush it into the room and out again, in one continuous movement."

Lawrence looked at him, and across at O'Dwyer, who stood silently behind him. He shuffled forward until he was on the edge of the threshold. He closed his eyes for a moment, hearing his worn-out heart beating in his ears. Then he took the longest step he could muster, right into the room. He was immediately struck by the smell of cigarettes, surprisingly strong, and the sharp tang of carbolic soap. The pink block of soap, he saw, sat where it always had, at the side of the oversized butler sink.

He took another step and looked slowly around, trying to take everything in, as tears poured down his face. He was standing in his old room from 1964, breathing the air he had then. A blunt, square room without windows, roughly six meters across. His old desk faced him; Kirsten's smaller table hard against it. He recalled how he would glance up from his work and be looking right at her, a sudden powerful memory. Sometimes they would share a look. A smile.

He inhaled again and there was no doubt, he could smell her, like she was there.

His desk was messy, as his workspaces always were, with a pack of Players, his silver lighter, and a Guinness ashtray, the one he had stolen from a pub in Cambridge. There was his battered, scribbled-over blotter and the old flintlock mechanism he used as a paperweight holding down a scrappy pile of papers. He had forgotten about that flintlock.

Kirsten's desk was neater, with carefully stacked books and papers, her pens stored neatly in a colorful papier-mâché desk tidy. Lawrence had forgotten about that desk tidy, but now he recalled it was a present, something that her niece had made for her, probably at school.

The only other furniture in the room was the big worktable.

He turned to look at the little group in the other room, and almost dropped his stick. The soldier still held the door tightly, McEwan and O'Dwyer beside him, but they were bleached out and wavering, like a television screen with a bad signal.

McEwan spoke, asking him something.

"What?"

McEwan was clearly speaking loudly, but Lawrence only just caught what he was saying, as if he was a long way away. "How do you feel?"

"Whatever it did to you, it isn't doing it to me."

"Can you turn the lights off?"

With the room having no windows, the only light came from two large, white globes, hanging from the ceiling. Lawrence reached out to the heavy, old switch and paused.

"I'm scared."

He took a long breath and flicked it off, finding himself instantly in almost total darkness. He could see the light from the doorway, like beams struggling through dark and viscous liquid, failing within inches. He switched the light on and walked further into the room, catching the clearest scent yet of Kirsten, her rose toilet water and her own clean smell; stalling at her desk to breath it in. A chiffon headscarf lay on her chair and he picked it up and put his face in it.

He made himself put it back and limped on, to pull his own chair out, catching the sharp odor of sweat. His own smell, he realized.

He flopped down with a grunt, stretching his tired legs and trying to focus on the group clustered beyond the door. He rubbed the old jacket sleeve between his fingers, amazed at how familiar it still felt.

Another distant shout from McEwan. "Can you check the telephone?"

The phone was an old, black Bakelite, but Lawrence ignored it, instead picking up the Players and flicking the cardboard lid. He expected the cigarettes to be ancient and dried up, but when he sniffed them, they seemed fresh. He shook one out and rolled it between his fingers.

"I haven't smoked in over forty years. Bad for your health, apparently."

He put the cigarette in his mouth and sparked up the big silver Ronson, surprised at the length of flame. He never could stop that thing from acting like a flamethrower.

He took a long drag, listening to the familiar crackle of tobacco, and blew out a stream of smoke.

He leaned back. "I'll probably pass out."

It seemed they had no answer to that. Lawrence took his time, smoking his cigarette but being careful not to inhale much, thinking he might indeed pass out.

"Dr. Juniper?"

"What?"

He had a feeling that they had called his name several times.

McEwan mimed picking up the telephone.

Lawrence picked up the receiver, surprised at the weight of the thing, to hear a comforting purr he hadn't heard for decades.

"The tone was so much nicer then. Friendly."

McEwan was holding up a card, showing a number.

"Who is that?"

"The Ministry of Defense."

Lawrence thought for a moment and then dialed a different number, waiting whilst it connected.

"Laurie?"

His mother sounded breathless, excited. Young. He had forgotten that she would often do that when he called; speak his name before he said a word. He dropped his eyes to the messy blotter. At first, he couldn't speak.

"Laurie?"

"Yes, Mummy."

"You sound terrible! Did she say no?"

"I haven't asked."

"Are you in a funk, dear? Your voice!"

"No, I'm ..."

"You're crying!"

"No, I'm not." He was, of course. "I've got a bad throat, that's all."

His mother sounded unsure. "Laurie, she'll say yes. She will. You have to pluck your courage up."

"I'll ask her."

"Do you have the ring?"

"In my pocket."

"Call me after, if that horrible Sextant man lets you."

"I'll call."

"Goodbye and good luck. You need to buy a bottle of cough medicine for that throat. And maybe a stiff gin."

The line went dead and he replaced the heavy receiver, stood, but then had to sit back down. He looked round the room again and again.

McEwan was shouting. "Dr. Juniper?"

"Oh, do shut up."

Lawrence got his stick under him, lurched to his feet, limped the few steps to the big table, with the crate from the Cathedral. Here too was the big ledger, with Kirsten's sweeping script open beside it.

He swept his hand over the creamy page, thinking that simple record keeping had its own beauty when ledgers and fountain pens were used. He tapped the date. "The exact day it happened. June 1."

Hurrying now, he scanned the materials on the table, comparing them to the catalogue. Finally, he picked up a tattered cream folder.

"I remember now. We were on our last item. She left to go to the ladies' room."

He could smell her strongly now. She had stood right here, maybe minutes ago. Seconds even. Time, it seemed, could not be relied upon.

"Whatever happened, I think it has only just occurred." Then, another thought, spoken in a shaky voice. "Maybe it's just about to happen."

117

O'Dwyer called out, "What's in the folder?"

"Nothing of significance, I'm sure."

But Lawrence flicked it open, starting in surprise; glanced up to see the questioning looks from the doorway.

"An unusual document, to be sure, but it doesn't begin to explain this ... phenomenon, I'm afraid."

"What is it?"

Lawrence leaned in. "A single page of real vellum, illuminated by a very talented artist from, oh, 1500. Something like that. It's in ancient Gaelic, not Latin, which is odd. Heresy, actually. Beautiful ornamentation."

"Can you bring it?"

"I can't touch an ancient sheet of vellum without gloves, man! What does it matter anyway? It's hardly in the same league as a time traveling room."

O'Dwyer, the short man's eyes even more intense, asked, "Does it have a title?"

"Yes, it's ... hold on a moment, my Gaelic is rusty." His lips moved soundlessly as he worked it in his head. Then he said, "*Scéal na laethanta.* The Tale of Days."

Lawrence looked up, his heart speed as something started happening by the door, some commotion. McEwan was shouting, "Hold it! Hold it!"

Lawrence could see the soldiers fighting desperately to stop the door closing, saw them failing. The last thing he heard before the door banged shut. "Oh Shit! Sergeant!"

*

When the door slammed, something doubled Lawrence over and he squeezed his eyes tightly closed. It wasn't pain exactly; something harder to bear.

He managed to open his eyes, immediately shouting out loud in shock.

"My God! Salisbury!"

He wiped his face with his hands and shook his head to clear it, but when he looked around him, his eyes widened. It seemed that he was in his old office from the sixties, although he knew that would not be possible.

He straightened and looked in confusion at his hand. For no reason he could think of, he was holding a walking cane. He threw it aside, noticing his surroundings as he did so and gasping in surprise.

Lawrence was shocked over and over again, catching sight of his old room, every time with no recollection of coming there.

Until, finally, he straightened his arms and back, rubbed his fingers through his thick red hair and wondered if he had time for a cigarette before Kirsten came back.

He had even taken a step towards his desk when the door opened, and Kirsten hurried inside, smiling, breathless, and more beautiful than ever.

"Sorry I took so long." She put her hand on his arm. "Owen was desperate to show me something about his Cathedral drainage project."

Then, "What's wrong? Laurie?"

Lawrence couldn't put a name to what was wrong; everything about the moment overwhelmed him. Kirsten speaking to him, *touching* him. It was simultaneously something that hadn't happened for a lifetime and something that had happened hundreds of times over; like a shuddering moment between two mirrors, the repeated reflection diminished into nothing. A thousand déjà vu's, falling into infinity.

The surge of longing he felt for her, the shock of that touch on his arm, as though he hadn't seen her for years. The illogical surge of real anger against Owen for delaying them, as though they could have been finished and out of there. As though they could have *escaped*.

She was standing in front of him, looking worried. "You're as white as a ghost. Do you want a fag?"

He touched the box in his pocket and felt himself steady, managed a smile. "I had a wobbly moment, nothing to worry about. Come on, let's finish this. Last one and we're done."

She was still looking at him uncertainly. "Why do you always say that? Last one and we're done."

He frowned. "I don't."

"But you said it twice, right there!"

He started to say no, I didn't, then shrugged. "Did I? Well, let's get it done before I say it again."

Kirsten moved quickly past him to the table and he caught her scent, heard the swish of her legs in their nylon.

She said, "This is a load of dross. Sextant is such a damned prig."

"So you keep saying. Once it's done it's done."

"So you keep saying."

Then she flipped open the last folder and said, "Oh."

The stunned way she had spoken, and her expression brought him round beside her. He said, "Oh."

"Oh, my God."

"Oh shit, Sergeant."

She put her hand on his arm in her surprise. "That's the first time I've heard you swear! What is this?"

He took a moment. "It's certainly vellum. Calfskin. Illuminated manuscript in Gaelic."

"Reminds me of the *Book of Kells*."

"Even more heavily illustrated, it must have taken a rather talented artist monk a long, long time. He would have been burned alive, writing something like this in Gaelic."

"It couldn't have been a monk. Not a Christian one, anyway."

"Why not?"

"Those symbols. The pentacle and the horned god. They're pagan. That big one behind the writing, like a big golden watermark?"

"The spiral?"

"I think that's the symbol for rebirth."

They stared at the illustrations for a long time, until Lawrence, excitement in his voice, said, "I've never seen anything like this."

"Scéal na ..."

Lawrence didn't know he was going to grab her arm until he did it. She looked at him, surprised.

"What?"

"I don't think we should read it."

He thought she might laugh, but she didn't. She was deeply troubled, he saw. When she spoke, it was in a whisper. "What is it?"

"You remember when I said, last one and we're done? Twice?"

Her eyes were wide. "Yes."

"I didn't."

"But I heard you. Like an echo."

He nodded. "An echo. Are you sure I only said it twice?"

She was about to nod, but then he saw the hesitation. The uncertainty in her eyes.

"Could it have been three times, Kirsty? Four? A thousand?"

"What are you saying?"

"I'm saying ..." He balked for a moment, then gathered himself. "I think we've done this before. Many times. I'm still hearing the echoes. Aren't you? Like we've said this too."

She was looking at him sidelong, but not telling him he was crazy. Her echoes might be different to his, he thought, but she hears them.

She said. "I feel it. How about I read it, but not out loud?"

He frowned, making himself focus and it was her who put her hand on his and said, "We've done that before too, haven't we?"

"I think so."

She grabbed onto him and he put his face into her hair, so he heard her when she gasped.

"What's wrong?"

She pointed. "Look at that figure, in the center of the spiral."

"The monk?"

"Don't you think it looks like ..."

"O'Dwyer!"

"Who?"

"I mean, Owen. It looks like Owen."

"I'm really scared! What do we do?"

He pulled away, took a moment to steel himself, then stepped to his desk and picked up his desk lighter, the big, silver Ronson with the ridiculous flame. Her eyes widened. "We can't! This could be the most important text either of us find our whole lives!"

Lawrence shook his head. "There's something wrong with it. Can't you feel it, Kirsten? It's got us, somehow."

He grabbed his long tweezers and tried to pick the vellum up, but it kept slipping and sliding from his grasp. Finally, panicking, he drew his hand back and pierced it through with the prongs, causing them both to cry out.

It billowed as he lifted it, writhing as though there was a gale, even though the air was still. He sparked his lighter and put the flame to it, hearing a screech like fingernails on chalkboard, but deafening.

Once it caught, the vellum burned hot and Lawrence winced as he held the pincers at arm's length. Then there were the words, like molten gold in the smoke, and he found himself reading them.

Kirsten grabbed his head and turned it. "Don't look!"

He pressed his head into her shoulder as she steered him to the big sink, pushing his arm over it until it burned to nothing. Shaky limbed, he turned the tap and rinsed the ash away, panting like he had been sprinting.

Kirsten, speaking in a tiny voice, said, "We did it."

"What did we do?"

"I don't know. But I do know that thing had us for a long time. I can still remember those echoes, like riffling the pages of a book. I recall it, but I don't feel it anymore."

He nodded. "It's fading."

For a while they stood there, stunned. Then Kirsten said, "We're free. I don't know what that means, and I'm not sure what we're free of. I only know it's true."

"Let's get out of here. Never come back."

Then her expression changed. She put her hands on his arm. "Owen."

It took a few moments before they could move, then they crept to the door and pushed it quietly open, to look out at their colleagues. Nobody looked up.

Owen was not at his table. He wasn't in the room at all. Sextant glanced up now, frowning in surprise as he caught sight of them, sitting all the way up. They were, Lawrence realized, standing with their arms wrapped round one another.

"Juniper? What is this?"

Lawrence tried to step away from her as the others started taking notice, but Kirsten only held him tighter. He looked at her and she shook her head. He cleared his throat, "Where's Owen?"

"Are you drunk? What is going on?"

"Sorry, Mr. Sextant, but it's important. Where is Owen?"

"Owen who, for God's sake?"

Lawrence was about to apologize when, at his side, Kirsten giggled. He looked down at her, hearing the edge of hysteria in there. She put her hand over her mouth, but couldn't hold back the bubbles of laughter. He was laughing too, he realized.

They stumbled into the center of the room, holding on to one another. Lawrence, a man who had never been drunk, felt drunk now, as though his veins were filled with Champagne. Dizzy, he whirled Kirsten round and around, then kissed her. Someone was shouting, someone was clapping.

Then she was pulling him, and they ran through the museum and out of the big front doors, ran into stunning sunlight and fresh air, ran like children, living the moment of their lives.

***

Letters of the Raj
by R. W. Warwick, Japan

From the Desk of Corporal James Wallace
15 May 1898

My dear Alexandra,

If these words somehow find their way to you, I wish them to bring you my goodbye, and with it my blessing for you to remarry should you find someone who can love you as much as I do.

It saddens me deeply to tell you that I have fallen victim to a bizarre and unimaginable accident which has changed me into something utterly contemptible.

I don't know if I can undo this thing that has been done to me, but I will strive beyond nerve and reason to pull myself back from it. Whether days or years of contention lie ahead of me, I will return to you as I was, or not at all.

If you can forgive the gloomy finality of this letter, I shall explain the strange and dire circumstance in which I find myself, if only to put your mind at ease. I suppose it began when I met the man, or perhaps creature would better define it, responsible.

It was a hot spring evening on the Bay of Bengal. A warm, salty breeze swept in from the ocean as I gazed at the burnt orange sunset which stretched across a clear and boundless horizon.

The market traders along the port had long since packed away, and the streams of merchant ships which filled the port of Calcutta by day, had docked or raised anchor.

I finished my tea as I watched my ship, HMS *Sutherland*, drift slowly off into the sunset. Then I collected my things, asked the waiter for directions to the train station, and left for my new assignment in Bombay.

As the waiter had promised, the station was easy to spot from the main road. So, unburdened from having to navigate the streets, I enjoyed the walk.

The clean, salty ocean air blended with the rich musk of herbs and spices left behind by the market. It was refreshing, and the subtropical climate enriched the aromas the farther I travelled from the port.

Horses heaved carts two and three times their size, piled high with crates of wonders from the Far East no doubt. Elephants, draped with lavish cloth of red and gold across their backs, plodded sleepily along the dust-ridden street, carrying men and women. The rich tapestry of the British Raj delighted me.

*

I first encountered the infernal creature in the dining carriage of my train, but to me he was only a man back then.

I had settled into my seat with a book when he caught my eye. An elderly Indian man, perhaps in his seventies, impeccably dressed in a black, buttoned, collarless jacket, loose black trousers, and thin brown sandals, watched me from across the aisle.

I shall never forget that black, penetrating stare. His eyes glistened as he smiled. I nodded politely and went back to my book.

Perhaps an hour after departure, I caught the old man in the corner of my eye, watching me again. He caught me looking at the peculiar card game he was playing.

"Have you played Kanjifa before?" he asked in a harsh and scratchy voice. He spoke with a strange intonation.

I shook my head. In hindsight, perhaps my dire fate could have been avoided there and then if I had left it at that, but curiosity got the better of me, I admit.

"What is it?" I asked, closing my book.

He invited me over, and never so ungracious as to refuse, I joined him.

"Rahul Jahan," he stated, extending his hand.

I introduced myself and shook his hand. Jahan instructed me on the finer points of the ancient Persian card game. As we played, we talked. His English was excellent, but from time to time he would drop in foreign words I did not understand.

In the beginning, I was utterly charmed by the man. I found his conversation and worldview to be both refreshing and fascinating. We talked of our countries and the state of things, and I found him to be a keen historian.

For all his charm, he was a queer sort of man. His mannerisms were at times almost vulgar, he would spit for no reason or snort like a hog, and his peculiar accent, which I couldn't quite place, bothered me no end.

It was perhaps around midnight that I was introduced to arrack, a terrible eastern drink made from the sap of a coconut and sugarcane, not unlike rum.

"First, we agree the stakes," he croaked after the third or fourth glass.

My head was swimming in arrack, but I understood his meaning. He placed a trinket on the table between us, a small metal box, about the size of a snuff box, with a wide-eyed demonic face carved into its lid. A forked tongue protruded from fanged teeth, and peacocks were carved on each side of the face. The design was intriguing, but I saw little value in it.

Jahan's eyes swirled like two dark whirlpools, and his face seemed different than before, more youthful, as if our conversation had rejuvenated him.

"I have nothing to offer," I explained.

My words drifted through the empty carriage like a stale smell. For a moment, the only sounds were the clicking of the pistons and the rocking of the train along the tracks.

"We can worry about that later," he groaned at last.

The card game was long and complex, I suffered through it. At my defeat, he asked me for his winnings, and I repeated that I had nothing to offer. He smiled and slid the small box towards me.

As I touched it, he grabbed my hand. I tried to pull away, but his grip tightened like a vice and I swear his touch became warmer, almost unbearably so. Then he laughed. His deep, scratchy voice filled the carriage and became louder and deeper until it was almost inhuman. How little I knew back then. A streak of light rippled across his eyes which were like pools of thick, black blood. It oozed down his cheeks.

I was drunk and in agony, unable to put up much of a fight. For a moment, I thought that the flesh would melt from my wrist. I groaned from the pain but nobody was there to hear my cries. All I can recall after that is the deafening, droning roar which surrounded us before I blacked out.

Even now, as I write this letter, I cannot say with any certainty what occurred in those final moments, but whatever happened was unnatural, perhaps evil. The creature I encountered on the train from Calcutta to Bombay was not of this world, of that I am certain.

The train jerked suddenly as it pulled out of a station, and I awoke to the worst headache of my life. I was disoriented and a little confused. I looked out the window to see where we had stopped, and gasped in horror as I caught my reflection in the glass; the long, grey beard, the tired, wrinkled eyes, the unhealed scar beside the right eye. The creature had given me its body.

Of course my first instinct was to panic. I struggled for breath, and my hands shook uncontrollably. I thought that Jahan must have disembarked at the station, or at least that was my hope. I scrambled through the carriage and grabbed a waiter by the collar, demanding to be let off the train, but he only shook his head and muttered something in Hindi I couldn't understand.

I rushed past him out to the small gangway between the carriages, and leaned over the rail. As the train picked up speed, the station faded into the night. The dark desert stretched out ahead of us as far as I could see. If I wanted to find the creature before he disappeared, I had little choice but to jump.

I climbed over the rail and balanced on the ledge. The ground rushed by faster and faster. I tried to see where I would land, but it was too dark. The vast black landscape filled me with dread.

I would not have found the courage to take that final step if the waiter hadn't tried to stop me. The moment I heard the door handle squeak, I glanced at him through the small round window, and pushed myself away with as much force as I could muster.

The fall, as you might imagine, was brutal. I hit the ground hard and rolled a good distance before I came to a stop. It might have killed me if I hadn't landed on the edge of a patch of grass beside the tracks.

As I tried to stand, I doubled over from a sharp pain in my chest. I must have cracked or bruised a rib or two. I shouldn't have jumped, but the limitations of the tired, old body were still new to me and extremely frustrating. As I nursed my aching bones, the streaming python of smoke disappeared into the dark distance. The clacking of the wheels along the track became quieter until it disappeared completely, and I was utterly alone.

I wasn't far from the station. As I staggered towards it along the tracks, my eyes adjusted to the darkness, and the moon and stars lit the landscape for me.

It was a strange place for a train to stop. Alone in the vast and arid landscape, the station was little more than a small stone hut which straddled the railway line. The only sign of life was a dull glow from one of the windows, so I headed towards it in search of help.

My progress was slow but quiet. I wanted my approach to remain undetected. The creature was surely close by, and I was counting on him not anticipating my dramatic pursuit. If he believed that I was still unconscious, steaming off into the night onboard the train to Bombay, all the better. The element of surprise might work for me.

I glimpsed him—rather I glimpsed myself—a few hundred yards from the station, and I froze, shrouded in the darkness. He was walking away from the station along the only road in sight, a single dirt track which disappeared into the darkness.

We were in the desert and I could see very little in any direction. I thought that someone might be waiting for him farther along the road, so I followed him. Then, when he suddenly veered off the path and headed into the vast, empty desert, I stopped again and watched.

As strange as it seemed that the creature inexplicably left the comfort of the train to wander across the desert in the middle of the night, I felt no surprise. My experiences with him had apparently jaded my sensation of wonder. I watched the creature until he was almost out of sight, and then I slowly continued my pursuit.

The temperature dropped throughout the night and it eroded my determination not to let the creature out of my sight. Creeping across that dry wilderness, I lost all sensation of time and my surroundings, until I caught the first glimmer of sunrise on the horizon. As that fierce white ball emerged from behind the distant hills to the northeast, it reinvigorated me, and its warm rays penetrated my cold bones.

We had walked for hours, much longer than I had anticipated. I still had him in sight as the sky became brighter, but I dropped back until he was only a dim, black silhouette wading ominously across the dunes like a distant specter.

Perhaps the lack of water, or sudden rise in temperature had affected me, but the thing I was watching so carefully slowly began to change. Its shape remained like that of a man, but I knew better. Its arms swung back and forth, and its strides across the sandy dunes were long and slow. Without any detail for my eyes, my imagination filled in the blanks. I became convinced that the foul and otherworldly thing was a demon of some kind. What else could wield such power on this earth?

Suddenly it stopped and turned to face in my direction. It looked right at me from across the barren expanse. I froze. It was still too far away for me to see in any detail, but I could feel the demon's black and savage eyes scanning me.

An intense throbbing pain in my chest suddenly brought me to my knees. The demon watched me for a while longer and then continued on its way, disappearing slowly behind the dune. As it vanished from my sight, the pain began to subside, and it occurred to me that the vast ocean of sand between us meant nothing. In that moment, as I was caught in its stare, there was no space between us at all.

When I finally regained enough strength to stand again, I continued along the demon's path. Now that I had lost the element of surprise, I did my best to close the gap between us.

I passed over the dune where the demon had stopped and finally discovered its final destination. He was still some distance away, striding across the sand towards a solitary stone structure jutting out of the ground. I was relieved. My strength may very well have surrendered, had he maintained the pace for much longer.

The lonely sandstone triangle gaping out from the sand like a gateway to the underworld, left quite an impression on me. Its peculiar sharp edges and pale walls were quite unlike anything I had seen before. At an angle, I saw that the far side of the triangle sloped down, and was partially buried. The great pale spike reached out from the stony depths, and hinted at something much larger beneath the surface.

As the demon approached the entrance, the structure dwarfed him. Its dramatic shape possessed an ominous presence which loomed over him. He did not stop or slow his approach, and the dark chasm quickly swallowed him.

A sandstorm appeared out of nowhere on the far side of the structure. I wrapped my scarf across my face, but I knew I needed to find cover soon. I had little choice but to follow.

The storm grew worse at an alarming rate, and I was grateful for the structure's protection. I stood in the mouth and gazed down into the black tunnel. It sloped downwards; God only knows how deep into the earth it reached. I felt the demon's presence. He had seen me, and somewhere within that abyss, he was expecting me.

The tunnel eventually levelled out into a round chamber with three smaller tunnels leading off it. Torches were mounted to the walls at each entrance, but beyond them was utter darkness. I watched the flame of each torch carefully for a moment, and then settled on the tunnel to the left. A gentle breeze flowed out from the shaft which caused the flame to flicker more than the others. It was my only clue that something might lie ahead.

The walls became narrower and it grew colder the deeper I went. I must admit, as I staggered through the dark passage my imagination started to wander, and it painted visions of all kinds of demonic creatures leaping out at me from the abyss. It was then, as I stood alone, surrounded by shadow, that I caught the faintest rumbling just ahead. I froze and waited for it to pass. When it finally did, I crept the rest of the way as quietly as I could.

A stale dampness hung in the air, and a biting breeze rushed at me as the tunnel opened into a large cavern. I had stumbled upon some kind of twisted, sunken church. It was longer than it was wide and the walls were jagged and wet. Ahead of me, rows of pews crudely carved from rock faced a large, flat stone altar at the far end. Upon it the demon sat with his back to the entrance.

A handful of torches glowed dimly along the walls. It was difficult to see the demon in much detail. He was sat cross-legged, groaning in some kind of meditative trance. The guttural growl I had heard earlier had come from him, and it was getting louder.

I waited by the entrance to the cavern and waited to see what would happen next. Even as I write this letter, I can scarcely believe it myself, but I swear upon my eternal soul that these next words are the truth as I know it.

A crack of light ripped open in midair in front of the demon and flooded the entire cavern with light. The hole became larger until it was almost the size of a man, and in moments the cavern was as bright as day. Suddenly aware that I was in plain view in the mouth of the tunnel, I went to hide, and then hesitated, realizing that the demon must have detected my presence, even if he didn't show it.

I had finally caught up with him, but I wasn't quite sure what to do next. I watched him in his meditative trance. The rift grew larger. Then the trinket from the dining carriage caught my eye, glimmering beside him on the altar.

He had used it to curse me, and now it was here, close to his side. It was more than coincidence. It occurred to me that if I could recreate the circumstances which did this to me, perhaps it could be undone.

Slowly, a thin blue mist emerged between the demon and the rift. I waited a little longer for my moment to strike. Then, as I moved in closer, I realized that something was happening to him. The mist was drifting towards the rift from the demon's body, my body. I wasn't sure what was happening, but it seemed to be in pain.

I focused on the trinket beside the demon, and went for it. I ran towards the altar as fast as I could, but strangely the demon didn't turn nor twinge, even at the echo of my footfalls. I grabbed the trinket and still he didn't move. Then I wrapped my arms around his shoulders and held on as tightly as I could.

The mist quickly began to dissipate and I finally drew a reaction from the demon. He groaned and threw his arms into the air, trying to free himself. I tightened my grip, moving one of my arms around his neck, and noticed something in the rift's fading light. A face, black and charred, scowled at me with furious yellow eyes. It didn't quite seem real, like a reflection in a window. It opened its mouth to scream but I heard nothing. I moved my free arm across the demon's chest and felt it heave with each labored breath. He tried to scream also but I could hear nothing.

Eventually, the rift began to close, and the face within the light faded away. I was speechless and unable to comprehend what I had just witnessed.

In the seconds before I passed out, the demon craned his neck and gazed at me one more time with those black and soulless eyes. I realized with alarm, that he had aged considerably. His hair was grey, and crow's feet weathered the corners of his eyes, my eyes. In that awful final stare I saw something which terrified me.

*

Alexandra gaped at the last word, hypnotized. She scarcely believed it to be true, and she might not have if the letter hadn't been written in James's own handwriting.

She turned the page but it was blank. It seemed strange that James would end a letter without a word of what had happened to him.

She put it down on the desk and searched the package for the missing final page. Inside she found a small square object wrapped in a tattered, old cloth. She opened it and dropped it on the desk in fright as soon as she saw what it was. She immediately recognized the trinket that James had described in his letter.

The devilish eyes and forked tongue seemed to mock her as she stared down at it with curiosity. She might have been tempted to pick it up if she hadn't been wiser for her husband's warning.

She moaned in anguish. Not knowing her husband's fate these past weeks had been agony.

She leaned over the trinket for a closer look, careful not to touch it, but before she could pull away, a thin blue mist streamed out from its demonic face.

Alexandra leapt back but it was too late. The smoke surrounded her and drifted into her eyes, nose, and mouth. She staggered backwards to the door and collapsed as a strange cloud descended over her vision. It blinded her, and a moment later she passed out.

*

Following his horrifying ordeal, Corporal James Wallace felt relief more than anything else when, against all odds, he arrived home in London as himself.

The struggle had taken its toll on his body and mind, and years from his life. It had left him with a feeling of uncertainty about his future. It was difficult to imagine how a man in his late twenties, with the body of a man in his late fifties, could continue a career in Her Majesty's armed forces, or worse yet, how he could return home to the woman he loved. He no longer resembled the fresh-faced young corporal that Alexandra had married. Her reaction to the change occupied his thoughts constantly.

It was a quiet Sunday afternoon when James returned to his home on the outskirts of London. He opened the front door without knocking, hoping to surprise his wife. He ran into the living room, but there was no sight of her. He ran up the stairs and opened the door to their bedroom, but it was empty. As he turned to leave, something on the corner of the desk caught his eye.

He walked over and picked up his letter. He smiled at the thought of her standing in that spot, reading his words, but when he noticed the trinket on the desk in front of him, his eyes widened with horror.

For a moment he couldn't breathe. He backed away but stopped at the sound of his wife's voice in the doorway.

"You don't look well, my dear" she said. Her tone was flat.

Wallace turned. He tightened his jaw at the sight of her. She smiled and stared at him with those black, soulless eyes. She took a step closer and Wallace instinctively took one backwards. He moved his hand over his pistol, and Alexandra grinned.

"Are you going to shoot me, James?" she asked, bemused.

He didn't want to reply, but a small inaudible sound escaped his throat. Alexandra took another step closer and stopped when Wallace unclipped the cover over his pistol. His face had turned sour.

"We haven't seen each other in a long while, my love," she said "but I can't believe you would shoot me. We're so close after all."

She passed him and walked over to the window, ignoring the pistol he now had aimed at her. She leaned against the tall window frame and gazed down at the street below.

"Is she dead?" Wallace finally uttered.

The demon looked at him through his wife's eyes and shook her head. "No," she replied softly.

"Why are you doing this?" he asked

The demon stared at him, but it no longer had the hypnotic hold over him it had back in the desert.

"It must be resolved, this thing between us," she said.

The demon unhooked the latch on the window and pushed it open. Wallace's hand shook as he tried to hold his arm straight. The demon glanced sideways at him. A breeze flew in and swept his wife's hair across her face. She was more beautiful than he remembered.

Wallace's jaw quivered and the pistol shook harder. He pulled back the hammer with his free hand and pleaded with his eyes.

"Do you know what you interrupted? Out there, deep in the desert?"

Wallace swallowed. He shook his head.

"That ritual was more than six hundred years old. What you did," the demon's head shook, its mouth slightly open, "closed the gateway forever." A flare of anger lit up his wife's face. "Forever!"

Her voice suddenly changed. It wasn't Alexandra's voice anymore, but something harsher and deep, a wretched voice. "I would spell it out for you if it did not dishonor her name. You saw her, didn't you?"

Wallace slowly understood, and he nodded.

"Say it! Tell me you looked into her eyes before you killed her."

"I saw her," Wallace muttered.

"And?" the demon cried.

"I understand what I did," Wallace added.

"Good," she replied. Tears dripped down Alexandra's cheeks. "I was going to bring her back. I could have, but now I will never see her face again."

"Who was she?" Wallace asked.

The demon shook its head. "Nothing more to say," it replied. "Nothing more to say now. This must be resolved."

The demon climbed onto the ledge and turned. Wallace waved his pistol and groaned, but the demon forced a smile through its anger.

Suddenly, Wallace dropped the pistol and fell to his knees. He cried and begged her not to jump.

"Take my body, is that not revenge enough?"

The demon scoffed and leaned out the window.

"This isn't justice," Wallace cried. The demon stopped and turned back one more time.

"I didn't ask for justice; revenge will do for me." Its voice was cracked and broken.

"You had your time," Wallace implored "the two of you, but now it's over. Why would you deny me the years I have left with her?"

The demon hesitated. Its black eyes fiercely focused on Wallace. It turned back to face the window and took a deep breath, and then in the breeze, blue mist drifted from Alexandra's nose and mouth, and faded into the sky. Alexandra fell backwards from the window ledge, and Wallace caught her in his arms.

*

From the Desk of Corporal James Wallace

23 December 1898

Kabir, my dear friend, as promised I write to you with warm tidings and a warmer heart, from my own desk, in my own hand. It is to you that I owe a debt which may never be repaid. I am certain that I would have perished out there had you not discovered me wandering along the edge of the desert.

Those final weeks I spent in the hospital in Calcutta were perhaps the most difficult of my life. Many times I recall death's ugly visage emerging to claim me, only to find the strength I needed to recover in a stranger's friendship. Thank you, Kabir.

Those missing weeks were difficult to explain to my superiors as you might imagine. I have only my aged appearance—and you, of course, after discovering me in such a state—as evidence that any of it happened at all.

As for my mind, that will take a little longer to heal. My dreams are still haunted by flashes of dark and violent memories. I believe that they are those of Jahan, the man I spoke of, and the other victims, or perhaps the demon itself. I pray I never find out.

As for the demon, the source of such chaos, I can only speculate. I must assume that Jahan, that poor wretched fellow, was merely another of the demon's victims, like myself. I pray that his soul finds the peace that he was denied in life. I dread to think how many of us there were across the six centuries the demon claimed to have performed its ritual.

The trinket which was sent anonymously with part of my letter, to my home in London, now belongs to Her Majesty's government. I fear that I may never discover the identity of the sender, and this troubles me deeply.

I do not know if the demon still lives, I hope not. I wish for its death. Not out of malice, or fear that it might darken our doorstep again someday, but out of pity.

I have never seen a creature go to such lengths for love. It was a remarkable thing, and beautiful in a strange way. Such pain echoing down the centuries, burning for so long surely shows us that for all its otherworldly powers, it was as mortal as you or I in its search for love. I hope that we will meet again someday; I would like that very much.

Your dear friend, James Wallace

***

Bathtub Sleepers
by Ann Stawski, United States

I pulled back the shower curtain and found a dead guy in our bathtub. I wanted to assume he was sleeping. That would be the right thing to do.

The night before, Caitlin and I threw one of our impromptu parties with people we didn't know. For some reason, the really inebriated ones liked to sleep it off in our bathroom. I myself had never tried sleeping in a bathtub. It didn't look the least bit comfortable, but then again, I'd never been so drunk that I ever got to the point of thinking a bathtub was a good place to sleep. Sure, there were plenty of times I'd fallen asleep on the couch or underneath the coffee table, but never in the tub. One time last year I fell asleep on the bathroom floor next to the toilet, but I was legitimately sick with the flu and didn't have the energy to crawl back to bed after puking out every last bit of matter from my insides.

I really hoped the guy in our tub was just sleeping it off. Wrapped in only my bath towel, ready for my shower, I was running late for work. I poked his arm.

He didn't move.

At this point, my annoyance skyrocketed. I didn't have time to deal with leftover drunks, let alone a cadaver. I'd been late for one too many Sunday shifts at The Patisserie Café, and Chad, my manager, made it clear that if my tardiness continued, I'd be looking elsewhere for a job. Let's face it, restaurant jobs were fairly easy to come by in the city, so it's not like I'd be out of a second job for long. My real job was as a marketing assistant for a real estate firm, but the extra cash came in handy. And the truth was I loved working at The Patisserie. Their croissants were the flakiest and most buttery I'd ever eaten, like edible heaven. After my

Sunday shift, I'd come home with at least one free dozen to last me through the week. I sacrificed sleeping late to be at the café by eight on Sundays for those croissants—and I never sacrificed my sleep for anyone. That's how good they were.

So while I should have been hurrying toward the smell of buttery nirvana four blocks away, I was poking what looked to be a junior Paul Bunyan.

He was a good-sized guy, all two hundred pounds of him in his dark jeans and red and blue plaid shirt. He was probably twenty-five, with dark hair, sporting a full beard. I'm not a big fan of the whole beard trend. Most of the hipster guys look like they're lumberjacks. I'd grown up in upstate New York where logging was serious and men worked in the woods. I didn't expect to see any of them in the city either, until this whole beard trend started up, gained steam, and somehow these posers survived through several seasons. It's unfortunate most guys my age look like they should live in an upper-Midwest logging camp in the 1920s. Except at nearly one hundred years later, I could probably guarantee that ninety percent of these pseudo-looking lumberjacks whose work boots were artistically and carefully scuffed in all the right places, had never picked up an axe and certainly didn't know what real outdoor work was. Some of my family was in logging, so I was familiar with what it took to chop down trees and clearcut the land.

I sighed at the prone figure in front of me and then poked him again and again. In his arm, his leg, his tummy. Finally, I lifted his hand and shook his arm, rather violently.

He didn't move.

The hand I held was as soft as my own and had never seen a hard day of work in its life. It was also dead cold with a faint blue tinge around the fingernails.

I dropped his appendage and retreated out of the bathroom. Not bothering to knock on Caitlin's door, I jumped onto the bed next to her. She groaned and turned over, right on top of whoever was under the covers with her. I grabbed Caitlin's shoulder and hissed she needed to wake up.

One bloodshot eye opened and glared at me with all the angst of a raging hangover. "What?" That one word held the promise of pain if what I was waking her up for wasn't life or death.

I was shaking from adrenalin, certain it was death. Death came for the lumberjack.

"Bathroom, now." I tugged at her arm with one hand while holding on to my towel with the other. If I had known I wouldn't be in the shower yet, I would've put on my robe instead. Goosepimples rose on every inch of my exposed skin.

Caitlin tossed back the covers, sat up, and then swayed for a moment. She put her head in her hands, her raven hair sticking out in every angle. "Oh, one sec," she groaned.

Impatiently, I rewrapped my towel and glanced at the clock. I'd have to forego the shower and go to work with last night's party stink still on me.

She took a deep breath in through her nose and stood, lamenting, "Shots. Why do I do shots?"

"Because you have to." I helped her stand. She kept one hand at her temple as she followed me.

I pointed to the tub.

Squinting, Caitlin took it in. "Ah Christ," she grumbled and sat down on the toilet. "Not another one."

I shrugged.

The dead hipster in our tub was the second one this month and the sixth so far this year. It was only April.

"Wish I knew how they were chosen. I almost had sex with him last night." She reached to the sink, turned on the cold water, bent over and drank direct from the tap.

I leaned against the towel rack. Her adventurous sex life was none of my concern. "Don't know, don't care. I gotta get to work. I'll be back by two. Can you get your, ah, guest out of your bed and the apartment without him or her using the bathroom? We can take care of this one when I get back."

She nodded, grabbed the Tylenol bottle from the medicine cabinet and walked out. Just as she reached her bedroom door, Caitlin called out over her shoulder, "Bring me home an egg and bacon croissanwich, would you? I'm going to need the energy."

*

When I returned home from The Patisserie carrying an aromatic box of croissants and a small white bakery bag, Caitlin had everything ready. The tarp, tape, and rope were laid out in the bathroom. I appreciated that Caitlin was thorough. I didn't have to remind her to do things. We'd lived together for three years, brought together because of our heritage.

She sat on my bed, eating her sandwich and drinking a vanilla latte while I changed into old jeans and a sweatshirt. In between bites she told me, "I dumped his phone in the gutter a couple blocks away. Near the subway. He could've been heading anywhere."

"Any idea who he is? Who he was with last night?" I tied my hair up in a do-rag with a bandana and then slid on my sneakers.

She washed down the last bite with the latte, swallowed, and then said, "From what I can remember, he came with someone who knew someone that we might know. Maybe. No connection."

"And your guest?" I moved past her into the bathroom, not wanting to waste any more time. I wanted the body out as soon as possible.

Caitlin followed, shaking her head. "She had no clue. I gave her tea before she left, a parting gift, if you will. She won't remember a thing. We're good."

"Good." I climbed into the tub and maneuvered behind the lumberjack. It was a tight squeeze with me and him in there, but bracing myself against the wall, I managed to get a grip under his arms. Caitlin grabbed his legs.

"On the count of three," I instructed, and then together we hoisted the body out of the tub, dropping the dead weight unceremoniously with a thud onto the grayish black tarp laid out on the bathroom floor. By the time we got him situated on the plastic and dragged him out into the hallway where there was more room to properly wrap the body, we were both breathing hard and sweating.

We might have been a little rough moving him, but it had nothing to do with him personally. If I had a preference, it was always easier when some little bulimic party girl expired in our place. We could put her in the large suitcase and just wheel her out the door. A guy the size of a small bear required arrangements. But the choice wasn't ours. We just passed along whoever came our way.

Fifteen minutes later our doorbell sounded. Caitlin buzzed the building entry and soon Peter was in the hallway, knocking at our door. He came inside. "Cart's in the hall. Van's out back. Everything's set. So, who do we have here?" He squatted down and tugged at the tarp.

I pushed his hand away, which wasn't exactly like flicking away a gnat. Peter is one hundred ninety pounds of lean muscle and a hardened certitude. He doesn't mess around and is really good at what he does. If he took the tarp apart, we'd have to rewrap the guy and that took time. I didn't want him to disturb our handiwork.

"Goofy looking lumberjack hipster. No idea who he is or if anyone'll miss him. You can check him out later."

Peter nodded in understanding, then stood. He looked back and forth between Caitlin and me before he smiled in what looked to be an appreciative manner. Sometimes it's hard to tell if he's pleased because Peter always looks like he's leering. He's got a scar that runs from outside his right eye down to his chin and pulls up one corner of his mouth. It's a reason he's not out in the city on a regular basis. He weirds people out.

"I don't know how you ladies do it, but Miss Margaret will be happy. Very happy indeed."

I looked at Caitlin and we shrugged. When you had the Angel of Death in your family, acquiring dead people wasn't a noteworthy accomplishment.

*

We wheeled the lumberjack down the elevator and out the back of the building to the waiting van. Ten minutes later, the four of us were speeding north away from the city toward a little town halfway between Albany and the Finger Lakes. We'd be in Poestenkill in under three hours.

We arrived as the sun was setting.

Caitlin sighed as we drove through the small town. "Think there's any chance we could just drop the guy and get back to the city?"

"Doubt it. You know the drill," Peter replied, saying what I was thinking. I'd been doing this since I was eighteen and never once had the ritual changed. We all knew how long it would take and when we could leave.

"It's just I've got a work meeting first thing tomorrow. End-of-month reports are due and I need to get there early. I forgot to bring an energy drink." Caitlin yawned big and noisy. She worked in accounting at one of the top fashion magazines. Even though she was a whiz at it, or maybe because it came that easy to her, nothing bored her more than tallying numbers all day. At first she tolerated the fashion industry with all its petty people and shallowness, but once she befriended the wardrobe editor after she showed him how he could bill cab rides he never took on his expense reports and pocket the extra cash, then her job became a bit more interesting. Caitlin became the editor's pet and go-to girl when he had extra clothing samples. Deep down she's a girly girl who loves pretty clothes, so this made her happy. Caitlin's kind enough to share her cache with me as she couldn't possibly wear all the items he gave her to work without arousing suspicion. There were no designer labels necessary for our task at hand, though.

A few miles past Poestenkill's tiny downtown, we turned off the main road onto a long driveway marked by a small wooden plaque hanging under the mailbox, listing an M. Karosserie, DVM. At the end of the drive, we approached a large Victorian farmhouse wrapped on three sides by a wide porch with white spindle railings. Peter pulled the van around to the back of the house. The home was lit up from the inside, giving off warm and inviting vibes.

Looks were deceiving.

"Ready, ladies?" Peter waited for us to nod, then turned off the van and opened his door.

We left the lumberjack while we went inside the house. We had things to do before we needed him.

*

The smell of apples and cinnamon greeted us as we entered the kitchen. My mouth watered. I'm a sucker for bakery. It's my biggest weakness. "Mmmm, German apple cake."

"She probably got tired of hearing you talk about the croissants." Caitlin smirked. "You just never shut up about them."

"They make my heart happy. You know how good they are." I flicked the light of the industrial oven unit on and peered in at the rising cake. Nearly done.

Peter cleared his throat and we followed him into the living room. Even though we had just been there a few weeks before, I was always apprehensive. While Caitlin seemed to think there were corners that could be cut or steps that could be skipped, I knew better. They were called rituals for a reason. We had to follow everything as prescribed.

Miss Margaret sat on a wingback chair near the front window, reading. She set the book aside and smiled. "Well, good evening. I didn't expect you'd bring me another one so soon. But I'm so happy to see you again."

I held my tongue. Miss Margaret knew exactly when we'd be coming back. After all, she was the one who caused the lumberjack's death. She liked to put on the pretense of politeness. It was all part of her public personae. With us, though, she didn't need to pretend. We knew most everything that was going on.

The three of us sat on the large sofa to her left, across from the fireplace with the mantle displaying a large grouping of family photos. Caitlin and I were in one photo on the left, from a picnic last summer. There were others of families and newborn babies. Peter was in a photo with his brother Marco. His brother used to help us with transporting the bodies and all that followed, but Marco messed something up and Miss Margaret would not let him participate anymore. I never got all the details and didn't ask. There were just some things that shouldn't be questioned.

Miss Margaret asked about the drive and we made small talk for a few minutes. It was like visiting with a grandmother, except she wasn't ours. And I could guarantee no one had a matriarch like her in their family.

She didn't have children but managed to look grandmotherly with rosy cheeks, her short, curled hair dyed a golden blonde, and a chubby, petite figure. She was dressed in sneakers, jeans, and a sweatshirt from SUNY I vaguely remembered being on one guy we brought in a few months earlier. I shrugged to myself. Recycling clothes was an act of goodwill—we weren't a wasteful group.

The oven timer sounded from the kitchen. "Well, a little cake and coffee before we begin." Miss Margaret stood and returned a few minutes later from the kitchen, setting a tray laden with the still-steaming cake, a carafe, cups, and plates on the coffee table in front of us. We made short work of the nourishment with unspoken eagerness. Caitlin drank three cups of coffee and looked more alert. We were ready to get started.

As we stacked the dishes on the tray, Miss Margaret lit a three-wick sandalwood candle on the mantle. Then we stood in the middle of the living room and held hands. Miss Margaret stood between me and Caitlin, with Peter completing the circle.

She looked at each one of us and smiled. Her eyes seemed to burn a bright amber color. Raising our hands up to chest level, she spoke in a slow, purposeful voice. "I am so proud of all of you. You make this life so much easier. I know this isn't what anyone dreams of, but we have all made it work. You are good to me and I hope that in return you believe I am good to you. Your reward will come one day, when it is your turn. I just want to say thank you."

Overcome with unexpected emotion, my eyes started to well with tears and I glanced across at Caitlin. Her eyes glistened, too, and she gave me a sideways smile. We were never asked to be a part of this. It came with our heritage. It was who we were, like it or not. But it was nice to be thanked.

Peter even looked a little choked up. He cleared his throat and then said, "Miss Margaret, it's time. The girls have to work in the morning, you know."

She grinned and shook her head. "Yes, sometimes I forget. Next time have one of your Friday night parties, then you can stay longer on a Saturday."

She let go of our hands and covertly Caitlin rolled her eyes at me. No doubt we'd have another sleeper in our bathtub within the next few weeks.

All sentimentality evaporated. Time to get down to business.

*

Caitlin, Peter, and I brought the lumberjack into the clinical workshop next to the garage. During the week, the room served as Miss Margaret's veterinary surgical clinic. Her animal surgeries were few and far between as she had a limited practice and only kept it running to avoid any suspicion that locals may have.

Even though she had acted surprised to see us, Miss Margaret had the room ready with the equipment, utensils, and tools we'd need. A Frank Sinatra CD was in the sound system, the concert he recorded in Paris. We had listened to it so many times I could mimic all his cues and witty dialogue. It was Miss Margaret's favorite and we never asked her to change it. Or maybe Marco did once.

We donned protective suits, gloves, and hair coverings and stood over the lumberjack laid out in the stainless steel embalming table, the tilted kind with high sides and a drain at the lower end. We removed all his clothes and then stared down at the naked body. His torso and arms were covered with tattoos. He was also heavily manscaped—his entire pubic area clean of all hair.

"Looks like a little boy." Peter stood behind me and glanced over my shoulder at the bare area. He harrumphed. "What woman wants that?"

"Or man. Let's not be exclusive." I nudged him with my elbow. Peter scoffed, then chuckled.

"He should have thought about waxing his legs. Those are obscene." Caitlin pointed to the lumberjack's calves that were covered in thick, black hair. The area by his ankles was still matted down from the socks he had worn. "Hopefully no one gets any hairs in their product."

Miss Margaret cleared her throat, indicating observation time was over. "Let's just be thankful he showered on a regular basis."

We nodded in agreement. We'd had some fairly ripe bodies come through before and had to bathe them before we could begin. As someone who showers once day, I'm always surprised by those people with poor hygiene.

Caitlin and Peter grabbed his clothes and bagged them. They argued about what to do with the boots. Caitlin recognized them as designer and could resell them for good money. Peter wanted to donate them to the local shelter.

I tuned them out as Miss Margaret closed her eyes and held her hands above the body, moving them over the lumberjack from head to toe. She opened her amber eyes and smiled at me, saying, "He is clean. No diseases. All is good. We can begin."

"These seem to be getting more frequent, Miss Margaret," I said, handing her the portable jigsaw.

She nodded, turned on the saw with the extended blade and cleanly cut into the lumberjack's neck. In one swift move, she severed his head, not even hesitating at his spinal cord. Before anything began oozing out of the neck, I grabbed his head by the hair and set it next to his arm, the one with the merman tattoo extending from his shoulder to elbow. We had placed him on the table so his head was down near the drain, and with the help of gravity, the blood began to flow out of his body and down the pipe.

"Well, the demand is growing. We won't do more than we need. But they keep asking," Miss Margaret said as she moved to his legs and began to massage his limbs. Caitlin and Peter joined us, and we acted as pumps to get the blood moving through the body. If we didn't help it along, it could take a while to drain.

Once the blood stopped trickling out, Miss Margaret cut into the torso and disemboweled him. All the innards were placed in stainless steel trays and set on the counter.

"How much is more?" We weren't arousing suspicion from anyone, so I wasn't worried about getting caught. Technically Caitlin and I weren't killing anyone. The deaths were random and with no connections to us, but I was getting a little bit tired of this work. In all my childhood dreams of growing up to be an actress or a singer or a famous explorer, never once did it occur to me I'd be most active and good at grinding up dead people.

"We'll see. No more than we're doing right now." Miss Margaret was moving on with the jigsaw again. She started cutting through the limbs. First the feet, then at the knee, finally through the hip area.

No more meant we'd continue with two bodies a month. That was manageable. It wasn't difficult to get people to come to a party where the booze was free. We made them disappear easy.

While we cut through the body, Caitlin and Peter put the pieces into the grinder. We couldn't talk over the sound of the bones being pulverized and the saw cutting its way. Even Frank Sinatra was drowned out.

Next off were the hands, then at the elbows and then at the shoulder socket. All that remained was an empty torso on the table.

I flipped it over and Miss Margaret began working the saw again. Cutting the body apart down alongside the spine, and then in various spots under the ribs and below the clavicle, she made quick work of it. That came with practice. My estimate was I had been involved with at least ninety of these, and she had been doing this for much longer before I ever came along. I wasn't really sure how old she was, either, or if we were the only ones who brought bodies to her. She could be doing one body a day.

Once the entire body was pulverized, we placed the remains into four large soup stockpots. Miss Margaret and I took off our suits and deposited them in black plastic bags. Then, the four of us each took one pot and carried them into the kitchen. The industrial oven had six large burners on the cooktop and I turned the flames to high under the four corner burners. Caitlin and Peter went back to the workshop to clean up while Miss Margaret and I worked in the kitchen.

I brought out two large plastic canisters from the walk-in pantry. I'd seen similar containers at a spice shop in Chinatown where they sold product in bulk, but what was in these jars was not found in any store. Miss Margaret bought the components for the mixture direct from Germany. Probably from another community like ours. It usually came packaged as veterinary supplies. She never told us what was in the shipments, but whatever it was, her customers were willing to pay big bucks for the final product.

She opened the two canisters and divided the contents equally into the four pots. Then I added a gallon of water to each and mixed thoroughly. While it came to a boil, we brought out the quart-sized canning jars and lids from the pantry and waited for the mixture to cook and thicken.

When Caitlin and Peter completed their cleaning duties and returned to the kitchen, we were ready to begin the canning process. We worked as an efficient assembly line and when finished, forty-eight gleaming jars filled with a thick reddish-orange jam-like substance filled the kitchen table. Caitlin and I carefully applied the labels.

Miss Margaret's Homemade Compote - Liebe vom Körper

That was German for "Love of the Body."

*

Miss Margaret's Homemade Compote was a best-selling product on the Home Remedies website. The customers spread it like jelly on their toast and English muffins. They raved about it on the review page, consistently giving it five out of five stars. It made them feel invincible. They didn't get sick, never experienced the flu, had their symptoms repressed, and some reported experiencing the best sex of their lives.

The customers were select. Miss Margaret only shipped to those who were members of our clan. Some were still in Germany, but most were in the United States. The product worked best with our DNA. Anyone else not associated with us received a message saying the product was sold out and they would be notified when more was in stock. They never received that email.

Peter packed the jars into individual boxes, using the preprinted shipping labels from the online orders. We carried them to the van, placing them on the spot where the lumberjack had lain hours earlier. After driving us back to the city, Peter would ship the boxes on his return to Poestenkill in the morning.

We had everything cleaned and put away just as the grandfather clock in the living room struck two o'clock. I let loose with a big yawn. It felt like days since I had discovered the sleeper in the bathtub.

"Wonderful job tonight. Our customers will be very pleased with this batch. Something about young men," Miss Margaret mused, lovingly patting the one jar on the table. She kept a sample of each batch and her cellar was lined on three sides, all jars identified by date.

We said our goodbyes standing on the back porch, the cool spring night air misting around us. Miss Margaret handed Caitlin a bottle of tequila. "Remember, host a Friday night party next time so you girls can stay a bit longer."

Caitlin nodded, took the bottle and hugged it to her chest. She said goodnight and then climbed into the back of the van, sliding the door closed. I knew she'd be asleep by the time I climbed into the passenger seat.

Miss Margaret gave me a hug. "You did real good." She reached out, flicking something off my bandana. The piece landed at her feet. "Oh. I think that was his fingernail."

I ignored that. "I'm curious, how does it choose? I mean, they were all doing shots. Caitlin too. But only one dies." I knew that whatever Miss Margaret put into the tequila wouldn't affect us. Again, something about our DNA.

Peter pushed himself off the railing, his face twisted into an amused look. He'd been involved with this for so long that I assumed he knew the details. He and Marco used to host the parties that Caitlin and I now do until his accident and the scar scared people away. He gave a wave of goodbye to Miss Margaret and climbed into the driver's seat.

"Drive safe, Peter." Miss Margaret turned back to me. "It just knows. It knows to pick the weakest one, the one who is going to die the earliest. It just speeds up the process."

"So if they lived, they might last only another month or something?" All our guests were young. No one over thirty came to our parties.

She shrugged. "A month, a year, five years. There's no telling."

I didn't respond, looking down at my feet. She wasn't telling me the whole story, but it was enough.

Miss Margaret tilted my chin up. "What is it?"

"Well, it's just that there's this woman at work. She's really horrible to me and just about everyone else. I was thinking maybe I should invite her over ..."

Before I could finish my thought, Miss Margaret grabbed my chin with a fierceness I had not seen in a while. She was angered. I had made a mistake.

Her face was inches from mine as she said in a low, slow voice, "We do not target anyone because of personal issues with them. If you do that, you taint the product. If the product is bad, we could harm one of our own. This has to be random. Do you understand me?"

I struggled to nod with her hand still gripping my chin. It was unwise to anger a woman who disemboweled people without thinking twice, even if she did look like a grandmother who baked an amazing German apple cake.

She gave a half grin and released me. "Don't be petty with people. That's not healthy. If someone is bothering you, talk to her. If that doesn't work, give her space and avoid her. Rise above this." She stroked my upper arm, her face softening with concern. "People don't die because we hate them. They die because we need them. If you target them, then it becomes killing."

I nodded, struggling to resist massaging my chin where her fingers had dug into my skin. "I'm sorry. You're right. I won't do anything like that." And I wouldn't. Our clan didn't tolerate disobedience. I had seen how Marco had been treated.

She reached into her apron pocket and pulled out a small Tupperware container that held no more than four tablespoons of the mixture we made that night. Miss Margaret pressed it into my palm. "Here. You seem stressed. In the morning, put a little on those croissants you love so much. You'll feel better."

***

Clay Figures
by Valerie Lioudis, United States

Her parents were always fighting. Normally, they would place her in the craft room and shut the door. The discussions always began with angry hushed whispers and ended at full out screaming matches. They believed they were protecting her from the brunt of their issues, but like most children, she was neither stupid, nor deaf. So, she sat in the craft room trying her best to wall off their nonsense, hoping the angry gurgling of her anxiety riddled stomach would end if she could just find a medium to create something truly special.

All other attempts had been in vain. Crayons broke in her hand as she held them a bit too tight during the loudest moments. Marker tips would wear away and become virtually useless. Paints would spill causing her mother to scream loudly at her, eventually apologizing for losing her temper, always destroying that apology with the word "but." Sophia had given up on finding that perfect item when she spotted the corner of a worn wooden box.

She fished it out from behind the coloring books and stared at it curiously before deciding that if it was in the craft room, it must be for her. When her parents had moved her away from all of her friends and family to a state thousands of miles away to get what they called a "fresh start," promises were made that she would have a special place that was all her own. This room was the only promise her parents had ever followed through with.

Her tiny fingers searched the box for an opening. Her father had been a fan of puzzle boxes, but as of yet, she wasn't allowed to touch his collection, she understood the concept from watching him work his way into each new one. There was always a trick. Sometimes it was a loose piece, or a secret button. It took skill and patience to be able to find out what it was. Some of her father's boxes had taken him days to break into. She was determined to work faster than that.

The screaming in the other room hadn't stopped. Sophia was no longer listening. For the first time in her life, she was able to tune them out. She would have been grateful if she had noticed, but that recognition would have pulled her out of the trance that was keeping their anger at bay. The gurgling ceased, and her body became calm. Concentration had replaced nervous fidgeting.

There were countless ripples carved into the wood. The swirling channels were perfectly sized to fit the tip of her index finger. She followed each path like a maze hoping to feel something different than the smooth wood below. Every path played a song in her mind. Simple notes hummed along with the turns, dips, and hills. Time itself began to slow to match her heartbeat and the songs its tempo.

Her eyes shut, and she fell more into the box's spell. A voice that wasn't quite her own sang along, adding words that were so old no one alive knew the name of the lyric's language. Her foot began to tap as she slowly rocked back and forth rotating the box over and over following the carvings with a speed that was soon undiscernible to the naked eye.

For Sophia, though, everything around her had slowed down. She was unaware of the magic spell the box had cast on her. That was until her finger found the tack. Peeking through one of the channels was a small metal spike, just large enough to nick her finger as she passed it. Blood smeared down the rest of the smooth wooden path. Sophia cried out in pain and dropped the box on the floor. It hit the ground and broke into two pieces exposing the treasure held within.

A lump of dark green clay rolled under the table. She was too busy with the cut on her finger to notice the box had opened. Although she knew it would probably get her in trouble, she ran out of the room to get her mother's help. Even with a legitimate reason for her interruption, Sophia ended up with a Band-Aid and a grounding. "You should have been more careful. I don't even know what you could have cut yourself on. You are so careless. That is something you inherited from your father," she said as she applied the bandage with little motherly care.

*

Darla had never wanted to be a mother. She had dreams of being a famous actress when she started dating Colin in high school. His dreams were much closer to the ground, and all he ever wanted was to travel the country like his father as a trucker. The open road called him, so did Darla's beauty. They had been oil and water since day one, yet couldn't seem to stay out of each other's lives.

Darla took off right after graduation, running towards the bright lights of the big city and their promise of stardom. Colin went and got his CDL and rode along with his old man for a few years. It wasn't until the big city had beat the hope out of Darla, and casting directors started pushing her towards the role of mother at the ripe old age of twenty-seven, that she dragged her tail back to her hometown. Colin was road weary, and had taken a job at the local gas station spinning wrenches when he saw her pull up to the gas pump on the way into town.

"Well, well, well, if it isn't miss glamour and glitz herself gracing our small-town gas pump with her presence." His accent was thick, and as much as she hated to admit it, the sound of his voice made her heart skip a beat or two.

"Colin Jenson. I thought you were headed out of this town. What are you doing at Rusty's?" she asked genuinely curious and without a hint of sarcasm.

That was the one thing he hadn't expected. She was far too tired to banter like they had in the old days, or maybe she just didn't have the fight in her anymore. He was drawn to her like so many times before, but this time with his guard down completely. It was her lack of hostility that tricked him. Unfortunately, he made the mistake of believing that she had changed while gone, not realizing that those changes could be temporary.

It didn't take long for her to move into his small one-room apartment. No one wants to move home at almost thirty, and they were sleeping together every night anyway. It was one of those unceremonious moves where suddenly you realize the other person hasn't left in a few weeks, and now stores all their crap in your space. He didn't mind, though. Everything was going so well that those weeks had flown by.

Things only began to sour after they both believed it was too late to find their way out. She was frustrated with his lack of ambition, and he with her incessant need to micromanage him. He had the tendency to want to retreat into his anger, often hiding for hours in his truck instead of going home. She, on the other hand, grew more volatile, losing her temper and erupting like a volcano more frequently. They both chalked it up to the pregnancy, saying that the hormones were in control.

It never really was hormones. Their initial honeymoon period was the exception, and not the rule. His mother urged him to find them a counselor. Hers suggested that she leave and have the baby with them. Colin and Darla were too stubborn and proud to admit they were wrong and that their union was doomed from the start. The baby needed both parents, they would rationalize. She wouldn't thrive being shuffled from house to house. Darla would imagine a nightmarish future where her child went to the arms of Daddy and "new" Mommy. No one would raise her child but her.

Sophia was born on a frozen winter night in the back of Colin's truck when they missed their window to leave in time for a hospital birth because they had been too busy arguing over some hypothetical parenting situation, just like every other night that entire month. When Darla had told Colin that she was feeling contractions, he had assumed she was using the baby yet again to win a fight.

Colin took to Sophia immediately, and that made Darla even less likely to pull her baby close. She was just another invasion into a relationship that already lacked intimacy. Colin's initial love became cold indifference when Sophia developed colic. She would spend hours screaming in her crib as Darla downed one glass of wine after another waiting for Colin to finally pull into the driveway. The moment he walked through the door, she would head out to the bar three doors down, so she could turn that buzz into a blackout.

Eventually, Darla's mother stepped in and began to watch the baby. She pushed her daughter out to get a job hoping it would get her out of what she assumed was a bout of postpartum depression. Depression doesn't get cured by activity, and Darla didn't have a temporary illness. If her mother would have looked back, she would have remembered that her daughter had never been pleasant, and no amount of wishing would fix that. Instead, she stayed in blissful ignorance hopeful that her granddaughter would eventually have the family that she deserved.

Mick had graduated a few years before either of them, and was a regular haunt at the bar where Darla spent her down time. Darla had decided the only place she was willing to work would be her escape, so she got a position waiting tables and tending bar depending on the need of the night. He was getting divorced for the third time, and was actively shopping around for a replacement. Darla was immediately swept off her feet once his attention shifted in her direction.

Always one who needed mounds of validation, Darla was an easy target for a serial monogamist. The trail of broken hearts and families behind him meant nothing to her. The only thing that mattered to her was his near obsessive level of attention. Each whispered compliment built her up, and he made sure to tell her she would never have to worry about a thing again. He was going to take her away from this shit job, her pathetic little apartment, and take care of her for the rest of her life.

One night, the drinks flowed a bit too fast, leaving what was left of her morals and inhibitions at the bottom of the empty glasses, and she fell into his arms. She should have felt guilty, but instead she felt free for the first time in longer than she could remember. That night she didn't go home, and she made no attempt to hide what was happening from Colin. Actually, she went out of her way to rub it in that someone still found her attractive.

Sophia spent most of her first year at her grandmother's home. There was never an official passing of custody, neither Darla nor Colin wanted to be around a screaming baby, nor each other. There she sat, cradled in the arms that had rocked her mother, screeching the days away until she was old enough to sit upright. Her parents never noticed that she had stopped screaming. What should have been a celebrated moment passed by with not a peep from any of them.

"Heading out again, Dar?" he seethed.

"I am going to work. What do you care anyway?" she spat back.

"I care that I look like a fool in front of the whole town. You leave me here, stuck with the kid, while you shake your ass for anyone who will throw you a bit of attention," he accused her.

"That isn't true, and you know it. I have her all the time, and so does my mother. You have done nothing but hide from the both of us since she was born. I am not going to sit around here and wait for you to love us."

"I love her." he lied to himself. "You, on the other hand, haven't been someone worth loving in a long time. Plus, I hear you have someone sniffing around you anyway. What are you waiting for, Dar, him to propose? You don't get to string me along until something better comes along," he yelled.

"Something better comes along? *Anything* is better than this! You don't get to ignore me, and then get mad when I walk away. I wish I never met you, Colin Jenson. You have been nothing but horrible to me since day one!"

"If you walk out that door, Darla, don't expect the lock to be the same if you try to come back." His tone was flat, and his face showed nothing.

"Please, just another empty threat. You couldn't do this without me. You can't handle a baby on your own," she mocked him.

"Yeah, Dar, it is really hard to leave the baby at your mother's for days at a time. How will I ever manage?" He stayed stoic.

Sophia began to scream from the corner, and for the first time it was due to their fighting, and not pain in her little body. The door slamming just made her scream louder, and her father unable to connect with her, bundled her up in her coat to take her to her grandmother's home. It would have been best for all if the three of them parted ways right then. Sadly, the adults were selfish, and wouldn't stop the merry-go-round of drama, anger, and recovery. Round and round they would go for years to come.

*

"Sophia, why don't you go make Daddy a picture or something for his work?" her mother said as she shut the door behind her.

Sophia searched the shelves for the box that had cut her last night. Her mother had sent her to bed, and as usual had straightened up the craft room before falling asleep herself. If the home was neat and tidy, it must be filled with love, right? Sophia always found this ritual ridiculous. She was just going to play with the things the next day. She never understood what it hurt to keep them out overnight. The shelves were stacked neatly like they always were, with her supplies on each level and a small label that matched the items in each plastic tub.

She shuffled the boxes around hoping to find the worn wooden box, so she could try to work her way into it, this time being more careful not to cut her finger on sharp edges. All the shelves were occupied by their normal items, and nothing more. Disappointed, Sophia slid down the wall with her back to mope on the floor. That was when she spotted the lump of clay under the table. Her mother must have missed it in her whirlwind cleaning session. She almost believed it could have come out of her normal supplies, that was until she lifted it up off the floor.

The familiar sensations of cool smooth clay were replaced with a vibrating warm ball that felt like it would spring to life at any second. She smushed it between her fingers. Normally, she would mold her favorite animals out of clay. This lump of clay was calling to be shaped into something a bit more advanced. She could see two small creatures in her mind. Intricate details of their faces flashed over and over as she worked her hands bringing her vision to life. Hours passed, and she was only partially done with one of them when her mother burst in the room.

"Clean up, Sophia. It is bedtime."

"Yes, Mother," she said as she snapped out of her trance. "I will be up in a minute."

"Make it quick. I am heading out and your father wants you asleep before I go."

Her eyes rolled as she turned to find a place to keep her newfound toy. If her mother was going out again, she knew for sure that tomorrow night she would be locked away in the craft room while her father ranted about his disgust with her mother's choices. The difference this time would be her enthusiasm to get back to her project. She still had to finish the creatures, and the thought of them brought on an uncharacteristic smile.

Tucked away in her bed, Sophia fell fast asleep without her normal tossing and turning. Her imagination was vivid like all other children of her age, but on this night her dreams were especially colorful and lively. The two creatures danced and frolicked in the background as Sophia chased after them, never able to get close enough to interact directly.

She called to them to come closer, but their attention was somewhere else. Each step she took forward would push them further back, leaving her longing to be close to them. She woke up well rested, yet wishing to return to her dream world. The pull was strong enough that her mother had to drag her down to the breakfast table with the threat of being grounded to her room that evening if she caused them to be late for school. The thought of being unable to keep working on her creations pushed her out of the room.

*

"So, he gives up on you and I am just supposed to take you back like nothing happened?" Colin sounded exhausted.

"I left him," she proudly announced.

"We both know that is a lie, Darla. You never leave them. They get fed up with how high maintenance you are, and then you come running back to me, always expecting that I will just accept you back because of Sophia."

"You are my soulmate." She cried softly as she cradled his face.

He tore away from her. "Then why can't you just be with me? If that was true, you would be happy with just me loving you."

"It's not you, Colin. It's me. There is something broken in me. I want to be here. I want our life with our little family."

"I'm not falling for it again, Darla. If you are coming back, something has to change. Something real, and big. You need to leave the bar."

She gasped. "I can't leave the bar! We need that money!"

"I wasn't finished. If you want me to take you back again, we are going to leave this town. We need to leave the state. Hell, we need to cross the country and start over for real." He stared her down looking for a reason to throw in the towel.

"What about my mother? Who will watch Sophia?" She grasped at the only straw that she believed would change his mind.

"We'll figure it out." He wasn't going to back down.

"Fine," she said.

"Fine?" he said exasperated. "I want more than fine, Dar. I want you to get it. This is our last chance."

"No, I get it. I love you, baby. I will do whatever you want. Let's start looking. Where do you want to go?"

Sophia had her ear pressed against the bedroom door. It was when the screaming ended that her troubles always began. Now, they were taking her away. They never thought of her when they made decisions. Maybe they would let her live with Grandma. She doubted it, though. Tears rolled down her cheeks as she huddled under her covers crying until she fell asleep.

*

It took three nights of sculpting and shaping. The two creatures from her dreams stared back at her in perfect detail. Her little fingers shook

153

with excitement. She ripped through the boxes on the shelves looking for a container that was perfect to keep her prized possessions safe. Behind one of the plastic tubs sat the puzzle box. This time it opened easily, and she saw the inside was lined with soft purple fabric. She laid the creatures in the box carefully, closed the lid, and snuck past her fighting parents to go relax in her bed.

Sleep came fast and heavy. She was taken back to the land of the vivid dreams, though this time the creatures were sitting at a table surrounded by flowers with a pot of tea. They both looked up smiling from ear to ear as she approached. Normally, smiles are comforting, but on an oversized cat-like creature, it came off as menacing.

"Sophia!" the feminine creature exclaimed. "Come, child, we have been waiting for you!"

"You have?" she asked as she walked towards the table.

"Of course, my dear. Who else would this party be for?" she replied.

"But the last time I saw you, you kept running away from me." She pouted.

"There are rules, little one. You had to create us before we could be with you. You worked really hard to get us here. Thank you." She pulled out one of the chairs and motioned for Sophia to sit down.

"Who are you?" Sophia asked, never flinching as the creature's claws fumbled with the fine china in an attempt to pour her a cup of tea.

"You don't know?" the masculine one asked, straining his face to make it appealing to a small child.

"Why do you two keep doing that to your faces? It is making them look weird."

"Doing what?" he asked.

"Smiling, I guess. At least that is what I think you are doing. It looks weird. You should stop. I made your faces the way I saw them in my dream. They are beautiful," Sophia said.

"You are weird for a little one," he said.

"You are weird for a clay man," she pushed back.

"I like her," he said to his partner.

"I hope so," she responded. "We are going to be with her for a long time. That is if she will have us."

"Of course, I will have you!" Sophia exclaimed.

"You don't know what you're agreeing to, little one," he said. "We need you to be sure."

"This is something really big. We want to spend forever with you, Sophia. You have been picked out of all the little ones in your time to be a family with us, but this gift doesn't come for free. Nothing good in life ever does," the feminine creature explained to her as she wrapped her paw around Sophia's small hand.

Warmth spread through Sophia's body. It engulfed her from her head to toe. She had spent her short lifetime acting like her parents' lack of caring didn't bother her. When she was out of the way, they didn't yell at her, and all she wanted to do was stay out of their fights. But really, deep down something had been missing. True acceptance and unconditional love were two things that she needed, yet never knew were missing. In that flash of heat, she was petrified that the creatures would take it all back, and she would be forced to go back to just existing.

"Sophia, are you willing to give up everything and start anew?" he asked.

"What do I have to give up?" she wondered aloud.

"Everything. Anything. It could be the smallest thing, or all in your life. If you say yes, we will stay with you forever. We will love you, and help you grow into the amazing being we know you could be. If not, we will disappear forever. I am sorry you don't have time to think about it, little one. We need to know now, before you wake up."

Not wanting this moment to end, Sophia agreed. Tears streamed down her cheeks as she said, "Just don't leave me. I don't want to be alone anymore."

"We'll never leave you, Sophia. All you have to do is wake up," he said with a devilish grin. This time one hundred percent real and absolutely petrifying.

*

Darla went into the craft room expecting to see her daughter seated at the table as usual, instead this time the room was empty, and spotless. At least the little brat had figured out how to put things back where they belonged. She had spent hours putting together a playroom that looked beautiful when posted online. It made her one of the better mothers. Everyone who liked and commented on her posts said so.

So far, Sophia had been unable to really appreciate the gift that she had given her. Her childhood would be filled with memories of her perfect space made for a princess, and even though she had created it, Darla resented her for it. Her own childhood was filled with nothing but her parents' missed opportunities to help her fulfil her dreams. Sure, they drove her to auditions and acting lessons. She always wondered, were they ever really supportive, or were they just going through the motions?

Colin huffed his way into the room. "Come on, Sophia. Time for bed. Your mother wants to go out." He was trying to rush the child so the fight could end. Though, the fight never really ended. It just moved time or location.

"She isn't in here," Darla snapped.

"Well, where is she then?" he asked accusingly.

"How should I know. You were in charge, too. I am sure she is in bed," Darla yelled at him.

They rushed to her room, not out of fear for the child not being in her usual location, but in fear that it would disrupt the plans they both had for the rest of the evening. Darla already had one foot out the door, and Colin was impatiently waiting for her to leave so he could get high and forget it all.

They opened the door to their daughter's bedroom without the scared "heart in your throat" feeling that any good parent feels when their child is missing. Instead, both Colin and Darla felt annoyed and inconvenienced. A beam of light from the streetlight outside Sophia's window landed perfectly on her sleeping cheek. No sigh of relief was breathed, and the door was about to be closed without a goodnight kiss for yet another time.

Darla saw them first. They stood tall in the shadows behind Sophia's bed. She would have easily missed them except the whites of their fangs flashed bright against the dark background. Frozen in place, she was unable to run or even warn Colin. Little did she know, he was also stuck in place awaiting his fate. The creatures lumbered over to the unfit parents and pushed them out of the child's view just in case she were to awaken. They didn't want her to see what they needed to take in order to stay with her, though the male creature guessed she might enjoy it.

Screams echoed in their minds, not from their mouths. Sophia's head rested still in a perfect slumber in the other room as her parents were punished for the sins they had committed on the child. Pain ripped through their bodies, but not a mess was made. Then the home was still.

*

"Sophia darling, come down for breakfast, sleepyhead. You need to get your energy up so we can start packing. We are going to head back home. This place doesn't suit us anymore. Nanny says she misses you," her mother called from the kitchen.

Sophia rubbed her eyes, and pinched her arm. She had to be dreaming still.

"Sophia, hurry up! We miss you in here. I made your favorite, dippy eggs and a French toast bagel," her father yelled.

She pulled her bear close, and slipped her feet onto the floor. This had to be a trick of some kind. If she wasn't asleep, then something else must be going on. Her parents had never made her breakfast together. Maybe, they were finally getting a divorce.

As she turned the corner, she saw her father twirling her mother around as the radio in the kitchen played music that she didn't recognize.

"Sophia!" they exclaimed at the same time, as they rushed over to pull her into their dance.

"What is wrong with you?" she asked as she backed away from her parents.

"Wrong, little one? Nothing. Everything is right in the world," her mother cooed.

Sophia's eyes locked with her mother's.

"Little one?" she whispered.

A smile spread across her mother's face.

"The smile looks so much better on that face, Mommy." Sophia giggled.

"Yes, it does, little one," she said as she pulled Sophia in tight, using this body in the way it had been intended since the beginning of time.

***

Blessing

by Charlotte Platt, Scotland

Rosy had made many wishes when Leon was a child, whispered many prayers as she watched him grow. As a journalist in the Dirty War, she had known he had many troubles coming. So she wished and prayed, hoping the world would have more kindness for him than it had for her.

Her last one was answered. It had been a muttered prayer after she'd been shot in her garden one balmy evening, the consequence of her story exposing a politician abusing sex workers.

"Dear God, please don't let my son die by violence," she had whispered, hands covering the holes in her abdomen. She staggered towards the house: fear spiked her blood. They had gone in after Leon's screams. He was only six. She heard shots ring out, but Leon came running. He had held her, screaming for help, and she shushed his worry. She could accept her death as long as he was safe.

*

While Rosy had prayed to her own God, that deity had taken a stance of inaction after the murder of his son by man and was not about to start intervening. An odd angel might intercede, but no miracles were coming for Leon. A miracle was not what he had received however: it was a blessing.

His grandmother discovered it after a drive-by.

Leticia had been in the borough a long time, she was used to the sounds of the guns at night, but she knew they could scare Leon. He slept under a soft blanket in the summer heat and that was poor comfort for a frightened boy.

She stopped in the door of his room, startled by a silhouette beside his bed. Tall and lithe, wrapped in a long, red dress, the woman was looking at Leon. She would be pretty, Leticia supposed, but the pretty ones got in trouble too.

"If you are hiding from the police, I won't call them," Leticia said, raising herself to her full height. "But I must ask you to leave. I don't want his sleep disturbed."

"That will not happen, Leticia Nunez," came the response, a reedy voice that scraped along the goose bumps it raised.

"How do you know my name?"

"You know me, Leticia," she replied, glancing over her shoulder. Her face was smooth yellowed bone, the smiling jaw hanging loose. Leticia crossed herself, fear coating her chest.

"I would beg you to take me. I knew Leon shouldn't have lived that night, that those men who shot my girl would have him too. If there is blood to be paid, please take mine. He is so young, his mother was so young too. I have lived well. I would walk into the next world with you." Leticia knew she was committing a sin in offering her life, for was it not suicide? But she couldn't lose her grandson. Rosy's death had shaken her heart from her chest and left a throbbing wound. She would not survive Leon being ripped from her too.

"You do not need to beg," the voice dismissed, turning away. "He is mine and he will not to be taken until his time. I am not here to take him from you." The jaw didn't move.

"Why are you here, Lady?" Leticia whimpered, tears of relief brimming over.

"He is marked as mine. His mother's blood paid for him. Violence will not kill him, though luck or illness can. He can be injured, he can be hurt, but he will not die. When it is his time, I will come, and he will serve me in watching the dead and observing their festivals."

"Mictecacihuatl," Leticia gasped. "The Pale Lady watches my boy?"

"It is nice to hear the old names," the woman's sigh was close to a laugh. "Until his time here is fulfilled, I will ensure his safety. I grant many favours, Leticia, and I demand many things from those I favour. I will demand much from you. Teach him my worship, keep a shrine for me. Show me how well he does and I will bring good fortune. I will not rescind my gift, but bad luck always stalks around. Give me reason to keep it from your door."

"Yes, Lady," Leticia nodded, clutching her rosary and squeezing her eyes closed against tears still burning there.

"I will never be cruel, Leticia," the Pale Lady promised, stroking a bony hand over Leon's brow. "Gods have time to see things grow, and I would see mine do well."

Leticia nodded, unable to say anything past the lump in her throat.

When she looked again, the Pale Lady was gone and Leon slept on, blanket tangled around his thin legs. She crossed herself and moved to her kitchen, looking for space. She cried as she cleared beside the stove, a good spot for worship. She set a picture of Rosy alongside it and noted shops she could go to buy an effigy. She would take Leon with her. Death was not to be feared, but Leon would have to be braver than most. Her priest was going to think her mad.

*

Whether or not his grandmother was mad was not something Leon would tolerate being discussed. He didn't care if she was. He had grown up in her house, received her care since his mother was stolen from him, and he would defend her honour and her home as long as he had the chance.

He was currently exercising such a chance, staring down two junkies trying to break in. One carried a crowbar and the other simply glowered, fingers twitching at his sides.

"You're not welcome here." Leon sighed, tapping his bat against the doorjamb.

"No one will help you stop us." Twitchy smirked.

"I don't need help. Don't you idiots know this house?"

"Those rumours don't mean shit, that's just your crazy grandma spooking people," spat Crowbar.

"I wouldn't insult the lady; she tells the truth."

"Shut up and let us in, kid."

"Oh, you can come in." Leon laughed back at Twitchy, sharp and bright. "If you can get past me." He rolled up his sleeves, folding the cuffs as he watched them.

"You're about twelve, you think you'll stop us?" Crowbar laughed, pushing Twitchy forward.

"I'm nineteen, fucktard, and why don't you come try?" Leon held his arms up, welcoming the attack. He wasn't disappointed. Twitchy pulled a blade and made to stab him. Leon leaned in, smirking when the knife slid home. It stung, of course, but it wouldn't last. He smiled wide at Twitchy, swinging his bat up one-handed.

"Want to try that again, friend, or will you find some other house?" Leon asked. The knife was pulled back and thrust again, a vicious jab Leon suspected was meant to sever something important.

"Your friend seems to have gone mute," Leon called to Crowbar, tapping his bat on Twitchy's head. He could smell the sharp tang of his fear and sneered, "I'd take him away before I'm forced to defend myself."

"Antonio, what's going on?" muttered Crowbar.

"He's a little shocked his trick didn't work is all. Move him, or I will."

"You won't do shit," mumbled Twitchy, yanking the knife again. Leon tsked, gripping the bat in both hands and swinging up, cracking Twitchy in the jaw. The man's head snapped back and he staggered, blood pouring down his chin.

"You little shit, you think you can do that? We're part of Francisco's crew, you'll be in the river before nightfall," shouted Crowbar, yanking Twitchy away.

"Let me know how that goes for you." Leon shrugged, resting the bat on his shoulder. "And don't come bothering my grandmother's house again."

He slipped out of his shirt, tossing it onto the sofa. His vest was ruined. He sought the shrine in the kitchen, kissing the picture of Rosy and whispering a prayer to his benefactor. His grandmother had never lied to Leon about her. She had told him not to tell people why they prayed to Santa Muerte and simply remind them all houses need luck.

Leticia had been shunned at church, the thundering minister disavowing her one Sunday morning. Leon never forgot how she had stood, taken his hand, and walked out. She had kept her pride. She still prayed, Leon heard her at night, whispering petitions to her god and kissing her rosary. Leon didn't hold much truck with that, but he knew it comforted her.

He washed the blood off, running his fingers over the smooth richness of new scars. Another for his collection: a life of risky behavior mapped.

The door opened behind him and he yelped, charging towards it. He was greeted by his grandmother's huffing face, her basket overfull as always. He laughed, tugging it from her and pecking her cheek.

"You should have taken me," he chided, ushering her towards her chair and bringing a cup of cool red tea.

"I didn't want to wake you," she shushed, sipping gratefully. "Though I did spy a nice boy. He's on Miguel's stall."

"You can't be matchmaking for me when I'm already claimed, Grandmother." Leon rolled his eyes at her.

"You aren't claimed yet, Leon, you may as well enjoy yourself. Since you insist on rushing towards the Pale Lady, I may as well get to see you enjoy yourself too."

Leon smiled, plucking his own tea from the fridge and sitting across from her. "It seems bad luck to invite someone else."

"Your mother would not want the life she bargained for to be a lonely one," Leticia stated, sipping again.

"I don't know what sort of life she expected but the college didn't agree with her vision."

"They were scared: it is not the same. They lost many. They still remember the four hundred dead at Tlatelolco. And your mother."

"They should not be cowards while espousing the virtues of learning," Leon muttered, chewing the inside of his cheek.

"Not everyone is as brave as you, little lion," Leticia smiled, eyeing his slumped shoulders. "And not everyone could survive what you have, blessing or no. Have you been fighting again?"

"Two of Franciscos tried to break in."

"They must be new. Francisco is better than that." She frowned, peeling an orange and handing him a segment.

"I don't think any of them are good, Grandmother."

"None of his would have killed your mother," she said pointedly.

He chewed thoughtfully on the fruit, running his tongue over the flesh. "It's not exactly a high standard."

"But it is the one we have for now."

"You're right, for now it is." He nodded.

"Do you want to come to the market tomorrow? Miguel asks after you. And I could introduce his new boy."

"Why is this boy so nice?" Leon asked with an indulgent smirk.

"He's a fine boy. Foreign, I think, he's a bit pale, but tall and polite and a lovely smile." Her eyes twinkled. "He looks strong. A little skinny, but I would fix that for you." She winked and Leon snorted into his tea.

He listened to her gossip from the market, smiling at her stories. He was lulled close to dozing by the time she finished; the familiarity of her voice mixing with the morning's heat.

He stood, stretching before kissing her on the head as he tugged his shirt back on.

"What trouble are you off to now?" she asked, following him into the kitchen.

"Just to work," he said, kissing the photo of Rosy. "You want me to pick anything up?"

"No, I brought back half the market, we'll be fine."

*

He loped out of the house, buttoning his shirt as he went. The bar wasn't open for a few hours but he liked to be in when the delivery arrived. He wasn't officially on the payroll, but Naima, the boss, liked having him around.

The truck was pulling up as he arrived, the chubby driver, Jorge, scrambling out of the cab. Leon nodded to him, kicking at the dust coating the tires.

"Naima about?" he asked, wiping sweat off with a much-abused handkerchief.

"I'll check," Leon said, walking through the back and calling out.

"What do you want?" she shouted.

"Jorge wants to see you for the order," he yelled back, wedging the door open.

"Always some other thing," she muttered as she came, wiping ink off her hands. They moved to her dark hair, twisting it into a bun. "What is it?" she barked at the driver.

"We had to switch out the anejo, because of the festivals. You have extra vodka instead."

"Is that all? No one cares." She ran a critical eye over the dispatch sheet, then scribbled a signature. The pen went into her bun and she clipped back into her office.

"You cared enough to order it," Jorge muttered, helping Leon unload.

"She's busy. It'll be a better day tomorrow." Leon shrugged. He was grateful for his lack of vest, he was already sweating.

"If you say so." The driver sighed, waving his cap for some breeze. "You and her a thing?"

"No!" Leon laughed, shaking his head.

"What does she keep you around for then?" Jorge asked, eyeing him.

"I'm security."

"You're tiny. Strong looking," Jorge added hastily, seeing Leon's glare. "But tiny."

"I'm good at what I do, short guys have better reach. I can get in and have your kidneys for pie before you've even hit me." Leon laughed, swiping the cap from pudgy fingers and planting it firmly on Jorge's head.

"Point taken." Jorge grumbled, shutting the back and climbing into his cab.

"Safe trip back," Leon called after the truck. He trotted back in, a crate under one arm.

"You need anything or want me out of the way?" he called to Naima.

"Out of the way, I need room to do my work."

"All right, I'll finish off the delivery. Where's Alicia?"

"Doctor's visit, she'll be in just before opening."

"Want me to do the tables then?"

"If it will keep you out of my way, yes."

"All right, boss," he nodded.

The morning went quick with the work, the bar stocked and spotless before the chef rolled in.

"How goes the day, David?" Leon called, leaning at the galley window.

"Terrible, some jackasses broke into my daughter's flat!"

"Sorry for your troubles."

"They didn't even manage to take anything, just busted in her window, then scarpered."

"At least it's just the cost of the window then?" Leon asked.

"I suppose so. It's poor, though, the police aren't bothered."

"They never do when they're getting paid to look the other way," Leon agreed, and the chef clapped a hand over his mouth.

"Sorry, Leon, I should never have said that."

"It's fine, it's true. Alicia and Elizabeth should be here shortly, the delivery is in the storeroom."

"That's great, thank you. How is the queen?"

"Needs peace to do the books. She'll be sunshine once they're done."

"I'll make her favourite as the special then, sweeten her up."

"Good plan." Leon winked, ducking away from the window and wiping the bar down again.

*

Leon opened the shutters and took his spot at the bar, flicking through his dog-eared copy of *Fahrenheit 451*. He had read a lot, and loved many, but Bradbury created a world he could feel. He was here for a few reasons, to keep the peace and to help out behind the bar when things got busy, but he got to read during the quiet times.

"What has that frown on your face, young one?" Elizabeth asked, leaning against the bar. Her plump chest sat on the wood and Leon studiously looked away. She knew his leanings and delighted in being inappropriate.

"Just thinking about things," Leon said, sipping his lemonade.

"Heavy things if your brows are anything to go by."

"I need to speak to Francisco."

"Why would you go riling that old dog?"

"Two of his pups tried breaking into the house."

"Silly boys," Elizabeth sighed. "You caught them?"

"Got one of them in the chin with my old baseball bat." Leon smirked, winking at her cackling laughter.

"That's our Leon, always looking after us," she grinned, ruffling his hair.

He rolled his eyes and combed it back to his preferred neatness. "Less of that, I can't defend you if I look like a scruffy thug."

"I'll leave you be. Can you help out with the food today? Alicia is slow and we don't want grumbling customers."

"Hurt her ankle again?"

"Not that, no." Elizabeth leaned in, beckoning him. "She's in a woman's way, but she isn't telling anyone yet. Rafael can't get the priest to marry them until next month and they don't want people to know until after."

Leon nodded, glancing over at Alicia. He imagined the ghost of a bump under her apron and smiled. She returned it in a bright flash. He went back to his book, eyeing the tables.

*

They were recovering from the lunchtime rush when the stranger arrived. He sat at the bar, a few seats from Leon, and ordered a rare steak with strong beer. His accent was off, almost local but rough round the edges, snagging Leon's ears. His skin wasn't white but he was certainly paler than anyone else.

"You work at Miguel's stall?" Leon asked, glancing up to meet his eyes. They were the rich amber of a cat's.

"Yes, how did you know?"

"My grandmother met you this morning. Stocky lady, streaks in the front of her hair."

"Leticia! She was charming. Miguel mentioned she had a grandson, but he spoke like you were a child."

"He remembers when I was, I've lived with Grandmother a while." Leon shrugged.

"I'm Michael," the stranger grinned, holding a hand out.

"Leon." He took the hand, shaking it firmly. It was cool from his beer.

"So why are you lurking in a bar on a lazy afternoon, Leon?" Michael asked, slicing into his steak. Blood ran onto his plate, settling around the crescents of green beans.

"I'm the help. I keep out ruffians and cover the occasional table."

"And how do I get you to cover mine?" Michael asked with a flick of his eyes to the stool beside him. His hair rustled in its low pony tail, catching the lights of the bar.

"You're already next to me, is that not covered?" Leon laughed, tapping his fingers along his book.

"Maybe I feel the need for extra protection? I'm new here, I need someone to show me the town."

"I'm more well known for the bad side, aren't I, Elizabeth?" Leon asked, laughing at her blush.

"He's a lovely young man who has a habit of getting into fights," the older woman commented, busying herself with taking the empty bottles out.

"Fights?" Michael asked, watching Leon.

"I have a low tolerance for violence. I tend to stop it."

"By getting involved?" Michael chuckled, those amber eyes flicking over Leon's chest. Leon saw why his grandmother said skinny. The man was thin but his shirt stretched nicely at the shoulders and his arms ran in smooth curves under the sleeves.

"Ending a fight is important." Leon shrugged, his face heating. "How old are you?"

"Twenty-three," Michael replied with a scandalised laugh, "Why, do I seem old?"

"No, I just wondered why you were working with Miguel."

"That's just for money. I'm traveling. I get to a place and then earn enough for moving on. Working a stall lets me see the borough while still having some free time. Speaking of which, when do you get off?"

"I finish at six."

"Take me sightseeing."

Leon coughed his sip of lemonade back into the glass, eyeing the man over the rim.

"I can't tonight," he said after he recovered. "But I wouldn't mind another night."

"Touring some other starry-eyed young thing round the town?" Michael asked with a tilt of his chin.

"No, I have to sort out something for my grandmother."

"Want a hand?"

"You don't even know what it is," laughed Leon.

"So long as it's not skinning dogs, I'm certain I'll be able to assist."

"I would need you to sit in a bar."

"Oh no, a bar! How will I cope?"

"It might take a while," Leon continued, rolling his eyes.

A sound caught his attention: the clean crunch of glass breaking. He looked up, seeing a stricken-looking Alicia at a table with two men. Leon could see she was near tears and hopped off his seat. "Save that thought," he told Michael, brushing his shoulder as he passed.

"You stupid cow, now look what you've done," shouted an unfortunately familiar voice.

"I didn't touch the jug, sir, he was pouring it," Alicia said. Leon could hear the tremor in her voice and slipped next to her.

"Do we have a problem, gentlemen?" he asked with a tight smile.

"What are you doing here?" spat Twitchy. A wonderful bruise was blooming purple along his jaw.

"I work here. What happened, Alicia?"

"They wouldn't let me pour their water, the short one grabbed it off me," she whispered, sniffling.

"You go get a fresh jug, eh?" Leon suggested kindly, steering her away and glaring at them over his shoulder.

"I want my meal free, she got water all over me," Crowbar near shouted.

"You keep the noise up and I'll have you out the door. I already dealt with you once today."

"What you gonna do?" Twitchy sneered.

"I'll go home and get my bat."

"Let's leave, Antonio," Crowbar said, jostling Twitchy out of his seat. "You wouldn't want food that's been near that freak anyway."

"Such assholes," muttered Leon, returning to his perch as they traipsed out.

"Troublemakers?" Michael asked.

"Just some druggies not on their leash yet."

"Addicts can be assholes," Michael nodded, sipping his beer.

"They'll be better once their boss has them trained."

"And until then?"

"We keep an eye on them. They misbehave then ..." He punched a first into his palm and smirked at Michael.

"Direct action, I like it," laughed Michael, amber eyes sparkling. Leon hadn't seen eyes like them before. He wanted to see them more.

*

They passed the remaining hour in comfortable chatter and Leon was happy to clock out.

"Don't they need someone for the evening?" Michael asked as they meandered towards Leon's house.

"I have my grandmother to worry over, so I just do the day."

"You love her a lot."

"She took me in when I was six, raised me up. It was risky, I could have been targeted for a contract, but she did."

"Your mother?"

"Killed."

"Shit, sorry."

"It's fine, same old story. She was a journalist, pissed off the wrong politician, got shot. One of many, it's just what they did back then"

"The Dirty War was brutal," Michael hummed.

"But Grandmother took me in anyway. She had to sacrifice a lot for me, so I look after her."

"A grandson most could only dream of."

"I try."

"Most of my family aren't around, but that's because of work. They all moved for different jobs. Event organisers. Lots of following the crowds for festivals."

"Sounds exciting." Leon smiled, letting his hand brush against Michael's. Michael gripped Leon's little finger in his own, giving a short squeeze. "I bet they're busy with the new year coming, big parties for the new millennium."

"They just adore it: the crowds, the drinks, the energy. It's in the blood."

*

They reached Leon's house and his stomach dropped. The door was open: no lights. His heart hammered as he bolted forward, pushing through the door and shouting for his grandmother.

He stopped as he reached the kitchen, a howl ripping out of him. The smell of the blood was heavy, cloying in his throat and strangling off his cry. She was on the floor, face down, one armed stretched out towards their shrine. There was an ugly gash down her neck and blood pooled around her head in a dark halo. No breath disturbed it.

Rough hands were pulling his shoulders, manhandling him away from her.

"Don't look," hissed a voice in his ear, tugging him close and backing out of the room. He was dumped into a chair and immediately made to get up again, receiving a rough shove to the shoulders. "Don't look!" Michael repeated, pinning him down with his weight.

"I need the shrine," Leon choked out.

"You need to call the police," Michael countered.

"They won't do anything, the boss pays them off." He was too hot, the living room too small for both of them and his rage too.

"Shit."

"I need to go to the shrine. And I need to cover her. Get that blanket." Leon pointed numbly to his grandmother's chair. Blood was loud in his ears, rushing through him like a river. Michael grabbed the wool cover and passed it to Leon's hands, standing in the doorway.

"I can do it, if you'd prefer."

"No," Leon said, pushing past him and swallowing against the smell. He gently rolled her over, putting her hands on her chest and her rosary on top of them. He closed her eyes, draping the colourful blanket over her and kissing her forehead. She was cold.

He moved to the shrine, kissing the photo of Rosy, then focusing on the grinning skull icon. He stared hard, tugging on his connection.

"Why do you call to me?" He heard her behind him, a voice of dead leaves and dust creeping over his scalp.

"My grandmother is dead, murdered."

"Yes."

"We are protected from violence," Leon cried, his voice cracking as he glanced to the body.

"You are protected," the voice replied. Leon turned and saw a tall woman with the face of a skull and robes red as his grandmother's blood. He looked away again, his sobs shaking his chest. "She has my favour, and I will take her over the river to the next world, but your mother's prayer was only for you."

"Does my protection still stand?"

"Yes, it will until it is your time." The voice made underneath Leon's skin seethe: he wanted to scratch until blood poured down his arms.

"Then I ask for your kindness in taking her over."

"She already has that. She served me well with you."

"She didn't believe in you. She still prayed to Him."

"She did," the skull agreed. "But many people pray to more than one of us."

"Can you tell me who did it?"

"Why do you ask me a question you already know the answer to?" the voice was a droll whisper, the itch under Leon's skin near unbearable.

"For confirmation, Lady. Never to waste your time."

"It was the two you interrupted."

"Thank you," Leon said, kneeling before her.

She was gone in a rustle of dead things and Leon saw Michael leaning against the door.

"When Miguel said you were touched by death, I thought he meant you were unlucky," he said, his brows high.

"It's been argued I'm both."

"Are you going to call the police?"

"No. I'm going to have my meeting."

*

The place Francisco ran was a pretentious thing, mood lighting and knock-off art to mask the mob rooms in the back. Leon stalked through the gloom towards the stools, nodding to the bartender.

"Julio, can you look after my friend?" Leon called, clapping Michael's shoulder.

"Of course," Julio replied, a smile ruffling his tufted moustache. The bar was busy and Michael should be safe.

"I'll be back shortly, have your beer."

Michael nodded, slipping into a stool and chatting to Julio. Leon didn't know why the foreigner was still here but it helped focus his mind. His coat billowed out as he jogged up the stairs, blood pulsing at his temples. He barged through the door.

"Leon, an unexpected pleasure," Francisco smiled. He didn't move from behind his desk. He was a toad of a man: thin hair slicked back and gold glittering at his throat. His suit, valiantly stretched over his stomach, was shiny under the electric lights. Two guards flanked his desk, eyeing Leon.

"If I'm unexpected, then your crew is getting slack on you, Francisco." Leon's gaze flicked to the men.

"Truthfully, they aren't. I did hear two new ones tried to break into your house. I've explained our understanding."

"One of them stabbed me," Leon barked, yanking his shirt to show the new scars. "And when they knew I was at work, they went back to the house and killed my grandmother." The smell of smoke and leather was grating in his nose, the hot lights burning his puffy eyes.

"No one in my crew would hurt Leticia, she's off-limits."

"No one else would be stupid enough. I know it was them."

"You saw it?" Francisco challenged.

"I asked those who did."

"I'll deal with them." The older man shrugged.

"Not good enough."

"Leon, I cannot be seen to be handing men over, that's preposterous," Francisco laughed.

"Give me them or I will take them. You know I can."

"I know you have been very lucky despite interfering with my business," Francisco replied, leaning over his desk. "Luck can run out."

"Do you want to have one of your statues test how lucky I am?" Leon asked, slipping his bat free. "Feel like paying someone to get blood out of that suit?"

"We can take him," the left-hand goon muttered, hand slipping into his jacket.

Leon smirked, blowing him a kiss. "Try it."

"Fine, get rid of him." Francisco sighed, nodding.

A pop sounded and Leon felt the bullet go into his chest, laughing through the burn of it. Pain was an amazing focal point. He took a deep breath and turned towards the man, gripping his bat. Leon leaned into the swing, the dull twang of metal confirming connection with the man's skull. The man groaned and folded in half, onto his knees. Leon raised the bat high and brought it down sharp. A cracking rippled through the room and the body flattened.

"You next?" Leon panted to the other one. The bullet was still a bright heat in his lung and he knew he would have to cough it out.

"Don't just gape, kill him!" Francisco shouted.

The goon lunged, a blade drawn. Leon swatted his arm away and grabbed on, twisting around his thick torso to avoid being crushed. A hand grabbed him, yanking his jacket and bringing the blade arcing into his stomach. Leon hissed air and brought his fist down on the man's wrist, jarring the hand open. They scrabbled for it, but Leon got purchase, stabbing the man's throat and ripping the blade forward. He spluttered against the stream of blood that poured on to his face, gagging and rolling out from under the weight of the gasping man.

"Where are they, Francisco?" he asked, palming the switchblade and standing. He shuddered at the kick of four bullets pounding into his chest, coughing up some of the blood he'd swallowed.

"What the fuck are you?"

"You know me." Leon smiled, his teeth red and blood slick down the column of his throat. "You know why our house was left alone. Now you can keep wasting bullets on me, and watch me keep talking to you, or you can tell me where they are."

Leon leaned over the desk, pressing his forehead into the shaking pistol Francisco held. "Which would you prefer?" he asked, eyeing the cartel leader along the barrel.

"They're in the stockroom."

"Thank you. If there are guards—"

"There won't be." Francisco spat, wiping his gun down and slipping it away. "I won't throw more men at you, devil."

"Good to know we understand each other," Leon nodded. He scooped up his bat, leaving the office. He jogged down to the steps towards the store room, the switchblade nestled in his pocket.

*

He found Michael still at the bar, sipping something expensive.

"Julio thought I might need something stronger than beer," Michael supplied to Leon's raised brow.

"Surely the decor isn't that bad," Leon scoffed.

"He said you were getting killed and this was to lessen the shock."

"Polite of him, we must tip." Leon glanced to Julio and flashed his stained smile. The smell of the alcohol was starting to give him a headache, though that could also have been the adrenaline.

"You have blood on you." Michael ran a finger along his neck, just below the collar line.

"I'll fix it back home."

"You're going back there?"

"I need to call the police about Grandmother."

"Now you want them?"

"They'll do their part," Leon shrugged. "The rest is dealt with." He began to cough, spitting into a discarded glass. If Michael heard the clink of metal, he was polite enough not to mention it.

They walked back towards Leon's home, silent in the warm evening.

"You think there will be retaliation?" Michael asked as they passed the threshold.

"I don't think Francisco wants to lose more people yet. Maybe in a while."

"Will you wait for it?"

"I don't know," Leon replied, huffing at the smell of blood still seeping through the house.

He stalled as he entered the living room, the Pale Lady sat neatly on his grandmother's chair.

"You have been busy, Leon," she said in her wheezing whisper.

"I have." He nodded, glancing at Michael. He was watching the skeleton-faced woman. "I sought vengeance for Leticia."

"She would not have approved of your methods."

"It's the only thing they understand," he shot back, forcing the bristling out of his shoulders.

"Humans are always so sure of absolutes," she breathed, the eyeless skull looking over him. "Gods know things are and aren't, and reach everything between."

"I don't understand, Lady."

"I am tired, Leon. I have a proposition."

"Yes?"

"I have undertaken this role for hundreds of years and my face has changed as my people did. I wish to rest, and I wish to live. For that, I must find someone to do as I did. I want you."

Leon felt his world tilt sideways and it wasn't until Michael's hands were pulling him upright he realised he'd collapsed. His head rang with the breathy words. He noted the uncomfortable itch of another bullet coming up his throat.

"Why me?" he choked out, coughing around the metal leaving his body.

"You understand the price of death, and have dealt it. I do not kill, that is my husband's role, but I help souls pass on. You have the kindness and the cruelty to do this."

"And what about your husband? If I take your role, he will be without a wife."

"Our kind are not really of your genders, Leon," the woman laughed, chiding. "You make us these for your worship, but souls do not have such a thing. You would not, if you took up my mantle."

"Could I leave?"

"As I have, yes."

Leon hugged his knees to his chest. He thought of his grandmother and seeing her in the afterlife. His mother, her smile and gentle voice.

"All right," he whispered. He stood and moved towards her. "Yes."

"I am pleased," she hissed, standing to embrace him, "Mictlantecuhtli has been so impressed with you." Leon tensed, a chill moving through him.

"Mictlantecuhtli?"

"My husband, the Pale Man."

"I thought I was only watched by you."

"Only she watched you growing," Michael said, stepping into the room and smiling at Leon. He had too many teeth, his hungry grin showing them crammed in close together, and he stroked along Leon's arm with his cool hand. "But I do look forward to seeing what you become. And to continue our sightseeing."

"You want me after those murders?" Leon croaked, crowded between the two beings.

"I wanted you after your decision for vengeance, though I appreciate humans tend to require a little more time."

Leon nodded mutely, his heart hammering in his throat.

"Let me show you," the Pale Lady said, taking his face in soft hands and bringing it to meet hers. He fell into the kiss, the rushing of his blood, and Michael's hum of approval guiding him to the sound of a great river.

***

The Toughest Nut To Crack
by George Karram, United States

"Gooooooooood evening, ladies and gentlemen, and welcome to another edition of America's favorite family TV game show," (together with the audience, the announcer shouts out in pacing fashion) "THE ... TOUGHEST ... NUT ... TO ... CRAAAAAAAACK!!!!!!!!"(Accompanied by the sound of crackling thunder.)

"And here's the star of our show, America's leading nutcracker, Wiley Jack Smiley."

Wiley Jack enters smiling and waving to raucous audience applause. Armed with his twelve-foot bullwhip and dressed in his traditional black three-piece suit, Wiley Jack doffs the ten-gallon hat that bears his initials in silver and heads over to the podium, calmly waiting for the hooting and hollering to subside. The two torches that light the podium with their flames give Jack a sinister glow.

Removing the bullwhip from his shoulder, Wiley Jack places it lovingly on the podium in front of him and in a display of affection, raises his index and middle fingers in tandem to his lips, kisses the tips and tenderly places them on the bullwhip. Speaking softly, Wiley Jack intones, "Crack well tonight, Bertha. Help them (the audience joins in) SEE THE TRUTH!"

Jack continues, "Our show tonight features three active addicts who just won't get clean and sober, or won't stop gambling. The winner tonight gets an all-expenses paid, one-year stay at the world famous River Palms Rehabilitation Institute, located in Beverly Hills, California, whether they like it or not! And the losers? The losers get to go back to their lives of desperate insanity; dying a little more, one day at a time." (The audience boos.)

"So let's go meet our contestants." The lights darken on stage as a booming drumroll heightens the anticipation of the studio audience, and three ghostly figures walk unsteadily to their appointed podiums. Wiley Jack continues, "First up is a suspended grammar school gym teacher from Independence, Missouri, Ms. Janice 'Apples' Martin."

Wiley Jack takes his bullwhip, rears back, and with a practiced flick of his wrist, cracks it over her head as a spotlight from above illuminates a startled and scared Ms. Martin. "Say hello to the nation, Apples." Dressed in an orange prison jumpsuit and looking like a bus hit and dragged her fifty feet, she smiles a weak, fractured smile, waves to the audience, and says, "Hi everybody. My name is Janice Martin, and I think I'll be the toughest nut to crack!" The audience jeers derisively as Janice, gaining confidence, just waves them off.

Looking down at his podium, Wiley Jack continues by saying, "So Janice, can you tell us how you got that adorable nickname, Apples?"

After repeatedly clearing her throat and coughing, Janice regains her breath and composure and begins to explain, "Well, Jack, I ..." Jack interrupts her by asking, "That's quite a cough you have there, Janice. Smoker's cough? Perhaps you'd like a nice cigarette now to calm your nerves?" Nodding gratefully, Janice reaches into her jumpsuit, pulling out a cigarette and lighter and begins the process. At which point Wiley Jack once again rears back, and unfurling his whip, yanks the lit cigarette from Janice's astonished face, raising a bright red welt in the process. The audience roars its approval as Jack kindly says to her, "Perhaps later, okay, Apples? So you were telling us how you got your nickname before I so rudely interrupted you. Please continue."

Rubbing her still smarting cheek, Janice continues on. "Well, Jack, I like to drink, and I discovered apple martinis at the age of fourteen. I liked them so much that I started bringing them to high school in a plaid Thermos®; my teachers thought it was the beverage from my lunch box for lunch, and (giggling) it was, so nobody bothered me as I got lit up day after day in high school. I make the best apple martinis, Jack, and neither you nor the audience can stop me from drinking them all day, every day!"

The audience begins to clap and chant in rhythmic fashion, "CRACK HER JACK, CRACK HER JACK." Jack raises both hands, palms facing out toward the audience and gently bounces them downward in an unspoken sign for the audience to simmer down, and says, "Patience my friends, let's meet the other contestants first, shall we?

"Contestant number two is an unemployed methamphetamine cook awaiting trial, hailing from Lubbock, Texas. Mr. Rafael Serrano." Jack takes his whip and flicks it over Rafael's head as the overhead spotlight illuminates a frail and scrawny young man with long, greasy black hair and green teardrop tattoos running down from the corner of his right eye. Rafael's wearing a black Oakland Raiders skullcap doesn't sit well with Wiley Jack. So once again he flicks Bertha and in the blink of an eye he removes and retrieves the skullcap and in the process he draws blood from Rafael's forehead, causing the green teardrops to mix with red. The oohs and aahs of the amped-up crowd bring a warm smile to Wiley Jack's face.

"Sorry about that, Rafael. I thought the producers told you only I get to wear a hat on this show. (The audience giggles in appreciation of Jack's dry wit and Rafael's pain, causing Jack to wait patiently for the laughter to peter out before continuing.) So you're an unemployed meth cook? That must be tough on your two wives, four girlfriends, and, how many is it, (looking down at his notes) eleven children? Your mother must be so proud of you."

A defiant Rafael dabs his bleeding forehead with the back of his hand, turns his head, spits on the floor, and snarls, "That's what I think of you and Bertha, *tu madre gringo*." The audience roars with laughter as Wiley Jack, feigning hurt feelings and holding his hands to his chest, soulfully replies, "I'm so sorry, Rafael, if I've hurt you and your feelings. However, Bertha here isn't so forgiving, (holding up the bullwhip and talking to it) are you, girl?" Wiley Jack cracks the whip again and Rafael wails in pain as the tip of the whip bites into his left earlobe; tearing out a diamond stud earring in the process. With blood now trickling from Rafael's ear and forehead Wiley Jack says to no one in particular, "Will somebody please get this man some tissues for his issues?"

Acting with one mind, the entire audience reaches under their seats, grabbing handfuls of white tissues, and proceeds to turn the studio into a snowstorm of waving Kleenex®. Wiley Jack is moved by the response. With tongue firmly planted in cheek, he says, "Thank you, audience. Your concern for our friend Rafael is heartwarming."

Wiley Jack continues on. "Hey audience, perhaps you remember our third and final contestant, a compulsive gambler, and ex-hospital administrator from Ft. Lauderdale, Florida, Mr. Tom 'Action' Jackson. (The audience jeers.) Tom was convicted for embezzling nearly five million dollars from The Children's Cancer Hospital building fund, causing its ultimate collapse and irreparable damage to dying children and their families." Jack cracks Bertha once again over the third contestant's head, and Tom "Action" Jackson emerges from the darkness under the glare of a white hot spotlight.

Appearing calm and collected, Action Jackson waves to the jeering crowd. Wiley Jack looks down at his notes and continues, "It says here you were a guest of the State of Florida for eleven years at Ocala State

Prison. You must have been very popular with the other inmates, being locked up for stealing money from sick children and all. Care to share some of your fun times with the studio audience, Action?"

Slightly bent at the waist and leaning on his podium with his forearms, hands clasped in front, Action begins tapping his index fingers together while thoughtfully replying, "Actually there's not much to tell, Jack. Coming from a legal background to the job as the chief financial officer of The Children's Cancer Hospital, other inmates came to me to help writing their appeals. My writing skills helped to free quite a few fellow prisoners, and at the same time won me a certain level of protect—"

Wiley Jack had heard enough, and rearing Bertha back, he cracked his bullwhip and cleanly split Action's upper lip, causing blood to spew from his mouth. The crowd started chanting, "We want the twins, we want the twins." Wiley Jack acquiesced by slamming the red "Medic" button on his podium.

Red lights begin flashing, accompanied by an overhead siren, signaling the arrival of an ambulance. But it wasn't an ambulance that drove onto the stage; rather it was an enormous Harley Chopper ridden by Dr. Lauren 'Twin' Peaks.

Dressed in a shiny black leather jumpsuit that may or may not have been painted on, open to the waist, revealing the endowments that earned her the well-deserved nickname of "Twin Peaks," Dr. Peaks climbed off the motorcycle and carrying her black medic bag, scurried over to a profusely bleeding Tom Jackson.

Cracking her gum, Dr. Peaks turned her back on the audience and bent over to more closely examine Action's injury, eliciting whistles and catcalls from the mostly male audience. Ignoring the audience, Dr. Peaks gently places her hand, led by her index finger, under the chin of Action, and with thumb and middle finger, raising his head ever so slightly to stem the flow of blood. Turning to Wiley Jack, in a high-pitched, little girl voice, Dr. Peaks said, "Geez Jack, you really got him good. I'm going to have to sew him up right away with no anesthesia!"

Looking down at a surprisingly calm Action Jackson while still cocking his chin skyward, Dr. Peaks reached into her bag with her free hand, removed a needle, thread, and gauze pad and in one lightning fast motion, cleaned and sewed the wound up tight as a drum. Looking down at her new patient, Dr. Peaks offered him a mild scolding, "Now you be a good boy, Tom, okay? No more upsetting Wiley Jack for you, mister. And, oh yeah, you might want to go see a plastic surgeon today, okay, honey?"

Turning to Wiley Jack, Dr. Peaks asked, "We still on for dinner later at my place, Jackie?" Jack smiles and says, "Sure thing, ding-a-ling, I'll bring the motor oil and the marshmallow fluff. See you at ten."

The woofs and catcalls from the audience cause Dr. Peaks to blush and wave them off with two hands. Climbing back on her Harley, she starts it up, revs the engine a few times, and peels out to flashing red lights and wailing sirens; and the audience loves it.

Wiley Jack begins to explain to Action why Bertha entered the fray. "So how's your shoulder Tom?" Lisping painfully through a split lip, a confused Action says, "My thoulder is fine, Jack, why do you asthk?" Wiley Jack smiles and says, "I thought it might be a little sore from patting yourself on the back. Ya' know, that making lemonade out of lemons kind of thing. Helping your fellow convicts get out of jail; very admirable indeed. Except, who helped the sick and dying children, who is now helping their shattered families?" Wiley Jack's smile turns dark and foreboding. "Not you, of course, you didn't have the time. You chose to help your cellmates because there was something in it for you, right, Action?"

The audience boos and jeers are near deafening, and Wiley Jack has to raise his voice to be heard. "And who's going to help your parents and two brothers, who you forced into bankruptcy after your release from prison by telling them you were going straight, begging them to put up their homes and the family plumbing business as collateral so you could begin 'restitution' to the families you harmed, because it was the 'right' thing to do; except you kept gambling, and losing, until all their money was gone too?"

Raising his voice even more to be heard above the increasing din of the audience, Wiley Jack roared, "How do you sleep at night, Tom? What do you see when you look in the mirror?" Seventy-one-year-old Tom "Action" Jackson closed his eyes and silently began moving his lips, lost in thought and deep in prayer.

Wiley Jack lets his questions to Action hang in the air for a moment, knowing no answers are forthcoming from the praying mantis that is Tom Jackson. Turning to the studio audience, Jack asks the question they've been waiting for. "So audience, are you ready to have our contestants stroll down Memory Lane?"

The audience begins a rhythmic chant, "We want the cones, we want the cones, we want the cones!!!" Jack smiles at the three contestants and says, "You heard 'em, panel, it's time to sit down, relax, and take a hard look at what you've done. Maybe that will help crack your shells, (smiling at the audience) sort of like dropping a cold egg into boiling water." This time the audience participates by hungrily flipping open the left arm of their chairs to remove the handy three-pack of rotting eggs graciously provided by the producers, viscously hurling them at the contestants with vim and vigor as the five-second overhead clock ticked down to zero.

Wiley Jack, who was ducking for cover behind his podium to avoid the fusillade of eggs, re-emerged unscathed with three towels slung over one shoulder and Bertha over the other. He then walked over to the dripping contestants, quickly wiping down their startled faces and tossing the used rags to the ground.

Turning to the audience, Wiley Jack asked rhetorically, "Where were we? Oh yes, the cones!" He then unfurled Bertha, and with a flick of his practiced hand, attached his bullwhip to an overhead lever situated above the contestants' heads and gave it a pull. From the floor below the contestants, out popped three straight backed metal chairs with matching armrests. The force of their appearance, coupled with the simultaneous tilting backwards of the floor on which they were standing, causes the contestants to lose their balance and plop into the chairs. The harsh, white spotlights fade as garish and glowing red lights that adorn the outline of all three chairs come to life.

Instantly, gleaming metal straps from the arms and legs of the chairs slam shut on Janice, Rafael and Tom, locking them in place. While all three knew this lockdown was coming, the gulf between expectations and reality is great indeed. Janice and Rafael are wide eyed and sweating profusely, nervously clenching and unclenching their newly immobilized hands, their eyes darting between Wiley Jack, the audience and each other in anticipation of the horror to come. Not Tom though. Tom stares straight ahead with unfocused eyes, looking like a man aimlessly waiting for a dental appointment.

Turning his attention from the contestants to the audience, Wiley Jack hushes the pulsating crowd by placing his index finger vertically to his lips, and reluctantly, silence is finally heard. Wiley Jack seizes that temporary silence to continue the proceedings.

"Before the show, we had our contestants draw straws to determine who would be first in line to view the carnage they've caused, and Apples, you were the winner. Sir Reginald, her mask, please."

From offstage enters Sir Reginald, a very tall, thin man in his early sixties, with long, flowing white hair surrounding his balding pate, walking extremely erect and wearing a black tuxedo with tails. In his white gloved hands he carefully carries a purple pillow encrusted with sparkling diamonds and sapphires. Atop the pillow rests a silver half-mask that would ensure Apples wouldn't be able to close her eyes during her time under the cone; as tiny, painful hooks on the inside of the mask were designed to pull open and keep open the eyelids of the contestant.

Sir Reginald gently placed the pillow on the floor next to her, and with both hands, gingerly picked up the mask, pinkies flaring, as if he were carrying a hot bowl of soup. He then affixed it to Janice's face, ignoring the yelping and moaning from her. After a bit of tugging and straightening of the mask, Sir Reginald turned to Wiley Jack, and sporting a toothless, decaying smile, gave him two thumbs up. In his cockney English accent, Sir Reginald declared, "She is prepared for the viewing, sir."

The audience applauded its approval, whereupon Sir Reginald faced them, bowed deeply, and slowly strode from the stage.

The red lights embedded in Janice "Apples" Martin's chair begin to flash, as a transparent, Lucite cone slowly begins to descend from the ceiling. Approximately six feet in height, with a circumference of the same, the cone is a circular movie screen that rotates around the viewer. Atop the cone was affixed a flat lid and black cable that was the feed to the screen. Hermetically sealed against all noise, and climate controlled, the cone had the appearance of a clear stick of dynamite with a fuse. Which perhaps, in a way, it was.

Wiley Jack adjusted his microphone and said, "Can you hear me, Apples?" Janice nodded her head in affirmation, whereupon Jack turned to the studio audience, and raising his voice declared, "THEN LET THE HEALING BEGIN!!!"

The audience settled in, reaching under their seats for their Wiley Jack Accessory Kits. Each gift box contains 3D black glasses, a small bag of popcorn, Twizzlers, Milk Duds, and three three-by-five cards containing a colorful hologram of each of the contestants. As each card is slowly turned by hand, the picture morphs from a smiling, happy contestant into a miserable, snarling monster.

On the back of each picture is a compilation of vital statistics that painted a gruesome and comprehensive picture of the contestant's offenses; dates of arrests, felony convictions, people harmed or killed, prison time and the like.

The pictures acted as interactive Playbills; much like the kind handed out by those lovely old tip-hungry ushers at a Broadway show. The audience donned the glasses, the house lights faded to black, and the show began.

Apples is suddenly surrounded by the sights, sounds, and smells of her drinking past and present. Ever so slowly, the screen begins to turn. First up are Janice's high school days. Dressed in a green plaid skirt with a large gold safety pin at mid-thigh and button down white blouse, brown hair pulled back into a shoulder length ponytail, Apples seems to be a painfully shy and quiet fourteen year old. Walking the hallways alone of her new high school, keeping the comfort and safety of the walls close at hand, she has the look of someone who would rather be elsewhere, anywhere but here.

The hallway scene slowly spins from view, replaced by Janice sneaking her first apple martini at a Memorial Day barbecue in her backyard. The transformation from shy and awkward to outgoing and self-confident occurs quickly as Apples becomes the life of the party, telling jokes and dancing barefoot in the grass without a care in the world.

The backyard scene fades as the new scene comes to life: Janice filling her Thermos® with apple martinis late at night with her parents sound asleep in front of a blaring TV. Quietly and carefully measuring the correct amounts of vodka, green apple schnapps, and lemon juice, one eye on her sleeping parents and one on the all-important pour, Janice completes her task and breathes a quiet sigh of relief. She then replaces the missing alcohol with tap water, knowing her parents won't be able to discern any difference, blaming the watered-down version of vodka and schnapps on the poor, inexpensive quality they buy.

Moving on, the screen proceeds to the night of Janice's senior prom. Drunk and sloppy, Apples is coaxed into a classmate's Chevy van, where three young men are lying in wait to sexually assault her. Hands fly and clothes are torn; however, the proceedings end prematurely when Janice vomits on her attackers, causing them to howl and curse. They then toss her half-naked body into the parking lot, whereupon they speed away into the night.

Janice has no recollection of this happening to her, and like the audience, is seeing this for the first time. Onstage, she is a terrible sight to behold; thin wisps of blood adorn her cheeks from the hooks in her mask, her eyes pulled open and terror filled. While she can't hear the audience's catcalls, she can see the venom being spewed at her.

And the screen rolls on ...

To a mid-twenties Janice, now a college graduate and gym teacher at Thomas Jefferson Middle School in Independence, Missouri. As an appointed chaperon for the Spring Fling Dance for the middle school children, Janice is supposed to show up at seven p.m. to help set up and decorate the school gym. Except on the way there, after having one too many apple martinis, Janice loses control of her car and drives onto the lawn of Mayor Albert Tanis, killing the family dog while his stunned children watch in horror.

Janice staggers out of her car, walks over to the crying children surrounding their newly crushed dog, belches, pats one of the mayor's twins on the head and mumbles, "I'll buy you a new beagle, or bulldog, or whatever the hell it was." She stumbles back to her car and drives away, drowning away the memory of the accident by downing the contents of her ever-present Thermos®.

She was never prosecuted for this as the four-year-old twins were unable to give police any help in identifying either her or the car.

This time, Apples has a vague recollection of this incident, but to the ex-mayor and now Governor Tanis, and his now fifteen-year-old boys, who were seated in the front row in the 'victims' section, this was grim and upsetting news indeed.

Still the screen rolled on ...

After two DWI arrests and convictions, Janice, now thirty-five, goes on a union-imposed two-month paid leave of absence, vowing to all she was going clean up her act and seek help. Yet the movie shows Janice driving three or four towns away, drinking where no one knows her, alone, and continuing to put her life and the lives of others in jeopardy every day.

Until one evening, when Janice permanently altered the lives of so many. Driving home at four thirty in the morning, drunk and sleepy, she veered into oncoming traffic and hit the Robinson family, all eight of them, head on in a horrific explosion of metal, tires, glass, and flames. The Robinsons were on the way to the annual Robinson family reunion attended by hundreds of Robinsons from around the country. But they never arrived.

The turning screen slowed to a crawl as the Robinson family's demeanor devolved from joyous singing, to concern, to abject terror as they realize this car is coming right at them. The ensuing explosion is deafening as five of the family members are ejected through the crushed front end and propelled to their deaths at sixty miles per hour. A torrent of severed limbs and bloodied luggage fly onto Apples car as she blacks out, bleeding from a superficial scalp wound.

Cleaning up the carnage is a living nightmare for police and EMS workers, as many vow to never go back to their jobs after what they witnessed here today. In total, seven Robinsons expire in the crash, with the eighth, a ten-year-old boy who had both legs crushed in the collision, in a wheelchair next to the Tanis clan, a blank look on his young face.

The screen goes dark as the house lights come up. Wiley Jack stands solemnly at his podium as the cone begins to rise from Apple's chair. The arm and leg restraints immediately snap open and a stunned Janice begins to fiddle with the mask, trying unsuccessfully to painlessly remove it. Jack says, "Be still, Janice, you'll only make it worse. Sir Reginald, please come and assist our guest."

Out strolls Sir Reginald, stiff backed, with a clean, white towel draped over his right arm. But Janice "Apples" Martin either doesn't hear or doesn't comprehend the commands coming from Wiley Jack. She begins screaming and with both hands begins to tear the mask off her face, ultimately taking the better part of her eyelids with it. The audience lends its support to her by chanting, "Rip it off! Rip it off!"

A bloodied and permanently bug-eyed Apples runs off stage, with Sir Reginald in close pursuit. Wiley Jack watches in amusement at these proceedings, turns back to the audience and says, "One down, two to go. We'll be right back after a word from our sponsors." Jack unfurls Bertha and cracks it at the camera lens, missing it by a hair.

*

Upon returning from the break, the camera finds Wiley Jack and Sir Reginald bantering back and forth. Standing side by side, Wiley Jack reaches way up with his left hand, and patting Sir Reginald's shoulder says, "Tell the audience what you just told me, Sir Reginald." Sir Reginald stares ahead, perfectly erect, a blank, impassive look on his face, and says, "Mr. Rafael Serrano wishes to decline the mask, sir. He says in his case it will not be required."

Wiley Jack looks to center stage, where Rafael and Tom are seated in their chairs, strapped in, eight feet apart, chairs slightly angled to see each other and still face the audience. Wiley Jack slowly walks over to the pair and stops and stands behind Rafael's chair, placing his hands on the contestant's shoulders. While looking over the chair toward the audience, Jack begins to speak to Rafael.

"Sir Reginald tells me you don't want to wear the mask, Rafael. Is that true?" Wiley Jack reaches down and with forefinger and thumb and gently rubs the earlobe he split open earlier, causing Rafael to wince. Rafael doesn't answer, prompting Jack to squeeze a little harder. "I asked you a question, Rafael. Can you hear me now?" Rafael yanks his head away from Jack's fingers, shaking his long, greasy hair in the process, and says, "Oh yeah, I can hear you fine, gringo, and I don't need no pussy mask to face what I've done and where I've been. *Tu sabes?*"

Wiley Jack pats Rafael lightly on the head, looks out at the audience, and asks, "What say you, friends? Mask or no mask?"

A few in the audience begin chanting, "Headgear, headgear, headgear!!!" Soon the entire audience picks up the chant and starts rhythmically clapping and chanting, "HEADGEAR, HEADGEAR, HEADGEAR!!!" Wiley Jack mulls it over, quiets the crowd, and says, "Let's give him a chance, friends. Let's see how tough he really is." Looking down, Jack speaks quietly so only Rafael can hear him, "If you look away for one second, or close your eyes, I'm going to put you in the headgear myself. Tu sabes, my friend?"

Not waiting for a response, Wiley Jack turns heel and heads toward his podium. Reaching into his pocket upon arrival, he pulls out a Wash-N-Dry Towelette, rips it open while scowling and muttering, and begins cleaning his hands, finger by finger; for the touching of Rafael has left Jack feeling dirty. Without missing a beat, Sir Reginald produces a clean, white terrycloth towel, which Jack gratefully accepts. Sir Reginald stares impassively straight ahead, waiting patiently for Jack to complete his task. Tossing the towel back to Sir Reginald, Wiley Jack looks into the camera and bellows, "LET THE HEALING BEGIN!"

Looking straight ahead, Rafael smiles his best "whistling past the graveyard" smile, baring his mouthful of gold-capped teeth in the process. Once again, as the cone descends, the red lights in Rafael's chair begin to flash. The mixture of flashing red lights bouncing off Rafael's faux smile of gold throws off an orange hue, kind of like an evil laughing pumpkin.

The cone now snugly in place, Wiley Jack asks Rafael, "Can you hear me, Rafael? Are you ready?" Rafael responds by giving Jack the worst half of the peace sign from his strapped in right hand. And the movie begins ... The first scene shows a six-year-old Rafael at his Uncle Arturo's thirtieth birthday party. The music is Latino and very loud; everyone is eating and drinking and having a wonderful time. Uncle Arturo is the overlord of the largest street gang in drug-infested Paterson, New Jersey. He wears his black leather jacket emblazoned with Latin Death Squad on the back proudly and with no fear. A large red "J" on the left front breast denotes what everyone already knows; Arturo is the *jefe*, or boss.

Little Rafael understands this and worships his mother's brother as he slowly rubs his little hand up and down the cool leather arm of his uncle's jacket. Uncle Arturo smiles and asks his nephew, "You like my jacket, Rafael? Here, it's for you!" Whereupon Arturo removes his jacket and places it on a beaming Rafael, to the appreciative laughter of all.

The screen turns to later in the night, when Rafael learns the first of his many drug war lessons. At the height of the merriment, three masked rivals come blowing in through the front door like an angry hurricane, and open fire on the room's occupants. Being in the bathroom at that moment subsequently saved Rafael's life, as Uncle Arturo, three of his top enforcers, his mother, and one child, Rafael's younger sister, Angelica, are shot dead in a victorious coup of Arturo's budding drug empire. And the screen rolls on ...

Police arrive long after the murderers are gone, to find only young Rafael alive among the carnage, clutching his uncle's jacket and sobbing uncontrollably. Child welfare services arrive to whisk Rafael away from the crime scene, and into the system.

Rafael is unmoved by the events onscreen, and true to his word, has not blinked or looked away from the massacre. And still the screen rolls on ...

To a now ten-year-old Rafael being admitted into The Latin Brotherhood, the newest and most ruthless drug gang yet to surface from the pock-marked streets of Paterson. The gang uses very young boys and girls to transport daily drug supplies around town via bicycle and backpack. Called *muleros chicos*, or baby mules, these fearless youngsters are immune from both prosecution due to their age, and consequences due to their gang affiliation.

By the age of thirteen, Rafael earned the first two of the seven green teardrops that now adorn his face by killing rival drug runners who were cutting in on his turf, and to Rafael, the entire city was his turf.

The screen moves on in time to a sixteen-year-old Rafael, who has physically outgrown drug running and realized that the big money was in cooking his own product, the crystal meth, or ice, that was now the rage.

Becoming the finest *cocinero*, or cook, of crystal meth in the city became an obsession for Rafael, and the movie rolls on to reveal long and dangerous hours of "cooking" that were as far removed from the sanitized, Hollywood version depicted in the AMC monster hit, *Breaking Bad*, as the three-thousand-mile distance suggests.

Filthy cooking pots and utensils, cigarette butts, and half-eaten day-old sandwiches are strewn about. The only concern of the kitchen being the cook yield and profits. The screen portrays a loyal and energetic crew that works for Rafael, as his employees are painfully aware of the consequences of a lapse in either.

The green teardrops have grown in number from two to four as Rafael passes his twentieth birthday. A young woman accused of thievery from Rafael's kitchen had her father and mother turn up dead and was then forced to work for free for the man whom everyone knew had done the dirty deed. This "two birds with one stone" approach to Rafael's shrinkage problem did not go unnoticed in the small but violent world of the local drug trade.

The screen rolls on to show Rafael hosting meetings with other local drug lords, sitting at the head of the table, in his mid-twenties and at the very top of his game. And Rafael's game remained strong and focused until his twenty-ninth birthday, when he started to sample his own product, and loved it.

Little by little, Rafael began sliding down the slippery slope of drug addiction, sniffling and sweating, with wild mood swings in his behavior that became apparent for all to see; especially his rivals. They began to perceive weakness in Rafael, and like hungry lions that can smell fear and uncertainty when on the hunt, he became a target to be devoured.

Rafael begins to squirm in his chair, eyes darting from side to side, knowing what was coming next onscreen. Without hesitation, Wiley Jack removes the headgear from underneath his podium, purposefully strides over to behind Rafael's chair, and slams the headgear onto his head. Jack steps away and removes a small remote control device from his jacket pocket, aims it at Rafael, pushes the button, and the headgear begins the activation process.

A metal stabilization bar rises from the back of Rafael's chair, and instantly his headgear is thrown back against it, riveted in place by magnetism, for the headgear is made of iron. Inside the headgear, the same tiny hooks used in the conventional mask, through radio control, bite into Rafael's eyelids and raise them to the completely open position. Finally, and perhaps most eerily, the mask conforms to the exact likeness of Rafael's face, albeit a startled, frozen, silvery version. And the screen with no conscience mercilessly rolled on ...

To Rafael's own thirtieth birthday party. Like his beloved uncle Arturo before him, Rafael was now "the man" in the drug world of Paterson. And just like his uncle before him, he stayed too long in the game and was slipping. His use of his own product had loosened his vice-like grip on his operation, and his underlings saw an opportunity, and seized it.

The screen shows lifelong friend and now bodyguard Caesar Fuentes arming himself for Rafael's party; not an unusual occurrence, as Caesar hadn't left his home unarmed since the age of eleven, almost twenty-one years. What is different, however, is Caesar knows his sterling silver .44 Magnum, truly a hand cannon, is meant to execute Rafael, not protect him.

Caesar is shown looking into the mirror in his apartment, staring at his reflection, steeling his courage for the night ahead. He hurriedly makes a haphazard sign of the cross, raises his right fist gently to his lips and kisses his clenched index finger, glares back at his image one last time, and heads out to the getaway van.

Waiting in the front passenger seat of the dark blue, late model Chevy van with the blacked-out windows is Caesar's brother Gustavo, and behind the wheel sits their brother-in-law Tito. All three are very nervous as they know that if their plan fails, not only will they not make it out alive, but their families, who will also be in attendance at the party, will also be executed, children and all, right before their very eyes.

Back in the studio, Rafael is making unintelligible moaning and muffled screaming noises through the sealed and skintight headgear, as two tiny air holes for the nostrils and quarter-sized holes for his eyes, mouth, and ears are the only way air or noise get in or out. And the screen rolls on ...

To the three killers entering Rafael's warehouse, where the party is in full swing. The music is Latino and loud, with horns blaring and harmonizing tenors singing in Spanish. Rafael is seated at the head table, surrounded by his current wife and six of his children.

Rafael waves the three men over to where he's sitting, unknowingly inviting the gun play to begin. The tension in the audience becomes palpable as the screen slows to a crawl. Tito arrives first, and in slow motion whips out his sawed-off shotgun and aims it chest high at Rafael and pulls the trigger. Nothing. The gun misfires. Rafael, in turn, pulls his pearl-handled .44 from his waistband and fires back at point-blank range at a dumbfounded Tito. Rafael's gun doesn't fail, blowing half of Tito's head clean off his shoulders.

Gustavo and Caesar step up and shoot at Rafael a combined nine times, while hitting three of his daughters in the process. As Rafael falls to the floor, he empties his gun at the feet of his attackers, hitting both in the lower shin and ankle. But on his way down, his first shot goes astray, hitting his two-year-old pride and joy, little Rafael Junior, killing him instantly.

A bloodied and crawling Caesar pulls himself up alongside Rafael and whispers to him in pained and broken English, "Whether you live or die, *esse*, it doesn't matter, your time on the throne *es finito*."

The movie screen then shows Rafael passing out from the loss of blood, with the images becoming blurry while skipping backward and forward in time, which elicits a disappointed, collective groan from the audience. The movie then stabilizes and resumes its frenetic pace, and the groaning audience reverses course with a smattering of light applause as they witness one of Caesar's underlings, as per prior instructions, pick up all the guns and head out into the night.

Ambulances and police arrive quickly and the carnage is sorted out. Police find no weapons at the scene, and nobody gives the police a single clue as to what just transpired.

The studio lights come back up as the cone holding a screaming Rafael starts to rise. The arm and leg irons snap open as Sir Reginald slowly walks toward him, pressing the remote that demagnetizes the metal bar behind Rafael's head, allowing him to stand, with the frozen silver headgear with the startling likeness still in place. Rafael claws at the headgear in a desperate attempt to remove it, to no avail. He turns to face Wiley Jack, and now has the freedom to give Jack two separate half peace signs.

Jack smiles back and declares, "Well put, my friend. Except perhaps you should look in the mirror and repeat that silent statement. Extensive surgery and many skin grafts will be required to even remotely resemble your old self. You see, Rafael, that headgear will need to be cut off."

Rafael begins to lunge at Wiley Jack, but Sir Reginald is too quick, and incredibly strong to boot. He picks up a kicking and struggling Rafael by the back of the neck as easily as one would pick up a ten-pound bag of garbage, and carries him offstage.

Wiley Jack looks into the camera and says, "Hoo boy, what a show tonight, huh folks? Two down, one to go—our compulsive gambler, Mr.

Tom 'Action' Jackson." Turning to face the remaining contestant, Jack continues, "How about it, Tom? Are you ready for this?"

Tom closes his eyes and again begins moving his lips, deep in prayer. Looking back to the camera, Wiley Jack quietly says, "Pray hard Tom, maybe it will help. Or maybe it won't." Unfurling Bertha, Wiley Jack Smiley rears back and aims at the camera lens again, barely missing it by a hair once more. "We'll be right back ..."

*

Except, Tom wasn't praying hard. In point of fact, he wasn't praying at all. All his life, as far back as he could remember, when Tom was jammed up, or in a place he didn't want to be, he developed the ability to close his eyes and make time stop.

As a young boy, in his mind's eye, just before the beating would start, he would imagine being at a baseball game, the baseball game, watching his team win the seventh game of the World Series. The fans in the stadium would be roaring in ecstasy with young Tom screaming for joy as loud as he could, unable to hear his own voice, his own screams; blending into his surroundings until he ceased to exist.

He would envision running down to the front row seats, floating like a ghost, and leap the fence that held the celebrating fans at bay. Then running full speed toward the pitcher's mound to join the forming mountain of newly crowned world champions, exulting in their hard fought, improbable victory. Diving into the happiness pile and being buried by the sweating, dirty, bodies of his heroes, a sense of peace would envelop young Tom, safe and secure. Oh so safe and secure.

Tom "Action" Jackson's closed-eyed reverie is broken by a sharp, persistent pain emanating from the top of his skull. "HELLO IN THERE, ANYBODY HOME?" Wiley Jack has moved behind Tom's chair and is rapping with his knuckles on Tom's head. "HELLOOOOOOOOO?" Jack picks up the pace of his rapping as he raises his voice to secure Tom's attention.

"Welcome back, Tom, where've you been? We've missed you so." Wiley Jack moves alongside Tom's chair, and rests his elbow in chicken-wing fashion upon the chair's top, interlocking his fingers together in a clasping fashion, palms down. He is standing on his right leg with the left crossed and bent, the toe of his pointy left boot dug into the floor for balance, heel up. Tapping his thumbs together, Wiley Jack looks like a man who really enjoys his job, and has all the time in the world to do it well.

Suddenly, from offstage, a loud argument can be heard, accompanied by the sounds of breaking glass and broken furniture, followed by a loud silence.

Seeming to be momentarily disoriented, Tom looks up at Jack, a glint of recognition in his eyes, and quietly says, "I'm right where you left me, Jack." Continuing sheepishly, "I guess I just spaced out for a bit."

In a tone reminiscent of a kindergarten teacher correcting a misbehaving student, Wiley Jack looks down and slowly says, "Okay, Tom, but please be sure to pay attention and be on your best behavior for the next part of our show. Okay?"

Looking offstage to his left, Wiley Jack summons Sir Reginald. "Sir Reginald, the mask please." Sir Reginald enters as before, elbows at ninety degrees, erect, stiff backed, stone faced; carrying the royal pillow with the mask perched upon it.

Except this time, instead of wearing a black tuxedo with tails, Sir Reginald is wearing a glittering red tuxedo, à la Liberace, all sparkles with a white fluffy blouse and red, old school Converse high-top sneakers. The new look is topped off by a dazzling red bowler. (The audience oohs and aahs.) Hearing the audience's reaction, Sir Reginald stops dead in his tracks, slowly turns and faces them, glaring. Instantly the audience becomes deathly silent. He then continues toward Tom's chair.

Wiley Jack finds the scene amusing, and while rubbing his forehead with his index and middle finger, he begins to chuckle. "What's with the new duds, Reggie? You look a little out of sorts, old friend."

Sir Reginald carefully places the pillow on the floor beside Tom "Action" Jackson, and turns to face Wiley Jack. "It's the wardrobe department, sir. They insist I become more 'colorful,' more 'with it' in accordance with today's clothing trends. So I grudgingly accepted their advice, sir, although I did feel it was incumbent upon me to express my protestations concerning my change in attire, as you may have heard." He continued, "May I adorn our guest with the mask, sir?"

"Certainly, Reggie. And might I add that I think you look simply smashing in red glitter." Turning to the audience, Wiley Jack asks, "Audience?" At first the audience is silent, not wanting to upset the giant that Sir Reginald is. A smiling Sir Reginald turns to face the audience and spreads his arms in an unspoken "how do I look" stance, but the smile fades to black when the audience fails to respond. Wiley Jack jumps into the uncomfortable silence, and raising his voice implores, "AUDIENCE, DOESN'T SIR REGINALD LOOK SPECTACULAR?" The audience explodes with a roar of approval, and Sir Reginald once again smiles that decaying, toothless grin.

He begins to affix the mask to Tom "Action" Jackson's face and upon completion, turns to Wiley Jack and says, "He is prepared for the viewing, sir." Sir Reginald grins at Jack, and proceeds to give him the two thumbs up. Slowly and gracefully he begins walking off the stage to the audience chants of Reg-gie, Reg-gie, Reg-gie!!!

Wiley Jack returns to his podium, places both hands on the lectern and announces to the audience, "Let's hope third time's a charm, folks. And so, LET THE HEALING BEGIN ..."

With that, the stage lights darken, and Tom's chair's red lights begin to flash as the cone begins its descent from above; finally settling in and sealing itself to the floor.

The screen comes alive, showing an eight-year-old Tom with his two best friends, Irving and Brian, flipping baseball cards in Irving's garage. The game is called Topsies. Each player, in turn, flips his card with a flick of the wrist toward the back wall of the empty garage. As the floor becomes littered with cards, the first player to land any part of his card on another, wins, and picks up all the cards in the process.

Tom is good at this, but his older friends are better. Tom loses his entire stack, and runs home crying. Upon arrival, no one is home, but an idea begins to take shape in young Tom's mind. He sneaks into his two brothers' room armed with a needle nose pliers and the burning desire to win his cards back.

Closing the door behind him, Tom takes his oldest brother's piggy bank and turns it upside down, revealing the plastic stopper belly button. Carefully prying it open, Tom "borrows" three dollars, carefully reinserts the pig's navel, and hustles down the street to Murray's Ice Cream Parlour, which doubles as Tom's first casino. There he purchases two dollars and eight-five cents' worth of brand-new baseball cards, saving the last fifteen cents for a chocolate ice cream cone with chocolate sprinkles.

With a smile on his face and a ring of chocolate around his mouth, Tom runs back to Irving's garage and re-enters the game of Topsies, winning back his old stack, and then some.

From behind his mask up on stage, Tom "Action" Jackson smiles warmly at the memory of this day; a day he made right with a perfect ending. His oldest brother Vincent, sitting in the "victims" section, doesn't quite see it that fondly. Until now, he had never known his brother had not only cost him his home and business, but had even violated his little bank as a twelve-year-old boy. He absentmindedly clenches and unclenches his rough, gnarled hands; made arthritic and stiff from many years of wielding heavy wrenches and cast iron fittings. Sitting next to Vincent is the middle brother of the three, Phillip, who gently pats his brother's twisted hand with his own version of the same, and the movie rolled on ...

To Calvin Coolidge High School, where Tom first earns the nickname "Action" Jackson. While other kids were getting groomed and dressed up for Friday night dances and grope sessions, Tom was riding his bicycle to the downtown underground card game, where he honed his skills of how to cheat at cards and still look the victim right in the eye, and teaming up with other players to take down the new pigeons in the games. For to Tom, all was fair in love and gambling. And Tom really loved gambling. But gambling didn't love Tom back.

The movie rolls on to Tom, at age twenty, getting caught cheating in a high-stakes card game in lower Manhattan, where he is dragged outside, kicking and screaming, and has both legs broken with a baseball bat and left in an alley, where he was no longer able to kick, but scream he did. This brings a rousing cheer from the bloodthirsty audience.

This painful lesson caused a re-focusing of Tom's priorities, and so he made the decision to clean up his act and go into white-collar crime; where the punishment wasn't as brutal and the payout was much higher.

Moving on, the screen rolled on to Tom enrolling in Brooklyn Law School, Class of 1979. Home at his parents' house for Thanksgiving in the fall of 1978, they are fawning all over their son, the soon-to-be lawyer, so proud to have a professional in the family.

Except the next scene shows Tom at a local bar playing Liar's Poker Thanksgiving night with a long-time gambling buddy. His friend, Ted "Le Baron" Ames, so nicknamed after a horse they won big on, remarks to Tom, "Never figured you to be a mouthpiece, Tom, you telling me your life of action is coming to an end? Four sevens." Studying his ten-dollar bill and Ted's confident smile simultaneously, Tom makes a decision, and offers up a confession. "CHALLENGE, Theodore, my boy, I've got none!" Ted groans the groan of a loser and says, "I've got three, you haven't got any!? Let's see."

Tom proudly waves his ten-dollar bill in Ted's face to show him indeed, he has no sevens on his bill. Grabbing the bill from Ted's hand, Tom goes on, "I'm only going to become a lawyer so I can walk in the front door of a big company and steal them blind. No more sneaking in the back door for me, trying to pick up crumbs."

Ted mulls this over and smirks, "We'll have to change your nickname to 'Front Door Action,' huh?" They both have a good laugh over this. Ted continues, "Like what, banks, colleges, insurance companies?" Tom considers this and says, "Maybe, I don't know for sure. I was kind of thinking about hospitals." Ted pulls out a twenty, snaps it in front of Tom's face, and says, "Double or nothing?" Tom reaches for his wallet, opens it, pulls out a twenty, and smiling says, "Three sixes."

Being smarter than the average bear, Tom is shown graduating from Brooklyn Law and entering the workforce. The screen shows Tom working and scheming, filching from every company he works for. Always moving on before he's detected, or involving his superiors in his murky plans, using that as leverage should the noose tighten. Most companies, when confronted, simply ask the perpetrator to move on, not wanting to risk public embarrassment or even worse, expose their own ineptitude.

The screen briefly lights up with Tom getting married, having three daughters, and living a life of duplicity of biblical proportions. Sadly, Tom's youngest daughter develops a brain tumor and is treated at The Children's Cancer Hospital, where she goes through a brutal regimen of chemotherapy over four months, and due to the tenacity of her medical team, she is miraculously healed. Tom intuitively knows this is his chance, for in his mind, the stars have aligned.

Tom asks for and gets a meeting with the hospital's board of directors, begging them to let him start a building fund, with their backing, to build a bigger and better, more advanced, state-of-the-art, brand-new facility that would save children the world over. Feigning gratitude and crying crocodile tears, Tom has the board eating out of his hands.

He deftly plays to their egos by describing how the medical world will be in awe of their new facility, and knocking each other over to work there, which will bring in more revenue, more acclaim, more social events, more country club memberships, more expense accounts, and last but not least, more children will go home with their parents.

When Tom finishes, there isn't a dry eye in the room, for Tom has given the performance of a lifetime. He has used all his acquired skills of manipulation, funneled all his "education" into a scalpel sharp enough to cut the board of directors into tiny, manageable slices. They agree unanimously and wholeheartedly to go ahead with the project. Led by Tom "Action" Jackson, Esquire, a building fund is created with bad intent.

The audience is stunned into silence as a parade of charity balls and charity auctions go merrily careening across the screen, one more ostentatious than the last. The "victims" section is squirming as if their pants are full of ants, made unbearably uncomfortable by the events they are seeing for the first time, crossing and uncrossing their legs and clearing their throats, looking away from time to time.

Not Tom, though, for he is unable to look away. He is visually surrounded by donors, sick children, and their grateful families. He watches himself become the fox who guards the hen house; a house he entered through the front door.

So the money came rolling in, and Tom quit his day job and devoted all his time to building the building fund. Up. And bigger. And larger. For all the lunches and dinners he paid for to secure new donors, he needed an American Express Card. So he got one. And a MasterCard. And a Visa. And a brand-new Mercedes limousine. And a driver, so he could spend his travel time working the phones looking for more donors for the building fund, *his* building fund.

His wife turned a blind eye to all the wealth, to the dresses, the jewelry, and the vacations to exotic islands. Which is why when their world came crashing down, she chose to turn State's evidence against her now ex-husband. After all, she still had three daughters to raise with no visible means of support, and she couldn't do that from a jail cell. At least not until the book deal was finalized.

Meanwhile, as hopes were raised across the country of families desperately seeking help from this hospital-to-be, families turned down local treatment in the hopes of being the first to be admitted.

A skeleton of a structure slowly crosses the screen, as Tom committed some of the fund to perpetuate the lie. And that's as far as it got. A bony, lifeless skeleton. Rather apropos, all in all. But the buzzards were circling overhead, and would soon take him down.

Moving ahead, the screen shows Tom being led out of his office in handcuffs by federal marshals, who alerted the national media in advance so Tom could do his now infamous "for the children" perp walk, which went as follows:

Reporters are gathered at the entrance of the hospital that held Tom's office, and when he appeared in handcuffs being led out, a reporter asked him, "Why did you do it, Tom?" Tom stopped, smiled at her, and said, "Why, for the children of course!" He then broke out in hysterical laughter and was led away into a waiting car.

Most of the money was never recovered, and while it's hard to estimate the effect Tom's actions had on children and families he would never know, it's safe to say his actions had a deadly impact on many.

The lights onstage come on as the screen is lifted. And there sat a nonplussed Tom with tiny rivulets of blood running down his cheeks.

The wrist and ankle bands snap open as Sir Reginald walks over and not so carefully removes Tom's mask, causing Tom to yelp in pain. Rubbing his wrists, Tom matter-of-factly asks Wiley Jack, "Is that it? Am I done?" Before Wiley Jack can answer, Tom's brother Phillip jumps out of his seat and yells, "Oh yeah, you're all done, brother!" Phillip reaches in his inner jacket pocket and pulls out a .357 magnum, aims it at Tom with fire in his eyes, but begins to tremble and shake. Sir Reginald seizes the momentary hesitation, and with two great strides, leaps into the victim section amid screams from both the women and men, and tackles Phillip, disarming him quickly. Holding up the gun, Sir Reginald calmly says, "I've disarmed him, sir. Shall I hold him for the police?"

Wiley Jack walks over to the edge of the stage, extends his right hand toward Sir Reginald, and says, "Nah, Reg, no harm no foul. Here, let me give you a hand."

After he helps to pull the giant back up to the stage, Wiley Jack says to Sir Reginald, "Hey, let me see that gun, Reggie. I want to see if it's loaded."

Jack takes the gun in hand and looking down at it, cracks open the barrel to discover, indeed, the gun is loaded. Staring down at the gun and running his fingers over the barrel, Wiley Jack begins to address a still-seated Tom Jackson.

"Tom, you don't remember me, do you? About fourteen years ago, I got the worst news a father could get, the very worst, Tom. A doctor told my wife and me that our little four-year-old, Jack Junior, had inoperable brain cancer, and he had about six months to live." Wiley Jack starts to walk slowly over towards Tom Jackson. He continues, "We attended one of your charity functions, and gave you all the money my wife and I could raise, fifty-eight thousand dollars as I recall, because you gave me your word, *your* word, as one father to another, that you would put us at the top of the original patient entry list, and you were certain that your soon-to-be completed hospital could save little Jack's life."

For the first time, Tom "Action" Jackson looks worried, and with good cause. Wiley Jack continues as the frozen audience breathlessly looks on. "We all know how that turned out, Tom, don't we? But what you *don't* know, Tom, is my wife cracked under the strain of losing Jack Junior, and took her own life soon after he lost his battle." Wiley Jack raises the gun to Tom's head, and asks, "Any last words, Tom?"

In a dry-throated, hoarse whisper, the last thing Tom "Action" Jackson would ever say is, "Do it."

*

Epilogue

Janice "Apples" Martin was subsequently convicted of vehicular homicide and sentenced to five years in a minimum security prison. The public outrage over the lenient sentencing, led by Governor Tanis, caused a new law to be written. Dubbed the "Apples" law, drunk drivers that are convicted of a homicide behind the wheel of a car will be given a minimum of twenty-five years in state prison, with no chance of parole.

Janice serves eighteen months, gets released, and returns to her home. Unable to withstand her snarling surroundings, she decides to sell all her belongings and move into The Mount Carmel Convent, where she currently resides; the only nun in the convent permitted to wear sunglasses.

Rafael Serrano was convicted of possession of a controlled substance with intent to distribute, and sentenced to a minimum of ten years in federal prison. He joined a Latin prison gang, called The Mighty Latins, and is currently working his way up the ladder, one body at a time. He chose not to have the silver mask removed via surgery; rather he decided to paint nine green teardrops on it. He thinks it looks cool.

Dr. Lauren "Twin" Peaks moved to The Congo to work pro bono for Doctors Without Borders. She fell in love and married Chief Ngomo Andugo, and lives a sparse and happy life as wife number seven, although at times she does miss the motor oil.

Sir Reginald decided to chase his lifelong dream and became a certified ballroom dance instructor in Laramie, Wyoming. He may be seen on Dancing with the Stars on May 23rd with his partner and lover, Tyra Banks.

Wiley Jack Smiley is still languishing in his prison cell, awaiting first-degree murder charges. Shown pacing in his cell, he stops, and looking into the camera, unfurls a phantom Bertha, rears back, and snaps his empty hand at the camera. At which point he breaks into a devilish grin as the camera fades to black.

***

Mama Bear
by Kathryn Collins, United States

Three generations of hands had worn the glaze from the rim of the fine
china plate. The young mother sometimes brushed the backs of her
knuckles against the raw places, scraping the tender skin there. It took
some getting used to, being the mother. Some evenings, as she ran the flat
of her thumb over each plate before placing it in the cupboard, she
thought that the gritty band was wider than it had been before her
scrubbing. Like the creases in the sheets she tried to meticulously fold and
the pink-scrubbed faces of her children, the polish of her life was giving
way to the rawness beneath. Every year the ivy threaded deeper through
the gaps in the doorframe.

When the last plate was tucked into its place in the cupboard and the
sink was wiped and shining, the mother glanced out through her window.
Like the grooves on the plates, she noticed the thinning window lip, the
grease from fingers that always gripped too tight against the wood.
Beyond the pane, which she would have to clean again, she could see the
workmen. They were a brawny bunch, with arms that bulged even when
they were only lifting their lunch pail or coffee mug. Scars laced over their
arms and faces, a funeral shroud they wore until their bodies were
returned to the earth they worked. They would have neat plots in town
while other men battled against the wilds, and the pretty girls they told
dirty stories about would bring flowers every weekend until another man
swept them off their feet.

Behind the workmen was the woods. Though the trees were fewer
these days, hacked back to make room for new homes, she could still see
every bough, every turning leaf as it had once caught the sun. She had

once meandered barefoot among mulch and pill bugs and bristling needles, before her paths had been furrowed up under the weight of the heavy carts. If she opened the window now, she knew that she would smell only draft horses and hear only the low laughter of the men, but she had known the taste of peat in her nose, and the chitter of life in her ears.

A clatter on the stairs roused her and she straightened, pulling fingers away from their familiar holds on the window ledge. She turned, catching glimpses of her boys as they tumbled through the hall, half out the front door already, some with only half their clothes about themselves.

"Michael!" she snapped, catching a more worrying glimpse, hurrying forward to catch the boy before his feet could cross the threshold. "What did I tell you about putting on your human face before you went outside?"

"But Muuuum," the boy wailed, looking longingly after his brothers as they tumbled and wrestled through the sun. "They're gonna leave me!"

She shook him, hard enough to bring his attention back to her, leaning her face in, letting a little of her own monstrous teeth show. "They'll see you dead and buried if you walk out that door, young man!"

Pouting, he took deep breaths, closing his eyes. The mother loosened her grip on his arms, but didn't release the child. They'd been known to run off after a pretense before. Slowly, a pale human face appeared through her cub's furry snout, until only a brown-eyed boy stood in wrinkled clothes before her. Satisfied at last, she cuffed him once across his ear and turned back to the kitchen and the window that needed to be cleaned. "You have to be careful!" she called after the boy as he disappeared out after his brothers, across fields and out toward the yet unconquered wood. She doubted he even heard her.

Her eyes lingered on the men swinging axes as they marched back to war with the forest, and she pulled out a cloth to dry the dishes. As she worked, the light slanted through the window, sparkling from the dirt. Her hands passed in and out of shadow, the dappling light comforting. It reminded her of a song that a bluebird had taught her once, and she hummed it as she finished the dishes and turned to the next cleaning task.

She glanced out of the dirty window, surprised to see that the workmen were gathered in a cluster at the edge of the forest. Her voice stilted, then stilled. In the space her song left there was no clamor of axes, no manly grunting and groans; only voices rising steadily in a chorus of chaos and beneath it all, the squeal of an animal.

She'd know that squeal anywhere.

The door tore at the hinges as she passed, bits of her dress catching on the fracturing wood. Outside, the empty field between her and the forest stretched impossibly far and she was running, running, running toward the screaming cries of birds launching into flight. The field was uneven, with fresh lumber stacked in piles and dirt shredded by the weight of the carts. She stumbled. Her arms splayed out, the heel of her palms sliding in the loose dirt, her elbows hitting with a grunt.

She had no time for this nonsense. With a sharp ripping, her favorite pale-blue dress became little more than tatters, as the illusion holding her in disappeared. Her brown fur was spotted with grey these days, but few would notice anything but the hundreds of pounds of fury barreling toward them. On all fours she made better time, gaining speed as her nose gave her direction. She could smell the men's fear and the soft musk of her babies' fur forms. The growl that rose in her throat wasn't enough. Her roar shook the leaves on the trees.

She rammed into a deep clearing where there was barely enough light to see the men scattering. Instinct was taking over and she strained to keep her head about her. All three of her cubs were pressed against the crumbling rock of a hillside, mewling. Their clothes were ripped and dirty, their fur matted. This close, she could smell Michael's blood, wet and hot, everywhere.

She roared, turning on the nearest man. He'd fallen, and his arms flailed as he pulled himself away from her. She rose up on her hind legs, feeling all the weight of maternal instinct settling across her shoulders. She would funnel that energy down to the sharp points of her paws. She would crush and maim and murder the creatures that dared make her baby bleed. She could smell the man's piss and it smelt right.

A new scream from one of her babies caught her off guard. She strained to see him, but she was too lumbering, too heavy. Her cub called again and she fell to her fours so she could turn to him.

Only now did she see the creature slinking behind her cubs. Its hide was mottled greys; its snout sharp and long. Her babies' blood dripped from its snarling maw. Of course. She was a fool to think the workers would attack her babies armed only with mallets and saws. It was her time-old enemy; it was always the time-old enemy, a wolf.

She roared and charged. Tangled behind the cubs, the wolf yelped as it scrambled away. It wasn't fast enough, tripped up by her cubs as they rolled out of her path. She didn't bother really snapping at it, but let her weight plow over the creature. It snarled, then yelped. The quarters were tight and the wolf was now below her. She reared back, stumbling out of the way. It had already turned, maw wide and snapping. She swung her paw and it was only luck that it connected. The wolf went flying, yipping.

She spun to press her back against the cliff face, her cubs scrambling to get behind her. Her eyes had adjusted now and she could see the empty clearing. The workers had fled into the forest, their shouts lower and less frantic now. The wolf staggered to a stand, slinking low. The two faced each other.

The wolf began to circle, edging the mother closer against her cubs. She lumbered carefully, their mewling cries bleeding across her senses. She tried to push them backward with her hind legs but they clung to her in their fear. Her legs quivered a little as her rage cooled enough for her to watch the wolf.

A shiver ran down the wolf's fur and she tensed. The wolf didn't lunge, its head tilting to the side. She shifted uneasily, her arms already beginning to ache with tension. The clearing was quiet and she could hear the wolf's paws upon the ground and her own panting breath.

It was too quiet. She turned her head just enough to see her cubs at the edge of her vision. They cowered, frozen by something behind her. Knowing the wolf would lunge any minute, she turned to stare up to the top of the hill.

The man at the top of the hill looked nothing like the workers. Where those men were all brash and brawn, he was slender and quiet. He wore perfectly ordinary looking clothes, but there was nothing ordinary about the way he was staring at her. There was no fear in his gaze, no ordinary human anger. Human emotions were harder for her to understand in this form, but she was sure that the expression on his face was that of pure, writhing hate.

A small sound warned her of the wolf's approach and she spun, ready to knock it back. There was more than one wolf now. Along with the limping, injured beast nearest her, three other wolves were stepping out of the woods. Adult bears did not feel panic, she couldn't risk it. Instead, she reared back, roaring louder than before, charging the wolves before they could charge her cubs.

They all knew the drill now. The wolves snapped and lunged at her, quick and too many to keep track of. She was nothing but rage and strength, flinging the creatures back. Her claws caught on flesh, and she was rewarded with yelps and howls. She was in the peak of health, easy human living had kept the hunger of winter at bay for years, and it was easy to break bones with the force of her rage.

Until the cry of her youngest cut through her focus. This instinct had nothing to do with her bear-form, she simply had to turn and look. The injured wolf was moving in toward her cubs. They had formed against each other, growling back.

The distraction was enough. One of the wolves bit deep into her side. She roared, but she was already staggering to a fall. She couldn't fall. Her babies needed her.

A snarl cut through the familiar sounds and she turned. Something large and golden wove through the wolf pack, not quite wolf, but definitely not bear. She rallied against the wolf at her side, knocking him away so that she could focus on her new attacker.

The golden creature didn't attack her, though. It turned on the wolves, snarling and biting and clawing. She turned on the other wolves. Two were moving on her cubs and she charged them. The wolves fled from the approaching weight of her, yipping retreat. The rest of the pack followed, darting out and away. When she looked for the man atop the knoll, there was no one.

Her cubs were bleeding, hurt. She needed to see to them, but she could smell the other creature now. A cat, large and tawny and impossible. She faced him, too injured to properly loom. If the creature wanted to attack her, it might just succeed.

It did nothing of the sort. Instead, it lay on the ground. She might have thought it was trying to be submissive, but its hide was spotty with blood. She approached slowly, cautiously. It lay sprawled on the torn ground.

Before she could get close enough to smell whether it was dying or not, something shifted. It was a shift she'd watched a thousand times, but she still reared back in surprise. The cat thing was becoming a man. He was lanky and tall, with a workman's beard. Any clothes he had once had were long gone, replaced with blood and hanging skin and broken bones.

He spoke, and she nearly jumped. "Your cubs. You. Saved me. Save me?" His eyes held hers for a long moment. She understood. His secret, like hers, was in danger now. If the other workmen figured out exactly what had happened, they would both be hunted out of their homes.

She didn't hesitate. Her dress was in tatters, but there was enough of it around the clearing to serve as bindings. She was in human form in a thought, on hands and knees as she scrabbled to gather the cloth. Her cubs came to her and she bound their bites and cuts, kissing their crying faces. For all that they were hurt, none of them were as wounded as the man. She led them home with the man draped over her back in her bear form. Whatever was coming for them, they would meet it together.

***

The Gift

by Jonathan Palmer, United Kingdom

Bless her heart. Bless my soul.

If I close my eyes, I can see her. One leg folded back under her body, the other sticking out at an impossible angle. Unseeing, milky eyes stare into the distance. A spectral ribbon of smoke twists and twirls from a cigarette clenched between cold, stiff fingers.

She's pretty and young. Too young for me at least. Her raven hair fans out in a pooling corona of blood, blouse is open, exposing a porcelain white chest. A thin gold necklace, spelling the initials S.K. catches the light and sparkles.

Somewhere, a clock ticks, but that is all.

If I look down, I'm holding a knife and my hand is slick with blood, a scarlet glove.

I'm sorry.

I don't know who you are, because I haven't killed you yet.

*

I open my eyes and walk on unsteady legs to the window. My eyes are raw, like they've been peeled and my throat's sore like I've been shouting. Or screaming. Maybe I have, I don't know. I live alone with my cat, Monty, and he's not telling.

I pull the curtain back and peer into the garden. I've no idea what I expect to find, but there's nothing new to see: the old oak tree still claws at the night sky, next door's television casting its upper branches in a flickering monochrome. The neighbour's cat is perched on the fence, its siren wail piercing the silence. A bloated moon slips behind a puff of silvery cloud and plunges the garden into darkness.

I stroke the curtain back into place and take a seat at my writing desk.

A letter sits on the leather desktop, half an inch off center. I move it back into place, tilting my head to gain perspective. A drawer holds two more letters and a battered red notebook. I put the letters on top of the first one, squaring the pile, and slip the notebook into my pocket.

My leg starts aching again. I push myself up and hobble to the fireplace. Reaching for the mantel with my left hand, I grab my ankle with my right, pull my leg up behind me and count to ten. Where there should be framed photos of laughing grandchildren and family dinners, there's nothing but dust. The empty mantel mirrors my barren life.

I don't want your sympathy. Let me be clear, this was entirely my choice.

*

I can't say why it turned out like this. An old man, living on his own with only an overweight cat for company. I was an odd child—I knew from an early age I was different—I just don't know why. If I had a penny for every time I'd asked "why me?"

There was no bite from a radioactive spider, nor was I adopted from a dying planet. I climbed trees, scraped my knees, and picked my nose like every other boy my age. A late developer—I didn't speak until I was five—and then, according to my long dead mother, I didn't stop. Around then, I remember the looks I'd get. Eyes would widen, mouths would drop. Nervous smiles hinted at an ill-concealed fear. I can't say for sure what it was that provoked these reactions. I mean, not specifics, but I can hazard a guess.

Mother doted on me. She tried for ten years to conceive and when I came along, she never let me out of her sight, although I must have been enough hard work to deter her from giving me a brother or sister. Father was affectionate too, albeit more distant. He'd return home exhausted, but still find time to bounce me on his knee and read me my favourite books. One night, I must have been seven or eight, I turned to him mid story and whispered in his ear, "Mummy has a poorly tummy."

Less than eight months later, she was in the ground and Daddy never looked me in the eye again.

I learned to check myself. I learned I was "different"—not everybody had the insights or revelations that I did. I learned the hard way that not only did I scare people, but their fear almost always turned to anger. They didn't understand me or my gift and this shocked and repulsed them in equal measure.

Staying quiet became the new speaking up.

After Mother died, and in what I now see was an indecently short time, Father declared he couldn't cope. The widow from across the street moved in, and I was shipped out.

It was decided I would be better off staying with Nanny, Mother's mother, who lived in an eighteenth century stone cottage on a blustery Norfolk coast. The trip from my old house took half a day by bus, and over the next six months Father's visits tailed off, until eventually they stopped altogether.

Nanny worked tirelessly to give me the stable home I craved, and given what she had to work with, was surprisingly successful. To this day, I can't smell a slow-cooked stew without seeing her puttering around the kitchen, chopping vegetables and humming gently. Most evenings we played cards at the kitchen table but not on Sundays. Sundays she'd fetch an old biscuit tin from the cupboard under the stairs and I'd sit cross-legged on the floor, surrounded by photographs of Mother growing up. Nanny was desperate for me to make friends my own age but I was always happier on my own. One time she invited a neighbour's son to play. After less than an hour, he appeared in the kitchen, face pale and streaked with tears, begging to go home.

I spent school holidays scrambling up sand dunes, jumping dykes, and scribbling the name of every bird I saw in the little red notebook that went everywhere with me. I also used that book to record my visions. For all intents and purposes, I was a normal, adventurous boy, albeit one with a dark secret. They were halcyon days, the only time I can ever remember being truly happy. The near isolation meant the chance of me being exposed was slim, and, although my notebook began to fill with dreams, it was the closest I ever came to a normal life.

*

I take the notebook from my pocket and flick through the pages. Here's one entry, 3rd September, 1961, so I must have been twelve. It's the first day of autumn term in the second year of seniors and Mr. Bingleton, the headmaster, has summoned the whole school into the main hall. A rumour spreads through the ranks that we're finally getting a swimming pool and the air is crackling with excitement. He walks slowly past us to the front of the auditorium, climbs three steps, and leans wearily against his lectern. The chatter stops and he tells us in a shaky voice that Rupert Somers in year three had drowned over the holidays.

A stunned silence falls over the room, eventually giving way to muffled sobs and cries. Students hold onto each other or sink to the floor, but not me.

I already knew.

I'd seen the quarry, I'd seen poor Rupert, bloated and blue-faced, rocking gently against the reeds.

We never did get the swimming pool.

TERRORS UNIMAGINED

*

To this day I think Nanny knew I was special. She'd tell me to "pay no mind" to name callers and contacted the school to complain on more than one occasion. I took great care to avoid touching her. When she moved in for a kiss, I'd dip my head and she'd brush my crown; when she came in for a hug, I made sure no uncovered skin touched hers. She was the only person who made me feel normal and I loved her with all my heart. I couldn't bear that I might foresee how she'd leave me.

But of course, eventually she did, although in what was a new experience for me, it was a complete surprise.

Stirring soup at the stove one night, she stopped mid-sentence and jerked her head violently to one side. I watched from the doorway as she slid to the floor, mouth frozen in a silent scream. She lay propped up against the cupboard, her left leg twitching, the rubber soles of her slipper squeaking comically against the linoleum. Her head rolled onto her left shoulder and a silvery line of drool stretched to the floor. She began panting like a dog, short, rasping breaths until, finally, she sighed and fell still. I stepped over her body and took the soup off the heat.

In the absence of a better idea, I carried on like nothing happened. Every morning I packed my satchel and walked to the end of the lane to catch the bus to school. We lived like hermits, so this state of affairs continued for nearly two weeks. Then came the knock on the door. Nanny was a regular at the bridge club—she hadn't missed a Monday night in twelve years—and her card partner turned up to check on her. I reluctantly opened the door and muttered something about Nanny being out but she elbowed past me. The smell of the decomposing body was so overpowering she fainted and for one awful moment I thought I had two dead bodies in my kitchen. When she came around, she called the police and a kind-faced lady from Social Services took me away.

I had two choices: move in with Father, his soon-to-be-dead wife, and their two ugly children, or convince Social Services I could look after myself. At seventeen years old, assisted by an Oscar-winning performance, I started life on my own. I was given a two-room bedsit on an estate near Long Stratton and it wasn't too long before I found myself a girlfriend, Jenny-something. She was a sweet, lanky girl with dancing eyes and a mouth framed with metal braces. I loved her the way only a teenager can. My first love, and my last.

Things began to look up. Independence suited me and Jenny made me blissfully happy. Pretty soon my troubled past became a distant memory. We took long walks hand in hand, kissed in the back of the cinema, and earnestly planned our future together; all the things teenagers do. Before Jenny, I always buried my feelings, but when I was with her, my gift quietened and I could relax and be myself. When we touched, there were no visions, just smooth, warm skin which shot bolts of electricity all the way down to my balls.

Looking back, I can see this made me complacent.

Jenny had a dog, a border collie named Archie, and they were inseparable. Alike in so many ways, they shared an infectious enthusiasm for life and would take seemingly unlimited pleasure in everything they did. It all ended the day I stroked Archie. She didn't like it when I told her Archie was going to die and she liked it even less when he went under the wheels of a council truck.

Darling Archie. All big brown eyes and slobbery kisses. A scream of brakes, a puff of smoke from the tires, and he was reduced to a steaming pile of viscera.

I heard Jenny before I saw her. Her wails floated up to my bedroom window before she reached the front door. I stiffened, guessing what'd happened. She leant on the doorbell and kept her finger pushed in. I slowly opened the door, full of shame at hiding my secret from her. She stood on the front step shaking with anger, hot tears streaming down her face and snot puking from her nose.

"HOW DID YOU KNOW?"

I told her I'd seen the truck coming and the moment of impact, a week before it happened. A ten-second vignette: a series of flashing images like a film on fast forward. It felt such a release telling her but I'll never forget the look in her eyes. After an unbearable silence that lasted an eternity, she broke eye contact and slowly walked away. She never looked back and that was last time I saw her. Love lost, lives ruined, and innocence dead.

I've never felt more alone than at that moment and I swore I'd never share my gift with anyone again.

*

When the whispers and sideways glances became too much to bear, I applied for a new council house. A new area, a new beginning. I took to wearing gloves when I went outside, psoriasis as good an excuse as any. The gloves and my self-imposed isolation meant fewer visions, but the dreams never left me. Most were innocuous, a builder falling off a neighbour's roof, the checkout girl pregnant with twins—they didn't bother me and were easily kept to myself.

I flick through a few more pages of my notebook.

A dream about the FA cup final in 1978—a shocking win for Ipswich over Arsenal—bought me a three-bedroom detached house.

In 1981, I invested in a small company called Apple. I no longer check my bank statements, but last time I looked, my holdings were worth in the region of twelve million pounds and so I treated myself to a shiny, red Jaguar. I only drove it once, from the showroom to my house, and it's sat in the garage ever since.

I turn another page and stop in my tracks. Not all my dreams were nice, some hit me like an express train.

I didn't leave the house on September 11, 2001. I unplugged the television from the wall, removed the batteries from the radio, and spent the day with Monty on my lap, stroking him with gloved hands. I felt no need to watch those chrome missiles, gleaming in the Tuesday morning sun, slice into the twin glass monoliths. I'd already heard the scream of metal on metal, felt burning aviation fuel on my face, and breathed deep the fetid stench of burnt flesh.

Some dreams would take years to come good; others would become reality within hours. Many haven't happened yet. Prince Harry gets overexcited on a state visit to Guyana and produces a half-caste heir to the throne. A plane crash into Canary Wharf is used as a pretext for a foreign war, but is simply the result of an exhausted pilot, a first-time dad, losing concentration. I have no doubt all this will happen, but not in my lifetime.

Which, by my reckoning, only has a few minutes left.

*

I put the notebook back in my pocket with a sigh. It's been nine days since the chain of events leading to my current predicament started. A hammering on the front door had woken me from a post-lunch nap and went on for so long, I eventually rose from my easy chair to investigate. I would have been perfectly happy to wait for the racket to stop, but my visitor must have seen the curtains twitch, beginning a ridiculous game of who'd get bored first—me hiding, or her knocking.

"I know you're in there, Mr. Swann," she shouted. "Social Services, I need five minutes of your time." A pause. "Did you get my letter?"

I did consider opening the door, but instead peeked through the letterbox and went nose to nose with a fleshy, pink gargoyle—wobbly jowled and beady eyed—capped with a shock of black hair and a scar of red lipstick. Think Susan Boyle in a wind tunnel.

"I'm not going away until I'm satisfied, Mr. Swann" she said, and the thought chilled me to the marrowbone.

I opened the door an inch to tell her to go, but she put all of her not inconsiderable weight against it, forcing her way in. Before I could stop her, she'd reached out and was pumping my hand.

Neurons fired in my limbic system, stars danced in the corner of my eyes and ... bang. There she was. Eyes glazed and mouth open in shock, trapped upside down in an impossible tangle of twisted steel. A blue flashing light cast long shadows of the police crowded around the wreckage. One of them was leaning against a tree, retching; another had removed his hat and was shaking his head. Somewhere, what sounded like an animal, was screaming.

I took a deep breath, composed myself, and said to my guest, with no small degree of sarcasm, "Well, please do come in."

My porcine intruder introduced herself as Ms. March and followed me to the lounge. I switched off the television and offered her a cup of tea, saying a silent prayer she'd refuse.

"Yes, please, Mr. Swann, and do you have any biscuits? I have low blood sugar."

Monty shot me a despairing look and, deciding it was every man for themselves, bolted out of the room and up the stairs. Not having that luxury—as tempted as I was—I bit my lip, smiled awkwardly, and disappeared into the kitchen. Filling the kettle at the sink, a thought occurred to me, if that's Ms. March, what's the rest of the calendar like?

She must have used those five minutes to rehearse her speech, which began the instant I stepped back into the room. It appears my new neighbours had taken exception to the state of my garden, and not seeing me for a few weeks, had put two and two together and got five. In an unwelcome and dubious act of civic duty, they were kind enough to tell the council I was not in a position to look after myself. Ms. March proudly told me, spraying crumbs all over the carpet, that I had been put on the council register of "vulnerable people," and would be assigned a caregiver

As she droned on, my heart beat faster and bile rose in my throat. Down by my side, nails dug into the flesh of my palms. I tuned back in to hear her say the details hadn't yet been finalized, but the council would be in contact shortly. She stopped talking and arched her eyebrows like she was expecting me to say something. I couldn't think of anything to add— well, nothing civil at least. Finally she broke the silence by asking if I would be kind enough to complete the online satisfaction survey, which I could find on the "yougov community support platform," whatever the hell that is.

Maybe it was the glare that started the coughing fit, but more likely it was the biscuits she was shoveling in at an alarming rate. Her huge, pendulous breasts bounced with every hack like two children trying to fight their way out of a sack. Unable to take any more, I thanked Ms. March for her time and led her by the elbow, protesting all the way, to the front door. She was still talking as I nudged her out and shut the door. I stood there on the mat, arms crossed, until she fell silent. Eventually she turned and waddled down the path, shaking her head and muttering to herself.

I returned to the comfort of my armchair, switched the television on and considered the consequences of this unexpected development. As the afternoon wore on, I slowly began to warm to the idea. It's true, I don't enjoy cleaning the house, or washing my shirts, so that would be a bonus. After some consideration, the only downside I could think of was if the council cut my grass, the value of my neighbor's house might go up.

That night before bed, I poured myself a large whisky in place of my usual warm milk, and when I started up the stairs, it was with the quiet realization that I was looking forward to some company.

I rose early the next few mornings and waited anxiously for the postman, but it wasn't until four days after Ms. March's invasion that an official-looking letter landed on my mat. I picked it up, half ran to the kitchen, took a seat at the table, and placed my reading glasses on the end of my nose.

The letter was a pro forma, signed by Ms. March, in which she expressed her pleasure in meeting me. She went on to say that I could expect a visit on the twenty-ninth—five days from then—at 10:30 a.m., from a Miss Sofya Kaveloski, and that I should use the time before then to think about what she could do for me.

Of course, I did that very English thing of spending a whole day tidying, dusting, and vacuuming in anticipation of the visit. I went to the corner store to get some tea and came away with a mixed pack of Earl Grey, oolong, chamomile, and all kinds of brews I'd never heard of before. The afternoon found me walking around town, from one barber to another, until I finally found one with rubber hygiene gloves. Freshly groomed, and back home, I fished out a shirt from the back of my wardrobe, gave it a sniff, and ran an iron over it. All was set for my visit from Miss Kaveloski.

Then I had the dream, the dead girl on my living room floor.
S.K.

*

Life's strange. It has a habit of pulling the rug out from under you. I never subscribed to the "old man sitting on a cloud playing a harp" fantasy. Life is random, life is cruel. Wait, no. Cruel's the wrong word. Life is harsh. Cruel denotes intent and implies some kind of natural order. Bad things happen to good people, and good things happen to bad people. There's no celestial reward system, the world's too full of grieving parents and orphaned children for that to be true. What good comes from a coal tip swallowing up a school and snuffing out hundreds of young lives? What's the point of an entire continent ravaged by an incurable disease or a tsunami claiming a busy seaside town? And you can save your breath with your "he moves in mysterious ways" claptrap. It's intellectually lazy and morally repugnant.

I don't know why fate dangled the carrot of someone new in my life and I don't know why I embraced the idea so entirely.

What happens if I take my gun, put the barrel in my mouth, and decorate the sitting room with my brains? If I don't kill the girl, does she stay un-murdered, or does some unwitting substitute step in and restore karmic order? It seems impossible that I'd kill her, under any circumstance. Do I see the future and decide the world's a better place without her? Is it self-defense? Is she even the S.K. from my dream?

As unlikely as it sounds, and this I know from experience, the stars will align and make it happen. S.K. will die a brutal, violent death. I don't have the answers, hell, I don't even know half the questions, but I cannot and will not sit here and do nothing. This is my last chance to jam a stick in the spokes of the cosmos and regain some foothold on my destiny. I get to wrestle back some control. What if someone steps in to finish the job? There's nothing I can do about that, but there is something I can do to ensure it's not me that kills that girl.

This is my gift to her.

I cross the room and old-man-sigh myself into the chair at my desk again. I hold on to the letters with one hand and lift the lid with the other. Inside there's a book of stamps, and Father's old service revolver. I take both out and lower the desktop, spreading the letters out in front of me and sticking a stamp on each one. One inch from the top, one inch from the left.

The first is addressed to the political editor of *The Guardian*. A warning about a young, rising star of a right-wing party. His tailored suits, brilliant smile, and easy-going bonhomie belies the blackness in his heart. After Germany in the 1930s they said it could never happen again. They were wrong.

The next letter is to a pharmaceutical regulator warning of an unfortunate side effect of a promising new asthma drug. The fallout will be measured in human misery and misshapen fetuses.

The last one is empty and simply labeled "Sofya Kaveloski." I remove the red notebook from my cardigan pocket and slip it into the envelope.

I take some thin leather gloves from my other pocket and pull them on, finger by finger. Monty senses my mood and fusses around my ankles, purring loudly. Easing myself out of my chair, I bend down and he raises himself up onto his back legs to help me. I carry him to the kitchen and take a can of food from the cupboard which I fill his bowl with and watch him eat, his purrs replaced with little chomping noises.

I return to the lounge and pick up the gun, weighing it in my hand and deciding my next move. It always surprises me how heavy it is. The banality of my final moments forces a chuckle. A thought occurs and I go back and shut the door.

Monty doesn't like loud noises.

***

Man-i-kin

by Matt Kolbet, United States

Terence avoided looking back at the glass-paneled doors and exhaled noisily. He refused to look at the walls, too. Though he'd entered the mall willingly, he didn't want to add anything to his growing index of regrets. No more being stuck. Still, life had taught him knowing where the exit was seldom meant the same thing as reaching it.

Today's exodus was hardly biblical, wending a path past a table of shirt-and-tie combos.

Escape would come later, after he found some new clothes to lift. He didn't know exactly where he'd be going later. Nonetheless, he planned to look the part.

Terence kept his eyes down, dodging the saleswoman on the floor. It was easy. No one expected teenagers to be schooled in social graces. Besides, he didn't need to look around to confirm someone was watching. He was used to eyes following him in stores, part of the legacy of being black. He wished he'd brought some music with him, though, to help in his sartorial attempt at discretion: gray hoodie, jeans, sneakers with an emphasis on the sneak part.

Unfortunately, he'd left his ears open. No trouble there. Best to know what people were saying. Was there a way to avoid being seen though, just slipping through? Invisibility began as a fantasy in childhood. By the time you grew up, it was more than a dream, becoming an idealized state—the world leaving you alone for once.

Terence's parents thought he was back in classes today, an auspicious beginning of the week and a robust response to the agreement they'd reached. He'd deceived them, as well. After Marina's text on Monday night, he didn't want to be anywhere near the high school.

The Friday before, Mrs. Beihler, the school counselor, had arranged a meeting with Terence's parents. His father grumbled about having to leave work early, though he made no objections to the counselor's suggestion that Terence simply work harder. It thrilled his old man, who wouldn't have to change at all. Tough love and high stakes were unshakeable tenets of the community.

"Terence misses too many classes, too many days," Mrs. Beihler said. "When he's here, he doesn't go to every class. Sometimes he misses the entire day."

"So he needs to buckle down." Terence's father had heard all he needed. "Someday you'll have to pay to learn. Success depends on showing up." So money had joined this conversation, too.

"Yes, studies on absenteeism do suggest a correlation."

"Good." His father glared. "You need to be here to get it. Got it?" Terence nodded. "Face the future directly. Keep your eyes on it." For his father, the future was always a deficit. Money was tight at the best of times. New clothes came as gifts or wishes.

Mrs. Beihler turned and began talking to Terence's stepmother. His father was done listening—to him, his son needed nothing more than a swift kick and a reminder to straighten up, a generational atavism. To be a real man. Not a return to living in solitary caves, just learning how to be a social animal. Always with his eyes forward. No more cutting class. No more angry tweets. No more mistakes.

"As if there's another way to grow up," Terence muttered. No one heard him.

"I think Terence is turning a corner here," said Mrs. Beihler. "He may have slipped up, but he's got a chance to learn from his mistakes. No permanent errors. Nothing hardened. Nothing set in stone."

The counselor's well-intended words meant nothing set against the details: weekly check-ins, a homework contract with his math teacher. More than boxes that needed ticking, Terence thought of Marina. He wondered what his parents, particularly his father, would say when they discovered he too had fallen in love with a woman of another race.

All Friday, Terence hadn't heard anything conclusive from Marina. The silence unnerved him. His palms and neck blossomed in sweat. He caught his father eyeing him. The old guy appeared gratified. To men of his father's generation, discomfort was a precursor to decision, to finally tackling the problem, and his father was probably only thinking of school. It was all academic.

When Terence returned to school on Monday, it was mainly to please Mrs. Beihler. He wanted to show her he could be trusted. His math teacher smiled when she initialed the contract. Marina had told him she'd have news before the end of the day, that they didn't need to worry, and that she loved him.

Today, Tuesday, Terence pushed those smiles and Friday's meeting from his memory. Mrs. Beihler had probably been notified after he missed first period. He had math third period and he would be absent then as well. Most of all, he did not want to think of Marina's face. His disappearance had betrayed them all.

Marina's text arrived late Monday night. Terence hid in his room, listening to "Light the Sky on Fire" on repeat, dreaming of being a racecar, a vehicle so fast he was uncatchable. He sometimes thought his father's record collection was the best thing about their relationship. His stepmother, like Terence's mother before her, was a white woman whose protectionist attitude preordained a distance. They'd never be close because Terence would never be himself with her, but always a stranger, someone molded to fit her expectations. Besides, his stepmother had just appeared out of nowhere. He did not remember a courtship. There had been no discussions with his father.

The divorce had followed the same pattern. Even before she disappeared, Terence couldn't imagine how his mother had fallen in with his father.

The test came back positive. That was all Marina wrote. She was pregnant. The baby was his. There were other possibilities, of course. Marina was an attractive girl, and Terence wasn't her first love interest. Some old boyfriend might easily have come back into the picture, he told himself. The lie did not stick. It was unfair to denounce the girl he loved with a stereotype, stenciling in her a simple frame. Society did enough to make women feel culpable. Though Marina was white, her skin wasn't always a protection.

After he had read the text, Terence's mind blanked. He wasn't paralyzed by too many options. No, the choices were all too clear, whether it came to staying with Marina or keeping the child. Terence just needed time to figure it all out. It was easy to decide to be somewhere else when the school day started on Tuesday.

Shuffling his feet, Terence walked toward the center of Nordstrom's, past mannequins wearing suits and others in bright dresses that managed to look sexy without being too short. Marina had been wearing something like that when he took her to Winter Formal. He tried to remember the hue and failed. After the dance, they'd gone to Terence's car.

It was too conspicuous to sit under the parking lot lights as the dance emptied and everyone else drove away. That would lead to more rumors, the kind they couldn't handle by ignoring them. There had been enough talk to *accidentally* overhear and dismiss when they'd started dating. Besides, it was too cold.

Terence had turned the key, happy the ignition caught immediately, and relieved from the pressure of conversation by the radio, a mindless song that sounded like a dozen others currently in rotation. They were all clones. As he drove, happy to be warm and alone with Marina, the sound of the radio faded away. Terence began telling her about his father's record collection. It was a way to discuss the old man without saying anything personal, hinting at Terence's role model, his dreams, and everything he didn't want to be. In twenty minutes they reached the city park on the far side of town, at the top of Century Drive.

Terence shot his eyes at the sign and tried to sound light. "This place has been here a long time. Not quite a hundred years, though. Still, I bet it's seen a lot." He became conscious of his voice as the only sound in the car. At least they were alone. They could make their own choices without worrying about hallway gossip. Or their parents. "What now?"

Marina hadn't replied, not even to protest how late it was. Terence readied his argument—"Nah, it's still early"—knowing the contradiction was futile, but she merely studied him with soft eyes, the kind that caressed you and made you enjoy the reflection. The February cold squeezed the molded sides of the car. Marina leaned over him and kissed him hard.

"Listen, we don't have to wait for prom."

"For prom?" Terence asked stupidly.

"You know," Marina lifted her eyebrows delicately. Terence understood. There were other ways to keep warm when the world froze you out. Their love had been clumsy, hasty, yet evidently effective.

Presently, Terence approached a female mannequin and ran a hand over the hem of her dress, a lustrous orange affair that simultaneously attracted and warned. If the figure was appalled, it remained mute.

"See anything you like?" asked a voice behind him. Terence turned to see a young saleswoman. She was cute. Even if her smile was false, it never wavered. He wouldn't mind watching her for a while, to avoid thinking about tomorrow and facing Marina again.

"I was just looking." Terence dropped his voice into maturity. "For my girlfriend."

The saleswoman did not challenge him about his age or relationship. She seemed to believe what she saw. Terence straightened, trying to make himself into a college student with a day off.

"Love is in the air?"

"Something like that." Terence chuckled.

"Let me know if you need anything." Terence nodded and moved away from the dress. The mannequin's legs were immobile, useless, but the eyes managed to stare despite their blankness. Like the old park, they'd probably seen a lot.

After Marina's update about her pregnancy test, Terence knew he couldn't show up to school. The first day of news was always the worst. Gossip raced against truth and won easily. Marina was sure to have told one of her girlfriends, one she claimed to trust, but this news was too big to keep under wraps. It would grow and be seen, demanding to be noticed. Girls would stare at Terence. Some would think him a rapist. Guys might offer high-fives, not caring if they'd only understood half the story. Marina would be angry with her confidant, though not enough to stop trusting her completely.

Yet if Terence were there, Marina would be overjoyed to see him. They would need to talk and have to ditch at least one class. He didn't think he could bear being alone with Marina right away. He might end up seeing himself reflected in her eyes. He doubted the image, frozen in fright, would be pleasant.

He wandered toward the glass watch display. No one wore watches anymore, not since phones did everything. No one needed to, though Terence supposed they added a nice touch to a professional look, a flash of gold or silver, something to catch the eye.

"Business is about being noticed," Terence's father had said countless times at the dinner table. His father ran a garage, so this wisdom did not generally apply as much as his second dictum: "Business is about results." When he gave one of these aphoristic prologues to a lecture, neither Terence nor his stepmother dared contradict him.

After Marina's message, there would be no gainsaying his father. Terence didn't delude himself. News of an unborn child was the kind they built expansive narratives around, weaving endless threads to clothe a whole universe of characters. For Terence, the time until the birth entailed months of uncertain waiting, confusion about who he was and who he might be. The whole business angered him. He wanted nothing so much as escape.

Despite his desire to rush away, the glass case fascinated him. In addition to watches, there were imprisoned necklaces, trapped tie clips, and immobile gloves, everything an accessory to some greater whole. He brushed a hand over the glass and his nerves jangled. If only he could outrun that feeling.

There were cameras sprinkled throughout the mall, but in .Nordstrom's they had people to watch every movement. Terence would have preferred being at the other end of the mall, where the stores were just as big, a last-gasp Sears or a Target, only the clothes weren't as nice. If he was going to face his father later, he wanted to look his best. More than that, Nordstrom's was closest to the exit. When he was ready, he would not have far to go.

He leaned over the case and glanced over his shoulder. He hadn't attracted the attention of anyone except the mannequins, who held him in their unwavering gaze. Terence stared back at one, as if to voice his defiance: *Well, what did you expect? You got yourself into this.*

Not me, though, Terence thought. Somebody might try to corner him, but he would fly. He mentally located his car in the parking lot and envisioned speeding away.

No salespeople lingered at the accessories counter. When Terence saw an elderly man approaching on tottering legs, he stepped back. He didn't need to buy a watch or any other means of marking time's lethargy. Marina, their future child, and Terence's fretting father would fill that role relentlessly. The salesman paused to catch his breath, a eulogist who knows he's next. Terence nodded perfunctorily and moved on, his limbs beginning to tire. What he really needed was something to make him seem responsible, to convince Marina he could be a better version of himself. When the time came. Someday.

He looked at the mannequin again. Its sandalwood face was too light for Terence to see himself in it, too dark for the women in his life. All around, mannequins scrutinized him, doing the twin jobs of security and the ambling salespeople. Terence walked in small circles, pretending vague interest in different styles of spring clothes. Each set of molded dummy eyes was disturbingly real, not the empty lizard glowering of most mannequins, the same gaze he got from his father. But then, his father was a man who ate crab apples.

Strangely, it appeared someone was in the mannequin, waiting.

No, impossible.

People looking at Terence constantly—seeing him for what he really was—probably scared him the most. When Marina gave birth, he'd have too many people to face. The waiting would be over. His dad might have foregone screaming by the baby's birth, and maybe hitting too. He hadn't really cuffed Terence for years, and maybe love for a grandson would override everything else. Terence's stepmother would be supportive without doing more than his father permitted, her silence like a dirge. Marina's eyes would implore him, one question after another: Where would they live? Should she quit school? What plans did he have? Worst of all would be the child's eyes, shifting between the joy of new life and the agony of helplessness, always accusing Terence of screwing up. *Too early, too early* those eyes would say. If Terence wasn't ready, looking smart in a new set of clothes, avowed joy would quickly become a burden.

He remembered how his mother apologized before she left, telling Terence she'd wanted to love his father, had even given birth to salvage the relationship.

"Now it's too late." She'd kissed his forehead and walked away without looking back. Terence felt on the verge of vanishing as well.

Once more, he felt a mannequin's stare creep over his neck. This time Terence chuckled, picturing a game show, an eternal staring contest in the malls of America. He wanted to look, even when he didn't want to.

Terence strolled to a section where he could loiter without anyone asking questions. Perhaps the store manager told the salespeople to leave customers alone in young men's fashion. Perhaps there was a second black kid for them to follow around.

It was an area for teenagers to find themselves, to risk something in the safety of trends. A lack of resolve might mean buying two or three shirts instead of one. Security cameras scanned it more than any other part of the store, but unless some bedraggled mother was hauling her son through, the salespeople evaporated.

There *were* some shirts Terence liked. He looked at one price tag. Unbelievable, seventy bucks for a simple cotton shirt with a short collar. A nearby mannequin was wearing the same shirt in a different color. Terence looked at the dapper dummy and laughed quietly.

"Ready for all kinds of weather," he observed. "But you don't have to worry about sweat, rain, or spaghetti stains."

He thought of his unborn child, aged the kid two years, and saw small hands affably flinging noodles and sauce onto a white floor while Marina, harassed but hopeful, gazed on. He would work during the days, and they'd trade off evenings for community college classes.

Looking up to the mannequin's face, he mused. If I were an oversized doll in a store, Marina would always know where to find me. Would she recognize me? Would she stay for a chat? She might position his arms into a gesture of embracing, but there was no simple movement to denote duty.

His parents couldn't stand the mall, probably because nothing seemed permanent, which to his father's mind meant nothing dependable. Too crass, his father would say, everyone pretending. No one real. And then, they might not bother trying to locate Terence at all. He could hear his father's voice: "If my son's run off, he isn't worth chasing."

The only other dummies Terence knew were dolls for practicing CPR on in health class. They were improbable vacant shells who never *seemed* real. More like suicide than restful death. He'd doubted his ability to save a life—flesh felt so different from a practice dummy. Still, Terence knew a bit about mannequins. Marina wanted to work in fashion and had studied up, dolls included.

"Sometimes they use models first," Marina had said and Terence heard her desire to be the model for something. Now she would be, to their child. "Of course, there's no perfect body, but models help with the face more than anything. The heads are rubber. They make them look the same for each store. You can't have different noses or anything like that. Hands and arms just get reproduced, one after another." Terence learned some mannequins were made with PVC. He'd thought it was only for pipes.

"We could use the old dummies for sprinklers." Marina hadn't found that funny. Instead, she explained with deliberate patience that mannequins were art.

"They can be more than just one person. That's why they work. The mannequin models clothes so shoppers see themselves in the outfit." She sighed, struggling to articulate her vision. "Somehow, it's more than we are." Terence hadn't agreed, though he hadn't argued either.

"How are we now?" asked a voice. Terence recognized the same female floorwalker as before. Their collision was mere happenstance, not her following him. And if she wanted a commission, he was the wrong guy. He'd get his hands on a few shirts, maybe a pair of pants, and run for it, disappearing into the rest of his life.

He folded the flattering shirt and set it back on top of a stack of duplicates. The saleswoman did not re-do his work. Not then. She would probably stroll through later and straighten the entire section. Still, he hadn't seen the woman since she caught him fingering a dress. Maybe management assigned staff to particular customers, especially when they weren't white. Or was this zone defense?

It was not worth thinking of distances inside the store in miles or even half miles. Likely the saleswoman was simply bored on this slow Tuesday. Terence could posture, pretend he was looking for clothes to match the dress he'd been eyeing earlier. Or the girl who would wear it. He'd already succeeded there.

Yet why did he feel desperate to avoid Marina and their new reality? He kept his phone off, resisting its phantom pull, knowing he would have numerous texts from the would-be mother of his first child.

"I'm ... I'm still looking." To his ears, the answer sounded listless. Perhaps he was more weary than he thought.

"Take your time."

"Yes, I'll have to, won't I?" The woman paused, not taking this invitation to ask more, to discover why he was here, why alone, or how much time he could still claim as his own. She almost let Terence be invisible, perusing the frozen volatility in his face. She told him she'd be nearby if he needed help.

He did. Just not the sort any saleswoman could offer.

Absence from school might cause the day's gossip to elongate a bit. Terence counted on Marina to protect him. She would assume he was ill, since he wasn't answering her texts. It was likely she'd called too, waiting through four rings to confirm her theory. He was ill. He needed time to sort himself out, from the outside in, and a place to do it.

Terence hadn't even decided which clothes he wanted to steal and already it was nearing midday. His stomach complained, but only growling, not gnawing. In a playful reflection, he envisioned himself as Corduroy the Bear before he was adopted, sitting idle on a shelf.

"Except I'd have better clothes. No missing buttons." He gazed again at the mannequin wearing the shirt he liked. The less playful version of his thoughts was a troll, doomed to terrorize the store without the possibility of acceptance or adoption. No bridge to hide under either.

Yes, it was a nice shirt. Out of his price range, but that didn't matter. He stretched his fingers. Today the mall was for liberation. He sought deliverance. The saleswoman had drifted away. There was no one else around. He could just grab a shirt from a nearby stack and go.

Despite turning his face from the mannequin, his eyes, guided by some preternatural force, were pulled back. He heard people talking in other sections. No matter how slow the day, there were always handfuls of perambulating customers, people looking for something. Probably they'd laugh when they spotted Terence ridiculously gawking at a mannequin. He stared. And after that, his father and Marina and a child with years of demands. They'd catch him all right.

In a shimmer, Terence felt his body disappear. His frame vanished in an instant.

A new perspective. His legs were no longer tired, and he felt, he was, taller. Glancing down past his shaped nose, he wore the shirt he'd been admiring. From his elevated position he could see more of the store, its intimidating dimensions. A space easy to get lost in.

Immediately, Terence was jubilant at this transformation. He would not have to face his father or Marina or the unborn child. The break might even be a nice vacation.

Terror now. He realized his new eyes could never close. In front of him, an elderly woman stood shaking her arms freely.

Terence couldn't narrow his eyes, yet he intensified his focus on the woman. Where had she come from? Moments earlier, he'd been standing alone with the classy shirts. There was no accounting for her sudden appearance. She was undeniably old, her body frail. Nonetheless, as he watched, the old woman skipped away, careless of her aged bones. She sprang at decades ahead of her, not mere months. She had taken this day to break out, for it was Tuesday, a slow day, a day for bewitching.

Terence understood. The old, white woman, someone's lost child reformed into no one's mother or stepmother or grandmother, had freed herself from the mannequin at his expense. It was a pattern he knew well. Even his father might find something to laugh at in this cosmic joke.

Now Terence would have time to work on his gaze. It was imperative to catch someone's eye, though facing things was not something he'd ever been good at. He wondered if he might end up a corpse before he slipped the collar of the mannequin, or if his soul would stay there forever, shrinking, wilting behind a façade, re-dressed occasionally to fit the changing seasons.

***

Lakeside Park

by C.M. Saunders, United Kingdom

"What's the name of this place again?" Paul asked.

His travelling companion, Dennis, still gripping the steering wheel in his hands, glanced sideways for a split second. "Lakeside Park. Not very original, I know. But it's better than the alternative."

"Which is?"

"*Parc Llyn Glas Dwfn.* Welsh for Deep Blue Lake Park."

"Yeah, it's a mouthful. So ... is this lake as deep and blue as the name suggests?"

"Ha-ha! As deep and blue as any other lake."

It wasn't much of a park. Not yet, anyway. Situated on the banks of a large, serene-looking body of water, which certainly did look both deep and blue, it was more like a storage facility for touring caravans when they weren't in use, along with a handful of RVs and camper vans. A fence ran around the outside, and there was a gate at one end of the enclosure. The site was located at the bottom of a lush valley, flanked on both sides by huge, rolling mountains. There wasn't a building in sight, and it was so far out in the sticks there wasn't even a proper road. Instead, it was served by a long, gravel path just wide enough to accommodate a single vehicle.

As the car rolled to a stop at the gate, Paul opened the passenger door, stepped out, and slammed the door behind him. Then he opened the back door and pulled out his rucksack and suitcase. Dennis got out of the driver's side, a set of keys jangling in his hand, and unlocked the gate. It swung open with a loud creak. "You been out this way before?" he asked, cocking a bushy eyebrow.

"Nope," Paul replied. "Kinda looking forward to the peace and quiet."

"Well, you'll have plenty of that. Nearest village is Wood Forge five or six miles away. Nobody ever comes out this far. I'll bring you some supplies every week. You can give me a list. Unless it snows. Then you'll just have to manage 'til it melts. Won't be too hard. Your caravan is fully stocked with tinned food and stuff. There'll be plenty of time for hiking and fishing, if that's your thing. The lake's fully stocked with trout. That's if the pike haven't eaten them all. No telly, see. Just a DVD player."

"Not a problem. Is there Wi-Fi?"

"Nope. Might be able to pick something up on a clear day. Not too sure how that all works, to be honest with you. Radio works fine, and the mobile phone signal comes in and out. If it's an emergency, you might have to climb up to higher ground and try from there."

"But if it's an emergency, I probably won't be able to go climbing."

Dennis shrugged. "I'm sure you'll be fine. As agreed, you'll be here throughout the off-season. It'll be quiet 'til about March. When the weather breaks, I can start the development work. Have a proper road put in, a shower block. As you can see, at the minute it's just a place for people to store their caravans. Brings a bit of money in. You'll just have to keep eyes around the place. Do a couple of patrols a day, take care of any maintenance, and keep any vandals, trespassers and stray animals out. Before people start coming to collect their 'vans, you'll have to wash them down and check the tires and shit. Pretty straightforward stuff."

"Understood."

"If it goes well, we can look at extending your employment. You'll be staying in that caravan there." Dennis nodded at a compact-looking tourer parked next to the gate. "Four-berth. Separate bedroom. Chemical toilet. Be fine for just the one. Like we discussed, it's not much money on offer. But you can stay here rent free, and you have power for the lights and heating from the generator. It's all hooked up and filled with petrol. Just turn it on when it gets dark. Go easy on it, though. Petrol's not cheap. I'll fill it up and service it every week when I bring your shopping. Make sure it doesn't pack in. And if anything does happen, just give me a ring. I can be here in about an hour. Maybe an hour and a half."

When Paul answered the help wanted ad on Craigslist, he wasn't really expecting to get the job. Who would give a rootless forty-four-year-old recovering alcoholic any kind of responsibility? Not that he'd put that in his application, of course. He could only assume there hadn't been many other applicants. Dennis wasn't lying, the money was terrible. But like he said, there would be no outgoings, so any money would just sit in the bank gathering interest until next March. By then he'd have worked out what to do with it. Maybe go on a long holiday, or start a business.

"What happened to the bloke that did this job before?" he asked, absently.

"Must've gone a bit doo-lally," Dennis replied. "Was only here two weeks. Being stuck out here in the countryside can do that to a man. 'Specially a man who's not used to it. I came out one Friday afternoon to give him his shopping and found the 'van smashed up, and him gone. Damage cost a few hundred to put right. Fucker smashed the window and everything."

"Where'd he go?"

"Fuck should I know? He's not been seen since. Obviously couldn't hack it, so good riddance to him." The man held out a bunch of keys and after a moment's hesitation, Paul took them. "What you have there are the keys to the front gate and your 'van. There's a board on the wall inside with the keys to the plots, all numbered for your convenience. Like I said, prob'ly won't have to bother with them 'til after the winter. Any questions?"

Paul thought for a moment, then shook his head slowly. "I don't think so, Dennis. Thanks for the lift up, and the opportunity."

"I know you've got it in you. I have your number, and you have mine. Like I say, feel free to call if you need anything. I'll check in with you once a week or so at least. You know, just to see how you're doing."

"No problem." To Paul it sounded like a spiel. Something Dennis said to everyone coming up here to do this job. For all he knew, he was just the latest in a long line. But as he said that last part, something dark and duplicitous seemed to shift behind his eyes before quickly being suppressed.

Paul watched the man get in his car, do a three-point turn, and drive back up the gravel path leaving him alone in Lakeside Park. He stood still for a moment, wondering if he was doing the right thing. Suddenly, everything seemed terrifyingly real. Was he really going to shut himself away from civilisation for six months?

Then he decided even if he wasn't doing the right thing, it was too late now. He was stuck here. Gazing out at the lake, he saw rays of sunshine penetrate the clouds to sparkle on the gently rippling surface. If nothing else, it was a beautiful setting. Just what he needed to wean himself off the booze.

His attention turned to the little caravan Dennis had said he would be staying in. It looked a little rundown, but fit for purpose. It was positioned in such a way as the big main window faced the gravel path, and the door faced the gate. That lake view would be nice to wake up to every morning.

Picking up his rucksack and suitcase, he went over and tried the door. It was locked. Eventually locating the right key, Paul inserted it into the lock, turned it, and pushed the door. It swung inward on a small living area containing a table, two cushioned benches, and a kitchenette. Against one wall was a row of shelves containing a stack of DVDs, some paperback books, a torch, a radio, and several ornaments. A musty, slightly damp smell hung in the air. The place looked clean, but obviously hadn't been aired out in months. Wrinkling his nose against the stench, Paul cracked a window, noticing that the adhesive holding it in place appeared to be untainted and new. That must be the window the last guy smashed.

Paul carried his bags through to the bedroom. It was tiny, just big enough to accommodate a single bed and a wardrobe. Two pillows and a rolled-up duvet lay on the edge of the bed, and a fishing rod and a tackle box were stacked in the corner. Next to the bedroom was a tiny washroom, just big enough to house a chemical toilet and a wash basin. The tiled floor slanted toward a drainage hole in one corner, and a showerhead was fixed to one wall.

Dennis had been right. The caravan was fully stocked with supplies. There was even a four-pack of beer in the fridge. The first thing Paul did was open each can in turn, tip the contents down the sink, then throw the empties in the outside bin so he wouldn't have to contend with the smell. After drinking himself into oblivion almost every day for the past twelve years, he had been clean and dry for four days now, almost five, and didn't want temptation to be an issue.

The beer problem taken care of, he poured himself a glass of water instead and sat at the table. So this was his home for the next six months.

It didn't feel like home. Not yet, anyway. The silence was disconcerting. Dreamlike. He'd lived in cities all his life and grown used to the steady hum of traffic and background noise. Out here, there was nothing. Nothing at all.

Something akin to a mild sense of panic washed over him and he leapt from his seat, making the caravan rock slightly with the sudden movement, and went to examine the radio on the shelf. It was clockwork. Genius. He wound the handle a few times and turned it on. The Police rose above the static singing "Message in a Bottle." Anything was better than the unnatural silence.

Water finished, Paul decided he should take a look around the enclosure to familiarize himself with the place. It probably wouldn't take more than twenty minutes to do a circuit. He checked his watch. It was almost three p.m. Starting tomorrow, he would do three patrols a day. Morning, afternoon, and evening. He knew how important it was to devise a routine and it would at least break the day up. He might even set an alarm and come out at night too, that probably being the time when the park was most vulnerable.

Leaving the radio playing, he stepped out of the caravan into the afternoon. The gravel path extended to the far end of the enclosure, the "plots" being allocated areas of grass-covered ground. He heard it rained a lot in Wales, especially in the winter, so he imagined much of his spring would probably be spent digging caravans and vehicles out of mud. He counted seven small tourers altogether, as well as five static caravans. They were going to be bitches to move. Camper vans occupied three other plots, the most impressive being a huge, sleek-looking Volkswagen. There was even a speedboat in one of the plots, covered with tarpaulin weighed down with bricks. Several other plots were empty. He went right up to a few caravans, looked through the windows, jiggled the doors, and generally made some noise and looked busy, just in case anybody was watching. Everything seemed to be in order. He didn't know how he would feel if he ever caught a trespasser in the compound, but right now, his patrol amounted to nothing more than a pleasant stroll.

His curiosity satisfied, Paul made his way back to his caravan. As he went to open the door, he noticed for the first time several scuffed dents around the doorframe. There were also several deep scratches which had apparently been covered over with filler.

What the heck?

Dennis had told him the previous occupant had smashed up the caravan, but why would he be smashing up the door frame? It almost looked as if someone had been trying to break in.

That must be it. There must have been a break-in at some point in the caravan's not-so-distant past. That would explain why Dennis was so keen to have someone here keeping an eye on the place. "Fucking hooligans," Paul muttered.

Back in the caravan, he flopped down on one of the cushioned benches. He was already looking forward to his next patrol, but he guessed the enthusiasm would pass. It was quickly becoming apparent that his biggest enemy out here was going to be boredom. He set about unpacking his gear and putting it away. He hadn't brought much except some clothes and toiletries. The truth was, he didn't own much more than that.

His eyes were repeatedly drawn to the window, and the expanse of water that lay beyond. There was something strangely alluring about it. Almost like the lake was calling him.

Llyn Glas Dwfn.

Deep Blue Lake

He didn't know how deep it was, but the lake was certainly blue. Not like the usual kind of brown-green you would expect.

Then he remembered the fishing gear in the bedroom. He had several hours to kill until his next patrol. Maybe a bit of fishing would help him relax and acclimatize.

Half an hour later he was at the water's edge, threading line from the reel through the eyes of a rod. Overhead, a bird of prey circled and a light wind troubled the surface of the lake. Paul hadn't been fishing since he was a kid, but found that once he'd started examining the tackle, memories came flooding back in waves of sepia-tinted nostalgia. In his mind's eye he saw himself at the riverside with his dad. He must have been nine or ten. Back when life was simple and he was unburdened by the pressure that would practically crush the life out of him as an adult. The biggest problem he'd encountered was finding bait. A quick dig in the mud turned up a solitary earthworm. Dragged out of its earthy home, it wriggled in Paul's hand as it searched in vain for an escape route.

Gritting his teeth, he unfolded the blade of the knife he found in the tackle box and cut the fat, slimy worm in half, putting the knife in his pocket afterwards. A little bit of clear liquid squirted out of the creature's bisected body, and fleetingly, Paul wondered if it could feel pain. The wriggling intensified, only now there were two worms wriggling independently of one another. He remembered something his dad told him. People say that if you cut a worm in half, it will grow into two worms.

It isn't true.

One half can grow a new tail so that will survive, but the other half can't grow a new head and will eventually starve to death. Not that this worm was likely to live long enough for that to happen. Paul pierced it with a hook, and cast out into the lake.

Then he sat on his haunches and waited, eyes fixed firmly on the float bobbing ten yards away so he would be able to see if he got a bite. Time passed. An hour. Two. One of the best things about fishing was the almost zen-like state you fell into whilst waiting for something to happen. He could picture himself doing a lot of this during the winter months. He could even take the fish home and cook them. Providing he caught any, of course. Dennis hadn't said anything about not being able to. He—

The float moved.

It was moving constantly with the motion of the water, but this time it moved unnaturally, as if something had brushed against it. Paul felt his entire body tense up. He knew what to do. The moment the fish took the bait and the float disappeared beneath the surface, he had to yank the rod hard to embed the hook in the fish's mouth. And then, battle would commence.

There it was again. An almost imperceptible twitch. Either the fish was sniffing around the worm, deciding whether or not it was good enough to eat, or it was eating the worm right off the hook. That would suck.

Paul's eyes narrowed and he held his breath as he watched.

Suddenly, the water erupted. Paul let out a shocked gasp, let go of the rod and fell on to his back.

What the fuck?

In a fraction of a second his mind registered something coming out of the water, something far too big to be a fish. It was bipedal, and dark-coloured. Like a man wearing a scuba diving suit.

Only different.

This creature had huge, oversized yellow eyes. Like those of a snake. And it was covered head to toe in what appeared to be mottled grey scales.

A shower of ice cold droplets drenched Paul, splashing his face and eyes. For a moment, his vision blurred over. He pawed at his eyes with his sleeve, then looked back at the spot where the creature had emerged, fully expecting to find it towering above him.

But there was nothing there.

Scooting back on his hindquarters, he tried frantically to look all around him at once, convinced he was under imminent attack. But he was alone, and all was still. The only tell-tale sign that anything had happened at all was in the water, which was still disturbed. Ripples radiated out, and a layer of foam now floated on the surface. The atmosphere had also changed. Now it felt dense and charged, as if something was about to happen.

Paul scrambled to his feet and hurried back to the caravan. He didn't know what he had seen, but recognised the need to get out of the open. As he entered, he looked again at the dents and scratches around the door frame, and suddenly knew what had made them.

The thing from the lake.

He also understood why the last guy to have this job had left so suddenly. It was the creature him who had smashed up the caravan. The question then became, did the creature get him?

That was something Paul didn't want to think about. He went inside, locked the door behind him, and sat at the table. He was shaking uncontrollably, and his breath was coming in short bursts. He was hyperventilating. A small piece of his mind, perhaps as a last-ditch self-defense measure, tried to tell him he had imagined the whole thing.

But he knew he was fooling himself.

It was just after seven o'clock. Outside, the light dimmed as night began to fall. Pretty soon the caravan would be in complete darkness. He needed to turn on the generator. But that would mean going outside. Paul didn't think he was ready for that. Not yet. Maybe he could call Dennis. Tell him the deal was off and he could come and pick him up right now.

But that would mean explaining what had happened at the lake. Or at least inventing a suitable lie. Paul sighed, trying to force his mind in a different direction. It was useless. Maybe just talking to another human being would make him feel better. He could call Dennis under the pretense of checking in. At the same time he would be giving the impression he was a conscientious employee. That would work.

He snatched up his phone from the table and turned it on. The face immediately illuminated the dim room, making him look around anxiously. He hadn't considered the fact that it would light up the caravan like a beacon. He quickly scrolled through his saved numbers, found the one he was looking for, and hit CALL.

The phone rang. And rang. Nobody picked up. Taking the device from his ear, he stared at the screen in annoyance. There was no signal. Fuck.

He could do what Dennis had suggested and see if he could get reception on higher ground. But that would mean going outside. In the dark.

He resolved to try again in a few minutes. He lay back on the bench, pulled his knees to his chest, and closed his eyes.

Sometime later, his eyes snapped open and he sat bolt upright. He must have fallen asleep, then something had awoken him. But what?

That was when he heard the noises outside. A single footstep, on the gravel path just feet away from the caravan. It sounded deliberate, stealthy. Paul's blood ran cold. His eyes went to the window. It was almost pitch black outside, and he couldn't see a thing.

Why hadn't he drawn the curtain?

It meant anything outside could see right in. Could even be watching him right now. Who knew how long it had been out there, circling the caravan, looking for a way in.

He tried his phone again, shielding the glow it emitted with an open palm. Despite the chill in the air, his hands were clammy. Still no signal. Only one thought was going through his mind. Had he locked the gate?

Then he remembered something.

Reaching into his pocket, he pulled out the fishing knife and opened the blade. Now he was armed.

Suddenly, the silence was shattered by a loud crash. Paul jumped in his seat, dropping the useless phone and instinctively thrusting the knife out in front of him.

Another crash.

It was coming from the door. The *only* door. Standing, he pushed himself against the far wall, as far away from the door as he could get. He thought about locking himself in the bedroom or the toilet, but knew that from there he had nowhere else to go, and was reluctant to box himself in.

Now there were bangs and scrapes all along the side of the caravan as the creature made its way around. It was almost as if it were intentionally trying to terrify him.

The noises abruptly stopped, and Paul held his breath. Where was it? What was it doing?

He wanted the curtains closed. He felt exposed.

Slowly, silently, he crossed the room. As he neared the window, he strained his eyes to see through the glass. All he could distinguish outside were shadows and outlines of other caravans. Nothing stirred. Holding the knife in his right hand, he reached out his left to pull the window closed. As his fingers made contact, the creature reached through the window and grabbed his hand.

He let out a hoarse scream as the cold, wet fingers closed around his, and instinctively tried to pull away, but the grip was too strong. It was pulling him outside. Looking down, he saw the creature's appendage with sickening clarity, his eyes drinking in every detail. It was like a human hand in that it had four fingers and a thumb. But that was where the similarities ended. This hand was bigger than a human hand, thicker and more muscular. The lack of light meant that it was impossible to make out a distinct colour, but it was black against Paul's pale skin. Rotten looking. Most striking of all were the sharp, tapered claws on the ends of the fingers and the webbing in between them.

Feeling blind panic swelling in his chest, Paul raised the fishing knife high in the air, and brought it crashing down on top of the creature's hand. It sank in effortlessly almost to the hilt, causing the hand to spasm and jerk. At the same time, from just beyond the window came an inhuman howl, almost a screech.

Seeing his opportunity, Paul let go of the knife and ran for the door. Thumbing the lock open, he took a deep breath, then flung the door wide and leapt out into the darkness. Both feet landed squarely on the dirt track. The gate hung open, which at least answered one of his questions, and in seconds Paul was through it and running as fast as he could down the gravel path. Didn't Dennis say there was a village five or six miles away? Where there was a village, there'd be a pub. By the time he got there it would be opening time.

He didn't look back.

***

The Lifeboat

by Todd Zack, United States

The tropical storm had taken them by surprise. Maybe it was a hurricane, but that's what the captain had called it, "a tropical storm." The captain was very likely dead. Most everyone was dead. Last night, Cecil Brinkworth and nine other passengers had entered the lifeboat. In the chaos of crashing waves, driving rain, and whipping winds, three were blown overboard into the sea. Seven souls remained to see daylight.

It was a cruise ship en route from the Dominican Republic to the Bahamas. The storm came on them swiftly, a charcoal grey wall large as the horizon. Then the rain arrived, racing towards them in silver sheets. Heaven's shrapnel riding on fantastic squalls of wind. The storm continued to build itself up and up like a brilliant jazz number, aiming for transcendence yet ending, ultimately, in ruin. "Tropical storm," the captain had said over the ship's intercom. "Unexpected."

The Witness should have shown Cecil something, a heads up, three days out, two days out, the night before perhaps? But, no, there was no notice from The Witness. The storm came completely unexpectedly.

It was sometime after six p.m. that the ship began to list starboard. Dinner had not been served. Everyone on board felt it going, the insane geometry of the craft, windows looking down, *down* at the roiling sea outside. As the ship teetered, the high waves kept coming, great hydraulic dunes of them right up to the tilted windows, crushing them effortlessly, as if they were made of cellophane, and the wind came roaring through the shattered sills. "Lifeboats," the captain commanded over the intercom. A few people screamed and some children cried as they made their way towards the lifeboats. Cecil watched as many of them fell right then into the soaring waves, sucked over the side, swept away. Sprawling shadows in the white frothing air.

How many of the six hundred-plus passengers and staff made it safely into the lifeboats, and how many of those who did survived the storm's assailment through the thrashing night? Cecil knew of only seven, the lot of his lifeboat.

Most shocking thing of all was that he hadn't seen it coming, this storm, this disaster at sea. He should have seen it coming. Normally The Witness would have revealed this tragic event to him, before it happened, before it was too late to alter. Yet, The Witness had not. Not this time. Cecil Brinkworth was going to have to face the fact that The Witness would not always be there to prophecy a crisis. This was frightening and sobering news. Had The Witness abandoned him? If so, Cecil's fate was sealed.

The storm rolled away from them in an absence of understandable time and the long floating night was at last eclipsed by dawn. As a new sun's tangerine hues spread upwards from sea to sky, Cecil could see that the sea itself was a roiling vegetable green, quite unlike anything he'd seen before, an eerie shade of aftermath. The core of the storm had passed, but there remained a discomforting steadily blowing wind. The sea was no longer a fit of chaos, but it was restless and its entire plane seemed off, fit at a bizarre angle. This strange crooked green sea was now rocking the lifeboat in a metronomic lullaby, bow to stern.

Cecil had calmed. Most of his shipmates appeared otherwise. A few of them were bloodied and vomit stained.

Although they hadn't spoken much in a conversational way, the lifeboat people had communicated enough between themselves throughout the night for Cecil to know their names. Cecil took inventory of them now, printing faces to names conclusively in his mind.

There was Tim, a lithe and fit-looking young man, mid-twenties, dark hair and blue eyes, intelligent, capable, and brave. He was one half of a newlywed couple that also included Rebecca, his wife. She was a red-haired Scottish girl, petite, scholarly, and shy. Nervously constituted, she was just holding on to her wits. They huddled together at the starboard side of the boat.

Lucinda was a taut, athletic-looking woman in her forties. With straight black hair and high cheekbones, she appeared both Nordic and Oriental. She was roughish and stable, a tough cookie. She had taken up residence in the center of the craft, sitting cross-legged on the floor.

There was George, a short, kind-faced, barrel-chested African-American man in his sixties. He had a cool head, was a practical and faith-filled man, one half of an inveterate marriage that also included Eleanor, a doe-eyed, diminutive, and straight-postured black woman, somewhat senior in age to her husband. Cecil found her quietly thoughtful, attentive, and streetwise. George and Eleanor had stationed themselves portside.

And then there was this guy, a less than charming goliath sitting at the bow of the boat. Marco, a curly haired, lumberjack-sized man in his thirties with a broad vascular neck, puffy pink cheeks, and jaded eyes. He was cold and narcissistic, physically imposing and potentially psychopathic; dangerous. Just looking at him gave Cecil a headache. Cecil wasn't at all prone to headaches and the onset of one brought with it an oppressive and ominous feeling.

Satisfied that he had taken an accurate mental cartography of his companions, Cecil leaned back into the stern of the lifeboat. His buttocks submerged themselves in a pool of murky green seawater. With thumb and forefinger, he rhythmically stroked the stubble on his chin, thinking again, *I didn't see this coming. How did I not see this coming? What happened to The Witness?*

"Look," Lucinda interrupted Cecil's musings, pointing her long, jointed index finger out over the side of the boat. "Sun's up. Storm's over."

Tim rose to his feet and addressed them all, hands casually at his hips. "Sun's up! Yes, indeed, sun's out now." He cleared his throat deliberately. "Rescue boats will be launched, if they haven't already. And aircraft too."

He yawned and stretched his arms to the sky and his contrived nonchalance was so absurd that it was almost convincing. "'Here Comes the Sun,' ha, ha, the George Harrison song, right? Was that his solo stuff or was he still with The Beatles? Before my time really, and who cares anyway?" He smiled down upon his wife. "Rebecca? Sun's up, the sun is out, storm's over."

Rebecca looked up slowly and eventually managed to placate her husband with the slightest indication of a smile.

Cecil noticed how pretty she really was now, for the first time. That very whisper, tiniest hint of a smile was all it took. Cecil could imagine the breadth of the genuine article, a real smile on this pretty girl's face. Goodness gracious.

"Baby, I'm cold," Eleanor told her husband, shivering.

George wrapped his arms around his wife and squeezed her small bird-like frame to his bear-like chest. "Well, that was a cold storm, baby." He rocked his wife gently, comfortingly, as a small wave slapped the boat at their backs, flicking opaque globes of seawater into the air. "That was a cold storm and a bitch of a storm!"

"It's over now," Lucinda reminded them. She turned towards Rebecca, who was shaking like a chrysalis in its shell, reached over slowly and touched the young woman's knee with her long, open hand. "Hey, Honey. That is storm is over."

Marco, the lumberjack, intervened. "It ain't over 'til they find us. They don't always find people who are lost at sea, you know." With dark unblinking eyes Marco continued, "That dyke, Amelia Earhart—" He looked decidedly at Lucinda. "You remember her, right? Sure you do. Lost forever, she was. And lots of other people too, everyday non-famous type people, like us."

Lucinda smirked contemptuously, "Aren't you an adorable prick."

Tim stepped in carefully. "Ah, let him blow off steam. We're all stressed out, you know?"

"Stressed out," Marco said sardonically, relaxing his large body into the bow, hands behind his head.

"I ain't stressed out," Eleanor chirped. "I's cold! Cold! What be goin' on here? Ain't this the tropics?"

Rebecca giggled.

Everyone, even Marco, was taken aback by this, softened in their own way by Rebecca's little laughter.

Jesus, that girl is pretty, Cecil thought. *She's beautiful. Thank God for her.*

By the dial of the sun, the morning was halfway turned towards noontime when the naps began. No watch was designated. Everyone seemed to agree, without really discussing the matter, that sleep was needed and that it was not likely that they would fall so deeply, at least not all at the same time, as to be oblivious to the sight or sound of rescue. They were damned tired. And so the lifeboat passengers drifted along, at sea and into sleep, each in their own time down into their private wombs of the mind.

While being lulled towards unconsciousness by the rhythmic undulations of the lifeboat, Cecil heard the sound of a "click." Following the sharp tone, he floated freely away from his own body and discovered himself to be hovering a few feet above it like a lucid disembodied eye. He was not dreaming. He was having what he might later describe to himself as "an episode." The feeling of being bi-located, body below and mind above, was very clear to him and quite natural by now. He was familiar with it. Cecil entered the learning space. He was now The Witness.

As The Witness, Cecil was approached by a languidly turning opalescent globe, an object that was similar in scope to a camera lens and seemed to rotate in its own gravity as it neared; although it seemed to be located peripherally to his own center however he sought to adjust his view in this state. The globe, or orb, could not be viewed directly, but nor did it need to be to endow Cecil with its gift of second vision.

The orb came close to Cecil from one side of his vision and then, tentatively, the other, as if searching for an accurate entry point, finally encircling and then enveloping Cecil. It was an intelligent cloud of light, proceeding to interface with him and steer his consciousness. A countless flickering of stars softly moved through his mind and then suddenly, placidly, Cecil had, in effect, become the wheeling lens itself. A vision took shape before him, coming into form as a fast-action, self-constructing puzzle.

Marco and Tim were fighting at the bow of the lifeboat. The struggle was violent and full of desperation. Tim was noticeably disfigured. Blood was streaming down his chest from a shattered nose. Marco had Tim in a headlock now from behind. Marco was attempting with great effort and determination to break the young man's neck. In due time, despite Tim's defensive efforts, he appeared to succeed. Tim's limp and lifeless body was dropped by a drooling Marco to the floor of the boat.

Rebecca entered the vision. She was on her knees, in bloody water beside Tim's body. She was crying, shoulders heaving. Then she was screaming up at Marco, her face a torn spectacle of pain. Marco was hitting her now. Marco was delivering swift punches to Rebecca's face, one punch after another with murderous purpose. Rebecca was sprawled motionless upon the floor of the lifeboat. Marco was hitting her, hitting her still, the heavy machinery of his arms swinging down, his giants visage twisted in a maelstrom of madness.

There was a loud clicking sound and the vision retreated deftly, pulled backwards through the sky on some invisible cosmic tether.

Cecil came to consciousness, wakeful consciousness, with a gasp of psychic pain. He sat up quickly and looked around, blinking repeatedly. His boatmates, each one of them, were quietly asleep in the sun.

Cecil watched them.

The two couples were huddled together, each the others pillow in some fashion, Tim and Rebecca at the starboard side of the lifeboat, George and Eleanor at port. Lucinda was sleeping in a reclined position in the concave of the floor using a life preserver as a makeshift pillow. The murky green hybrid pool of rain and seawater had caught a length of her long black hair and turned it into a floating nautilus shell that hovered gently upon the surface of the water next to her sharp dry chin.

Marco sat like a presiding buffalo in the bow of the boat, his meaty forearms at rest upon his knees, forehead stationed upon the thick wrists of his two downturned hands. Cecil could hear the sound of the big man's breathing beneath the blowing wind. It was a sound like subterranean steam seething up from a fissure in the earth's crust. It was the breathing of a hibernating monster, a temporarily dormant demon playing dead.

When will it happen, the murder ... murders? And what will be the cause?

There's no way to know, and every second spent wondering will be time lost to affect any possible intervention on fates behalf. Cecil shuddered at the thought of this, this "possible intervention." There was, of course, no guarantee. He knew this. Cecil also knew, as much as it disturbed him, that there would be no better time for an intervention than right now, immediately, while everyone was dozing away.

So he intervened.

With the white noise of the wind serving him cover, Cecil slowly stood and moved forward from the stern towards the center of the lifeboat, being careful not to splash any water near Lucinda. Once there, he dropped quietly to one knee and proceeded to fashion from its metal clasp the starboard oar, switching his nervous vision from Marco to the others to the task at hand. Marco was motionless, sleeping. The other passengers were still.

After a few precious seconds of exploratory fidgeting, suddenly the clasp fell open in his hand. Cecil discovered that the oar could now be slid free lengthwise from the device. And a lengthy instrument the oar was, perhaps seven feet long. Cecil ran the oar out deliberately now, hand over hand, and took terrific caution not to let it knock against the body of the boat as the oar whispered free along its nickel track. But the process was not a smooth one. Cecil discovered that the unbalanced temperament of the oar's shape, combined with its gaining weight as it was removed from its mooring, made it a difficult object to make adjustments for.

The oar clocked the side of the craft once, and then again. Those clumsy noises were conspicuous, not wholly camouflaged by the wind. Against his better judgment, Cecil stopped pulling the oar. His body had frozen in fright. Cursing himself, he looked up and studied his fellow passengers, scanning them each for signs of impending wakefulness.

George was moving now, groggily raising his head from Eleanor's shoulder and turning his shoulders in Cecil's direction.

If George sees me, Cecil thought, *all he has to do is open his mouth, ask me what I'm doing. Anyone and everyone could wake up then. My plan could be thwarted, easily. If that happens, then two people on this boat will be murdered by Marco, first Tim, and then Rebecca, maybe more, maybe all of us.*

Cecil took a deep breath, drawing strength from the wind. He yanked the oar from its mooring in one decisive motion, claimed it in both hands, and raised its length to the sky.

George's body straightened up and his eyes slid open. He blinked twice and set them evenly on Cecil. "What's goin' on?" George asked, sleepily perplexed.

Cecil stepped to the center of the lifeboat, located his balance and estimated the spaces around him. As Cecil gauged his center of gravity, he turned the oar's handle above, rotating it in his grasp so that the flipper-shaped head faced Marco edgewise. Against his expectations, the wind quickly caught the face of the oar, like a sail, and the effect of this development was to push and nearly blow Cecil over the side of the boat, into the green-colored sea.

"Hey! Cecil! What the hell ya doin'?" George hollered.

Cecil compensated for his near disastrous portside stumble by applying brutishly all the strength his left leg contained against the upward curve of the lifeboat's concave hull. His wrists pained brightly in tandem. The long oar seemed to shiver with an electric current in his weakening hold, threatening to jump free from him, and all the roaming weight of it was bedeviling his command.

Marco then lifted up his head, in one short, mechanical motion, and looked at him.

Cecil, grimacing with the effort, jackknifed his body, fell forward, and delivered the oar to its target.

The oar struck Marco in the center of his brow with a rubbery watermelon thud. A thick gash opened fast, the white bone of his skull brightly visible in the sunlight. It seemed a few silent seconds that the bone was exposed, there between two aghast and lidless eyes, and then a curtain of blood poured out and down. Marco pulled his lips back, showing his teeth fisted together in pain. His eyes squeezed shut against the agony and the puckered sockets began to fill up with pools of running red. Marco's mountainous hands came up to cup both of his ears. This was a strange sight to behold, for it was as if the pain he was enduring was strictly auditory, a screaming voice ricocheting in his skull. His elbows dropped to his waist like pistons and with a rage of energy, Marco began to stand.

Cecil raised and recalibrated the oar and hit him again, this time a lesser blow that nonetheless knocked a rising Marco off balance and backwards. Marco collapsed into the bow on his back, blinded in his own blood, hands still clenching and twisting at his ears. A bloody grimace bubbled upon his face.

Rebecca, who was awake now and watching, covered her eyes and mewled like a feline, an inquisitive and infantile sound, as if to say "why" and "no" at once.

Tim was on his feet now and had Cecil by the hook of an elbow. "Hey!" he shouted. "Hey!" and began to pull Cecil backwards away from Marco.

Cecil, flooded with adrenalin, brought back the same elbow that Tim was holding on to, catching the young newlywed in the chin, forcing him to recoil. Tim moved backwards, tripped over his wife's feet, and spilled to the floor of the boat, landing on his buttocks with a shallow splash.

Freed from Tim's clutch, Cecil reestablished control of the oar. He changed his position, standing with one foot forward and the other back, anchoring his weight. The oar he turned out lengthwise and gripped it in both hands holding it over his right shoulder like a javelin.

Marco held up a wet, red hand, pleadingly. "Stop," he groaned through his agony. "Staaaah ... "

Cecil came at him once more.

When it was over, Cecil turned to face his shipmates. George was holding Eleanor to his chest turning her face into the crook of his arm. Tim was struggling to his feet beside his crying wife, one hand on her knee, the other placed to his jaw and looking up at Cecil in horror. Lucinda was crouched down in a defensive posture in a corner of the stern observing him with narrowed glittering eyes. A thrown drop of Marco's blood had painted her forehead, a solitary drop, perfectly centered.

"Jesus, Cecil." George gurgled.

Cecil emphatically dropped the weaponized oar, as if to say, "That's over. I'm disarming myself now, and I know there'll be some explaining to do." He understood that any explanation of his last actions would sound ridiculous; but knowing that he must offer one—at least attempt one—he decided to simply start talking and invent what he was going to say on the fly. It was the only plan possible and he'd better talk fast.

Cecil began, "This man that I just did this to ..."

"Murdered," Lucinda said icily. "You just murdered him. And his name was Marco."

Cecil nodded, accepting the charge. "Yes. This man I just murdered, Marco. Let me explain." He took a deep breath, standing there in the wind, Marco's obtuse fallen body crumpled and bloody behind him in the bow. "I knew Marco. Marco was a violent criminal and a murderer himself, many times over. I know this because ..."

Lucinda cut him off, "Bullshit!"

George and Tim switched their attention from Cecil to Lucinda.

"You don't know that," Lucinda said. "And so what if he was ... a murderer?" She jabbed her chin in Marco's direction. "What you just did to him, in cold blood like that. That was sick, unprovoked, and atrocious. You're the murderer!"

Rebecca was weeping, her crying sounds very human now. Tim had struggled to his knees beside her. He looked drugged and defeated, still recuperating from Cecil's blow as he tenderly stroked his struck jaw.

Cecil held up both hands, pleadingly. "Hear me out, hear me out now. I'll answer all of your questions in a minute, just hear me out first, okay?"

By asking for the ears of his audience, Cecil was buying himself more time to concoct an explanation. "Marco, understand this much, he was a violent and dangerous man. He was a criminal. And who am I to know this, you're asking? Well, I'm a corrections officer. I was transferring Marco—or I should say, in the process of transferring Marco from one prison to another."

There was now a long silence.

"On a cruise ship?" Tim mumbled disbelievingly.

George shook his head. "No. Not on no cruise ship. That's booshit what you tellin' us."

Jesus, Cecil thought. *If only they knew why I had to murder this man. And now I'm jumping through hoops. Imagine trying to explain The Witness to them, though. It would never work.*

"Well, it's a complicated story," Cecil tried, "because ... okay, look, I'm more like a bounty hunter."

"Like a bounty hunter?" Lucinda asked.

"Okay," Cecil conceded. "I *am* a bounty hunter. Not a corrections officer. We bounty hunters have a little more leeway in how we get to do these things. And, no, I wasn't transferring Marco from one prison to another. Obviously. Marco was an escapee from an institution for the criminally insane. This man had been on the loose for weeks. He was wanted."

So far, so good? Cecil couldn't tell if he had a working narrative going or not. He continued ...

"The most important thing that I need you all to understand is this ..." Cecil placed his palms together in a prayerful gesture. "I knew Marco, okay? I knew his case, his history, and I knew him a little bit even on a personal level. It happens in this line of work. You can trust me when I tell you that Marco was an extremely dangerous person. A lit fuse at all times. Marco was a man with multiple murders on his record. You see, Marco was a paranoid schizophrenic. That was his condition."

"Hmm," Eleanor grunted appraisingly. She had raised her head from the crook of her husband's arm and was watching Cecil deliver his oration as if she were a detective. Perhaps this sharp, old bird was in sympathy with Cecil's narrative intent.

Emboldened now, Cecil said, "And that's what made our situation here so dangerous. Marco was on numerous medications. I should know because I've been administering them to him, by force, for the last three days. Those medications were only effective for twenty-four hours. Well, less than that actually if they're discontinued." Cecil paused, letting this sink in. "Those medications went down with our cruise ship."

"Oh, my God," Rebecca said. She pointed at Marco's strewn body and turned her cheek, wincing. "That's why you ..." again she began to weep, now more out of sadness than terror.

"Yes," Cecil said pointedly. "Without his medications, Marco was a time bomb. The stress of our situation here, where we find ourselves, I don't need to belabor a point. This environment was not a healthy one for a man with Marco's issues. With nowhere for any of us to escape to, one of us, or some of us, or all of us would have become the victims of his rage, his paranoia, his violence."

The lifeboat people thought this over in silence for some time. Their heads hung low in contemplative depths as they each played judge and jury with their own conscience. As they meditated, all but Lucinda averted their eyes from Marco's bloody corpse. Cecil took note of this.

"But what you done," George began hoarsely, before Eleanor touched his arm quieting him.

Cecil nodded emphatically, acknowledging the breadth of George's concern. He took a deep wounded breath, and though it was showcased, it was no act. "I did what I felt I had to do, George, knowing what I know, to keep us all safe. I'm not proud of it. I'm sure as hell not happy about it."

"You ain't happy about it," Eleanor labored to agree with Cecil, and by doing so, defend him. "We ain't happy about it none either."

"No, of course you're not, Eleanor." Cecil sat on his haunches, rubbed his face with one hand. When he spoke again, his voice tone was somber. "George? Eleanor? Tim? Rebecca? Lucinda? I'm sorry you all had to witness that. I really am. It was ... I know it was awful."

Everyone was looking out, in different directions, at the sea.

"If there's an afterlife, I'll be judged, one way or the other."

For a long time there was only the sound of the waves, lapping randomly at the sides of the lifeboat, a tinkling of sea spray thrown hitherto by the wind.

Are they accepting any of this? Cecil thought. *Do they have a choice? What choices are these folks contemplating in their minds?*

Finally, "Shouldn't we say a prayer?" Rebecca asked meekly.

God bless her.

"Yes. Yes, we should," Cecil opined.

By their unified silence, everyone appeared to agree.

Eleanor, poignantly sad-faced, led them in prayer.

Soon after the prayer was said, Tim helped Cecil to load Marco's large lifeless body off the side of the boat and into the swallowing sea. Cecil cleaned up the blood alone, in a diligent manner, washing it overboard with many handfuls of splashed water.

It was later in the day, after the measured lunch of granola bars and bottled water that they'd found in the lifeboat's survival box, that Lucinda approached Cecil in a quiet way, at an angle, and spoke to him softly in wind-shrouded privacy. "They believe you," Lucinda said, "with that bullshit story." She lifted her eyes slowly up to Cecil's own and he saw that they were cold, marbled landscapes with two gleaming pupils of obsidian. "It's probably best that way for all of us that they do." Lucinda's words were quick and menacingly delivered behind a long, pointed finger. "But I don't. Not for a second, pal. There is something very wrong with you. I know. *I know.* So, watch yourself."

As Lucinda drifted away to her place in the boat, Cecil noticed that his shipmates had been watching them out of the corner of their eyes. He nodded his head aggressively in the wake of Lucinda's words, as if to agree with her. Perhaps the others wouldn't suspect that anything was awry between them. Cecil however knew differently. Things were awry between them. Lucinda was awry. She was very awry.

The sun diminished into the sea and the day came to an uneventful end.

There was no rescue.

That night, it seemed to Cecil that nobody slept a wink. The stakes were too high. To sleep may be to miss a sign in the sky or across the open sea. Or perhaps it was something else? Had a precedent been set? Last time the crew dozed off, they'd woken to the sight of a man being murdered. Cecil was suspect; an uncomfortable person to sleep in the company of. Who could blame them? They were all so tired and cold and frightened and quiet. It was a long and aimless night at sea. At one point Cecil addressed Tim.

"You got those flares ready, Tim?"

Tim didn't answer him. He was trying to avoid Cecil, maybe even to ignore him out of existence.

"You got those flares?" Cecil calmly repeated.

At last Tim responded in a low key. "Yeah, I got them."

"Good. Keep them dry. Keep them handy."

They were afraid of him, Cecil understood, all of them, even Lucinda. Be that as it may, and although they may not want to admit it to themselves, Cecil knew that they were glad that he had done what he had done. Yes, even Lucinda. Even Lucinda.

It was a long night. The sea had become placid, glassy black, and the stars were clear and sharp as pins in the heavens, but there were no signs of rescue in the sky, no lights placed upon the face of the sea. It was a sea whose horizon was lost in darkness.

Were there any rescuers even looking for them now?

Cecil didn't know.

None of them did.

The sea was a smooth, turquoise sheet and the morning sun was potent, rising like a helium balloon. It was a sharp, cloudless sky and the horizon was dizzyingly empty, rushing everywhere into a void. Cecil inconspicuously studied his shipmates. They all looked drawn, haggard, and less of themselves than yesterday, with the sole exception of Lucinda, whose metabolic strength and mental guile made of her person a comparative picture of aloofness. Cecil had on several occasions throughout the night felt Lucinda studying him from the far end of the lifeboat, her dark, interrogating eyes calibrating him with something far less than admiration guiding her interest.

Tim took a sip from his water bottle and stood up. He placed one hand to his forehead like a visor and stared out at the rising sun. "We're gonna burn today," he said. "You know that, Cecil? Do you? We're gonna burn in this sun. It could be a hundred degrees. No cloud cover, none."

Cecil could see that Tim was starting to come unglued, talking that way in front of his wife. It wasn't like him.

Rebecca looked up slowly from her feet and in a weak voice, barely above a whisper, said, "Somebody's going to come today, though, right, Tim? Cecil?"

Tim stared out in silence at the endless sweeping sea.

"Yes," Cecil said. "Somebody's going to come today. Today's the day."

Rebecca looked over at Cecil and provided him with the faintest indication of a smile before returning her blue eyes to the floor.

Tim was correct. They were all going to burn.

Well before noon the sun had already become an outrage, blazing down upon them unrelentingly from the icy blue shining sky. Eleanor huddled in George's lap and he used his broad arms and bearish chest to shield his wife from the sun as best he could. Rebecca clung likewise to Tim. Cecil could plainly see that her once fair skin had already turned past pink to an agitated stage of red. She was burning. Tim took notice of Cecil observing his wife with concern and at this moment something unspoken passed between the two men.

I can see that you're worried for her, Tim was saying. I appreciate that.

Tim touched his wife's brow and drew a lock of her hair down to cover her eyes and nose. Eleanor sighed painfully as George held her, rocking in place. "They comin', baby, they comin'," George reminded her.

Lucinda was stretched out in the sun, on her back, in the middle of the lifeboat with her eyes closed.

As the noon sun reached its brutal apex, Cecil lay down in the bow of the boat, the same spot where Marco had died the day before. Cecil had already made the observation that his shipmates avoided this area and this was, of course, understandable. The spot was as bright and absent of shade as anywhere else on the boat and certainly no more comfortable, but it was his spot now and he owned it, curling himself up to suffer the sun's scorching head with some semblance of privacy. He shielded his burning face with both arms and shut his eyes against the pain.

Cecil could feel the entire weight of sea undulating slowly beneath him; sense the silent fathoms going down, sideways, every way and beyond, the vast fantastic reach of the sea, floating amorphously within itself. *The sea is its own tomb*, Cecil thought poetically. It had never occurred to him before, this particular thought, but it was so strangely true, wasn't it? The sea is its own tomb. Those thought words echoed through the chambers of his disoriented mind as the sea itself seemed to rise up through the floor of the boat, dissolving the craft, dissolving his person and absorbing his consciousness. He was tired, so very tired. Cecil was going down fast into a dream.

From somewhere deep within the confines of his skull, Cecil heard a sharp abrupt "click." He floated up from his body, free as a ghost, and rose up over it as The Witness. He was approached peripherally by the glazing orb. It merged with him like a giant eye, urgently, and Cecil became the eye. A vision unfolded before him.

He was in the water, in the sea. He was swimming in place, treading water. The lifeboat was drifting away from him, empty, turning in circles. Water was stirring and churning violently all around him and the air was filled with diaphanous whipping mists. Cecil felt as if he were caught beneath the giant turbine of a tornado. Looking up, he could see the helicopter a hundred feet above, like a black praying mantis planted in the sky. The circle of its whirling blades splintered the screaming sun into innumerable diamond flashes. What Cecil came to recognize as an empty rescue basket was poised directly beneath the helicopter's open bay door, vibrating upon its tether. Through the flailing mists Cecil could discern four familiar figures seated inside of the helicopter, wearing orange life preservers: George, Eleanor, Rebecca, and Tim. Two other uniformed figures were up there. One was couched in the bay door and tending to the cable line, the other was standing up, waving his baggy arms, and appeared to be shouting something to the pilot.

Am I the only one left? Cecil wondered. *Where's Lucinda?* Cecil was wading inside of the whirlpool current, turning in slow cumbersome circles like a cork. A rift of sea spray lashed at his face and momentarily blinded him. As his blurred vision returned to focus, Cecil could see the rescue helicopter rise several feet in the air and begin to turn its tail around as it jockeyed for a new position. One of the uniformed men was bracing himself with both arms in the frame of the helicopter's door, leaning out, looking down and shaking a fist at Cecil as if to tell him, "Hold on, hold on. Your turn is coming soon. Just hold on." A feeling not unlike a religious rapture was coming over Cecil and it was stupendous in its glory. As he was presently The Witness, engaged in prophecy, he knew, with certainty, that he would be saved.

They all would be saved.

Just then, as he was celebrating in his heart, Cecil was assaulted from behind, grabbed, pushed down, and submerged beneath the water. It was a long-fingered pair of hands that gripped his neck with vice-like strength, engaging him in a strangle hold. The grim sea filled his eyes, filled his ears. As Cecil slipped down deeper beneath the face of the sea, someone was climbing up his back to position themselves atop his shoulders. Thighs became a scissor around his throat. Cecil could hear the knees lock over the back of his neck and squeeze at the base of his skull as if to pop it free from his spine. Long, witchy fingers dug into his scalp, knotting themselves in his hair.

It's Lucinda, Cecil suddenly realized. She's drowning me.

It was a dark understanding, getting darker as Cecil went down, down through the glassy green water, Lucinda kicking repeatedly from above. It was too late now. He was tired. No fight remained in him. Cecil's fate was sealed. He was going down, down towards the very bottom of the sea.

There was a loud "click" and the vision wheeled away from him. Cecil came to wakefulness with a gasp. With a heroic effort of will, he collected his reeling mind and looked around.

His shipmates were there, each one of them in their own spot, sitting sorely in the blistering sun, silent and suffering. But they were, of course, still alive, still there, adrift at sea, baking in the Mediterranean sun.

Cecil watched them.

George and Eleanor sat heads down in tandem, holding each other as the last vestiges of hope faded from their eyes. Tim and Rebecca were curled into each other in an angular collection of reddening limbs as each tried to shade the other in some fashion from the relentless sun.

Lucinda sat directly across from Cecil, Indian style, facing him from the stern of the lifeboat. Her long face was blank, her obsidian eyes unblinking.

She was watching him.

***

Dress Up
by Gary Van Haas, Greece

An anxious, nice-looking man in his forties, wearing a dark blue pinstriped suit was seated in a psychiatrist's office waiting room fidgeting restlessly. He got to his feet to leave, thought the better of it and sat back down.

His name was Bill Petersen.

The internal door finally opened and Dr. Ted Wilcox, forty-two, with greying hair, came to him.

"Well, hello, Bill, your call took me by surprise. Come in and we'll talk."

He threw his arm over Bill's shoulder warmly, ushered him into his private office. A large brown leather couch and glass-top desk with a few paintings by Dali and two tall ferns dominated the cheerful interior. Dr. Wilcox seated himself in his tan overstuffed swivel chair and motioned Bill to take a seat.

"Sit down and tell me what this urgent call is about. If it's about the golf game on Sunday, I'm coming."

Bill appeared restless and uneasy. "No, Ted, it's not about that. It's about something else."

"Is it about Sally again?"

"No, it's not her. It's me ..." he said with distraught, weary eyes. "I think I'm losing my mind."

"Come on, old buddy. I've known you half my life and never seen you like this."

Bill glanced at his friend, apprehensive.

"Okay, Ted, you tell me if you think I'm going crazy. It all started about two weeks ago ..."

He started relating the story, remembering back, gazing out the window staring blankly at a building across the street. His vision moved to a sign out front, BRAVADO ADVERTISING AGENCY, to the large plate glass window of the CEO's office at the agency. He was sitting gazing through the glass door at the frenzied activity going on within the agency's halls and cubicles. He looked at the computer on his congested desk, shook his head, and let out a fearful sigh.

Taking a deep breath, he continued telling the doctor. "My account exec, John Simmons, and the rest of us had been invited to a big client's annual masquerade ball ..."

In the ad office, Bill glanced up from his desk as John Simmons came through the door, grabbed a chair and brashly threw his legs up on Bill's desk, then leaned back arrogantly in his seat.

"Well, Bill, that wraps the Sartell account. Guess that makes a third bonus for me this week. Those dummies didn't have enough sense to get another bid. Jesus fucking Christ, I can't believe how gullible people are. Ha! But no sweat off my back."

Bill looked at him with distain.

"John, did you ever think that maybe those people trust you?"

"I can see you've grown soft, Bill. You gotta go in for the kill on these deals. Like W.C. Fields used to say, 'Never give a sucker an even break.'" John laughed as Bill handed him a note.

"I just received this from the Parker account," Bill told him. "It's an invitation to their annual costume ball and I want us both to be there to represent the company."

"Oh, man. Do I have to attend these silly things?"

"Yes, John, I want you to be there this year and no excuse this time." Bill leaned forward and gently removed John's legs from his desk.

"Okay, Bill, but I'm warning you, don't push. There's a hell of a lot of agencies that need a good rep, and I might take the Parker account with me, too!"

John got up in a huff, walked out, and slammed the door behind him.

The man was incorrigible. Bill shook his head and went back to typing.

*

While John was driving home that night, he spotted a sign over a small, unassuming shop on a side street. The sign above the door read "Marie's Costumes & Nostalgia Shop." He thought it curious after just getting the costume ball invitation.

At that same moment, the face of a mysterious, old woman peered out the window from inside, stared at him, then disappeared.

John parked his car, got out.

Entering the shop, the old place seemed deserted, with no sign of the old woman he saw previously in the window. The place was dimly lit and gloomy, seemingly untouched by time.

He paid no mind, began looking around at various costumes hanging on the racks. Most were a little tawdry and insipid, clowns and ghouls for the most part.

He continued fingering through racks of creepy clown costumes and started to pull one out when the old lady in her seventies with white scraggly hair and wrinkled face appeared from behind, staring out at him with wild steel-blue eyes.

"Oh wow, lady! You gave me a fright."

"My name is Marie. What can I do for you?" she inquired.

"I'm going to a ball and need a costume, something interesting. I hope you have something better than this."

"Perhaps I can show you something upstairs," she said. "That's where I keep the good ones. They're period costumes. Very realistic and some are authentic. Come, follow me ..."

She waved him to follow her as she walked up the creaky staircase.

She led him up into an attic where the air was stale and musty and the light subdued. John brushed away cobwebs as he made his way to racks where bizarre costumes and frightful masks hung from the rafters. It was a place out of time, untouched for years.

The costumes seem to glitter and sparkle as he passed them, and they appeared to glow oddly as John touched them. He smiled at the old woman.

"This is more like it. You should have this stuff downstairs, probably double your business."

He continued fingering through the racks while Marie watched him attentively.

"These costumes aren't for just anyone. They're special," she said. Then she pulled out a costume of a World War I, Doughboy Officer.

"Here, try this one. I think it suits you."

She helped him put on the jacket.

John saw a large antique oval mirror in the corner of the attic, walked over and stood in front of it gazing at his reflection wearing the jacket.

Then she moved behind John, gazing into the mirror as their images merged eerily together.

"Oh yes, see how you look. Do you see? Do you remember? Do you remember?"

John was staring eyes fixed at his image when the background in the mirror gradually changed to a rural countryside setting. Then he heard the distant sound of a cannon, and all at once there was a bright flash of light and his mind went blank.

*

The cannon noise continued in the background and suddenly John reappeared in a rustic cottage in the countryside in France. On the stucco wall was a calendar with the month of May displayed and the year, 1916, was printed on the bottom of it.

John, oblivious to the person he was previously, was seated at a large oak table in a sparsely furnished cottage in front of a roaring fireplace.

In the background, more sounds of distant cannon were heard. The door opened and a lovely, twenty-year-old disheveled woman in a red cape entered the room.

"They're getting closer!" she said worriedly. "They'll kill us if we stay. We must leave now!"

"I told you before, I can't," said John standing up putting on his Doughboy officer's jacket.

"What about the baby? You won't help your own child?" she pleaded.

He said nothing and was about to leave when she blocked his way.

"I told you before, you stupid peasant, I can't take you. Our unit is moving out," he said coldly. "Now get out of my way!" and then shoved her heartlessly to the ground.

"You used me, you bastard! You never intended to stay, did you?"

In the next moment, cannon shells began bursting and rifle fire rung out around the house.

"Yes, I used you," he said shamelessly. "This is war, and in case you didn't notice, everyone's expendable. Goodbye."

He ran out the door and once outside, found himself dodging bullets and explosions.

She chased after him, following out the door.

"No, don't go, don't leave me," she begged.

John heard her and ran by a tree when he was hit by a bullet, and fell to the ground wounded, moaning in pain.

"My god, I'm hit! Somebody help me," he cried, whimpering.

She ran to him, but as she did, she was also hit by a bullet.

"I'm bleeding. I'm dying ..." he groaned.

She crawled next to him, stretching her hand out to comfort him. "I'm dying too," she said sorrowfully.

With the last of her strength, she wrapped her arms around him and pulled him close to her.

"Now we'll be together, my love. Do you remember the good times we had when your regiment first came to the village? Do you remember? Do you remember?"

There was bright flash as a cannon ball exploded next to them. John gasped in horror as all went white.

*

Instantaneously, after the bright flash, John found himself back in the costume shop again, standing in front of the oval mirror. He was staring at himself in a trance-like state, his eyes wide with fear and confusion.

The old lady moved in behind him in the mirror, smiling benignly.

"Do you remember? Do you remember?"

John quickly snapped out of it, tore off the jacket, and threw it on the floor.

"What the hell was that? What are you talking about? Remember what?"

"The time ..." she said matter of fact. "Do you remember the time?"

He looked at his wristwatch, shocked.

"Oh, Jesus, the time ... it's seven thirty already. I've got to go."

"Do you like the costume, sir?"

"Yes, yes, very nice. Let me think about it."

He put on his suit coat, straightened his tie.

"I'll stop by tomorrow, if that's okay."

"Whatever you wish."

He went down the stairs where she showed him out the door, eyeing him inquisitively as he left.

*

Back safely at his home, John's family were seated at the dining table as he came racing in through the front door. His wife, Marjorie, and his sixteen-year-old daughter gaped at him inquiringly as he seated himself at the head of the table.

"Sorry I'm late, guys," he said, plopping some mashed potatoes on his plate. "Some business I had to take care of on the way home."

"Business always comes before your family," Marjorie said glibly. "What happened, a little extra overtime with your new secretary?"

"Very funny," he quipped. "No, I had to get a costume for a ball. Actually, I had a strange experience just now at Marie's Costumes. I tried on one of those old World War I uniforms and I had the funniest feeling I'd been there before."

"What, the costume shop?"

"No, in the middle of World War I!"

"Sounds like a déjà vu, Dad," his daughter said. "Everybody has them."

"Whatever it was, it sure felt real."

"What an imagination you have," his wife chuckled. "I think you've been in the ad biz too long."

"Well, where's the costume, Dad?"

"Haven't made up my mind yet. When I went in there, it was five o'clock and when I left it was damn near seven-thirty."

Marjorie glanced at him, apprehensively.

"Two and half hours and you didn't get a costume? Have you been drinking again? Wait a minute. What does this Marie look like?"

John had had enough badgering, threw down his napkin and stood up.

"Damn it, I'm telling you it happened just like I said. I wasn't drinking, and Marie is near seventy years old, so knock it off!"

"Fine," said Marjorie. "Let's finish our dinner and let it be, shall we?"

John sat down and they went back to eating.

*

In their bedroom later, in the wee hours before dawn, John had been tossing and turning and unable to sleep, while Marjorie snoozed peacefully by his side.

He found himself staring at the ceiling as he reflected on the costume shop and the old woman, with her haunting words ringing in his ears, "Do you remember? Do you remember?"

*

The next day after work on his way home, John went back to Marie's Costumes. He drove by the old brownstone, stopped in front and parked. He stared up curiously at the glittering sign on the façade.

Then, as if some hidden force were driving him, he got out of his car and entered. He called Marie's name and she appeared out of nowhere, grinning expectantly.

"Welcome. You've probably come for the Doughboy uniform, but I found something else you might like. Let's go upstairs. Come ..."

John followed her up to the attic. There was something different about the place this time. The overhead lights appeared to vibrate and the costumes on the racks glowed incongruously with a life of their own. Out the window, he noticed the last rays of daylight fading and he hesitated for a moment.

"Wait, it's late, I don't think I really want to see any more costumes."

"Nonsense," said Marie. "First take a look, then see what you think."

She moved through the racks.

"Ah yes, here it is. Try this on ..."

She pulled out a complete 1800s cowboy's outfit with Stetson hat, plaid shirt, brown leather vest, boots, and gun holster belt, but without the pistol.

John was somewhat amused as Marie placed the cowboy hat on his head. He eagerly removed his coat and strapped on the gun belt.

"Oh yes, it's more you," she said enthusiastically. "Take a look in the mirror."

He walked over and gazed at his outfit in the mirror.

"Yes, I like it. But where's the gun? There's got to be a gun ..."

252

As soon as he said gun, there was a bright flash of light and he was immediately transported to another time.

*

When John opened his eyes again, he had forgotten who he was before, and found himself in a ranch house in the 1800s where a pretty young girl with long black hair was cooking food in a pot hung in a fire hearth.

John was looking through the cupboards when the lady at the hearth turned to him. She was a stunning Mexican girl in her late teens, wearing colorful native dress.

She wiped the sweat from her brow and started putting food plates on the table.

"Where's my gun, Anita?" he said irritated. "I know I left it here last night."

She pointed to a side drawer, and he went over, pulled it open and took out his Colt .45.

"Sam Huston's gonna pay me good to fight and I don't give a good damn if they're Mexicans or Indians!"

"If you kill my people, Johnny, you kill me a little, too."

"Hey, I told you not to sass me about man's talk. Now get back to cookin'. That's all you folks are good for anyhow."

He strapped on his gun belt and headed for the door. She stopped her cooking and stood in front of him.

"No, Johnny, don't do it. Please!"

He paid no attention and slapped her.

"Get out of my way, woman!"

"You treat me like this and desert me? You never loved me. You were just in need of a woman, any woman!"

She quickly grabbed his gun from his holster and pointed it at him.

"Now wait a minute, honey," he said. "Think what you're doing. I love you. It's just that I gotta fight for us Texans."

"You're nothing but a lowly gringo dog and you will die like one."

"No Anita, don't. Please!"

With rage in her eyes, she pulled trigger. John went down with a look of shock, clutching his gut, screaming in pain.

Back in the costume shop, John lay on the floor in front of the oval mirror holding his stomach, moaning and groaning, writhing in fear ...

"No, don't do it. I don't wanna die!"

"Are you all right?" said a woman's voice, and when he looked up, he saw the elderly face of Marie staring down, leaning over him.

"Do you remember now? Do you remember?"

"Yes, yes, I remember!" he cried. "Make it stop, damn it. I don't want to do this anymore!"

"What are you talking about, sir? Stop what?"

John glanced down at his stomach, saw no blood. Embarrassed, he quickly composed himself, jumped to his feet, and angrily grabbed her arm as she tried to move away.

"All right, what the hell's going on, lady? I come here to buy a costume and I get a crazy side show. What's your game?"

She gazed at him cautiously. 'I'm afraid I don't know what you're talking about."

"You know what I'm talking about! You drugged me, didn't you?"

"You're hurting my arm, sir. Please let go," she begged.

He finally let her go.

"Okay, what was it, hypnosis or drugs? I can have your ass in jail for this!"

"I think not, sir."

"Why not?"

"Because I have other costumes to show you. Certainly you want the best one, yes?"

"Are you nuts? I'm not listening to any more of this. I'm getting out of this loony bin."

"Oh, there's no hurry, sir."

"There you go with the cryptic crap again. I don't have the time for this. I'm outta here."

"But I have plenty of time. You'll be back," she calmly assured.

He gaped at the old lady, stupefied.

"You better be careful. Somebody's gonna lock you away for messing up their minds spiking their drinks."

"But you didn't have anything to drink here."

He knew she was right. He gave her a nasty look, turned, went down the stairs and out the door.

In his car, driving home, John reflected on the old lady and her shop. It all seemed so real, he thought.

He glanced at his watch and noticed it was eleven o'clock at night already. He hit the gas pedal and sped home.

*

Arriving at his house, he found the place dark. He quietly and cautiously entered the living room and started up the stairs when his wife Marjorie appeared standing on the upper railing.

"John, where have you been? It's not like you to do this to me."

"I just had a little drink with the boys, dear."

"Really? Since when did you start going out with the boys?"

"Since now, that's when! A man needs to get away once in a while," he fended.

"I've heard enough. I think it's time we go to bed," she demanded and went into the bedroom.

*

Once again in the early hours of the morning, John had been awake, not slept a wink, tossing and turning, thinking about the costume shop.

At six o'clock in the morning his alarm went off and he stumbled out of his bed groggy-eyed and into the shower, getting ready for work.

Exhausted and bleary-eyed from lack of sleep, John arrived at his office disheveled and unshaven. His perky, blonde receptionist greeted him on his way in.

"Morning, John. Love your new stubble look. It's in style."

He hardly looked at her, 'Listen, I'm expecting a call from the Reardon account. Put it through to my office immediately when it comes in."

He leaned over, gave her a peck on the cheek.

"I like the smell of that perfume," he said

"It's called 'Le Dark Marie.' You like it?"

He was taken back when he heard the name, sloughed it off, and headed for his private office.

John walked into his office and sat at his desk looking at the piles of paperwork in front of him. Then he glanced up, saw Bill Petersen, the CEO of the company, walking toward him, and quickly acted like he was hard at work. Bill entered John's office in a smart blue suit with white tie and was surprised seeing his haggard appearance.

"My goodness, John, you look terrible. Are you ill? If so, why don't you take the day off?"

John managed a smile, 'No, I'm fine, really. Just didn't sleep well."

"Well, I want you looking tops for the Parker Costume Ball tomorrow night. Did you get a costume?"

"Yes. I mean, no," he fumbled. "I mean, I almost did, but didn't get it yet."

"Are you trying to get out of going?"

"No, Bill, I'll be there."

Bill glanced at John's artboards, noticed some of the type on the layouts was upside down.

"You sure you're all right?"

"Yes, I mean, no ... I have to tell you, Bill, there's something crazy going on. I went to a costume shop and things got weird."

Bill looked at him, puzzled, 'Weird, what do you mean weird?"

"I'm telling you, something evil is going on in that place. Some old lady named Marie there got me to put on a World War I officer's uniform and a cowboy outfit and suddenly I was transported to those time periods!"

255

"Come on," Bill laughed, "what's the gag?"

"No, I'm serious, I was looking into her mirror, when—wham—suddenly I was in another time!"

"John, have you been hitting the sauce again?"

"No. Look," he pleaded. "I don't know how to explain it, but it happened twice. I was transported back in time somehow."

"Well, everybody's had a déjà-vu ..."

"But it wasn't like that. Everything around me was real. I even saw the calendar date on the wall on one and it was May 1916!"

Okay, John, this is getting absurd. Are you sure you're not trying to get out of going to the ball?"

"No, I'll be there just like I promised. I'm telling you, there's something peculiar going on at that costume shop."

"Why don't you take the day off,' Bill said. "Go home, get some rest and get a shave, for God's sake, before you scare people off."

"Maybe you're right. I'll try and get some work done at home later."

"Good idea," Bill said patting John on the back. "Get some rest."

John gathered his coat from the rack and put it on.

"Thanks, Bill, and don't worry, I'll see you at the ball tomorrow night."

When he left, Bill was watching him, wondering about his mental state.

*

On his way home, John took the main road through town when he thought about the costume shop. He remembered he promised Bill he would get a costume for the ball.

"Hell, why not? I don't believe in this hocus-pocus anyway," he assured himself.

He turned the wheel of the car around and headed for Marie's.

In front of the shop, he sat in his car for a minute or two, staring blankly at the building with its red blinking neon sign. He then got out of his car and walked to the door.

The door slowly creaked open and Marie peered her head out, glancing around to see if anyone was with him.

"Welcome again, sir. Please, come in."

John hesitated a moment.

"Let's get this straight, lady," he told her emphatically, "I want a costume this time and *just* a costume. No tricks, okay?"

"No, of course not," she quietly replied.

He glanced around the dark interior trying to appear casual, but was still apprehensive.

Marie walked over to a small table in the corner and switched on an antique Tiffany lamp. She looked at John and smiled, knowingly.

"I told you you'd be back, sir."

"Yeah, okay, fine. I just want a costume and I'm out of here for good.

"Yes, sir, follow me." She led him up the old creaking staircase.

Once in the attic, Marie went to a rack of costumes, leafed through the garments, found one and pulled it out. It was a black felt cloak and hood with some kind of bizarre symbols and astrological signs stitched on it.

"Ah yes, this is the one. Try this on."

John was hesitant at first. "What the heck is it? I don't want to wear that. I want something more me. Don't you have ..."

But Marie wasn't listening and slipped the cloak over his shoulders. She quickly went to the oval mirror and turned it toward him.

"Oh my, that's it! See how radiant you look?'

A floating ethereal feeling came over John as he glanced down at the astrological symbols.

"Uh-oh, something's happening again. Why are you doing this to me?"

"Don't you remember? It was a long, long time ago ..."

*

A bright flash lit the room and the mirror instantaneously became an extraordinary doorway into the lush English countryside.

John was now in the Middle Ages where stately castles and thatched brick houses were seen in the distance.

John stepped out from the mirror and found himself in a medieval castle chamber, standing in the middle of a large magic circle with a pentagram and lit candles placed around it.

John began chanting, pouring various herbs and solutions on a smoking brazier in front of him.

"Come forth, Ashtoreth. By the power of Almighty Lucifer, I command thee!"

Slowly the smoke began to rise, taking on a ghostly form, then an unearthly demonic vision appeared and spoke to him.

"Master, why hast thou summoned me?"

John held up a small vial of potion and showed it to the apparition.

"You lied to me. I command thee to give me the secret to the Magic Mirror!"

The ghostly demon looked at him, 'I have told you, Master. You must show your gratitude with an offering of sacrifice. A sacrifice of blood, human blood."

John glared at the demon, holding out the vial threateningly.

"I don't believe you. Give me what I request or by the powers of Tetragrammaton I will banish your soul to damnation for eternity. I command thee!"

"I cannot comply, Lord, until you make a sacrifice."

*

In that moment, there was a knock at the door. John turned to see who it was and the demon swiftly vanished from view.

John called out, "Who is it and what do you want?"

A young girl's voice answered, "It is I, the chambermaid, milord. I've come to clean your chambers."

John put out the candles and let her in.

The girl was attractive, around the age of nineteen wearing rags for clothing and carried a bucket and mop. She immediately set about her chores cleaning the floor while John scrutinized her every move.

"What's your name, my lovely?" he casually inquired.

"Mary Hardwick, sire."

When she glanced up at him, John knew he had seen the same facial features before, but couldn't remember where.

"Won't take me long, sire," she said humbly. "I'll be out your way soon."

John stood next to a large oval mirror in the corner.

"Come 'ere, my dear girl. I want to look at you. Have you seen how lovely you are? Come ..."

She half-heartedly put down her mop wondering what he was up to, looked up at him curiously, brushing back her golden hair.

"Me, sire?"

"Yes, I am talking about you. Look at yourself. Come closer ..."

She stood up and walked to him in front of the mirror, studying herself, touching her face when John drew a dagger from his cloak and stabbed her viciously in the back.

A look of horror came over her, 'Why, sire? Why?"

Clutching her back, she staggered, knocking over the table where John had placed the vial of secret potion. The vile crashed to the floor where its contents spilled out mixing with glass and blood, and suddenly she vanished.

With bloody dagger still in hand, John stood thunderstruck. He glanced around the room bewildered, wondering how the girl had disappeared.

A second later, he heard his name being called faintly. He whirled around and realised the voice was coming from the mirror. He moved toward it warily and saw it was the young girl in the mirror calling to him.

"Why, John? Why did you do it?"

*

Another bright flash of light and John was back in the costume shop.

John was looking at his startled face staring back at him from the mirror, still wearing the cloak of the Magician. Marie slinked up next to him.

"Do you remember now, John?"

"How did you know my name? What are you talking about?" he protested, throwing off the cloak.

"The mirror does not lie."

John was beside himself, "What are you talking about? You don't expect me to believe this happened, do you?"

He grabbed a bottle from the table and raised it threateningly toward the mirror.

"I'm going to put an end to this right now."

Frantic, Marie lurched for his arm to stop him.

"No, don't!" she pleaded. "Our fates will be consumed forever in the mirror!"

"You're insane!" he said and threw the bottle, smashing the mirror to pieces with a loud crash. Glass and shards went flying, and in the next instant, they both vanished.

Only a small liquid pool of shiny silver mercury was left, mixed with broken pieces of glass and blood on the floor.

*

Back at the psychiatrist's office, Dr. Wilcox sat perplexed behind his desk staring woefully at his friend, Bill Petersen.

Bill had just finished his story what John had told him about the costume shop and was restless, pacing the floor anxiously, wringing his hands. Bill stopped, leaned forward and looked deeply into the doctor's eyes.

"And that's what happened, Ted. Now he's vanished.

I should have listened. The woman must've taken him back to different lifetimes."

Ted stood up from his chair, 'Come on, Bill, you're an intelligent man. You really don't believe that, do you?"

Then Bill reached in his pocket, took out a clipping from an old newspaper and handed it to him.

"Then how do you explain this. You met John, so how can this be possible?"

Ted took the paper and looked at it. It was dated May 2, 1916, and then he saw it. There was an old photo with the article showing the same John Simmons he had met, smiling out at him wearing a World War I officer's uniform.

"My God, Bill!" Ted cried, shaking his head. "I really don't know how to explain it either."

*

A few days later, two police detectives were browsing around the attic of Marie's costume shop investigating the mysterious disappearance of John Simmons and the old lady.

The detectives were looking through the racks of costumes when they noticed a large broken mirror. "Here's something, Hank. Looks like there's was some kind of struggle." He leaned down, picked up a piece of glass.

"Maybe it was an accident," Hank commented

"Doesn't look like an accident. There's an overturned table next to the mirror."

Jotting in his notepad, Hank said, "Still say the guy ran off with a broad, happens all the time."

His partner stooped down to take a closer look. There was a small pool of mercury near a broken shard of glass and he thought he saw something moving.

"What the hell's that?" he said, stunned.

They both looked closer and gasped when they saw John's face staring up at them from mercury puddle. John was frantically calling out to them in a muted voice, "Please, help me ... get me out of here!"

Shocked, Detective Hank reeled back in fright while his partner gasped, each looked at one another speechless.

Lost for words, Hank was trembling, "What are we gonna do, Mike? Nobody will ever believe this."

John cried out again, and in a panic, Hank stomped his foot down on the mercury, splashing glass and mercury in all directions, and all went deathly silent.

They both stood speechless for a moment.

"Jesus Christ, Hank. Why'd you do that? It was the guy, John Simmons's face from his wife's photo."

"I don't care who it was. I'm not writing this up on any report, are you? They'll think we lost our minds and will never believe it."

"You're right. I'm putting this down as a simple case of runaway husband."

"What the hell was it?"

"Forget about it, Hank. We didn't see nothin'."

The two detectives backed up slowly, turned off the attic lights, and started down the stairs.

"Yeah, let's leave be," said Hank fretfully. "Place gives me the creeps."

As they left and slammed door shut, an eerie silence descended over the shop. Then a few moments later, the faint cries were heard again coming from upstairs.

"Please, help me! Get me out of here ... please!"

***

The Toy-Doll from Her Youth
by Sergio Palumbo, Italy

Seen from the outside in that rural setting, the house looked a bit
outdated. Inside, however, Elixabete Moreish knew that it was spacious,
well furnished, and very cozy. The long slate roof, wide pine decking, a
peculiar stone fireplace, and the first floor en suite bedrooms were a few
of the special features it offered, and all of those memories flooded back
into her mind. Located on one of the most verdant country roads in
Chittenden County along which you could find an abundance of apple
orchards, the house was just three miles from the small town of Winooski.
It was a typical Vermont country home, built in 1921—*or was it 1922?*—
with open meadows surrounding it, but it had all the amenities and
comforts of a modern residence. The house had never been close to
shopping, but that wasn't important at the time, because she was very
young when she lived there. Her father usually drove her to school and
the stores in the city nearby.

That morning, the forty-seven-year-old chestnut-eyed woman with
frizzy fair hair—her curls having been recently dyed to a vivid blonde
color—had been driving for many hours along Interstate 89 that crossed
Chittenden County from east to west. She had then made a northward
turn, driving along the lake shoreline before getting to that rural area
outside Winooski where her childhood home stood. She had been
thinking about going back to that place for many months, wanting to
spend a weekend there perhaps, but she had been very busy until just
recently.

Now she had been forced to go there to finally settle the matter of
her dead mother's inheritance. It was obvious that the old house needed

renovations, which would take several months, if Elixabete decided to spend her money to fix it up. The intention of her last partner, whom she had left several months ago after a serious disagreement, had been to turn such an inherited worn-out stone-and-wood structure into a new mansion so they could spend their vacations there, along with another beautiful residence she already had in the countryside. But she had different plans for the house, her project ideas springing from personal reasons from long ago.

She was wearing a gray leather jacket with underarm and side gussets, over an expensive imported violet long-sleeve wrap dress that was endowed with a surplice neckline and a pleated skirt that showed off her long legs. Elixabete had been strolling the wide garden paths in her stylish and very fashionable attire, circling the building and examining many things that matched her past recollections from when she was a girl there growing up. Well, a few things were different from what she remembered, but most of them were still in the places she knew they had been those years ago. And, strange to say, it was as if she was circling around and around without directly heading for her real destination: the old basement of the house itself. In a way, she was afraid of what she would find when she finally went down there. Or, maybe, she was deeply afraid of *what might not be there anymore*, hidden under the floor, where it had remained concealed for years ...

After working up her courage, even if she was still dubious, thought it was time to go inside. As she entered, she immediately noticed that pictures of her mother and her family were still everywhere in the house: her father and her older brother were even in some of them as well. All of that reminded her of something she remembered very well, but something that she had tried to keep out of her mind so far. As Elixabete kept walking on, she went into the living room downstairs, with all those light-colored bookshelves, the Key Town coffee table she had always thought was a little outre, and the two Treylan corner chaises that she had snuggled into for so many hours. Rounding a corner, she finally spotted the family's old LCD TV. How many nights she had spent there, watching movies and new episodes of her favorite shows, staying up late while eating sweets or listening to her preferred MP3 files in the dim light of her Holtkoetter lamp situated along the opposite wall.

After a short stop to look at the nearby bathroom—and also to relieve herself after the long drive—her stomach began to hurt. She thought back on what she had eaten that day, but decided her upset stomach wasn't due to something she had ingested. No, it had to be something else. And then her eyes turned to the left, where the entrance to the basement was, and her heart began beating wildly.

Recollections, afterthoughts, even a few worries—many things were presently fluttering around inside her mind. After switching the light on, the anxious Elixabete finally went down the stairs into the basement of the old house that she knew all too well. It was down here that she had kissed her first boyfriend, during a weekend when her parents were abroad on vacation, but it wasn't just that memory that made her feel ill at ease now. She was about thirteen then, and she could still picture the blue sleeveless dress she wore—not that she had kept it on for long after they had started hugging and it all had become more passionate. She could still feel the touch of his lips, his warm breath and picture the short haircut he had, even though the details about his face were unclear nowadays. As a matter of fact, more than thirty years had passed since that evening, and she had been with many other young men after him.

The small window on the left let her see that it was already midday outside and the bars on either side made it clear that there was no way out. There had never been a second exit from that basement, there was only the entrance leading upstairs in this part of their house. That room had been used for storage for nearly twenty years before her father died, and she remembered that many old chairs, cabinets, and damaged tables were kept down there when her family decided not to get rid of them once and for all because of some emotional attachments. Some of those were still here, as she was discovering now.

Actually, there was a precise reason she had come here again, and it was not because she wanted to see the old house another time. It had been here that it all had started, when she was still very young—six or seven, she didn't remember exactly—and it involved that toy-doll she had been given as a gift some months before. It had become an object of entertainment—*her peculiar style of entertainment, of course.* The name of the doll originally introduced in the 1960s as the fictional boyfriend of famous female doll, it had a fantastically fashionable line of clothing and accessories, and it was very handsome to her eyes.

To be specific, the model her parents had purchased for her was the one built from 1977 on, that was much better and, in its latest version, featured a dimpled smile, a head that could swivel, bent arms, a more muscular physique, and underwear permanently molded to his body. The previous dolls had only straight, non-bendable arms, and a head that could only turn left and right. There had been many TV commercials about this doll at that time, the same commercials that you could see on the web today, and the sales of those toys had been very profitable for many years. Who knows, probably it was simply the beautiful features it had, along with all the movable parts its body was made of, that had shaped her following behavior or that had made her start thinking about what her relationship with the doll might turn into. Or maybe her deepest wild desires were already in her mind before she got the doll, but she couldn't be truly sure about it. The fact was that the toy-doll itself had proven to be a perfect target on which she could easily start practicing her dissections, along with hiding the severed parts.

It was strange to think that, as commonly happened, all young children loved to mutilate their most recent toy in order to see what lay inside, sooner or later. For her, things had been very different, as Elixabete liked to cut up the many parts of the body of the doll, even though not just to discover what was inside, but also she liked to hide the parts, unseen from anyone else, mainly in the garden of her family house, but not only there. And she didn't know if she had done it all on purpose, as if she was afraid in her heart that her parents would blame her for having destroyed her toy-doll afterwards. Instead, the woman thought she had acted that way because she felt ashamed—as if she knew that what she did was wrong and simply didn't want anyone to see the result of her violent cutting. From this game, it was a short step to her later behavior, when she had started killing and cutting real individuals instead of simple toy-dolls of a time gone by.

As the woman very slowly moved on, her feet walked over the heavy paving stones that constructed the basement floor, both eyes attentively looking at those as if she was searching for something in particular. She remembered that one of them had always been easily movable—even though it wasn't easy to locate it at present—and she had hidden one of her belongings under that stone long ago. Elixabete really yearned to find it again, hoping that it would still be there. That object truly meant something to her, without fail.

*

The small town of Winooski had never been a very crowded place, the same as the whole of Chittenden County, despite the fact that it was situated within the most populous county in the state. From 2000 to 2008, residents had left the area in high numbers for places outside Vermont, and the population of the locals had only increased slightly, mostly in part because of immigrants from other countries. The city's population was only six thousand when she moved away, so there had never been a lot of opportunity for her to find targets that she could practice her wildest and most bloody desires on, given the fact that any unexpected disappearances were soon noticed when they occurred. In fact, the city had a very low crime rate and alcohol was involved in most of such cases, all things considered. For that reason, she had always been forced to be very cautious when she lived in that small town. Eventually she had moved to New York, once and for all, where she got a job as a renowned lecturer.

She well remembered the first time she had done it, *the real first time*. That old woman, of about ninety, lay on the table. A whitish cover was on most her body, her wrinkled and pale skin ended just below her shoulders and seemed to be just waiting for the cut. Well, the poor one would have run immediately away from there and would have tried to defend herself if she just weren't tied, or if she had been strong enough; the same as she would have tried to save herself if her destiny wasn't already sealed. As Elixabete had begun her cuts and blood started spreading on the table itself and pouring onto the floor, across the room, the breath of life would soon move away from that old individual, and then the dissection would follow. Nobody was ever going to find the remains of the first of her victims, or any of her following ones, given her precise method that separated the severed parts of the dead body and buried them underground in different locations, being very far away from each other— at times as far apart as seventy miles. And that was where they would stay forever, unless someone found them by chance, one day, which hadn't happened so far. Probably the pieces of those ill-fated corpses weren't lucky enough to ever be discovered, the same bad luck as had happened to all the men and women they originally pertained to, before their final passing.

At times, she had also played that bloody game with her best friend, Patrizia, the only girl Elixabete knew who loved the murders and subsequent dissections of their victims as much as she did. In fact, Patrizia had proven to be much crueler than her at times. Anyway, that was just her point of view, given the fact that, from the perspective of the poor targets of their actions, it should have been really very difficult to exactly determine who was the more eager at making them suffer before putting an end to their lives. Strange to be said, Patrizia also was of Italian descent, like Elixabete, even if she didn't think that was the real motive behind their bloody merciless behavior. *Or was it?*

How many times had they looked in silence at the blood together and then at each other while a murder was in progress? Actually, it had gone that way for a few years before Elixabete was forced to resettle eventually, in order to start her new job elsewhere. Obviously, she had also been obligated to finally get rid of her friend and beloved playmate before moving away from town, as she knew that she would never leave any person alive behind her who had witnessed so many of her crimes and who might turn against her one day. Killing her and cutting her into pieces hadn't proved to be as enjoyable as it had been when Elixabete had previously played that game with other victims. Truthfully, it had left a strange aftertaste in her mouth when all was over. But the woman was certain it had to be done, so, no excuses, and no regrets.

Besides, many other changes had taken place when she started living in New York. Actually, Winooski had always been a quiet town where people lived peacefully, at least most of them, and where there had been only a very few CCTVs on the streets in downtown and even fewer on the outskirts of town. That fact had greatly helped her in finding, assaulting, taking by force and killing all the right targets of her bloody desires whenever the perfect moment came, according to her will and her experience. But things had proven to be much more difficult in New York where almost all the streets had security video-cameras watching the entrances of many buildings, costly mansions, old manors and modern facilities. So, she had to get accustomed to the new environment that surrounded her if she didn't want to be seen or imprisoned because she made a mistake, or because she was careless while committing her crimes. The good thing was that New York had so many people living there, an incredibly great number of citizens, that any one disappearance didn't raise suspicions as there were several horrible things continuously going in that there. *It would boggle the mind, no one could ever imagine, how many illegal actions and bloody assaults were perpetrated in that city night and day.*

Finally, she had gotten use to her new way of doing things, undoubtedly. After all, Elixabete had always been smart, malicious, fierce and very attentive. It didn't take her long before the first of her new murders occurred in her new city.

*

Suddenly, the woman stopped walking because her feet had finally reached the paving stone on the basement floor she had been looking for. After a while her eyes had recognized it: there was some dust on its gray surface, and some scratches indicated that something heavy had been previously been placed on top of it, or had been dragged over it, but now it was easily accessible. *If only she could move it again ...*

Patiently sitting on the floor cross-legged and using her delicate, though strong, hands to play around with it, Elixabete tried to lift and carefully set back the stone. It required some time, but it didn't turn out to be that heavy anyway. Actually, it had never been, otherwise she wouldn't have been capable of moving it the first time she had discovered it, when she was much younger. As the paving stone finally slid back, the woman found again that small hole in the ground, and she knew what had to be under it. *Exactly as it was when I was still a child, nothing has changed, she told herself.* That was the place where she had positioned the remains of her first action, long ago.

"Oh, my God!" she exclaimed in a moved voice, as her fingers searched the small hole and finally touched something full of muck. "It's still here, the same as I left it years ago! How incredible."

While stroking the old head of the worn-out male toy-doll of her youth as she was taking it out of the hole, the woman considered that, after all, over the course of her lifetime, she had never forgotten that first experience of hers, that first evil game. *In a way, it was so heart-warming and*

268

reassuring to look at that doll now! No one had ever found that part of her toy-doll, and no one knew about it, still today.

It was strange to think about the way things had gone. In reality, as a serial killer, Elixabete was rather uncommon, and her peculiarity was that she simply chose her victims by chance. So, depending upon the moment, the woman found someone that she could easily overpower or make unconscious, be it he or she, a lonely tourist, an aged individual who had come to Winooski from some other place, or a very old resident who no one else cared about anymore, she immediately acted, and her actions always ended up hitting the mark. You might think being she was only five foot seven, and not very muscular, that this could be difficult, but she had been taught to practice martial arts in a number of distinct styles since she was seven, both at home and in the only school in their small town. The girl had proven to be very skilled and promising in that field, insomuch as she had been asked a lot of times to continue such activities as a professional sportswoman when she grew older. Many people even said she might one day even become a representative of their national team. But she had always plainly refused, as a matter of fact, saying that she only wanted to learn martial arts for her own self-defense, and not to get famous. In reality, she knew that she didn't like that her hand-to-hand abilities were put on display publicly, more than was strictly necessary inside that school. She had learned at an early age how to use her dexterity, speed, and mental alertness only when she really needed those qualities: *specifically when she assaulted somebody by surprise, taking helpless people and turning them into her poor victims in the end.*

Of course, all of this hand-to-hand fighting had to take place before the dissection process started and the real game took place. The most enjoyable part of it all was burying parts underground, each one at a great distance from the other, the many parts of the corpses of her dead targets being hidden when the killing was over.

Well, when she had begun driving the car that she had been given as a gift from her family when she was sixteen, things had become ever much easier and more interesting, and the distance involved in it all—along with the different locations where she chose to put the several remains from time to time—had also grown larger.

Actually, Elixabete was aware of the fact that only one person seemed to have had some suspicions about her in the past. This man had seen her once, by chance, standing alone in the garden, cutting some parts off her new beloved doll, which was just one of the many she had had in her collection over the course of years, after all. It was her brother, more than thirty years ago, but he had died. She had killed him while the young boy was asleep, before making his body disappear forever.

Actually, it hadn't been easy, as it was one of her first murders, and for that reason her experience was just restricted, so several mistakes had been made in the process. More than that, her behavior long ago wasn't as precise and self-confident as it had become afterwards, but she had been forced to commit the crime, and in a hurry, as that morning her brother had seen her doing something unheard of to her toy-doll. Most girls wouldn't have done that awful thing, but she knew she had to accomplish her purposes before he told her parents about her strange actions.

After that, and the subsequent affliction all of her family had been thrown into—where she had to fictitiously show off, so as not to reveal her true feelings ... things had greatly changed. Actually, the woman had also used the opportunity to go more and more into the practice of martial arts, as her parents said that she had to be prepared, to become really capable of always defending herself against unknown assaulters or delinquents so as not to become the prey of some mad individual, as had probably happened to her unlucky brother, whose corpse had never been found.

As she looked around again, she noticed an old cabinet in the basement. She remembered the day she had taken the book from it, and the way she had used it. That was a medical book and there were many images of human bodies and human tissues within those colorful pages. It had led her to perform the many interesting projects that she had soon put into practice. The first one happening just two days later ...

*

Dissecting and studying the various parts of that poor, weak old man she had taken late at night, when he was entering his house, proved to be very spectacular. But it was also a very bloody event, much more that it had been all the previous times. As people had told her, a little knowledge could go a long way and it had taken her to newer, unexpected levels that she had never imaged reaching when she was young. In fact, she would never have thought about playing such new games on a living body if she hadn't stumbled onto that book by chance. And how entertaining it all had been in the end to her curious, tireless eyes.

She missed that moment. Not that she hadn't practiced the same thing on other victims later, but, as everyone knows, the freshness of a first experience can only happen once. During subsequent times you might add something else in order to turn it into a more interesting entertainment, but the pleasing sensations of those first tries of discovering and pushing herself even more was something that couldn't be possibly renewed again.

*

As the woman came to her senses again and stood up, her fingers stroked for the last time the severed head of her old male doll that was

270

full of dirt and in very poor condition. It was time for the moment to finally end, and all that remained of her first experience when she was much younger had to be pushed again in the same hole, under that gray paving stone, exactly where it had to stay hidden forever. Even if it was only a toy, and not a piece of a corpse who had been forced to pass away, that head still really meant something to her.

Certainly, there had been more than thirty dead people who had come after that first time, but she was still so fond of that childish accomplishment of her, that first dissection of her doll. Notwithstanding all the people she had killed afterwards, such an old deed still had a special place in her heart. In a way, that act was what had started it all, and she was pleased that such a plastic body part had remained in the same place where she had positioned it long ago, well hidden, without anyone ever finding it by chance. She was so proud of that fact, as it proved how cautious and clever she had been even in the beginning of her bloody hobby. No clues had been left behind her, no human remains had ever been found, just like the plastic head of her doll. Her skills had greatly increased over the course of the years, but you know, you can never forget your first humble steps.

By staring at that dusty severed head, which still looked so handsome, so dead, though also so artistic, even if it had no blood on it, no body fluids or pieces of cut tissue, the woman considered how wondrous it really appeared to be now. *You see, after all, the heart has its reasons which reason does not know.*

*

As the forty-seven-year-old woman exited the old house and headed for her luxury car, an aged female, a retired toy store owner with only a few hairs on her feeble head was walking along the road and she just happened to see Elixabete who was going away. Her old eyes weren't sure about it, but she thought that one might be the only daughter of the family who had once lived in that house.

If it was true, then that had been one of her worst failures, the old witch considered, as things hadn't gone the way she wanted them to go. The witch had gotten used to walking past that house from time to time, even though more and more rarely during the last few years, in order to remind herself of her incapacity to finally get what she really had on her mind.

She had always hated the father who owned that house, as that handsome man had rejected her, laughing at her love for him when they were still very young at school. So, she had decided to avenge herself, and the plan she had devised was easy. Getting hold of that doll—the toy-doll that was so fashionable long ago—and convincing the man she hated, to buy it as a gift for his daughter hadn't been difficult. Her intentions were to make the curse that the doll had been given—thanks to her evil sorcery—immediately cause disaster, death, and sorrow within that family. However, the only satisfaction she had gotten was the sudden disappearance of that father's oldest son, who was never found, and whose crime had never been solved. But nothing else. And this was not enough for that man to pay, according to her will. That family had had a long, wealthy life from that time on, so, where had she failed? What had she done wrong when she had conjured up such a strong, bloody curse long ago? She really didn't know.

As the witch watched the luxury car drive away, her eyes spotted the expensive dress the female driver had on, with the gray leather jacket and the flashy necklace. She deeply felt dejected. Nothing had gone as expected. Maybe she had just lost her touch with that curse. But then again, who knows? *Was it possible…?*

***

Boneglow

by G. Ted Theewen, United States

The closer they got to Jackstone City, the rougher the tracks became, jostling the cars from side to side, until it was impossible to keep a drink on the tables.

"Goodness," said a woman behind Sadhir. She had been a loud, pompous aristocrat all throughout the trip across the plains. "This car will be shaken to bits!"

Sadhir knew they would arrive within the hour and he would be relieved of her company. Outside the drab tan and gray hillsides rose and undulated like a child playing under a blanket. One glimpse was a leg under the blanket but after reading a few pages of his book, the next glance was a hand and perhaps a nose.

Daddy, why won't you play with me tonight?

Sadhir pulled out his Letter of Orders from the Duke of Finecut, whom the emperor himself put in command of settling efforts in the northwestern frontier. It was written on thick parchment with no less than three wax seals stamped at the bottom. Duke Redmont was a stern aristocrat with dwindling patience for the efforts of Baron Seton in the mining settlement of Jackstone City. Sadhir was being sent to assist the baron.

"This Letter of Orders hereby charges Sadhir Stapelton, a Trusted Citizen of the Kingdom of Rusitain under the rule of His Holy Emperor Charles IV, with the following tasks:

"First, to ascertain the efficiency of Jackstone mining operations in the frontier settlements in the territory commonly known as Boneglow.

"Second, to assert standard business practices when needed to increase efficiency of mining operations while seeking out new sources of profits for The Royal Frontier Mining Company.

"Third, to ensure the rule of laws set forth by our Royal Courts are properly enforced and to enforce or make judgments when deemed necessary."

The rest of the letter was filled with an assortment of dates and stamps as proof of the letter's legitimacy. When Duke Redmont gave the letter, he took Sadhir aside, glaring at him like an angry parent.

"If that baron is as incompetent as I'm hearing, send word and he shall be replaced at once. Our profits from these mines have been negligible, at best, despite a flood of people moving into this city."

"I will see to it, Your Grace," said Sadhir.

"I know it's soon, my boy. But getting back on your feet is the best thing for you," he said as he clapped Sadhir roughly on the back. "You'll see," he said as he turned his back on Sadhir and quickly walked away. The smoke from the duke's pipe lingered in the air for several minutes while Sadhir stood still and waited to be dismissed by the duke's staff.

As the train pulled into the station, the first thing Sadhir noticed on the platform were the children in school uniforms with model dirigibles floating above their heads, held by strings in fists, all held at exactly the same angles. They soundlessly paraded by him stern-faced with military precision as a line of porters pushing identical carts followed.

"Mr. Stapelton! Over here!" A young man jumped up and down while waving his arms with the enthusiasm of a Q'idjenball fan during the Prince's Cup Tournament.

"Mr. Stapelton," he gushed flamboyantly. "My name is Reggie Rasjani and I've been assigned to be your aide in Jackstone City." He wore a dark suit with bright accents and stitching. His hair was sculptured into the shape of a frying pan, as was the style amongst the youth that year, the trendiest calling themselves Pharaohs.

"I see," said Sadhir. "Then lead the way, Reggie." He found the boy's excitement amusing. Aides were always working to outdo each other's flamboyance like peacocks.

Reggie escorted Sadhir through the crowded station past a group pale, gaunt children singing in perfect harmony. Their voices resonated so well that Sadhir felt surrounded by the small chorus. As he put a shilling in the hat at their feet he noticed every child had brilliant green eyes sunken behind their dirty faces.

"They're Khadisha," said Reggie in a whispered tone.

"Khadisha?"

"They were the tribe who used to live here before settlement. You can tell by the green eyes."

Reggie motioned with his fingers at his own eyes.

"All of them?"

"They have some folklore amongst their tribe that explains it. Something about death blessing them or showing the living into the afterlife." Reggie shrugged and waved at their waiting driver in a manner that could only be described as a dancing hand.

He made excited small talk as their steam carriage chugged and puffed along. Banners of every color were strung across the streets. Written on them were slogans.

Prosperity Through Settlement! Frontier Today, Civilized Tomorrow! The Emperor's Foundation Supports Us All! Forward and Outward!

They passed a women's boutique with last year's fashions and jewelry in the windows.

What gem is local to where you're going this time, dear husband? I can't fit any more on my fingers!

Sadhir looked down at his pants and noticed they were no longer black, but a grayish brown from all the dust and dirt. Reggie saw this and handed him a cloth dust mask with a flourish that required both arms and an exaggerated head snap.

"Thank you, Reggie."

"Today's dust is tomorrow's concrete, Mr. Stapelton!" His grin never wavered. "Do you have a family, Mr. Stapelton?"

"No," said Sadhir. Saying it was truth, but felt like a betrayal to the dead.

Daddy, will you be home from work before I go to bed?

The carriage shuddered and coughed as they arrived at the baron's business office. The squeal of the brakes was ear-piercing. Reggie held the door open with a flourish that resembled a dance move out of a brothel's front window.

As Sadhir looked around at the various buildings, he noticed how each was adorned with a dead body. He scanned across the street and sure enough, it too had a dead body hanging from the second story. And another next door to it. The body hanging from the baron's business office was a fat man with a large belly roll.

Sadhir paused to look at the man and wondered why in the world would the baron do such a ghastly thing? Why would anybody string up a dead man's body and hang it from a building as some kind of morbid adornment? And why isn't anybody else looking up at this grotesque display with revulsion, or even noticing it, for that matter?

"Ah," said Reggie. "You're looking at our street lamps."

"I'm looking at a corpse, Reggie."

"Wait until sundown, Mr. Stapelton. You'll see."

The air inside of the baron's office building was stifling. Clerks shuffled between desks in wool business suits that stuck to their skin.

The baron's aide escorted Sadhir into his office with a flourish that put Reggie's to shame. It took several seconds and ended with a slow, arching stretch towards the sky, and a taunting gaze in Reggie's direction. Sadhir could hear Reggie's feathers ruffle.

The baron was a short, portly man with red cheeks and a wide, waxed handlebar mustache. His hair was a greasy sculpture that must have taken an hour to create in the morning. Sadhir wondered how he kept it in that shape after sweating so much.

"Mr. Stapelton," he gushed. The baron's clothing was soaked and he smelled like a locker room. "I must apologize for the heat inside this building."

"It's all right, Baron," said Sadhir calmly.

"Our engineers are working on the condenser manifolds, but please don't worry," he said quickly with his arms waving in front of him. "We're safe."

The baron waddled behind his desk, which was covered in files piled neatly with polished jackstone weights atop to keep them from flying away. Two aides with wide fans on sticks waved them up and down to cool the baron as he wiped sweat from his face. As the papers fluttered under their weights, Sadhir thought they looked like birds trying desperately to escape from under a boot, in a futile struggle for freedom.

Sadhir pulled a silk scarf out of his pocket, a gift from his wife on his birthday three ago, and wiped dust from his watering eyes.

"Please let me extend my heartfelt condolences, Mr. Stapelton. Such a tragedy to lose one's family."

"Thank you, Baron."

"I mean, a boiler explosion while asleep! I have kids of my own, Mr. Stapelton. As a father, I—"

"I appreciate your concern, Baron. As you know, Duke Redmont had some concerns about the operations of this town."

"Ah, yes. Yes, indeed. We have been working tirelessly."

"I would like to see your ledgers, Baron. Perhaps I can find ways of increasing efficiency and profitability."

The two men left the office and encountered three children clamoring for the baron.

"Daddy! We brought you lunch!" Two girls and a very small boy, all three with his familiar round face, carried a bag with them.

"They insisted upon bringing it to you today," said a woman from across the room. She, too, was round and smiled as the children hugged their father. The baron, with a look of embarrassment, led the children back to their mother.

"I'm sorry, Mr. Stapelton," he said wiping his brow. "It doesn't happen often, I assure you."

"It's all right, Baron," Sadhir said as he scanned the office. The workers glistened with sweat as they ran back and forth. "Do you have a desk I can use?"

Sadhir was escorted to his desk while the baron snapped his fingers. For the next few weeks, this would be his office, as he pored over ledgers and rows of numbers.

"Baron," said Sadhir. "One more question—why are there corpses hanging from the buildings?"

"They are our streetlamps," he said.

"Streetlamps?"

"Yes," he said. "Khadisha burial tradition. The probing mines have an algae deep within. When a corpse is embalmed with it, it produces light after the sun goes down."

"That sounds ghastly, Baron."

"Yes, but we don't have the land yet for a cemetery. I mean, with how fast Jackstone City is growing, the original planners didn't want prime land to be wasted on cemeteries."

"So, when somebody here dies, they are embalmed with this algae, and strung up like Queen Cassandra's Day decorations?"

"The Khadisha practiced this for hundreds of years in this territory and Barons before me kept that practice. It pacified the Khadisha, illuminated the streets, and solved burial issues."

Sadhir looked at the baron for a moment.

"Please, Mr. Stapelton," he said. "This evening you will see."

*

For hours, Sadhir carefully studied the ledgers of the Jackstone City operations of the Royal Frontier Mining Company.

"Mr. Stapelton," said Reggie. "It's past closing time. Everyone's gone home. Would you like me to lead you to your quarters?"

"I didn't realize the time."

"Hard work sets us free," said Reggie. Sadhir wondered how many of those slogans he would have to hear during this time.

Sadhir stood and stretched his arms high above his head with a yawn, then nodded silently, which made Reggie sigh and smile.

"Great! It's just a short walk."

As the two men slowly walked in the evening dust, both wearing cloth masks and goggles, Sadhir looked up at the buildings. The corpses were more than just lit—they sparkled. They emitted a slightly green glow that sparkled and glittered more radiantly than any streetlamp he had ever seen.

"It took me a while to get used to them," said Reggie. "I thought it was barbaric at first."

"How long do they last?"

"The light? All night, until dawn."

"No, the bodies."

"Oh," said Reggie. "Well, the algae feed upon the flesh until there is nothing left but bone. Once they do, there is no more light, and another body is brought in to replace it."

"How long does that take?"

"Depends. An adult male usually last about three months. A child, less."

"A child?"

"Yes," said Reggie. "There isn't a single cemetery here in Jackstone City."

Daddy, Mommy says if you come home early tonight, you can read me a story before bed.

Sadhir's apartment was just three blocks away from the office. It was suitable for his needs. The shower was extremely hot, but the water pressure was weak. Reggie had warned him about this, as Jackstone City was in an arid climate with scarce rain, but Sadhir didn't have time to take a hot bath.

After his story, can I get some help sleeping, dear husband?

Outside of Sadhir's window, across the street, was the corpse of a woman. She glowed warmly in the evening hours, the light piercing the dust and dirt that filled the city's air. Off in the distance, he could hear men hacking and coughing, struggling to breathe as they made their way down the street.

The light was too intense for him to sleep, and the curtain wasn't nearly thick enough to provide any shade.

Sadhir looked out his window at the body of the young woman. Her features were hard to make out from the glaring lights pulsating and sparkling inside of her.

Eventually exhaustion won over and he fell into an uneasy sleep.

The next morning, Sadhir went outside to examine the woman who had kept him up all night.

He gazed up at her as people walked around him. She was young, perhaps in her early twenties. There were no obvious injuries anywhere on her body that he could see from the sidewalk. There was something familiar about her.

*

The office was still hot and steamy. Baron Seton apologized repeatedly.

"I must say, Mr. Stapelton, our engine—"

"Please stop apologizing, Baron. Sometimes machines break."

"Yes," said the baron. "Sadly, they do."

"Why are you using privateers to haul raw jackstone from the mines?"

"Well," he said as he wiped the sweat off his red face. "By spreading out the income amongst company workers and privateers, it keeps more people pacified, and less likely to cause trouble."

"We have the largest standing army on the planet in case there is trouble, Baron."

"Yes, indeed."

"And construction costs for worker housing. Why so expensive?"

"The size of the apartments were too small to accommodate families."

"Families?"

"Well, yes," the baron said. "Some workers brought their families along. Plus, when we annexed this territory, several villages were destroyed and those people had nowhere to live."

"Those villages were destroyed because they rejected His Majesty's gracious offer to join his kingdom and instead chose to fight."

"Some, Mr. Stapelton. But most were women and children without homes."

"Baron Seton," said Sadhir, "you do realize this operation is supposed to be profitable, right?"

"Yes, of course. But—"

"His Majesty has a whole department that handles charitable projects. That's their job."

"I understand," said the baron. His shoulders slumped and he let out a long sigh. "I'm sorry," he said quietly.

Sadhir spent the rest of the day making notes on changes that needed to be implemented. That evening, he sent word of his findings to Duke Redmont on the wireless messenger box. Within minutes he received his reply. It was a single line.

"Continue appraisal and await adjudication next week."

That was it.

An hour later, Reggie was preparing Sadhir's briefcase, mask, and goggles in the office area. They were the only two in the building.

"Reggie," he said, "do you ever see a corpse light and recognize them?"

"Once. It was my neighbor."

"Were you scared?"

"No, I was young and he was a drunkard."

"Is it possible to look up who a corpse light was before they died?"

"No," he said as he handed Sadhir his hat. "Why would you want to?"

"No reason," he said quietly. "Just curious."

That night, Sadhir looked up at the woman who sparkled with radiant light. Her skin was smooth and her body was thin but shapely. The expression on her face was that of serenity as if the very act of illuminating Sadhir was bringing her peace and harmony within. It was the face his wife made when she sang lullabies to their son as he drifted off to sleep.

The baron had Sadhir over at his house for dinner. His wife cooked a humble but tasty meal of a bird indigenous to the Boneglow territory. After dinner, the baron sat next to his wife, holding her hand, as he read *Farley's Fables & Follies* to the children in front of the fireplace. His animation for the children even gave Sadhir a chuckle despite his best attempts at composure.

Sunday at twilight, Sadhir stood beneath her corpse again. A sliver of sunlight shot between two buildings on her thigh and arm. She had his wife's hands. As the sun sliver disappeared, a glow began to emanate from her, starting with her solar plexus, radiating outward until she was fully consumed by the sparkling and pulsating light.

That night Sadhir dreamed of his wife. She was getting into bed, and the expression on her face as she looked down upon him was of serenity and inner harmony, as if that very moment was the achievement of all her wishes. Her eyes closed and she began to glow, but her face remained the same. Sadhir tried to wake her, but the glowing just grew in intensity.

He woke up covered in sweat. Before drying himself off, he went over to his calendar, and counted the days until he could leave the Boneglow Territories.

"Ten," he whispered to himself. "If I work hard and push, I should be able to leave here in ten days, Gods willing."

That day at the office, Sadhir spoke to no one, remaining at his desk while he crunched numbers and scratched out notes.

"Tomorrow," he said to Baron Seton as he left the office for the day, "I will present to you a plan to make this operation profitable."

"Oh," said the baron as he winced. "Radical changes, then?"

"Very. But I shall require your cooperation." Sadhir put on his jacket while looking the baron in the eyes.

"Yes, Mr. Stapelton," he said. "I mean, of course. I just hope ..."

"You hope for what?"

"Nothing. It's late. I look forward to seeing you tomorrow," he said as he wiped sweat off his face with an already damp cloth.

Sadhir missed the glow that night. By the time he left the office and walked to where he was staying, the young woman was already engulfed in sparkling light that glittered from within.

"I'm sorry," he whispered. "I had to work late at the office."

As Sadhir drifted off to sleep, he heard the whistle of a train. He said a silent prayer he could leave before she was reduced to mere bones.

The next morning, Reggie was pounding on Sadhir's door, shouting his name.

"What in the Devil's na—"

"Mr. Stapelton! Come quick!" Reggie was panting and frantically waving his arms about.

A few minutes later they were in front of the office, where a steam carriage bearing the Royal Seal was parked, followed by a line of black carriages bearing flags of the Royal Frontier Trade Company.

Inside, Duke Redmont himself stood, glaring at the various clerks who had stopped trying to look busy. Several of the clerks looked at Sadhir with disgust as he entered the office.

"Ah, Sadhir, my boy!"

"My Lord, I wasn't expect—"

"I wanted to handle this personally. Squandering Royal funds on housing homeless and defeated insurgents, failure to use only company transport for hauling minerals, and falsifying records to cover up assistance to indigenous clans!"

"I never said—"

"No, but the baron confessed. I have his confession right here." The duke held a piece of paper with a desperate scrawl at the bottom.

"Where is the baron now, My Lord?"

"Out back, my boy! His Majesty's justice is swift!"

Sadhir slowly willed his legs to take him to a window, where several ashen-faced clerks were staring, to see what had been done. The body of the baron hung from a rope. A black hood on his head spared his family. The faces of the children were buried in their mother's skirt as she stared at her husband's corpse in shock while surrounded by black-clad security forces.

"My Lord, I never—"

"I knew what you would find, my boy. I just needed you to confirm it."

"But what about a trial?"

"He made a deal," the duke said with a dismissive shrug. "For his family, you see."

"My Lord, I—"

"You'll run this operation until Baron Van Gelder arrives in three months," the duke said as he strode towards the front door.

"Three months? But My Lord—"

"Is there a problem?" The duke stopped in his tracks, spun around, and looked down at Sadhir.

"I had hoped to leave Boneglow a bit sooner, perhaps," said Sadhir. His voice trailed off and the words became a whisper.

"Oh? What's so important back at the capitol you can't stay here?"

Sadhir sighed and looked at the accusatory glares around the office. He knew the answer the duke was asking for but he just couldn't bring himself to say it. As if the very act of saying he had nobody to go home to would shatter him like fragile glass.

"I just thought Baron Van Gelder might arrive sooner is all." Sadhir folded his hands in front of him and looked up at the duke.

"Nonsense. You're needed here." The duke gestured towards his entourage as they all migrated towards the door. "Time will go by quickly, my boy!"

Within a few short minutes, the baron's body was cut down, the Duke and his entourage were back on the train, and within less than an hour the train's whistle signaled its departure.

"Mr. Stapelton," said Reggie. "Is it always like this?"

"Yes, Reggie. It is always like this."

As afternoon slipped to evening, at twilight, Sadhir stood under the corpse of the woman. Her serene face took no notice of him. Her smooth skin slowly sparkled and glowed until it was so bright all that could be made out was her shapely form. A pit formed in his stomach as he looked at her torso and asked himself if it was any smaller than when he first arrived.

That night he lay motionless in his bed, staring up at the ceiling, watching the shadows created by the glowing corpse outside his window. After an hour, he got up, walked over to his briefcase, and pulled out stationery and a pen.

"Dear Reggie," he wrote. "Please have my body embalmed locally and mounted across from the woman outside this room's window."

Sadhir put the letter on his nightstand and then stood at the window one final time as hot water slowly filled the tub in the bathroom. He looked her fingers and toes closely, hoping for the slightest movement, just in case. But no, she was still dead.

When the tub filled, Sadhir took the razor from his shaving kit into the bathroom, and closed the door behind him.

***

Sins of War
by Shaun Meeks, Canada

Nothing is sacred in the fields of war. At times, morality has to be left at the door when you put your uniform on, or so Jess had been led to believe. His father fought in the war before, as had many of his relatives, and there was little doubt they'd be ashamed to see the path he'd taken. At first it sounded like a good idea. Derek, the one who brought the plan to him and the others, made a great case for it. Sure, there was greed involved, but it wasn't as if the people would miss the things they took. What could the dead really complain about? Jess wasn't one to steal, but when the war was over, what would he have left? Not much.

Derek's plan was to separate from the platoon and go to villages ravaged by Germans, and then take things the dead no longer needed. "Why leave it there for the Krauts to take back to Hitler when we can get it first? We deserve to get something out of this damn war."

Yet five days and three villages later, the group of them had little to show for their troubles. After all they'd gone through, their haul was a few pieces of silverware, some coins, and memories that would no doubt follow them into sleep and throughout the rest of their lives.

The villages were gutted, as were the villagers. Many lay in the streets, more in their homes, blackened from the fires, food for the bugs and rodents. The group seemed to have lost hope at a big score, at being able to go home with some treasure to allow them to live comfortably for a while. Yet, Jess still held on to hope.

"Look there," Derek called out as they moved slowly through the woods, snow crunching under their feet.

Ahead of them, over the tree line, Jess saw smoke billowing skywards. It was clearly not a chimney or campfire. The smoke was thick and black, signs of the destruction they'd come to know. Soon, the air was full of the unmistakable odour of burnt homes and scorched flesh. Jess didn't look forward to what they might see, but the thought of what they could find pushed him forward.

They crept to the edge of the woods, careful in case there were still soldiers in the village. Jess stayed close to Derek, while Marcus and Vincent stayed in line with one another. Nobody spoke or made a move. Jess felt as though he'd stopped breathing as they hid in the thick forest. Although there weren't any sounds aside from the crackle of fire ahead of them, they knew they needed to be careful.

Derek motioned to Marcus and Vincent to take the west side, then motioned to Jess that the two of them would take the east. Jess paused, looked into the village, and felt something gnawing at him, a feeling deep in his gut he didn't like. It was similar to the way he felt at the other places, so he brushed it off as the simple fact he knew what he was doing was morally wrong.

"You coming?" Derek asked and looked slightly pissed off.

"Yeah. Sorry."

"Just keep your head in the game, Jessie Boy. Don't be dumb."

Jess nodded, ignoring the name he hated, and followed the leader of their little band into the east side of the village. It was just as he thought it would be. Many of the homes and stores were smouldering piles of rubble; others looked like jagged, broken teeth poking out of a rotted mouth. They moved towards the house closest to them and as they did, Jess noticed something strange, something none of the other ruined villages in the hills of Hungary had.

There were no dead in the street. In the days since they left the platoon, following behind a group of Germans who ravaged anything they found, there was always death in the homes, stores, and in the streets. Usually there was some poor soul laid out, shot in the back as they tried to run from the fate that chased them down and took all they had left to give.

Here, there were none. He went to say something to Derek about it, but he had already entered a house, so he had to follow. As soon as Jess entered the small home, he was greeted with a wall of death. The smell was like meat left in the sun, feces, and a hint of sweetness which made Jess's stomach roll with a threat of sickness. He covered his mouth and nose, wanting to avoid tasting the air as much as smelling it, and then moved further inside.

Near the kitchen, they found the cause of the odour.

"Jesus wept!" Derek gasped and turned away.

Jess wished he'd done the same. He hadn't felt the urge to see what made Derek react that way, but it was too late. On the floor, by the fireplace, was what Jess assumed was a woman and a child. They lay there, curled in one another's arms. Most of their clothes were gone, only the remnants of a dress and a nightgown the child wore clung to their dark bodies. Thousands of maggots danced on the exposed flesh and Jess had to turn and leave before the bile that tickled the back of his throat could push its way out. He might have worried that Derek would yell at him, or even strike him, but his sergeant had already run out of there, no doubt as disgusted as Jess was.

Once out of the house, back into the air that was so much fresher than the house, Jess felt his head swoon and he crouched down to try to gather himself. He'd seen death before, people shot, blown to bits and even burned into a black statue of terror, but he'd never seen anything like that before. The whole scene seemed unimaginable

"How?" Derek whispered as he leaned against the house. Jess looked up at him, and was greeted by a face paler than the snow on the ground. "How could anyone do that?"

Jess could only shake his head.

"How do you skin someone while they lay holding a child? Skin not only them, but the kid too. Mother of God!" Derek nearly yelled and pushed off the wall. "Okay, forget it. We don't have time for this. We need to find some shit and get out of here." Jess could see him trying to brush it off, trying to stay strong and a leader, but his gritted teeth and shaking hands gave him away.

"What? But what about those bodies?"

"What about 'em, Jessie Boy? They're dead, we're not. We ... we came here with a plan, so let's not waste any more time. Just ... forget it."

Derek walked away, towards the next house, but Jess was reluctant to follow. He glanced back at the one they just left, and wasn't sure he wanted to stick around to see what else the village held for them. Nothing he'd seen to date could prepare him for that, and he just wanted to leave. He knew it was out of the question though. He was AWOL as far as the army would be concerned. If he stuck with Derek and the others, they could eventually head back to camp and claim they had gotten lost, trapped, and had to wait it out; something that sounded believable. If he left them right then and there, he was sure one of them—probably Derek—would make him out to be a coward and a deserter. Jess didn't like the idea of staying, but there really was no other option for him.

He followed along and walked into the next house, then a third, and a fourth. Each held more horrors, and nothing in the way of treasure. A family of four lay in their beds, skinned, with two of them missing their heads. In the fourth house they found only parts of bodies and pools of crimson and intestines piled on the dinner table. Jess saw Derek try to stay cool and calm through it all, but as each house was filled with insanity, it seemed like an impossible task.

They walked out of the fourth house and Derek was silent. He kept spitting on the ground and Jess was sure he was trying to rid himself of the taste of decay and old blood. Jess did the same as he also wiped the clotted blood off his feet in the snow next to the house.

"Maybe we'll have better luck there," Derek said, and Jess followed where he pointed to.

"You've got to be kidding, right?"

"Why not? I bet there's something other than dead bodies in there."

"It's a church! Are you really talking about stealing from the house of God?"

"Look, Jessie Boy, we've come a long way and have nothing to show for it. You really want to go home emptyhanded, after all this? It's a church, not really the house of any god. It's just a symbol, so, get your head on straight and let's see what's in there. I know they've got to have something."

Derek began to walk away, but Jess refused to go this time. He stood there, as fresh snow began to fall, and knew he couldn't do it. He'd been raised Roman Catholic, went to church every Sunday and sometimes on a weekday too. His family was very tight knit and religious, he had a crucifix in his coat pocket. He prayed every day in-country and knew there was a god who watched everything they did. Church wasn't a mere symbol to him, but the actual house of his Lord. So, there was no way he could steal from there and do it with a clear conscience. Years of Sunday school, and being told what happens to sinners, made him wary of what Derek suggested, even if he'd come along to steal from the dead.

"You coming?" Derek called out, halfway to the doors.

"No."

"Excuse me?"

"I'm not stealing from the church. I can't do it."

"Listen," Derek said as he strode back over to where Jess stood. "You're going to come in there with me and watch my back, or you're done."

Jess said nothing.

"You think when we head back I'll cover for you if you don't follow me now? Screw you, buster. You mess with me here and now and so help me God, I'll do everything in my power to see you court-martialled. So, you can walk with me, or just get the fuck out of here now. Got it?"

Derek turned and made his way back towards the church and Jess did the only thing he could. He followed. Jess took in the rest of the village as he went, seeing no sign of Marcus or Vincent. He was sure they'd found the same terrors in each home they visited, and wondered how long before they gave up and searched them out. He knew them both well enough that they'd want to leave as badly as he did.

"So, let's go inside so we can get out of here, and fast."

Derek pulled the tall doors open and they were greeted with foulness. There was a hint of death there, something lingering inside.. At first, Jess couldn't put his finger on what it was, thinking it smelled of rotten, boiled eggs; then it came to him. Sulfur.

Derek seemed to pay it no mind as he covered his mouth and nose and walked in. Jess did the same.

The church was dark, only lit by the light that came through the cracks of the shuttered windows. Part of him wanted to run over and push each of them wide open. There was an urge to let the light in, to take away from the creepiness that engulfed the small structure. There was something off about the church. There was no way to tell if it was Catholic, or another sect. There were no crucifixes, no paintings on the wall, no statues of Mary or any other religious figures. There was an altar at the front, pews in between and what looked like a confessional booth on the far left side of the room, but nothing else to suggest any sort of denomination.

"I think the smell is coming from there," Derek said and pointed to the confessional booth.

"So?"

"I want to see what it is."

"Why? You know that whatever is making that smell, it's going to be bad."

"I need to know what could make such a stench. Call it human nature."

Derek went to the booth, but Jess didn't follow. He had not an iota of desire to see what could be in there, if anything. Nor could he understand why Derek needed to go over so badly. The way the man had looked after going into the horror-filled homes, you would've thought he'd know better. Instead of following, Jess made his way slowly towards the altar.

Jess found a little relief in the fact that there wasn't any blood in the aisle or near the pews. He'd grown up believing that a church was the one place you could go and be safe from persecution, war, and murder, that some things were just to sacred to defile. Along the walls where pictures of Mary and Jesus would normally hang, there was nothing but the shadowed outlines of what could be paintings. There were also strange letters and symbols unlike any he'd ever seen before. They weren't written in English, Hungarian, or any other language he knew. Jess went over and touched one of them and found they were ash, his fingers blackened as he pulled his hand away.

It was just more of the strangeness the village held, that made him feel more and more uneasy.

"Jesus fuck!"

Jess turned as Derek cried out and saw him stumble backwards away from the booth. His gun fell to the floor as his shaking hands went up to his mouth. Jess went to him, not sure he wanted to see what would make Derek so terrified, but he couldn't help it. The door was still open and the mystery inside the small, dark place called out to him.

Nothing could have prepared him for what he was about to see.

Inside sat the remains of a man, who, judging by the tattered clothes he wore, had been the priest. He leaned back, his head tilted to one side and his legs splayed out towards the open door. His body was intact aside from the gaping hole where his chest and stomach had once been. White bones peered out of red pulp and from the center of the giant hole, a green mist floated skyward. Jess was horrified, but moved closer, having never seen anything like it before, as he tried to figure out what could do such damage to a person. It looked as though a bomb had gone off from the inside, exploding the priest outward while he sat in the booth.

Yet when he took his final step towards the dead man, he saw something less believable than anything his brain could have fathomed.

"How in God's name?" he whispered as he saw a virtual abyss leading into the man. Green light glowed deep down, maybe sixty feet in all as though whatever had blown up inside him, had blown downwards too. It was impossible, though, because the booth was undamaged aside from the gore that clung to the dark wood.

"You were right. We ... we need to get out of here," Derek said, and Jess could hear the sheer panic in his voice.

Jess backed away, ready to run out of the nightmare he found himself in. As he was about to turn towards the door, something caught his eye—movement from one of the pews. Pure reaction made him raise his gun and move towards it. There was a moment when he thought whoever or whatever had done that to the priest could still be in the church, hiding and waiting to attack, so he felt safer with his eye looking down the sights of his weapon.

"What is it?" Derek called out. Jess said nothing, just held up a hand and continued forward.

He was only three pews away.

Then two.

Then one.

His finger tensed on the trigger, ready to shoot at anything, even something marginally threatening. Since he had come to Hungary, he'd fired his gun more than he could count and killed more Germans than years he'd been alive. Yet, there was a nervousness that built in him with each step and every passing second. It was the unknown that made him hesitate, as fear crept across his skin. The memory of what he'd seen in each of those houses and the unfathomable sight from inside the confessional booth were the cause of it all. War was war, but whatever was at play in the village was something his mind couldn't fully comprehend.

He was only a step away; he could hear Derek stir behind him. He took in a deep breath and pushing aside any thought of hesitation, he stepped forward to see what awaited him.

"Please don't shoot me!" a voice said in Hungarian.

It was a woman, hands up as she cowered on her hands and knees. She wore a ragged and torn dress that was covered in a thin layer of grime, just as her hands were. He could hear her weep as she knelt in front of him, whispering prayers in her native tongue. She looked up at him, her matted black hair hung in front of her dirty face.

"Don't ... kill ... me."

"It's okay," Jess said to her. He spoke in Hungarian, slow and slightly broken as he wasn't nearly as fluent in the language as he should be. He lowered his gun and held a hand out to her. "It's okay. You're safe now."

"Who is it?" Derek called out, but Jess didn't look over at him.

"It's a woman. She's fine by the looks of it, but scared out of her mind." Jess motioned for the woman to take his hand as he put his gun on the ground. "We can help. Come, I won't hurt you."

She hesitated. Jess could see how terrified she was, and if she had lived through the hell that had taken place in the village, she had every right to be. He decided to try and win her trust, so he pulled out his canteen, opened it, and then crouched down so he was on her level. He held out the water to her.

"Here," he said and moved a little closer to her. "It's water, take it."

She looked at the canteen with fear and caution in her eyes, but eventually her thirst won over and she took it from him. She gulped the water down greedily, some of it spilled out the sides of her mouth and left streaks on her dirt-covered face. Jess heard Derek walk towards them, but kept his attention on the woman. He smiled at her in hopes that it would make her feel safe.

"Ask her if she knows what happened to the priest, to the whole damn place."

"Wait," Jess said. "She's scared to death."

"So am I. Maybe we should just leave. If she wants to come, she can, but I really don't want to be in this fucking place."

Jess ignored him and went back to the woman who had finished the water. "Come. Sit on the bench and tell me what happened."

She didn't move at all, just sat on the floor as she shook her head.

"What's your name?" he asked. Jess hoped to slowly break her down a bit, to earn some trust and maybe find out what had happened.

"Irma," she said low and quiet.

"My name's Jess, Irma. Did you see what happened?"

She nodded.

"To the priest?"

Nodded again.

"To the rest of the village?"

Same response.

"Was it Germans?"

This time she shook her head.

"Russians?"

Another shake.

"English? American?"

"Not soldiers. Demons," she said and began to cry.

"What did she just say?" Derek asked.

"Hold on," Jess said to him, then turned back to the woman. he asked, "What do you mean by demons? Evil people?"

"No. No, they were demons, straight from Hell. They ... they killed everyone," she told him and Jess translated it.

"Well, she's nuts then," Derek said, laughing nervously, but Jess knew he found nothing funny. "So, let her sit here and think about demons. We can get the others and get out of here."

Jess wanted to think she was crazy. Maybe she'd seen too much death and simply snapped. Yet when he thought of the skinned bodies and the priest with a hole in his torso and the green mist and light coming from him, it was hard to say she was off her kilter. He tried to get her to sit on the pew again, and this time she did, taking the canteen from him as she did.

"The priest, he was not a man of God. He took the paintings down, removed the crosses and spoke to the devil. He called them here and they ... came through him, tore him open. I ... saw ... saw them coming out ... monsters." She took a sip of water with shaking hands and the look of terror was on her face again. "I hid. They never found me. I hid and could hear everyone crying, dying, and praying for help. But none came. God didn't listen."

She started to cry and Jess put a hand on her knee and squeezed it. She put her hand on his hand and squeezed back.

"Come with us. We'll take you somewhere safe, away from this," he told her and hoped she would come. He didn't want to leave her behind. "You can come back to our—"

He stopped. His head perked up and saw Derek do the same.

"Shit," Derek said and ran to the window. He looked out through a crack in the shutters, and then turned back to Jess. "Fuck me! It's Germans."

He knew it would be, the sound of the tank was distinct and he felt like things were about to go from bad to worse.

"How many?" Jess asked and hoped the woman didn't understand any English.

"I don't know. One tank, and there are at least seven on foot. But there might be others. Damn it, there's no way out of this!"

"It's fine. Maybe there's another exit." He turned back to Irma. "Is there any other way out of here?"

"I don't know. Maybe in the back?" she said.

"She's not sure, but said maybe through the back," Jess told Derek. He moved to the window himself to see what was going on. As he did, he heard shouting and saw something that made his stomach drop.

The German soldiers had gathered in the center of the town, maybe fifty feet from the church, and there were more than seven. By Jess's count, there were closer to twelve, and they weren't alone. Marcus and Vincent were with them, unarmed and being shoved forward by a group of soldiers. Jess could see blood pour from a cut on Vincent's forehead, and more coming from the mouth of the other.

"We have to do something," Derek whispered as their two friends were forced to kneel in the middle of the street. "They're going to kill them."

"What can we do? Look how many there are." He wanted to help as well, but it was clearly a suicide mission. He turned and looked over his shoulder to where the woman was, as she sat on the bench where he'd left her. She had no idea what was going on.

"So, what? We let them die?"

"If we go out there, we're all dead. Maybe we should go now and see if there's a way out the back of here."

Before Derek could sound his rebuttal to the idea, two quick shots rang out and their gaze went back to the square. Jess turned just in time to see the red mist hang in the air above the falling bodies of his two friends and fellow soldiers. He felt cold inside, a wave of nausea at the sight of it, and knew it was too late to run now. With them dead, the group outside would no doubt split up again and hunt them down as they went looking for anyone else.

"We're screwed," Derek whispered, and Jess saw tears in his eyes.

Jess ignored him, not willing to allow that kind of thinking into his head, no matter how likely it seemed. He knew there had to be a way out of it all. Even as he looked back out through the crack in the shutter and saw his friends lying on the ground, turning the snow red, he knew there had to be some sort of hope to hold onto.

"Derek, go look and see if there's a way out back and I'll watch here."

"Why? If they're moving again—"

"Just go!" Jess ordered. It was weird to tell his superior what to do, but it worked. Derek began to walk away and left with his negative thoughts.

He focused back outside and saw the soldiers hadn't moved yet. They stood around the dead, laughed as many pulled out cigarettes and lit them. One of them nudged Vincent's body, said something that made most the others laugh, and then spit on each of their bodies. In war, most things weren't sacred.

"Bastards!" he whispered to himself and continued to watch.

"All right, all right. Enough fun," one of them said, most likely a captain, getting the other's attention. "No more fun for now. I'm sure these two weren't alone, so let's find the rest of the scum here. And the villagers too. Where is everyone?"

They began to split up, and as they did, Jess felt panic swarm over him. There were three that looked right at the church and he was certain they saw him. He was tempted to back away, to run and find some nook to hide in, even if it meant leaving the woman and Derek behind, but he refused to be a coward, despite the fact that running was an easier road. He stayed, waited to see them get closer, but they never did. Instead, something far worse than any German attack came.

The three were less than five feet away from the steps when a roaring growl echoed through the streets and the church. The sound was thick and heavy, vibrating Jess's very bones. The soldiers outside heard and felt it to. He saw them freeze in their tracks, look in all directions for a source, but seemed to find nothing.

"What was that?" Derek whispered as he came back into the main part of the church.

"I have no idea," he told him, and that was when he saw it.

From the right came something dark and fast. It moved through the streets, a black blur that left death in its wake. No sound of alarm was raised, not even a cry of shock or pain. Once the black thing moved past a soldier, they dropped to the ground. Some of them were missing their skin, others had no heads; all were dead before they even began to fall.

Jess said nothing as he watched the slaughter. He was in a state of shock, and before long, all but the three that had been heading to the church were left. They had watched the killings too, backed away from the town square as it happened, and in those few seconds Jess thought about letting them in. Whatever it was out there wasn't human and to let them stay out there to die like the others felt wrong to him. He hoped that there would be some sort of sanctuary in the church, but as he thought that, he looked over at the confessional booth and remembered the priest. He remembered the gaping hole in the man's chest and stomach, and imagined that it must lead to Hell, where the thing in the street must have been born from.

"Get away from the window," Derek whispered.

"Why?"

"In case the soldiers hear you," he told him and Jess knew he had no idea what was going on outside. He turned to look at his sergeant, who stood by the woman on the bench, and thought about telling him everything that had just happened. He decided against it.

"I just need to see something," he told him and turned back. When he did, he really wished he'd listened to Derek after all.

In the town square, among the red-soaked streets, were twins from a nightmare. They stood, slightly hunched over; their skin dark as oil and glistened with what Jess assumed was blood. They sneered as they looked over the carnage they'd brought; their snouts wrinkled in what must have been a smile. They draped the torn flesh of the dead over their bodies, like the robes of ancient Greece and finally turned towards the church. Jess worried they might see him, but that was when gun fire echoed through the dead town as the last three German soldiers raised their guns to kill the unspeakable creatures.

There was a roar, just like before, and the blackened monsters pounced on them. That was all Jess could take. He backed away from the window, ready to run out of any opening he could find on the back side of the church, ready to smash out a window if need be. As he turned to go to tell Derek and Irma to follow him, he froze in his tracks.

Derek was on his knees, in front of the woman, his hands moved spastically at his throat as a waterfall of red poured over his fingers. The woman, Irma, held a knife in her hand, a soldier's bayonet, and as it dripped Derek's blood from the tip, she turned to Jess.

"What the hell have you done?"

"What have I done?" she said in perfect English as she pushed Derek over. He fell without any fight and bled out there. "You mean to your friend? I gave him a way out. A higher purpose."

"What the fuck are you talking about?"

"Your friend, like the priest in there, is about to become a doorway, the key to our world." She knelt down and placed a hand on Derek's forehead. "Do you know what a conjuror is?" She looked up to Jess's face. "I assume by the look on your face, that is a no. We've gone by many names before, dating back to two centuries before Christ. My family has a rich history in this country. Some call us witches, others think of us as healers, but we can do so much more. We lived here in peace and quiet, helped those that needed it. Then Germany and you people come here and declare your little war, killing people without a thought or care, and the tides of Hell stirred."

"You just killed Derek!" Jess yelled, looking down at Derek's body.

"I didn't kill him. I'm giving him a chance to be more, to let him be the door to Paimon's hounds."

"Who the hell is Paimon?" Jess yelled, and as he did, thunder erupted behind him as the monsters beyond slammed into the door, trying to smash it in.

"Paimon is the true king of Hell, one of Lucifer's princes. His hounds out there, the ones I called forth, want in for you."

Behind Jess there was more crashing which was enough to set him into motion. He went to grab his rifle that was strapped to his shoulder, ready to fire into the face of the insane woman who had killed his sergeant, and then he would figure out what to do about the nightmare smashing into the door. Yet as he went to pull it off, he found nothing there, and then saw it on the floor a few feet away from where Derek lay. He cursed to himself, and felt the bleakness of it all.

"Those aren't the only hounds, though, stupid American. There are more down in the infernal world. They want to come out and taste the blood of the war mongers, to take the flesh of all you sinners back to Hell, down to Paimon. They want your sins; can taste them in the air like smoke from a fire. You've sinned, or they wouldn't be so eager to get inside. And soon there will be more. Now let me show you how I've given your friend here meaning."

As she remained kneeling beside Derek with her hands on his forehead, his neck ceased spewing crimson. Jess watched her, though he didn't want to. What he wanted to do was to run and grab his rifle, and blow her head off, but he felt stuck in place, rooted to the floor of the church as madness began to unfold. The room became still, nearly electric, as Irma began to mumble words Jess couldn't understand. She rocked back and forth, chanted until Derek's body jerked. Jess took a step back, fear gripping him at the sight. Her words became stronger and louder, and as they did, Derek began to jerk up and down at a faster rate until green mist began to seep from his chest.

Everything else moved in high speed.

The smashing at the door continued, but Jess's eyes were locked on what was taking place before him. The mist continued to rise out of Derek, and then a geyser of blood shot skyward in the church, red liquid mixed with chunks of flesh, bone, and Derek's uniform. Jess was filled with terror at what might come next. His mind raced with possibilities. There was a part of him that strangely wanted to stay and see what sort of abomination was about to take place; that was unable to turn and get far away from there.

A black arm began to rise from inside Derek, Hell born from death and it was time to move, or time to die. Irma's eyes were closed as she continued to chant and Jess pushed himself to move. He ran across the floor, snatched up his gun and ran for the back of the church.

As he made it to the door, he turned back and saw the twisted head of a monster rise from his sergeant's body, now a door to Hell. He forced himself to keep going. Jess turned away, heard another loud boom of the door and this time there was the sound of wood splintering as well.

The others were inside. He had to go—fast.

He went room to room, looking for an unlocked door, a way out and finally found one on the third try. Jess saw that luck was on his side because there was also a window in the room, his way out of the nightmare. He pushed it open, felt the cold air kiss his face, and then climbed out. The only way to get away would be to run for the woods. The dense forest would wrap around him like a blanket and save him from the things that came from Hell.

The snow had begun to pick up, but the trees provided cover as he ran, and ran, and ran. His throat burned as his breathing became laboured. His legs begged for him to stop, the muscles felt ignited, but he couldn't slow or give up, not with the end of sanity behind him. When he heard that roar, the one that set his nerves on edge, echo through the woods behind him, it made him run even faster.

Jess ran for what felt like hours, but it could have been days the way it his body cried out. Fear pushed him forward, terror at the beasts getting at him. Jess would have kept going if it wasn't for the unseen root that stuck up from the ground and tripped him. He flew through the air for a second that lasted an eternity. His mind thought of all the things those creatures would do to him the second they caught up to him. And in a way, he deserved it.

Irma had been right, he was a sinner. He'd killed people. Sure, it was in the name of war, but murder is murder. He'd stolen from the dead, lied, and he thought it was justified, but in his heart, he knew it was wrong. He'd believed what he'd been told, that in war, anything goes; morality didn't exist when you put your uniform on and served your country. Yet did God see it that way? Did a military uniform make Him turn a blind eye? As Jess fell to the cold ground, like an angel falling from the grace of God, he knew it wasn't true. Wrong was wrong, no matter how you sugarcoat it.

The air was knocked out of him and his rifle landed a few feet away. He reached for it, tried to catch his breath, and behind him there were more roars. So close. He thought of Derek with his throat slit and the doorway in his chest, Marcus and Vincent getting shot in the head, and the German's being skinned. He remembered the bodies in their homes, the dead woman holding onto her child, and he knew death was coming for him. Whether it was just fate that he should die there, or a cause of his own failings and sins, the roars that echoed through the trees made denial futile. He knew he could use his rifle and kill himself, but as a Catholic, he knew suicide was a sin and he'd be damned to Hell just the same as if he let those hounds kill him. So how could he save his soul?

Was there even a way?

He grasped his gun and knew what he had to do, the least he could do to save something of himself. He knelt down on one knee, looked down his sights, and waited to see one of the shadowy bastards. He whispered a prayer to God, hoped he would be heard as he asked for forgiveness for all his wrongdoings. He fought back tears and he spoke, prayed more, and then he saw one of them, dark and hulking as it crashed through the woods. He prayed for strength and for his bullets to work on the unnatural.

Then he fired.

The bullet found its target, and there was a sound worse than anything he'd ever heard. The beast stopped in its tracks, hands flew up to its chest as blue light exploded from it. Jess watched as the hound threw its head skyward and let out a sound that might have been a howl, but unlike anything he'd ever heard. The sound was like a mix of things: the screech of a train stopping, the howl of an injured cat he once owned, and the low rumble of distant thunder, but all mixed with some other terrible sound that made him feel as though his bladder wanted to let go.

He waited and watched it die, ready if any of the others would come, but was happy to know his bullets could kill them.

The creature was engulfed in the blue light. The light throbbed and engulfed the creature, swallowing him until there was nothing. Then, Jess saw another. And another. And another.

All three were there, near where their brother had died. Jess saw the anger building as their yellow eyes glowed against their dark faces. They turned to him just as he raised his rifle and pointed it at them. They saw Jess no doubt as the pathetic human who had just killed one of their brothers. There was rage in those eyes, in those faces, and Jess knew he couldn't hesitate.

He reloaded.

Fired.

Reloaded.

Fired.

As he went to reload a third time, he was grabbed and lifted off the ground. There were still two of the hounds alive. One bullet had killed a second, but the other missed and there were still two left alive. Jess watched as his gun was taken from him and snapped in two before he was pushed against a tree. One of the hounds held him there, and the other stepped close to his face. Jess could see there was a liquidness to its flesh, as though it flowed. The creature opened its mouth and there was a stench of sulfur and decay as it leaned forward as if to bite him. Jess could see flesh dangling from between its teeth as it sniffed the air around him. He closed his eyes and hoped sending those two beasts back to Hell would be enough to absolve his sins.

He would find out soon.

The humid breath of the hound was on him, the foulness of it turned his stomach. He imaged the pain, the fall into darkness as the life slipped from him, but the pain never came. Slowly, he opened his eyes and saw the beast had moved back a few feet and seemed to look at him strangely, almost tentatively. It looked just like a dog as it turned its head from side to side, confusion clearly visible in its eyes. To Jess, it almost looked afraid. The one holding him didn't let up, though; in fact, its grasp tightened.

He turned to try and look at the face of the one that held him, but it stood too far behind the tree. When he looked back to the one that had been about to bite him, he saw Irma beside it. She stroked the hound's head as the beast knelt at her feet. She spoke softly to it, in a language Jess had never heard, and then turned her attention to him.

"I see you were able to dispatch two of my hounds," she said as she walked towards him. "No worry. I can call more. As long as there is flesh close by, the gates of Hell are always open to me. Maybe you should be the next door. Would you like that?"

Jess said nothing, but shook his head.

"Why not? For the first time in your life you'd have purpose. And I mean real purpose. You'd be the mother and father to Paimon's hounds, an honour if ever there was one." She reached out and traced her finger on his cheek. "It is sin which makes all humans prey to Hell and those who serve it. And since you're all born with sin, thanks to the acts in the Garden of Eden, no flesh is safe from me. Every day people corrupt their souls and don't even know it. They break one of the seven deadly sins as if it were nothing, a mere triviality. You men are the worse. You look into mirrors every chance you get, horde money in banks, let machines do the work of your feet, eat until you're ill, lie with anything at the first signs of arousal, and so much more. Sin is so easy to your kind. Now we'll put those sins to good use, to feed my hounds and give Hell more of the world's evil."

She placed her hand on Jess's forehead and began to say the words he'd heard her speak earlier, just before Derek's chest had burst open. He struggled to move his head, to get her hand off of him, but it didn't lose contact. She continued to hold him and speak the secret language of Hell.

Behind her, the hound stirred and her words fell short. Irma paused and looked back at the creature. When she turned back to Jess, there was something in her eyes, a look of fear, just as he'd seen earlier when she had faked being scared in the church. Only it seemed genuine this time.

"What are you?" she whispered and leaned in. She began to sniff his face and neck, just like an animal. "You're human, no?"

Jess refused to answer. He had no idea what she was going on about, asking if he was human, sniffing him like she was a dog, and why did she look so afraid?

"You are human, right?" she asked again, this time with a blade to his throat.

"Yes."

"Born of woman and man?"

"Of course," he told her as he felt the pressure of the blade's edge dig into his skin.

"My hound says there is something about you, something to fear, but why should we fear the weakness of Man? What is there that a human can do to harm us?" She turned back to the hound behind her and spoke something in a fast and sharp language, words that were no doubt orders.

The hound reluctantly moved towards her and Jess, the beast's head lowered in what looked like obedience and fear, but fear of what? Her? Him? Jess listened as Irma spoke again and heard the hound grunt at her. Then, it stood tall, moved past her and was right in front of Jess. He could feel the heat of the beast's body, and then he felt the teeth of the monster as it bit into the meat between his shoulder and his neck.

Jess opened his mouth, wanting to scream out as searing pain exploded from the wound. His body tensed, but no sound came out, despite the pain that echoed across his flesh. It wasn't that he was unable to; it was the sight before him that stopped it.

The hound that bit him backed up. It convulsed and spewed globs of black from its open mouth. It looked to be choking as it clawed at its own throat, as if Jess's blood had poisoned it. Then the liquid black skin that had looked like oil began to dull, turned a weak shade of grey, and cracked like a desert floor which longed for rain. From the fissures in its strange skin, blue light began to seep out and then finally exploded in a brilliant, blinding flash.

Jess reached up to cover his eyes from the light, and then realized his arms were somehow free. He pushed off the tree and looked back to where the hound that'd held him was and saw it frantically wiping at its hand. There was something on it, red, and Jess could only assume it was his own blood. The hound whimpered wildly, trying to get the blood off of it, but it was already too late. The creature's skin had begun to turn the same ashy grey as the others and before long it too disappeared in a flash of blue brilliance.

"You!"

Jess heard Irma scream as the last of the blue light disappeared and he turned in time to avoid her blade finding his back. He grabbed her wrist as the two of them fell to the ground and struggled with the knife. She cursed and spat at him as they rolled on the snow-covered ground. He'd been trained in hand-to-hand combat and did his best to disarm her, but she was not human, or at least he thought not.

Yet when he freed the knife from her and sank it into her chest, there was no blue light, no change in her skin; only regular human blood bubbled from the wound as he pulled the blade out. He stood up as she tried to put her hand on the wound to stop the bleeding and he looked down at her.

"What ... are ... you?" she asked, her breathing hitched as life drained from her.

"Blessed, I guess." It was all he could think to say, because he had no idea what had caused it all to happen. He was no better than anyone else, had his own sins on his soul, so there was nothing special about him.

He wondered if it was his religious upbringing, the way he'd been taken to church by his mom and nana. He thought it could be his prayers as he felt the end coming, refusing to give it all to suicide, so God had somehow stepped in to save him. He placed his hand over his heart as he looked down at her, tried to think of an answer, and then had an idea.

Jess opened his jacket and grasped his military issued shirt. He was close to panic. He felt the urgency of the moment as he tried to unbutton it as quickly as he could. He could hear her breathing slow and knew she wouldn't last much longer. Jess needed to get answers from her before that happened. If she died, who else would give him some clue; provide the key to the puzzle before him?

The buttons weren't coming open. It was as though they were melded together, or his fingers wouldn't work the way he needed them to. Out of sheer desperation, he ripped open the shirt, and buttons flew in every direction. He pulled it open and told her to look at him.

"Is this why? Is this what did it?" he asked and saw her eyes widen as they fell on his chest.

"The ... mark! The Dayak!" she managed to say before her eyes fluttered and rolled back in her head. She let out a final gasp and was gone.

But she'd told him enough to know the truth.

Two years before, when he turned eighteen, his grandfather had taken him out to get his birthday gift. He'd been hoping for a new jacket, or even tickets to an upcoming Glen Miller show, but instead he was taken down to the docks, to a tattoo shop.

"What are we doing here?" he asked the old man before they went in.

"We have many traditions in our family. Some you know about; others you will learn as you get older. This is one of them."

"A tattoo. I'm going in the army, not the navy."

"Always a smart ass." His grandfather had chuckled and slapped him lightly on the back. "Every man in our family, on the day of their eighteenth birthday, is taken to get a tattoo. Not just any one, though, but a specific mark that is a family crest of sorts. We wear it over our heart for enlightenment, protection, and to allow the will of God into us."

"You have a tattoo?"

"As does your father and my father, and all down the line. Traditions are important."

"What's it a tattoo of?"

"In the old country, it was called Dayak, from a book called *The Anna*. In a way, the symbol is a talisman, set to ward off evil and protect you."

"Does it work?"

"Am I still alive?" The old man laughed again and unbuttoned his shirt. He showed his grandson the tattoo; a faded black line circle with a double crossed line in the center. It looked a bit like a crucifix, only with two lines going through instead of one. Jess had never really thought about getting a tattoo before, but the ones he'd seen and liked usually involved a pin-up girl, not a plain symbol like that. "You will get the Dayak and wear it and no evil shall be able to overtake you."

As he stood over the body of Irma, he knew it had actually worked, that the symbol had protected him from the hounds and the conjuring witch. His grandfather and family had passed something along to him that had saved his life, and his soul.

Jess took the bloody knife and cut away a chunk of Irma's clothing. He used it to cover the wound in his neck, and then tucked the bloody blade into his belt as he walked away from Irma's body. He wondered what other evils there were in the world. If things like the conjuror and the hounds were real, what other monstrosities must there be?

"And how can I find them and rid the world of them?" he asked himself, and disappeared into the dark woods.

***

Medium

by Philip Trippenbach and Blake Jessop, United Kingdom

When people tell you their dreams, they're usually rather neat. I mean that in the sense of clean, or tied in a bow. I'm jealous; mine have never made any sense at all. No narrative, nobody I recognize, except my mother, who I barely remember. So nothing real at all.

Mostly I dream of shadows, which is a daft thing to dream of when you're asleep, surrounded by them anyway. By shadows, I mean monsters, not the usual inanimate shadows you're used to.

Lately, when I dream at all, I dream I am the girl who screams at the darkness, and makes the darkness shrink away. My dreams are the only place it listens to me; the shadows certainly don't listen to me when I'm awake.

So, don't judge me. I'm crazy, okay?

*

The cancer ward is on the twelfth floor, so I'm supposed to have a nice view.

Some view. It's dark outside, with a dishrag sky dripping cold rain on the rooftops out in the gloom. Tomorrow morning a team of well-meaning NHS surgeons are going to cut a hole in my skull to see if they can figure out where the shadows come from.

On a normal day, it's just me and one of the monsters. For as long as I can remember, my companions changed constantly; it hurt my feelings. Do you imagine shadows as having personality? Look closer, they do. Mine aren't the kind of monsters most people dream up to thrill themselves or use as excuses for not confronting their fears. All they do is flicker like something lit by candlelight and make lowing noises.

My dream monsters sort of keep an eye on me, more collocating in my personal space than invading it. Now that I'm here, hair already shorn away, I seem to be getting a lot more popular with the things that come from the dark. When the nurse turns the lights off and my eyes adjust, I see lots of them, guttering about the pools of dusk cast by the solitary bar of light above my bed.

"Why did you bring friends?" I ask one of them, tangled in the sheets and hugging my knees. "Are you worried the surgeons are going to evict you?"

It breathes evenly, rising and falling. I've imagined these things, or they've imagined me, for as long as I can remember. Every time I fell asleep, there they were. Leaning over me, watching, and making that sound. I don't ever remember being scared of them, though normal for me may be abject terror for you. I don't know. I thought everyone saw them, until my father told me to stop talking about it. I learned not to tell other kids at school. Great way to not have any friends. Monster kid.

I don't draw them anymore, even though I'm quite good at it. I learned to hear and speak no evil early on, but deciding what to do about seeing it came later. I tried drawing them a few years back, when I turned fifteen. Isn't art supposed to set you free? Ms. Swift went rather quiet when she saw my accurately rendered charcoal ghosts, then quietly had my father book me to see a "special educational needs coordinator" in an office in town. Apparently my mother used to walk me around there, before she vanished into the shadows.

The specialist had to look my name up on his clipboard when we talked, though he put his hand on my arm just so, to show me he was listening. He asked Dad to leave the room.

"Now, Julie, this is confidential," he said. "Will you tell me, are you taking any drugs? Are you getting high?"

I told him no, and no, and got out of there as fast as I could. I am not agonizing over a boy leaving me or cutting myself. I am not anorexic or dyslexic. Those are serious things, and maybe he could even deal with them, but they are not what I have been trying to figure out, trying to hide. Not what has been trying to hide me. I'm not sure if that last bit is my imagination. It's just a sense I get.

Crazy is the wrong word. I get good grades, mostly, and I've been seeing the same boy since year eleven. I am not stupid; I just see better in the dark than you do. Every night. Days, too, if I run across any particularly good shadows.

That's the problem, and it's growing. I never used to see them during the day. You know when you glimpse something out of the corner of your eye and see something really distinct? It's like that, only you probably see a face in the curtains or the silhouette of someone about to cross the road. I generally see eyes, or the sockets where eyes should be, if they had eyes. They don't.

This October the fits started. I must have fallen asleep in class, because I dreamt of a cold place, a garden, and when I woke up, Mr. Kent was standing over my desk, clutching a dry erase marker while everyone else huddled at the edge of the classroom and stared. I'd been frothing, apparently, and howling. Not very social, even for me.

Dad took me to the emergency room so we could wait among the coughing hordes. They saw me more quickly than I'd like. The next day I was strapped rigid to a plastic bed, whirring smoothly into the tunnel of an MRI machine. It's like being slid into a tastefully lit coffin. They played lame music while they looked into my head.

Everyone's eyes went wide when the technician brought up the images. My brain looked like a pale grey cauliflower, shot through with spreading lines like the roots of some dark plant. My father displayed his usual composure, but his eyes were suddenly brimming.

It's curious, the doctor said. He'd never seen anything quite like this before, growing in a lattice through a whole brain like that. They asked me to leave the room. The doctor closed the door.

There was nothing to sit on in the spotless hospital hallway, so I stood around in my coat under the strip-lighting, next to a corkboard covered in flyers. My father's deep voice filtered out into the hall in indistinct dollops. When the doctor answered, it was in the same tone Dad uses when he's telling me to calm down. Words soft and final. I wish they'd let me stay. Not knowing is always worse.

Or it isn't. It took me a while to figure out my father's euphemisms, but it boiled down to them needing to start with the scalpels. Immediately. Open up my skull and have a look at the back of my brain, where the anaplastic astrocytoma is the most diffuse. That is really hard to say, and I started thinking of them as tentacles, like a cute little octopus was massaging the back of my brain.

So that's why I'm in the cancer ward on the twelfth floor, waiting for them to drill a hole in my head in the morning and maybe let the monsters out, those self-same monsters now looking at me from the corners like things grown organically out of the night.

They stand over me and sway, sometimes move around in the background where there's a smell like electricity. Not a bother usually, but I'm having a hard time not being profoundly terrified of what's happening to me. Monsters? Not a huge deal. I've lived with them. Scalpels to the brain? Shivers, and not the good kind.

"I've had such a long day," I whisper, "what do you want?"

The monsters move a half-step towards me, crowd me, like something is about to change—and vanish as if someone had flipped a switch. They always do that when someone walks in the room.

"Peter?" I say.

*

In a way, I think my father was kind of relieved that I have an impressive amount of brain cancer. I know that makes him sound like a monster, but he isn't. I know exactly what monsters look like. Trust me. I guess it makes him human, which isn't any easier, but at least it makes sense.

What I mean is that his generation aren't all that good at mental health stuff. You know how you have that one grandpa who calls chip shop owners *dagos* or whatever? It's like that. Not so much nasty as just *old*.

Last year Ms. Swift did a whole unit on mental health. We learned about autism, Down's syndrome, Bipolar Disorder, everything. It's like sex-ed, assuming you didn't look everything up on the internet when you were ten. Sex is supposed to be a big deal, but eventually you understand that it's just a thing you deal with. You deal with it, say *huh*, and move along.

I have a friend named Matthew. He got taken out of class and sent to a special school, eventually, but most of us still follow him online. Matty has Asperger's, so he was a bit of a berk, but if you got over that, he was kind of nice. Pretty cool, actually, because when he got into something, he really, really got *into* it, in a way I don't know if I can. All you had to do was try to get him interested the same stuff you were and he was great. Want to play Pokémon but there are too many monsters? Get Matty. He would memorize everything and help you out with it. I learned a lot from him.

The point is that's normal for us. For my dad there are only two kinds of people: crazy and not crazy. I think he had a really hard time understanding that I might be crazy. I feel pretty sane, of course. Pestered, tired, scared, and wanting chips, but sane. The dark shapes aren't crazy to me, they're just there. If that's insane to you, then I don't care.

So that's why my father is not a monster. He has an easier time understanding that the baby octopus cancer lump is putting pressure on my brain and making me see things than imagining that his daughter is simply certifiable.

It has made being here hard. It has made being me hard. Peter has made both things easier.

I was half dozing when he snuck in. When I'm almost asleep and the incoherent nightmares haven't started yet, I do the thinking about dying I avoid during the day. It's hard not to; I can hear the monsters better right before I go to sleep, like some kind of barrier is down. The dark is darker, the light is lighter, and I can't stop imagining what it's like not to wake up. Imagine what it's like not imagining not imagining. Does that make any sense?

You're not allowed to have visitors after nine at night, but Peter has gotten good at sneaking about. It's been a nice surprise; he's a really straight arrow most of the time. Hearing the tiny squeak of his trainers perks me up, but I stay still. I hear him take the visitor's chair by the bed and whisper my name. I lie there, breathe evenly, and pretend to sleep.

"Julie?" he says again, and reaches out for my hand, "you awake?"

He pauses.

"I've been thinking about us," he says.

Is he telling me he's breaking up with me? My head starts throbbing.

"This is pretty rough, right? I mean, I don't think either of us was expecting it to be like this. I honestly didn't think I was going to be able to tough it out, but it's weird, I'm sort of getting used to it."

No, he isn't. Okay.

"I never thought it was going to be this hard, coming back day after day, but I feel like I'm doing something right, something real."

That's actually pretty sweet.

"It's got me thinking. About you. I, well –"

Go on. Say it. Every part of me wants him to.

"I'm ... I'm not going anywhere."

Well, he almost said it, and I had to be unconscious. Whatever. I'll take it.

"Smooth," I say, and open my eyes. His eyes go wide and he gets the cute confused look on his face that means I've caught him.

"Seriously, I didn't know if you'd still like me with no hair."

He exhales in a whoosh.

"It suits you, actually. So, you weren't asleep?"

"What I do here isn't really sleeping," I say, and reach for his hand.

He didn't kiss me when my eyes were closed; he is a modern sort of boy. My eyes are open now.

It's been a while. Things have changed. We had a tough time when I started seeing the monsters during the day. I told him about it, moment of weakness, and he kind of just accepted it. I think he believes they're a metaphor for something; he was in Ms. Swift's class too. I really wasn't sure he'd stick around when I told him about the cancer. Dad even had a talk with me about how he might not be able to cope and that it was normal. Result: I was a bit surprised when he came to see me. When he started showing up every day.

This is far from the first time we've kissed; we've done rather more than that. It is the first time I feel like I know what it means. It's not a long kiss. His lips are soft. Everything tingles. I'm smiling as wide as I can when we pull apart, cancer or not.

"You are not bad, Peter. I think I shall invite you to stay."

Now he smiles. The shadow contingent has been watching all this, of course, but I've gotten exceptionally good at ignoring them when the mood suits. Peter smiles at me again, then says he needs a cuppa and goes off to nick tea from somewhere. His family are Jamaican, originally, but he's as Lewisham as it gets.

In the meanwhile, I look around at the monsters. There's an even bigger crowd now, which is odder still. There's just the one light on over the bed, so there's plenty of room. They pull away when Peter gets back with two paper cups, and I focus on the tea. We sip together. It's good to have him around. Great, actually.

After a moment, Peter glances over his shoulder.

"I will stay, Julie," he says shyly, "at least until things get going in the morning."

I've already thought of a few ways to tell him how nice that would be when he says, almost offhand, "By the way, who was that in your room just now?"

My heart and the tea hit my stomach at about the same time.

I look him in the eyes. I may be staring intensely.

"What did you see?"

"My mistake. Just out of the corner of my eye. A nurse or something."

"If it was a nurse, where did she go?"

He tries to shake his head and nod at the same time.

"I don't know. I heard a kind of braying. Is something broken in here?"

"Not anymore. Help me up, we're leaving."

I've never felt this way before. Maybe I'd started believing my father. I know I believed something.

"Leaving?" Peter stammers. "Slow down. What about the surgery?"

"Yes. About that. If *you* can see the monsters too, then why is it such a good idea for surgeons to drill holes in *my* skull?" I sit straight up and look around for my shoes.

"You think I can see the monsters? Julie, I don't know."

"Think hard, then." I think he's seeing something new in me. So am I. His brows knot.

"This is crazy, but maybe. It wasn't like a person, more like ... a shadow perhaps?"

"Right. Exactly. Off we go."

Peter digs out his mobile. Flashes a glance toward the corner by the window. I know what that feels like.

"We should call your dad," he says. "Call someone."

"Forget it; Dad thinks I've got an octopus tumor strangling my brain making me crazy."

"You do, though. I saw the x-ray."

I stare at him.

"Yes, but it's not making me crazy."

*

Did I mention there's music playing? I love music. This is the kind of thing you think about when your life changes all at once. Pointless little things.

Even when Peter is here, I get to choose what's on the Bluetooth speakers by the bed. I have cancer. The longer the hospital stay went on, the angrier I felt, and the more sense angry music made to me. Tonight it was some kind of tinkly folk band, except they get pissed off a lot and play metal. They're Swiss or something and I can't pronounce the band name. What I like is between songs there are haunting little instrumentals with bits of poetry. That's what was playing when Peter kissed me. I wasn't listening to the words.

Peter looks scared. I lean on him as I get out of bed. My legs feel weaker than I expected. Like I've never stood up on my own.

I close my eyes, just for a moment. I'll rest for a second, then go. Somewhere. I'm shivering, too, and the room swims. Someone is calling my name; a singsong lullaby from the far echoing depths, insistent and delicate. There's a cold place I can fall into, as soft and welcoming as snow.

The monsters reach out to catch me, and the darkness swallows me. While I fall, I remember the words to the song with perfect accuracy.

Where ere thou has been
here, or in yon world manifest
Canst thou tell what is, or what was,
or what is to come?
No thing shall last.

*

I awake into a buzzing disharmony, crouched and shivering on a smooth circular platform. In the gloom all around me, creatures sway and twitch, knotted tangles of translucent growth lean tall and stamp nervously, like horses do. They stretch scrofulous twists of pale root toward me, erupting new tendrils as I shrink away. Natural reflex; shy away from sickness. The air is full of their hollow chant.

I'm tired of this. Even in sudden clarity, I wish only an endpoint. You want to grow until you engulf me? Fine. Take me. I want a conclusion, either way.

Slowly, I reach out to touch a trembling, extended root. It retracts suddenly, then reaches forward again, wrapping a pale tendril firmly around my finger. Soft. Another stem touches the back of my head. A searching gesture, like it was tousling my hair. I notice my hair is back, flowing like I was underwater.

I turn and see it; a giant tussock of pale coralline tendrils, splitting into fractal tips so fine they lose themselves in the air.

It reaches forward with half a dozen tubers, touching my face and neck, and I know those tendrils' root-tips reach back down into the water at the source of the world, through the space between stars, to the heart of the network. Shape and colour riot in my mind, images flipping past too quickly to see.

It feels like getting hit by a giant wave while you swim in the ocean. I lose all sense of balance and direction. Cities grow through living rock, bored by centuries of roots. Cold descends from above, coming on stronger and stronger every winter. Seeds grow, are saved, deep where it's still warm. Nothing will live, the next time the ice comes. There is something they need me to do, before the snow falls. I tumble in the surf. The water is freezing.

"Listen well," someone says, "and think clearly. You can do this, Julie. I know you can."

The voice is familiar, female, hard and reassuring at once. I can't remember whose it is, but I feel my equilibrium return.

Through the flurry of images one catches my attention. A small figure unlike the others. A familiar shape. Peter, seen from above, struggling on the floor, drowning in shadow. Engulfed.

A hundred thousand voices whisper to me. Fine. I'm used to it. It's time for them to listen instead. With the sensation of breaking glass, I dive back into the world.

*

Tendrils reach up through the floor, into my mind, a feeling like cold water pouring down the length of my spine. The gate is open; the key has turned in the lock. I'm waking up. I can feel the cool tile under my palms.

I never knew whether I was dreaming. Maybe I was, but not this. I draw a line between sleep and waking, dark and light.

"Who are you?" My voice, without an echo, swallowed by the hospital room.

We are travelers in the dark. We have reached you, at last. We are connected, at last. Mind and minds. Your world and ours. Thanks to you we will not wither in the cold. Thanks to you.

"Why me?" I ask. It's the only question I've ever really had.

Why any of us?

I glance up. Peter is on his knees by the bed. I can't process how much has just changed, but they are touching Peter, and it's killing him. I know this. I can process this.

"You're hurting him."

I can see. They still aren't listening. What's the hardest you've ever fought to wake from a dream?

"Stop it!" I scream.

The hospital room snaps into focus. I regain medium awareness. I can hear them perfectly. My hands and feet are freezing. Two shadows hold Peter, their fronds now almost totally encasing his head. Two more, stepping gingerly toward me with many-toed feet, stop in mid-step as well.

I point to the ones holding Peter.

"Let him go," I howl, "he's mine!"

The web of waxy tubes relaxes, then slithers back. Peter draws in a great shuddering breath and paws his way up the bed. This time I'm the one holding him.

"Now," I snarl, "piss off."

*

We hold each other. The room is empty.

I have yelled at them many times in my life, but this is the first time they've listened.

I am the girl who screamed at the darkness, and the darkness shrank away. Cool.

There is a warm, pressing feeling on my neck. Peter, holding me so tight I can barely breathe.

"It's okay," I say, "they've stopped. For now, anyway."

"What," he manages, "the bloody hell?"

I look from him to the shadows. They're back, but keeping their distance.

They sway anxiously. I am not what they expected, apparently. Fine. Distantly, through the darkness behind them, I can feel the echo of the deep root we shared. I sniffle. It smells like iron. I wipe blood from my nose.

"This will happen on my terms," I say, "you sods."

"That whole time," Peter says, "everything you told me. That wasn't a metaphor."

"No, apparently," I tell him. "Not even a little."

"This is mad," he says.

I nod. It is, but what isn't?

"Why can I see them?" he gapes. "Wait, not because I kissed you?"

"I don't know," I tell him. I really don't, but that idea isn't crazy. It's the only thing we changed. When I felt like we connected, I guess we did.

How very romantic, I tell myself. Actually, scratch the sarcasm; it was romantic. I don't care who knows it.

"So you gave me an extra-terrestrial contact high?" Peter says, out of nowhere.

I will give him this; he makes me laugh.

*

We run.

I don't know where we're going, but the cool night air is like a river, washing away my doubts. My father is going to be furious.

What's strange about this? It's not the part where Peter started seeing the same monsters I do after he kissed me, or even the bit where I started screaming and bleeding from the nose. What's weird to me, truly odd, is where I am in the story. Part of me was getting used to having cancer. I honestly thought I was at the end, that the last chapter was written and I was going to miss all the crying in the epilogue.

I was wrong. There may still be tears, but I was wrong all the same. I have so much work to do, so much to learn, and I don't even know where to start. I'm not at the end of the story. I'm at the beginning.

"Are you okay?" Peter asks. He's breathing hard, and he looks more than a little freaked out. Not too bad, considering.

I smile at him. It may not be my best smile, but it's honest.

"So, what do we do now?" he asks.

"Get the tube," I say, "and some chips."

"I mean about this," he gestures at the shadows and rain.

"I don't know," I say, "I think I'll have to talk with the deep root again. Chips first."

He nods. I grab his hand, and we start down dark paths, chasing shadows.

***

A Beckoning Muse
by Jay Seate, United States

His hands rested on the kitchen table. The untouched eggs and coffee getting cold before him. "Fly away, Thomas. Come fly away with me," a voice gentle and pure whispered from some unknown place, a voice that reminded him of places now impossibly far off and inaccessible, populated with fading masks of the departed, somewhere far down the road from his world of aching joints, memory lapses, and a dismal prognosis. The beautifully pitched tone reminded him of someone who had mattered more than most. It stood in sharp contrast to news of disaster and death. Time could seem a shapeless lump of successes and failures, of pleasure and anguish. His personal setbacks combined with the woes of a world in chaos gave him cause to reminisce about his initiation to life—the Alpha and Omega. From the beginning to the approaching end.

He had survived childhood, adolescence, college, and Vietnam with all his limbs intact and without noticeable psychological damage, except for the dreams. He let his hair grow and lived on the beach as part of the freewheeling California lifestyle.

Like many of the young and restless of that era, he wanted to see and do it all. He soon pulled up stakes and crossed the Atlantic to the roots of western civilization, picking up odd jobs when his money ran low. He slept in first class Eurail Pass compartments, cheerfully annoying the European upper crust that travelled by train. In Paris, he danced beneath the Arc de Triomphe. In Budapest, he leaped from one twenty-story balcony to another to join a girl of unknown nationality because she smiled and displayed a bottle of champagne. Occasionally he spent evenings rollicking with females in one town or another. In truth, however, he would have preferred the company of his soulmate he had found, then lost amongst the flower children and the distractions of the West Coast.

Thomas's devil-may-care façade was not immune to moments of loneliness and guilt. This segue of autonomy from responsibility eventually came to an unceremonious end in a whirlwind of decaying memories. Back in the good old USA, he got someone pregnant, the cosmic powers-that-be providing a link to what mainstream society beckoned for—the roots of Americanism that promised a predictable career, marriage, rug-rats, conservatism, and seeing old age creeping ever more closely from a distant horizon. Normalcy prevailed and finally ruled.

For the next thirty years, the artistry of dance and of making music survived only as fading memories, yet time failed to totally extinguish Thomas's creative flame. And one day, he began to write and when the moment to retire from the cubicle-enclosed computer world blessedly arrived, little by little, fiction absorbed him.

First, he sculpted stories from his own experiences, then later from flights of fancy where bizarre beings and odd, astonishing beasts frolicked. He gave life to creatures that could achieve anything and trek anywhere. Sometimes his fanciful creations became gods and other times monsters gobbled them up depending on which light bulb in Thomas's skull shined the brightest. More and more his fertile mind lived in these amazing worlds where he could encompass the voyages and destinations lacking in designed day-to-day living.

Throughout his lifetime, doors of opportunity regularly opened and closed, but a final exit was too quickly approaching. About the time his efforts gained recognition, he found himself suddenly old. The kids were gone, his wife spent her afternoons with other women, and a nasty cancer grew inside him.

Cancer, sickness—words alien to him and his literary creations. Ugly words. Unjustly brutal in an age of high-tech, Band-Aid remedies. The powers-that-be, it appeared, had placed a time limit on the continuing development of his craft. He was fading away, becoming almost invisible to a dwindling number of acquaintances, to Gladys. He and she began as two people, then become one, then two again, facing in opposite directions. No one's fault. No infidelity. Nothing to blame but the parade of time.

In his study, Thomas deliberated over his souvenirs, knickknacks, and pictures—mementos of a lifetime, objects that melded his seventy years— and speculated about a future journey. If the struggles through life ended with dreams unfulfilled, why does one go through it? Simple enough. Because we don't know that until near the end. Though far beyond the days of youthful exploration, he wanted desperately to travel once more, while there was still time to experience another interlude like his college days, or his sojourn to Europe all those years ago.

The following day, his wife sat in the living room with a cup of coffee and her nose in a book—not one of his. The length of silence between them exemplified the vastness of the gulf which separated their lives. They had lived in the same house, under the same roof, for almost the whole of their married life. They had raised children here, but a wall between two bedrooms had separated them almost from the time the second and final child was born. They had been happy here once, but it was so long ago that its significance had long since faded with the old photos in an album. Except for the sturdiness of the rooms they shuffled through, they were unsteadily adrift and ignorant about how to change things.

"I'm going to the library to do some research," Thomas announced to his wife. "I'll be back in a few hours."

"Fine," Gladys softly replied.

Although he could research most anything on the internet, he wanted to get away from her. All that bound them now were their son and daughter, and that bond was mostly superficial since both had moved to different parts of the country. Thomas studied the woman he'd been married to for so long a moment longer, then he disappeared through the garage door.

Gladys sighed and returned to her book. "You won't be back until you get hungry," she murmured softly so he wouldn't hear.

What she didn't know was that Thomas wasn't going to the library. He had a more substantial trip in mind, one he hoped would satisfy some distant longing and make him forget, at least temporarily, the latest of life's challenges he had to face. He had planned it secretly for weeks, almost from the time he'd gotten the news from his doctor, in fact. This would avoid the cascade of questions or objections. Or maybe it wouldn't have mattered to Gladys at all.

His clothes were in the trunk of his car. He backed out of the drive, looked for a moment at the house the same way he'd looked at his wife. Once it had been nurturing, but now it was just a place to hold his inanimate treasures. He drove away from what was supposed to be a small version of the American dream, hitting the road like John Steinbeck had once done. He believed that observing some current component of the human condition might inspire him to a signature piece of work, but most of all, he wanted to come and go outside of expected routines with only a rudimentary plan—no phone, no pool, no pets.

Thomas stood on a balcony. His first stop on his road to rediscovery had a purpose: to visit the college town where his adult pleasures reached fruition. Upon his arrival, he found an old college buddy's name in the phone book. They had reunited only once in the forty-eight years since graduation.

In college, his friend Roy had been Joe Cool, but he would be old now and part of Thomas hated to see the result. Still, it would be worth a day to reminisce. He dialed the number. Roy answered. After the required dialogue between lives parted, they agreed to meet at the old university malt shop, now a bookstore.

Roy had planned and accomplished the American Dream: to marry the boss's daughter, raise two kids and live in the nicest part of town near the campus—a kind of latter-day Bobby Darin and Sandra Dee life. Thomas, on the other hand, had his own history to remind him that the accomplishment of a prefabricated plan seldom equates to happiness. But, perhaps it was only himself that remained unfulfilled. In America, at least, who could criticize an existence with every convenience and appliance desired?

It was a short walk across campus from where Thomas parked, but the walk brought back ancient memories that poured out steadily at first and then became a torrent of flashbacks. There were scenes of crisp autumn days when he walked to the football stadium with his frat brothers or with a date. There had also been the hot, humid days spent at the burger hangouts where bronzed teenagers chatted each other up and where he had always been on the make. The laughter of young girls was like no other sound.

"Not too old and worn out to remember." He smiled to himself. He had walked this path hundreds of times. It was a bittersweet path where hopes and dreams had blossomed, and where many of those hopes, he now realized, had dried up like the brown, shriveled leaves that swirled around his ankles. But the memories of good times added a lift to his step as he crossed the street and entered the bookstore.

Inside he browsed to see if any of his books had found their way onto shelves while waiting for Roy.

"Go team," a voice called. A clear, evocative voice from the past.

As Roy sauntered toward him, Thomas's jaw dropped as if unhinged. His old chum looked unchanged, still young, handsome, and wiry. A co-ed clung tightly to his arm like a crepuscular vine entwined into a rough surface.

Had strolling campus addled Thomas's brain? He had not been under the effect of hallucinogenic drugs since surviving Nam. Perhaps he was still inside the overly warm rental car, nodding off behind the wheel, falling prey to his imagination. Nevertheless, Thomas closed his mouth before anything flew inside.

"My man, Thomas." Roy offered his hand while the cute co-ed beamed coquettishly.

As they shook hands, something kinetic occurred. It coursed through veins and muscle, a connection generating new vitality. He felt as young as Roy looked.

"Take a load off," Roy said as a red Formica-top table with four accompanying chrome and plastic chairs materialized next to them.

"I'm a little confused," replied Thomas. "This feels like a fifty-year-old time warp, like we're still students. And your wife ..."

"You're still a doubting Thomas. That's later. It doesn't matter now."

A dream. It has to be. But the scene was not bathed in an amber haze of nostalgia. It seemed real. Thomas, Roy, and Beth handled chocolate shakes delivered by a beaming, fresh-faced lad with less intrusiveness than a transitory shadow.

They traded stories for what seemed a long while, like a dream that in truth may last only seconds. Beth chattered about her courses. Roy mentioned current events and knew of Thomas's writing, but that was the only tie with the present, the only sinew of reality to their visit. When Roy and Beth finally waved goodbye, the spell was broken. He was back in a bookstore. The rejuvenation within had begun to fade.

"Did we really meet?" Thomas exclaimed as a customer gave him a quizzical stare. The rational side of Thomas had difficulty accepting the encounter, but there was that tell-tale drip of chocolate on his sweater. He could not keep himself from gazing past the bookshelves in search of the disappearing ice cream counter. In our universe, anomalies occur regularly and for whatever reason the clockwork of cause and effect appeared to be on vacation in Thomas's present world.

He checked the directory again and was unable to find Roy's listing this time. "Old age, old man," he told himself. "You're flipping out." He left the bookstore, made a hasty return to the car wondering if all the marbles beneath his skullcap had been shot out of the circle.

A slow drive around campus temporarily shelved the bookstore/malt shop conundrum and instead sent him on a veil of matriculated reflection, maddeningly disrupted by modern buildings and too much asphalt. Where had all the ivy gone?

He had forgotten many names and places, but one location indelibly imprinted into his circuitry was a duplex just off campus where he had made love for the first time. He parked the rental car across the street. Sure enough, the wood and brick structure still stood, unchanged, holding his and Bonnie Sue's affair inviolate.

He and she had waited until college to go all the way. Thomas sighed and fast-forwarded the six-month melodrama through his mind. "You'll always be the first, Bonnie Sue." He wished to run time backwards and change the outcome of this fleeting romance—to imbue it with more longevity, but time only ran one way, at least till now.

"Hey," someone called from one side of the duplex. Surely not for him. "Hey, Tom."

A young girl wearing a pink bow in her bubble hairdo stood in the doorway waving. Thomas removed his spectacles and rubbed his eyes. "I've got to be dreaming again, fast asleep."

"Hey," she said a third time.

"Bonnie Sue?"

"Come in, silly."

Thomas slowly climbed out of his car and crossed the street. He looked back to make sure it was the 2013 Toyota and not his ancient Plymouth parked against the curb.

"Where have you been? It seems like forever." She kissed a befuddled Thomas on the lips, took his hand and perkily led him directly to the bedroom. Once again, the inexplicable had surfaced, arriving this time with nerve endings.

How this blazing swirl of momentarily reawakened passion compared to the old days in college, time spent with his traveling liaisons, or the early years of marriage he could not recall with certainty. Bonnie Sue's lips and tongue proclaimed a forgotten urgency between giggles, amazed at the feeling of their youthful desires welling up, strong and unencumbered. Yet in a languid moment of repose, he saw in her eyes what it had been like within the heart in that first innocent coupling. It had been the purest of shared emotions devoid of conquest or dishonor.

She extolled his virtues as they made love a second time. Although he again felt young and vibrant, his many years forced him to acknowledge this rendezvous was no more than a succulent dream. It provided all the more reason to linger in its impassioned embrace that possessed the power to seal him off from the abyss of requirement, the mundane, the reality of a life not utilized to its fullest potential.

He lay next to Bonnie Sue half expecting to wake up to the reverberation of his wife's snoring, but he tried to hold tightly to this current circumstance. The necessity of illusion, a feeling akin to the birth of a dance, the first few notes of a familiar song, or an inspired sentence in one of his stories, lingered over, the ever-present blinking curser waiting for more.

Then suddenly, he was transported to the duplex's living room sofa while in the kitchen, the twenty-year-old Bonnie Sue, her pointy brassiere, culottes and pantyhose restored and readjusted, prattled away about her daughters' careers and her husband's sudden death.

"Time to get home," she announced gently. "Have to get dinner on the table. Same time next week?" It was a statement more than a question.

He stood and followed her to the door and heard himself saying, "You know how these dreams are. You want to return, but you can't. I won't pass this way again."

With a smile and a wave, Bonnie Sue trotted down the street beyond his view, leaving him standing in the yard, the old and new askew, juxtaposing around him, current facts incongruously overlapping ancient history.

Thomas did not know exactly when reality returned, but apparently it had. The duplex looked dissimilar now with a decided change of color and superior tending to the surrounding shrubs. His delusion must have started before he had called Roy and the interlude with this girl certainly met the required stuff of dreams. But it was over now. The arthritis in his heel was kicking up, there was slight discomfort from the virulent and breeding invader within, and he still had hundreds of miles between his college town and the place of eternal sunshine where he had lost Sherry.

The sun followed Thomas across the sky. Ten very real hours of reflecting sunlight, squinting into the glare of headlights, and fighting off fatigue gave him time to think about the day's strange encounters and to brood over his past and the pursuit of happiness. The trip had become more than the search for an idea to share with a handful of loyal readers. Planned or not, it was now a continuing quest for what had been experienced and mislaid through time and age. He was not seeking a new adventure so much as he was searching for the graceful beauty and symmetry in the best of recollections gone by. *Little future, but oh what a past. Was that it?* Twilight had this effect on him—a time to reflect on what his existence had stockpiled—a house, a family, a wife, his stories— to what purpose? Only hedonistic pleasures or something of value to mankind?

Thomas pulled into a Motel 6 parking lot weary from miles of highway that had been all too real. And yet, he knew the magical quality of the trip thus far would continue in some manifestation. He sensed that something different waited under the red and blue neon behind the glass double doors. Instead of the usual overweight girl or Pakistani behind the counter, two young men in naval officer uniforms standing ramrod straight awaited him.

"Greetings, Thomas," they said robotically. "Thanks for reporting. Right this way."

"I'm not in the service," Thomas protested. "I served five decades ago."

"There's another war on and you owe Uncle Sam. Your time in the Reserves is never up."

His early past was not wholly one of women and sweet rose wine. The aforementioned dreams about the military lingered in dark corners like evil cherubs awaiting the opportunity to create mayhem. His ghost ship sometimes sailed into such a slaughterhouse that he would find himself hovering on the floor, the horribly disfigured imps dancing and playing tunes of their own creation until he struggled into consciousness. Was there ever a week that his military experience did not cross his mind and soil some pleasant thought? He knew his fictional fire-breathing monsters were an attempt to purge the gremlins of war in a socially acceptable way, but the knowledge provided little respite.

He dutifully followed the sailors from the motel office through a door and directly into the bowels of a naval ship. "How long must I stay? I've got a life, you know. How can I ..."

An officer raised a hand to silence him. "Why, when the war's over," he said. "Not like before, Williams. This time it's for the duration." Funerary marble could not have felt colder than this chilling utterance.

Thomas groaned. "I'm just taking a trip, for Christ's sake."

"Here's your rack and locker," the officers said in mechanical unison. "See you topside when you're squared away." They left him below decks in crowded sleeping quarters.

Thomas stood incredulously between all too familiar rows of canvas bunks four tiers high, alone in the ship's ambient belly with no sounds but the creaking and groaning of the iron creature as it shifted ever so slightly to remind him that it was a living thing not unlike being inside Jonah's whale or one of Thomas's own paper dragons. "I can't do this again. I paid my debt. I must wake up before we leave port."

But he did not wake up. He climbed ladders to the deck as the ship set sail into the ocean's unforgiving blackness. A huge deck gun exploded and recoiled, sending a missile en route to some unknown target. In the heavens, the cylinder abruptly reversed direction and circled toward him, becoming a Napalm-spewing dragon. A creation of his own making spiraled back from the sky to bring an end to him. The dragon belched its fiery breath in his face. He covered his eyes and cried out with enough truculence and anguish from the searing heat to jolt him back to a simple motel room where he lay in a tangle of sweaty sheets.

He wiped saliva from the corner of his mouth and stared wide-eyed at the nondescript walls of the room that possessed all the earmarks of Motel 6 realism. "Christ Almighty. The government is still after another pound of my flesh?"

He shuffled to the bathroom and drank a glass of water. He examined the small scar over his eye from his Vietnam days, courtesy of a ship's ladder in the middle of a storm, and felt thankful that it had been the only physical souvenir awarded while in the service of his country. "Once was enough. Please, no more carnage."

He returned to bed on tender hooks beseeching the fates to bring restful, mindless slumber before his odyssey resumed.

To sleep, perhaps to dream. Eventually he felt himself dematerialize into the core of oblivion, sliding downward into unconsciousness and once overtaken, it was the sleep of near death.

As the shroud of night slipped away, a sliver of sunlight divided Thomas's face into halves. The bed from which he awoke was lumpy, yet familiar. "The beachfront apartment, by God." The one he had rented for six months after the Navy stint prior to his barnstorming of Europe. "I've arrived. Somehow, miraculously, I'm here."

The room was as real as the motel had been with its own contribution to pedestrian detail. His bed was tucked into the corner of the two-room dwelling with a kitchenette that overlooked the Pacific. It had not changed from his memory, nor had he. He touched the edges of a still youthful beard that shadowed his face. Well-worn Hawaiian swim trunks adorned his flat midsection and muscular thighs. Still a dream, no doubt, but each journey to the past seemed to gain a substantive momentum.

He sauntered into the adjoining room. Glass balls of cool colors, blues and greens, drooped in a fisherman's net hung from the ceiling. One wall was covered in butcher paper where guests had been encouraged to write whatever their heart told them, a tribute to the thoughts and views of free-spirited souls in the early seventies.

A young surfer was scrawling a joke or epitaph as Thomas watched, a timely embellishment, since a party was in full swing. Long hairs and short hairs, colorful clothes, the smell of marijuana and spilled wine. The Moody Blues wailed from a stereo and girls with long straight hair parted in the center, some of them topless except for their strands of colored beads, danced merrily about. How much real time could the convolutions of a dream as elaborate as this require? The bare-breasted beauties reminded him of a story he'd written years later that started with a cabin in the woods. He tweaks the vision until it comes into focus:

I walked up the cabin steps and entered. The polished wood floor led through the living room into the next room where meals were prepared. Standing in front of the sink stood my Sherry, her raven hair shimmering in the light of a kitchen window, the curtains billowing as if reaching out to tease her smooth breasts. At the sound of the door she turned toward me. Her eyes were the color of lilacs, large like those of a doe. She wore nothing but a pair of beaded Indian moccasins. I took in her bright smile along with the rest of her. Her hands on my face smelled of soap and passion. She wasn't naked for the sake of exhibitionism or theatrics. It was because she knew I enjoyed seeing her this way. Any embarrassment had long since passed because of the love and admiration she saw in my eyes when she moved, when she smiled, when she embraced me. I wanted to be with her forever.

And there she was—sweet Sherry—standing in a corner, clothed this time, heavy into a conversation with his roommate. How many times had he envisioned her just as she now appeared? His heart thumped to the beat of a faster drummer. His skin warmed. She had been his first true love, a romance born out of folk music and protest during the time when young people thought more about making love than war.

A kindred spirit, Sherry had never fallen from the pedestal he had elevated her to, but by the time he returned from Europe, he had grown out of his idealism and felt the pinch of societal expectations, the need to be successful. The last Thomas knew of Sherry, she was living in Indonesia helping the disenfranchised. She took life as it came, turning it into spontaneous free-form expression. She had remained true to her principles and beliefs.

But here she stood, before all of that, naive and mysterious. He thought of her lips, her touch. Once upon a time, Sherry had cured his disillusionment by making love to him. And he had been infected by the cure.

If this seaside illusion could sustain itself until shadows fell, Thomas would take her to the water's edge like old times, and perhaps they would become intimate on an unlit stretch of beach.

"I wish this wasn't a damned dream," he said to a stranger standing next to him.

"Right on, brother. What *you* smokin'?"

Thomas's own acoustic guitar lay against the arm of a chair next to him. The Moody Blues receded as he picked up his instrument. At the twang of the first chord, everyone abruptly vanished except for him and Sherry as if the clock had struck twelve. He reached for her—a grab at emotional magic to stave off the coming night. The instant their hands touched—presto, change-o—they were in the wet sand striding barefoot along the ocean, sans guitar. The boardwalk was lined with wetsuit, poster, and T-shirt shops. It was the only place in America one might see a fifty-year-old man with no shirt on a skateboard with a Coors beer in one hand and a roach of killer weed in the other, his balding head with curls in back flying in the coastal breeze. Girls walked along the boardwalk or at the water's edge, featuring their long, blonde tresses and short, tie-dyed skirts allowing one to see their honey pots when they sat. But Thomas had eyes only for Sherry.

The sky turned the deepest blue, the stars were out while the moon watched with a vapid eye through the gloom of cirrus clouds. The water repeatedly crept onto the shoreline like an eyelid closing over the sand before returning from whence it came. A gentle sea breeze was as welcoming as a kiss. Someone unseen played Roy Orbison's "In Dreams" on a stringed instrument. They began to lose themselves in the music like they used to, then another magical change.

Leapfrogging time and space, he and Sherry were transported to Big Sur, then to the great redwoods, accelerating ethereally to wine country, all the locations they had once shared returned in a few sweeping, transitory moments of familiarity, capped with a glowing night of passion and song.

"No need to drive if our destinations materialize whenever I open my eyes," Thomas informed Sherry.

But too soon, much too soon, Sherry was waving goodbye, landlocked, as he floated above the landscape heading out to sea. He feared he would drop and drown, or be returned to the naval ship's deck in the midst of battle, betrayed by the dream masters, but instead he levitated higher and faster. No need for planes either.

"Why must we part? I don't want to lose her again," he whined in his reverie. "I'll forgo the rest of my journey and stop here if the powers-that-be ..."

Thomas awoke in an unfamiliar motel room near the beachfront. He crawled out of bed. His familiar boxers had replaced the colorful, semen-speckled briefs. The aches and pains of a seventy-year-old body were unhappily at hand.

With trepidation, he dressed and patrolled the neighborhood he used to live in only to find everything he remembered had disappeared except for the water and a Taco Bell. High-rise condos had replaced small apartments and bungalows. He smelled of seawater even though he had not been in the ocean except in his dream of Sherry. He craved to return to this other dimension he had been gliding in and out of. Reality was too grim.

It is within our dreams that we truly live rather than in our mundane day-to-day existence. A concept proposed by an off-the-wall professor during an almost forgotten conversation. Had that happened? Were his physical locations bringing forth dreams of people and places as they used to be? Had reality and dreams switched places? No more cause and effect? No, too much like an old *Twilight Zone* episode, but some altered state of consciousness was happening with increasing chronological regularity and he eagerly anticipated his next encounter.

When it came, he had been zapped to France and was riding a train. As the countryside swept by his window in blurs of color, a man bearing the demeanor of one not to be trifled with entered the compartment.

"Hand over your money, *monsieur.*"

Thomas recalled this event. In the real world, he had been robbed and made to feel a fool. Not this time. He stood and made a gesture as if to comply. When the man reached for the wallet, Thomas grabbed his arm and tossed him through the compartment's window and into space with one fluid motion as easy as you please. A regular James Bond move.

On this occasion the powers-that-be played the hand in his favor. In fact, if he wished hard enough, long enough, perhaps this quantum leap could make the exultant interludes of his life richer and alter or banish altogether the unpleasant moments. If he could change this event, could he stop the nightmares, stop the fear of the future and change the past? There should be more to the future than fishing in a lake of lost yesterdays. More dancing and playing. More traveling and more stories to tell, none more intriguing than that which he now found himself.

The prospect of change and the growing confidence that all would end well wrapped him in a cocoon of invincibility as he leaned against the cushioned seat and drifted to the clickity-clack of the steel wheels, expecting to wake up in another motel somewhere in California, but wishing, hoping for more.

Darkness shed its veil once more. When his lids rose to greet the setting sun, Thomas found himself again on a balcony one moment, and clutching a platform rail on the Eiffel Tower in Paris the next. Sherry stood at his side. He observed her with a mixture of melancholy and exhilaration, hoping her presence would prove more than another rapid speed, titillating taste of the past.

"I thought I had lost you again on the beach." he said to her.

"You never lost me. You just spent a lifetime apart from me. You needed to complete your original journey, run the gauntlet of your early life on your own."

She was right, he guessed. She had come onto the scene but for a moment and left quickly during his carefree years.

"You've had quite a trip thus far. I hope you're not going to finish the last part without me, the new part? That is, if you want me?" Her voice was different now. It held gentleness as tender and caring as an angel's song. He recognized it from not so long ago. It was the paean siren song in the voice that had beseeched him to come away. He was no longer perplexed by contemplation on his past and future, or the meaning of his existence that twilight often aroused. *He just was.* No more, no less.

They looked at each other as if for the first time.

"Will you be with me always?" Thomas dared to ask.

"I always loved you, Thomas. It was just that we were so young and unsure about everything. I thought I could save the world, but a Tsunami ended that. So I'm here for you now. I want to see the universe through your eyes and by your side. It is our destiny."

They took each other's hand.

"Don't be afraid," she said. "We can fly in dreams, you know. Just like Peter Pan and Wendy. Fly away with me now."

Sherry led Thomas to the top of the tower's rail where they balanced momentarily, then leaped together, dropping like stones.

"Try your new wings," Sherry shouted.

Sure enough, Thomas and Sherry had sprouted wings. He stretched his wing-arms as they soared above the City of Lights where day had turned into night just for them. The nexus between mind and body had been severed. He had pierced the veil of reality and could see into another realm.

"Will you play and dance for me, and do all the things you enjoyed in my absence?" she asked.

"Yes. Of course I will." Thomas's body had become nimble and quick again. No more arthritis, or creeping cancer, or fear of failing. Here was a refuge beyond his stories—a path not yet charted, a way through to another side where a clean and glorious story awaited. "Let's go to Greece. I'm going to dive from the cliffs, something I didn't have the courage to do alone. If I sing and dance, will you dive with me?"

"Anything and everything, my love. A world of exploration awaits," Sherry crooned, flying effortlessly next to him. "The world we knew couldn't save us or itself, but here we shall experience all the wonderful images our spirits can create. Let me touch your face and smooth the lines. Drink in your eyes and laugh within your soul. The cosmos never reaches an end and neither do we. The best in us survives."

They glided through the starlit night beneath powerful wings in this new ethereal world of contradictions. He looked at Sherry. She was shimmering now and a feeling came over Thomas that was akin to the moments after lovemaking, but it was more intense. It was spiritual. Forget the old codger who sallied forth on this adventure like Don Quixote might have. He could fly with her forever.

All was well in the land of Thomas. Memories of previous sins and selfish acts were cleansed like bleached bones in the desert sun. The ability to escape reality had become his grandest artistic creation. *The necessity of illusion, seldom found beyond the border of sanity.* He was anointed with calm. "Don't make me wake up ... don't make me ... don't make me," he repeated.

With Sherry's raven hair flowing in the breeze and her feathered wings shimmering against the lights of the earth, he knew she was his salvation, his angel come to lead him to the place where dreams last forever. He and she, sharing a tangled and inseparable destiny where past and present were the same, where time no longer crawled in an endless parade of minutes, where it didn't matter at all.

*

Gladys received the phone call at that time of night when a piercing ring causes stress. Everyone who had known Thomas was shocked when

325

they heard he had jumped from a hotel room balcony in a faraway place ... everyone but his wife. She looked out onto the world through a window in the private citadel that had been Thomas's study. Forty years of her life entwined with his like the weave of a blanket, but had she ever really known him? She felt both loss and anger at his act.

"Couldn't you cope with the world of reality any longer, Thomas?" she whispered quietly with the knowledge that he had felt cheated by his circumstance, and by the disease there was no escaping. She only hoped, at the end, he had not suffered too severely from the increasing pain or from his final decision. "Your flights of whimsy finally overtook you, didn't they?" she breathed with trembling resignation as she wiped a tear away.

She deliberated on her own future and then softly whispered to the world outside, "Sweet dreams, Thomas. May your fantasies come true wherever you may be."

***

To Catch a Dreamer
by Mary-Jean Harris, Ontario, Canada

It took four suicides and half a dozen failed police inquiries before the
members of the Order for Investigations into Curious Metaphysical
Phenomena raised their learned noses from the dusty tomes of the
ancients. I believe Matthew Wiggins still had his learned nose buried in
Aristotle's *Metaphysics*, but the rest of us had gathered at Farington's
House of Fine Arts to discuss the matter.

"I do admit this case is a strange one," Arnold MacRae was saying,
standing before a window of triangular glass pieces. The rest of us were
seated around a rosewood table with a pot of dried white roses at the
centre. Arnold was perhaps the only one of our twelve members who read
the paper in addition to philosophy, and so he was the only one who
could have discovered that something was amiss. Though how it related
to our order, I had yet to discover.

"Just this morning, the death of Miss Anna Finch was reported in the
Kentish Gazette. At half past two this morning, she ran from her bedroom
and flung herself out the window at the end of the hall, all the while
crying 'She's got me! She's coming!'" Arnold, his thick dimpled hands
halfway inside the pockets of his autumn orange waistcoat, tilted his head
as if considering the matter anew. His grey wig threatened to escape from
his head. "And what's more, last Wednesday, September 14, 1853, at two
thirty-seven—"

"My, Arnold, what has the exact time got to do with it?" William
Scott interjected, his dark eyebrows knitted rather philosophically.

"It may be important!" Arnold protested. "Indeed, one must not fail
to notice seemingly unremarkable details. It is like leaving the Good out

of Plato." A few philosophers nodded in agreement, but I for one wished they would get to the heart of the matter.

"At two thirty-seven," Arnold continued, "Sir Johnathon Brighton was on a bridge overlooking the Stour in a state of bewilderment, muttering, 'Dreams can't find me here ... oh, why must she find me? The red lady ...' Henceforth, he plummeted into the Stour. Moreover, the other two victims mentioned a 'lady of dreams' and a 'ruby death.' There is clearly a thread that joins these events together, gentlemen—*lady* and gentlemen," he corrected himself after a stormy glare from Belinda Hawthorn. "And the police are clueless about the significance." He smiled broadly.

Most of the philosophers seemed confused at his delight. William said, "What has this to do with us? I can't imagine something further from metaphysics as suicides!"

"A fine question," Arnold said, unperturbed. "And you will receive just as fine an answer, my friend." There was a pause, intended for dramatic effect, of course. I noticed that besides William and two other disgruntled philosophers, Arnold had caught the interest of the lot of us. And except for Louis, our youngest member, whose round head of flaxen curls and wide amber eyes hardly made him look philosophical, I was perhaps the most interested.

The purpose of our order is to investigate the phenomena that lie beyond the reason of the authorities, natural philosophers, and common folk alike. We are, in short, practical metaphysicians, though there are some who deem this an oxymoron, such as the notable Charles Lyell, who kindly informed us of his opinion upon the matter. In any case, that is what we are, and it has led us to investigate numerous peculiar practices and events, including embalming the dead and the effect this has upon the deceased's soul, the metaphysical status of poets, and the significance of the astronomical bodies discovered by natural philosophers. So you will understand my interest as I listened, grasping the velvet armrests of my chair tightly, memorizing Arnold's next words.

"The second victim uttered these words to a beggar upon her death," Arnold said while removing a piece of paper from his pocket. He brandished it above his head as if it were a fragment of the true cross. Though in our case, it would rather be a fragment of Socrates' bone.

"Are we to trust this beggar?" Belinda asked.

"Listen here! The lady spoke these words to the beggar only moments before cutting her own throat."

Louis gasped, and Sir Patrick of Marksbury said, "Upon Gabriel's horn! Cut her own throat!"

"We might learn some fortitude there, if not metaphysics," William added.

Arnold waved his paper to silence them. He read, "*I was awake in my dream, I know not how, and the lady, the lady of dreams, took me. She is in the dream, not my mind. It hurts so much, I can see everything now. I can see my husband's soul and it is as black as tar. I can see every ray of sunlight streaming down to Earth—I must leave at once. I warn you, and everyone you speak to, do not trust the lady! Do not tarry in her dream!*"

Another silence ensued. Arnold placed the paper on the table and sat in his chair. Sir Patrick coughed, Louis looked confused, but again, it was William who spoke. "So people are having strange dreams." The golden rims of the spectacles sitting atop his head of thick black hair glinted in a shaft of sunlight. "Perhaps they were given opium or another such substance." There was a general nodding in agreement. "Not that *I* have experience with opium," he added. This resulted in a more vigorous agreement that, oh, no, neither have we.

"Hardly sounds like a metaphysical curiosity," Belinda pointed out.

Arnold grimaced. "What if a spirit were communicating to these people in a dream state? What if there were a lady who entered their dreams?"

"Yes, and the police would have no hope in investigating such matters," Zeno said. His real name was Bartholomew Bloodworth, but everyone called him Zeno.

"Indeed!" Arnold said. "This calls not for idle speculation, but a proper investigation."

"And what if it is just opium?" William asked.

"The police would have found that out already," Arnold said with a sweep of his arm.

William scowled. His countenance was radiating irascibility across the room. I knew not why he was so indignant: he was never the one to endanger himself. Oh no, whenever there was a mission that involved even the slightest danger, the unspoken consent was that I was on the case—with, at most, one other martyred member to aid me—while the others concocted schemes and analysed my results.

I felt a pat on my shoulder from Zeno, who was sitting to my left. "What say you, Edwin? Are you ready to start?" Zeno grinned, revealing his rust-coloured teeth.

"I don't believe I have a choice," I said pleasantly. Not that I minded, but to see Arnold or William out investigating would have been more satisfying.

"Not at all!" Arnold agreed. "But we'll give you a companion, for this might be a thorny one." He knit his fingers together and looked about the room with a shrewd gaze. No one met his eyes except William, though his aggravation hardly volunteered him for the task. "Louis!" Arnold proclaimed with sudden inspiration.

Louis's eyes became veritable saucers. He had never been on an investigation before, though he was cleverer than he appeared, as I knew from reading his treatise on how to model Parliament on Berkeley's idealism. In any case, the other philosophers were eager now that the victim was chosen and it was not them, so offered encouraging remarks, such as Sir Patrick's "You might just meet Raphael!" Not that this had anything to do with Raphael, but Sir Patrick was currently studying the angelic hierarchies and had a knack for mentioning archangels at every opportunity.

"Arnold," I said once the commotion had died down and Louis had agreed to come—so long as he was girded with the Order's precious heirloom, Alexander the Great's sword, which was more likely to cause rusty cuts to its bearer than a mortal wound to the enemy. Louis, however, seemed to believe that it would be enough to give him the courage he required. "How is it that we might investigate dreams? I don't suppose it could be performed without dreaming ourselves."

"And then you will be in danger like the others," Belinda said.

"And entirely helpless, unless you can control your dreams," Zeno added.

"I'm afraid I cannot," I said. I glanced to Louis, and he shook his head.

Sir Patrick raised a long finger into the air and said, "Perhaps you ought to see ..." he seemed slightly timid, though forced himself to continue, "... a *mystic*."

There were two furious roars—William and Arnold, the latter of whom leapt from his seat and caused the table to tremble. Just about everyone else made their disdain known through complaints, gasps, and scowls. Sir Patrick raised his hands at the onslaught and said, "It would just be so that they can dream with a certain consciousness. After that, it would be purely philosophical!"

"We do not engage in the machinations of mystics!" Dr. Alastair Connelly said with a pound of his hand on the table.

"We've investigated into a great many mystics, and have found much of their practices valid and—"

"But never have we done such practices ourselves," Arnold declared. He did not sit back down, but instead looked to me and said, "This is a difficult task, for it does not take place in the world around us. But it is nothing that philosophy cannot surmount. Oh, no! You will just have to experiment a little. If there really is a lady trapped inside dreams, then it is up to you to find her. And discover her metaphysical condition: how did she get there? How is it that she can direct her will in dreams? What is the dream world really, and how does it connect with our waking life?" He was excited now, as were the others, since Arnold had alleviated their worry about the involvement of mystics. For if I were successful, they would have much to incorporate into their metaphysical theories.

After the incident with the mention of mystics, William had lost his spectacles and was overseeing Louis crawling all over the Turkish carpet to find them, but to no apparent success. It was quite fortunate, for William was in no state of mind to complain about the investigation, since if he did not find his spectacles, he would be unable to read philosophy, and that would be disastrous.

Like the other philosophers, I too was excited. But this was checked by my doubts. This wasn't a usual task where I might wander about and speak with people, record my observations and such. I would have to experience the world of dreams firsthand and hope to meet someone who had already driven four men and women mad.

Belinda, noticing my uncertainty, said, "If you keep in mind your intentions of meeting the lady throughout the day, she will be more likely to come to you in sleep. Perhaps repeat it to yourself often, as well as your intention to remain conscious in your dreams, so you may investigate."

"If only it were that simple," I said. I didn't mention that that was probably what a mystic would have suggested.

"You might as well try," Zeno said, patting my shoulder again. "If it fails, we'll all be crafting alternatives in the meantime."

"And remember, we have our finest investigator on the case!" Arnold chimed in. Whether that was supposed to comfort me or the rest of them, I was not sure.

In any case, it was all decided, and Louis and I soon set off to investigate dreams.

*

Later that day, Louis told me that although we had both been setting our intentions upon meeting the lady in our dreams, that we needed someone to keep watch while I slept, in case I woke up and tried to kill myself. Clutching Alexander's sword to his breast, he seemed to deem himself worthy of the task, and thus, was unable to engage in the dream investigation. How convenient, I told him, but I didn't argue, because he did have a point.

And so it was that early in the evening just as the sun was setting, I, cloaked in my intentions that now repeated through my mind with the regularity of a ticking clock, lay to sleep while Louis sat at the foot of my bed with his sword at the ready. It was not simple to fall asleep under such circumstances, especially as Louis had absolutely no idea how to hold a sword. Not that he needed a sword, but my explanations about the matter went unheard.

So I got up and taught him how to at least hold it properly, then returned to bed, covered my head with my blankets, and tried to sleep. *Come meet me, red lady,* I thought, though I felt ridiculous. Yet so too, afraid.

It took me over an hour to fall asleep, during which time I heard Louis set the sword down on my desk, tiptoe across the room, and snatch my volume of Kant's *Critique of Pure Reason*, evinced by the distinctive creak it made upon opening the cover. This—knowing that Louis was not brandishing a sword at the foot of my bed—was perhaps what finally allowed me to sleep.

I did not dream at first. Around midnight, I awoke to find a crescent moon smirking at me through a wisp of clouds out the window. Louis was fast asleep in my chair, the *Critique of Pure Reason* on the verge of tumbling off his lap. Horrified, I returned the book to the shelf, and then took the sword from my desk and hid it under the bed. I fell asleep much more quickly now. And this time, dreams came to me.

I was in a meadow of yellow, round-headed flowers. They each had faces of people I knew, such as Arnold, William, my mother, and my cousin Thomas. They smiled at me joyfully, but when they looked away from me, they gave each other menacing scowls. I was not fully conscious, for the strangeness of the situation did not strike me. I wandered through the field for what seemed like days, seeing the same faces over and over again, meandering about the flowers so as to not crush their faces. It was all nonsense, that is, until I saw a face I did not recognize. It was the face of a young lady, and she stared at me with blazing red eyes that looked like two rubies studded in a yellow paste of butter. At this moment, my dreamy oblivion left me, and I possessed a waking consciousness. I knew why I was here, and I knew the face on the flower must be the red lady.

The dream world then started to become unclear. I could no longer discern the faces in the flowers, and the blades of grass that had previously been finely chiseled were now smudged into a vague green mass, as if they had been part of a giant painting which the artist had smeared to start over. I felt myself spiraling as my consciousness slipped away—it was as though the universe had just realized that I was fully aware in my dream and was quickly endeavouring to correct the mistake.

But before I awoke, the lady in the flower spoke. She alone was clear and distinct in my vision, and her voice smote me deeper than Alexander's sword could have ever done.

"You are not waking up yet, *dreamer*," she said. Her voice was cool and calm, and it lingered in my mind like a beautiful swirl of frost. Then the flower was no more, and she was standing before me, immaculately clear amid the smudging world of green, blue, and yellow. Like her voice, she was beautiful. But I was not going to let that get in the way of my mission. She was tall and graceful, with long red locks that reached halfway down her back, curious bright blue eyes that might have been looking into my soul, and small lips that seemed to conceal a secret. She wore a long blue gown with translucent sleeves that flared out about her wrists, and skirts hemmed with scarlet embroidery of Celtic knots. There was also a ruby pendant like a bright mouse heart upon her pale neck. The ruby, the red lady. I had no doubt about it now.

I swallowed, and tried to speak, but she put a finger to my lips and I was mute. She then took my hand and the two of us whipped out of the formless meadow, vanishing into darkness. It was not a pure void, for as we travelled through it, I saw brief twinkling lights, stars perhaps, sprinkled in the canopy of darkness. I felt nothing but the lady's cool hand on mine, and I could do no more than wonder in amazement at this voyage. For although I came here from a dream, it seemed to be a real place that I was traversing through. I was going somewhere. It was exhilarating to say the least.

After some measure of time, we began to spiral downward, and with the pricks of light about me streaming in a blur, it felt as though I were entering a pinwheel. I gasped—my voice had returned to me. The next moment I was on my hands and knees, having landed on a hard marble floor that sent juts of pain up my limbs. I looked up to see the lady standing beside me, and quickly rose to my feet, instinctively dusting off my trousers, though the floor was clean.

"Madam," I said. "Would you please tell me what this is all about?"

She paid no heed to my question, but instead took my hand again and led me down the marble floored hall at a formidable pace that gave me little time to discern my whereabouts. What I could see was this: I was in a tall passageway with a floor of rose marble slabs lined with silver, and walls flanked with tall Grecian-styled columns that flared out at the ceiling to create arches high above our heads. There was no ceiling between these, but only the night sky, where the stars, so bright and unsullied by the lights of a city, dripped starlight upon the pale columns, causing them to glisten slightly. I also saw a great stone chair along the side of the hall, a kind of throne, and some doors with silver handles on either side of me.

The lady stopped before a door near the end of the hall. With a flick of her hand above the doorknob, it opened smoothly. I noticed that unlike the other doors, this one was lined with elegant silver hinges, and there were three keyholes, one on top of another.

The lady released my hand then, and gestured for me to enter.

"What is this?" I whispered. I peered inside hesitantly, but I couldn't see a thing. It wasn't that it was dark, but it was out of focus, uncertain. As if the universe hadn't decided what to put in there yet.

"Go in and tell me what you see," she told me.

Although I was curious, I didn't like this. I was supposed to be the one investigating, but it seemed that she was testing me. "I'd appreciate it if you would tell me something first: how is it that you are here? You seem to have been in the dreams of at least four others, all of whom met an unfortunate end."

"I am trying to find someone," she said coolly. "I will tell you no more until you enter that room."

So it was true: she was entering people's dreams of her own accord. "How do you do it?" I asked.

She grabbed my shoulders and pushed me into the room before I could resist. I fell into a wall of a thick substance, but it only lasted for a moment, as if a slimy sort of water were hovering in the air before the door. After passing through it, I could see the room clearly. It was a small chamber with a thick carpeted floor of pale purple and gold that muffled every sound, and fabric of deep purple draped about the walls and ceiling in a style from the East. The fabric glistened as if it was dusted with sand.

Yet this was merely the jewelry box to house a greater treasure. At the centre of the room, up a few marble steps, was a bronze-coloured pedestal. Upon it rested a beautiful old tome on a black velvet cloth. It seemed to emanate secret knowledge and wisdom, so I hastened toward it, the carpet muffling my footsteps. When I reached the steps, a voice caught me midstride.

"Come, mortals, and read my secrets. If you hail not from a greater realm, you die."

I glanced about, my heart beating keenly. I could see no one. The voice had been that of a man, and he'd spoken with a great profundity. It did not seem to come from any one place in particular, as if it were emerging equally from every particle of air in the room. It spoke no more, though I waited a good many minutes.

This must be how they died, I thought. *By reading this book.*

Now, upon such a realization, it would have been prudent to leave the room at once and endeavour to speak with the lady. Of this, I was well aware. And yet, I did nothing of the sort. My fingers itched to touch those pages, to open that smooth leather cover and discover the mysteries that lay cloistered within. It was a dream after all. Could I not do what I wished in a dream? However, I knew that this was surely more than a dream. Still, although I was not one to doubt the power of words, neither was I one to doubt the power of my own reason and convictions. I could handle this, whatever it was.

So I ascended to the pedestal and reached for the book. It looked ancient, bound in dark leather, and yet it was in fine condition. There were silver letters pressed into the cover in a language I couldn't read, but it used the Latin alphabet. I opened to the first page and found that I could understand the words. A subtle radiance emerged from the book in little golden lines, which I could see when I looked at it from certain angles. Just beholding the first page made my mind feel breezy, as if a bird were flying through it and stirring awake parts that had hitherto lain dormant.

I was already breathing heavily when I started to read; my eyes were watering and unable to shut. The words captivated me the moment I read them: it was about the start of the universe, and although little of it made much sense to my reason, I felt a glow of enlightenment nonetheless. That bird kept soaring through my mind, opening, opening ... and it hurt too, a pain that was penetrating deeper, and deeper ...

I heard a slam behind me, and turned—which was ever so difficult with the enticement of the book. Outside the room I saw the lady bracing herself against the open door, which had been flung open to its limit. She flicked a pulse of jagged red light from her fingertips down the hall.

"You're too late, Talverion!" she cried, then dodged a glowing white pulse that came from the direction she had sent hers.

Startled, I ran from the book, though in my heady state from reading it, tripped on the steps and landed on my stomach on the thick carpet. *So that's what the carpet is for,* I thought, pushing myself up. I passed through that strange wall again, and saw a man down the passageway. He was quite remarkable, and, as Sir Patrick would have said, *mystical.*

He was all night sky and starlight. He wore a midnight-blue robe, his hair was a long whitish-blond like starlight, and his face had precise and elegant features, from his narrow nose to his sharp cheekbones. He had sparks of blue eyes that, even from my distance, I perceived as ancient and penetrating, yet at the same time, full of wonder. He held an opal orb in his hand, and from it was tethered an eagle—at least, something with the shape of an eagle, for it was more the shadow of an eagle than the real thing. The eagle was sending out the blasts of light toward the lady with every flap of its broad wings.

The man, whom I assumed was Talverion, grinned and said, "Dear Lunora, don't you love my new means of destroying you? I thought the eagle was quite fitting."

The lady's ruby necklace was ablaze, and she seemed to be using it to gain strength, as if it were another heart of hers. I pressed myself against the wall, perilously close to the battle. I hoped I wouldn't cry out in terror, but I felt no guarantee that I could manage that.

Talverion's shadowy eagle was doing a fine job at deflecting the lady's blows, absorbing them into its dark feathers, which momentarily glistened the colour of whatever light they were absorbing, such as now, having taken on a glittery red. There was a strange beauty to it.

"And what have we here?" Talverion said, approaching us. "A British fop from a fractured world?"

"A fractured world?" I could not help but say, though my voice quavered.

Talverion had ceased his blows for now, apparently curious about me.

"I assure you, my world is as whole as ever," I added.

Talverion smiled pleasantly. "Charming creature, but of course, he isn't really here, is he, Luna?"

Lunora made no reply. She was walking out further into the hall, curling one hand, while sparks of blue crackled within it.

"Oh, I do hate it when you try to be crafty," Talverion said with a sigh.

Before he could go on, Lunora flung the sparks of blue toward him, and their speed was such that I only saw them leave her hand, and the next moment they were ablaze within the eagle. They also skirted about it and caught Talverion along the neck and shoulder, giving him a searing blue cut. He gasped, though in indignation more than pain. The eagle flapped about sporadically, trying to rid itself of the sparks. Talverion stumbled, but swept himself up before he fell, his robe billowing about him. He was in an absolute fury, and reminded me of an exploding star.

"I see you're not prepared for *everything*, radiant Talverion," Lunora said wryly. "Although you may bar me from the Secret, you may not bar the soul of one dreaming in a lower world."

Talverion scowled. "So you find the one flaw in my plan and push there. Clever, Luna, oh, but you will pay dearly for it." One hand was slowly stroking the cut on his neck, which had darkened to a blackish hue. His eagle, having recovered, gave a mighty flap of its wings, causing bands of black bolts to jut out from them and stream through the air toward Lunora. They snagged her neck and arms, holding her in place in the centre of the hall. She struggled, but only managed another feeble blow back to Talverion, which his eagle absorbed without harm.

Smiling again, Talverion waited as the eagle flapped its wings in small motions, then broadened its wingspan until the very air crackled with energy. I knew what was coming: some mighty blow that would destroy Lunora, trapped as she was in Talverion's black rope-like bolts.

I unconsciously took a step from the wall. The two of them were ignoring me completely, which was understandable, since I was useless in a magical battle such as this. That is, useless with respect to doing magic, but not *entirely* useless. Lunora was going to die, surely. I could see it in her eyes, for although they were strong and defiant, there was also an acceptance that Talverion had bested her, and she no longer struggled. I couldn't bear to see her like that, not with the wicked triumph on

Talverion's face. I bit my lip, my body tensing. I was asleep, was I not? *I couldn't die, could I?* I wasn't sure, but just as the eagle was releasing its final force of black energy, which coalesced into a concentrated orb of power, I ran from the wall and flung myself in front of Lunora.

The orb caught me full on the chest, and sent me stumbling to my knees. Pain crackled through my bones, snipped my veins, squandered my heart, and then ... nothing.

*

So this was what it felt like to be dead. Nothing, nothing at all. There was no body, no gravity, or anything of the sort whereby I might gain my bearings. But there was one problem: I could think. That, of course, meant that I wasn't really dead. Nevertheless, perhaps my *body* was dead. Though if that were the case, my body in the dream would have some sort of connection to my real body. It would be a curious metaphysical phenomenon indeed to bring that about! I knew not what I should do, so I waited, trying not to think too hard about my predicament lest it lead to panic.

Soon, I realized that I was not alone. It was an odd sensation, like something nagging at the back on my mind, something I had forgotten. A voice spoke to me, and I suddenly remembered the lady, Lunora.

"Edwin," her misty voice was saying. "Edwin. Can you hear me?"

I could not speak, but I thought, *Yes, yes I can!*

"Good."

You're alive then?

"Yes, and I thank you. Although to me, death is never the end, I hope to remain in this form a while longer. But listen to me now." She waited a moment before saying, "I am searching for the orbs of Malcuvian. You have aided me already, though I ask if you will help me find them. Leave your world, and voyage to others as I do."

I was amazed. Though the way she asked me was in a rather calculating manner, that choosing me was convenient, not her personal choice. *Why me? And why did you bring me to look at that book?*

"It was a test. Whosoever casts their eyes upon the pages of that book will have their soul stirred to a higher awareness, to be able to feel and see things others cannot. I sensed there was a soul in your land who had a greatness within it. Someone who might aid me in my task. Fortunately, I found you."

I don't understand.

"You didn't go mad when you read the book. Ordinary souls cannot bear such knowledge."

I gasped, inwardly at least. You mean ...

"Don't think about it."

But I must. You mean that all those people died because of me? Because you were looking for me, and when others failed the test, they went mad and killed themselves?

"Live with it. You have a great soul. Common people are expendable."

I almost regretted having saved her now. Almost—for if I had not, I would be no better than one of these strange wanderers who let innocents die so simply. Although I was curious, I couldn't let that get in the way. I knew that going with her would mean leaving the world entirely, and I couldn't do that. Whether out of fear or courage, I could not.

Well, I must disagree with you, I told her. *And no, I will not help you find these orbs. You'll have to make do without me.*

"Then I will continue to search for another soul."

No! No, you mustn't!

"Then will you join me?"

No, no, but ... I was thinking furiously. I couldn't tell if Lunora was a good person with immoral methods or a bad person with equally immoral methods. I was quite sure that this Talverion fellow was a bad person despite his amiable manners, so I was inclined to think that Lunora might be good, or at least, not as bad as him.

What happens after I die? I asked.

Lunora gave a slight laugh. "Wouldn't you love to know."

I would indeed! But what I really meant was ... I was trying to make a bargain.

"A strange way to make a bargain."

Yes, I suppose it is. Perhaps I should just say it plainly. I was hesitant, for I knew not what this bargain really entailed. I knew not if it were even possible. But I had to try. *If, after I die, my soul is released, then I will help you find these orbs then. But only if you cease taking people in their dreams and testing them as you have been doing. I will have no others die for my sake.*

I anxiously awaited her reply. It was a strange sort of anxiousness, for it was entirely of the mind. No pounding heart, clammy hands, or tensed muscles.

At last, she said, "Fine."

Really? You mean, you'll be able to find me when I die? My soul will be out there in the universe, and you will be alive then?

"I said fine. I agreed. I shall not answer your aggravating questions."

I was relieved. In one sense, at least. I had saved the lives of perhaps dozens of people, yet who knew what awaited me after my life. Though I did have the rest of my life to ponder the matter, perhaps think of a way to escape it, or at least prepare myself.

"Awaken then ..."

Wait. I was already starting to feel myself slip away, slip back to reality. *I did come here with the intention of conducting an investigation. I have indeed learned the cause of these recent deaths, yet I know very little of the dream world. Would you tell me something about it? Perhaps how it is connected to our world?*

"No."

I did save your life.

"Yes, you did. But that makes you no less impertinent."

I waited for a response. At last, Lunora said, "You will learn much in the future. But I will tell you this, so you may puzzle over it for the rest of your little life: there are many realms, and mortals such as yourself dream in the realm of their soul, not their body. Yet they would never know it, for most people are so entrenched in their mortal existence that when their body sleeps, so does their soul. They dream perpetually. That is all."

I knew not what to say to that. I hardly understood it, but it was fascinating nonetheless.

Thank you, I said awkwardly.

"Until death then, Edwin."

And then she was gone, swept far away, while I fell back, back, back ...

I awoke. It was a relief to regain my body, to feel a heartbeat, to feel the press of the bed sheets upon my skin, to hear the world, and not just a numinous voice in my mind.

I was stifling beneath my bed covers, so I threw them off, perhaps a bit too vigorously, because Louis yelped and leapt from the chair, his clothes and hair disordered from sleep. He frantically searched for the sword, and this task proving unsuccessful, he seized a poker from the fireside instead.

"Hold, Louis!" I said, raising my hands. "I'm perfectly all right, not about to kill myself."

"Did you do it?" Louis asked, tentatively taking a few steps toward me, the poker still extended. "Did you see the lady?"

I smiled, and Louis gasped at the notion that our plan had actually worked. Despite all that I had been through, I felt a remarkable sense of peace. Perhaps it was from my brief glance at that book. And although I had returned whole and well, the world seemed a bit different. Ever so slightly, so that I didn't quite know *what* was different, only that it was.

I came out of bed and walked slowly to the window. The sun had risen a few hours past, and although hidden behind a tower to the east, it cast its light in a gentle halo about the town and the surrounding moors. I didn't open the window, lest Louis take it as a suicide attempt, but I longed to hear the birdsong, and even the noises of the town from people at the market, carriage wheels across the cobbles, and the sounds of men working at their trades. I thought I almost saw a flicker of a thin golden line across the town, but this soon vanished, perhaps a memory from sleep.

For during my sleep, I had glimpsed something that none might take from me. And I had changed—just a little, but enough to sway my soul from where it had been sitting stagnant at the top of a safe little hill, push it so that it started to roll. It would continue to roll until it reached the vast ocean below, whose uncharted wonders I sensed flickering at the edge of my mind.

Seeing Louis standing hesitantly at my side, I said, "You know, Louis, the world is a strange place, full of all sorts of curious metaphysical phenomena. But I believe the most curious metaphysical phenomenon is what lies beyond it. Because that is where we're all headed, be we poets, philosophers, or any soul in this dreaming world. It is as Shakespeare told us: 'We are such stuff as dreams are made on, and our little life is rounded with a sleep.'"

***

Necessary Elvis
by Jerry L. Wheeler, United States

Nothing about this smelled right, least of all the inside of my Mazda.

It reeked of peanut butter, bananas, and Essence of Old Fart, which was no surprise since I had one sleeping in the passenger seat. His chin was on his chest, his white hair lush but lank, hanging over his blue eyes like a shredded shower curtain. He still wore his pajama tops and bedroom slippers from the nursing home, but I'd been able to get him into his leather jacket and put some jeans on his bony ass before the end of my shift when I'd snatched him. He didn't really look or sound like Elvis from what I'd seen on YouTube, but I told him I'd do it and I didn't have a Plan B.

My phone buzzed, nestled among the banana peels in the console well between our seats. I saw it was Carlos, so I turned it off. My jaw still hurt from the last time we got together, not to mention the ribs he kicked. Besides, I didn't want it to wake up the old dude. Fat chance. He was snoring so loud, he must have had adenoids the size of grapefruit. The moonlight along the canyon road shone down on his lap, one of those goddamn peanut butter and banana sandwiches in his gnarled hand. On white bread, yet. "It ain't grilled," he'd said, "but it'll have to do." Then he ate four. I glanced down. Four and a half.

Fuck you, I thought. *Fuck you very much*. Who's gonna get the chunky Skippy out of my cloth seats or clean all those little banana strings off my goddamn dashboard? Life-changing experience, my ass. I'm not sure I need a life-changing experience after all. Maybe all I need is to give Carlos back his ring, ditch the old guy who thinks he's Elvis, buy a box of pine tree deodorizers, and ride off into the sunset. But I'm not strong enough to do that. I wish I'd never started working at Arbor Rose Nursing Home or hooked up with Carlos at the Bar Nun. And I sure as fuck wish I'd never met Elmore, even though he looked a little like my daddy with those blue eyes and all. But mostly, I wish I'd never fallen for the old geezer's half-assed story.

It's the church I went to when I was a boy, rising up out of the river. My great uncle Gains built it for my mama. Says I'm welcome over the door. When I find it, I'm finally goin' to glory. You'll get somethin' out of it, too, don't worry. I ain't exactly sure what, but ...

"What?" he said, jerking his head up suddenly. Folds of loose skin stretched out beneath his chin like an aged basilisk. He coughed without covering his mouth, then looked over at me, all pissed off. "I was sleeping. What do the hell do you want?"

"Me? I don't want anything. You were snoring so loud, you woke yourself up."

"Your phone woke me up."

"My phone's turned off. Why are you always so goddamn argumentative?"

"I'm *not* argumentative."

I snorted. "Just ironic."

The phone buzzed from the well. Carlos again. "Shit, I thought I turned that off."

He pushed his hair back and gave me some side eye, automatically reaching to adjust the nasal cannula he wasn't wearing. "For a punk CNA who's about to receive a gift that's gonna change his miserable goddamn life, you're pretty snappish. Where's my oxygen?"

"All around you. Take deep, peanut buttery breaths."

I ignored him glaring at me for about five minutes.

"Are we there yet?" he finally asked.

"You tell me. It's your quest. I'm just the vehicle, remember?"

He dropped the half sandwich on the floor mat and wiped his hands on the headrest as he twisted around and grunted, reaching into the back seat. "Where's my damn guitar?"

"It's back there under the coats."

"We're near a river, right?" He threw some clothes aside and found the instrument, smashing it tunelessly into the dome light as he brought it up front and put it on his lap.

"Going through Glenwood Canyon, Colorado River off to your right."

He peered at the guitar. "Nope. Not even close."

"How can you tell?"

"The strings'll turn blue."

I lost it right there. Couldn't help myself. "Turn blue?" I said, laughing louder than necessary inside a closed vehicle. I raised a hand to my temple in mock horror. "Oh, Mister Frodo," I cried, "are there *orcs* nearby?" I almost pissed my scrubs I was laughing so hard.

He stared at me until I was quiet again. "Are you done?"

The look on his face reminded me I was up to my ass in this, and I *still* didn't have a Plan B. "Okay, okay," I said. "But you have to admit, it doesn't look like a relic. It's too new."

"It ain't no relic. It *is* new. Got it from Amazon Prime yesterday."

I shook my head and wondered if it was too late to go back to Carlos. He'd get drunk and say he owned my ass. He'd fuck me, then he'd beat the shit out of me, but at least I knew what to expect. "You're a fraud," I announced, wondering who the hell I was making that official to. "You don't look like Elvis, you don't sound like Elvis—give me a 'thankyavurrymush.'"

"A *what*?"

"You know, a 'thankyavurrymush.' Or play a couple of chords on that thing. Maybe bust out a little 'Heartbreak Hotel' or something."

He held up his wrinkled claw-hands. "With this arthritis? You got to be jokin', son." He pulled the leather jacket tighter around his thin chest. "I'm hungry. When are we stopping to eat?"

"Run out of Skippy?"

"I mean *real* food."

"Got any money? Cash. No cards. They can check those."

"Yeah, I got cash." When I looked over at him, he was grinning. "You turned the GPS off?" he said, nodding at the phone. "They can check that, too."

"*Shit*." I started to grab for it, but he held up one wrinkled hand.

"Don't worry," he said. "It'll take 'em a while to realize I'm not in my usual ten-block escape route. That's how I set it up. We got time for a meal. Y'think mebbe we could find a place with grits?"

"Colorado isn't exactly grits country."

"Damn shame," he said softly, staring ahead. "I'd kinda like grits and gravy one last time before I go to glory."

He sounded so old and so lonely and so pathetic right then, I remembered why I believed his crazy ass story in the first place. "I guess there'll be someplace off the highway up here by Glenwood Springs. We're not goin' anywhere near town, though."

He smiled. Did he even have teeth?

"And I'm not guaranteeing grits," I added, making sure I had my phone turned off.

*

"So, your manager, this Colonel Parker, was a vampire?"

"Yeah," he said, a dollop of gravy congealing in the grey stubble at the corner of his mouth. He dabbed it with a napkin. Grits and gravy wasn't on the Bluebelle Diner menu, but he'd summoned up a lopsided, blue-eyed, hunka-hunka-burnin'-love grin from somewhere and totally melted Brenda, the waitress, who had the cook fix him up something special. "But he wasn't the bloodsucking kind."

"There are *kinds* of vampires?"

"You got kinds of people, right?"

"I guess." I sipped my coffee. My scrambled eggs were runny, and she'd given me link sausage instead of patty, but the pancakes were sweet and steamy enough to melt the plastic butter she'd brought. "But if he didn't drink blood, what did he drink?"

"Talent. In my case, the gifts given me by my beautiful mother, Gladys." He paused, looking down at the table. He must have been thinking hard enough about something, because his spoon tipped and a glop of grits fell back into the bowl. "Motherfucker ate me up," he said, spooning it back. "He wouldn't kill me, and he wouldn't turn me. Just left me enough to keep the machine going. Makin' those stupid-ass movies. He would have kept me like that forever, except I got away from him."

"How?"

"Faked my death on that toilet," he said, grinning again as he went back to shoveling in the mess. "He knew it, too. But this ole country boy ain't as dumb as he thought. I got friends, too. Friends who showed me how to hide myself from him. He moved on right after I did. Left Parker's body to rot and leeched on to somebody else, I hear. But he ain't never bothered me no more. I lived quiet and simple until I broke my goddamn hip."

"And you rehabbed at Arbor Rose," I said. "But Elmore Pushkin? I mean, is that a name anybody chooses?"

His eyes got that faraway look again. "I wanted to be Jewish ever since I met Sammy Davis Jr." Then he resumed eating and talking. "The dreams started in the hospital. A river. A church. And me holdin' a guitar with strings of blue light. The rest you know. You gonna tell me about Carlos?"

The question caught me by surprise, like I'm sure he meant it to. "Carlos?"

"Yeah. The name I've been seeing on your phone every half hour since Topeka. He give you that big bruise on the side of your face?"

"Nah. I told you, Mrs. Brewer clipped me with her cast. Dementia and a broken arm isn't a safe combo." The pancakes were starting to taste too sweet. "What do you want to know about Carlos?"

He scraped the sides of the bowl with his spoon. "Tellin' the truth, I don't give a rat's ass about Carlos. I want to know why he makes you so crazy and desperate you actually believe any of what I'm telling you, let alone want to help me."

"Carlos is a mistake," I said. "A hot, drunken, big-dicked mistake—sorry. You wouldn't understand."

"Son, I was in show business for over twenty-five years. Just 'cause all my mistakes had big titties don't mean we didn't make 'em for the same reason." He pointed to my ring. "He give you that?"

"Yeah."

"So, you're married."

"Nope. He just gave it to me and pronounced us husbands."

The wattle under his chin bobbed as he swallowed the last of his grits. "Don't sound legal. You love him?"

Did I? Maybe I did until the first black eye. Now, not so much. "Doesn't matter," I said, shrugging. "I'm heading for a whole new life now."

By the time he'd put his spoon back in the empty bowl, his grin had turned into a chuckle that exploded into laughter, flecking my arm with gravy spittle. "Your poor, sad fucker," he said once he stopped wheezing. "You can move to another place or change your name or whatever, but no matter what you do, you just drag your shit along. Tell you what. Once you get me to where we're goin', I'll give you the guitar."

"I can't play that thing."

"Once I'm done with you, you'll be able to play as well as me. You want a new life, right?"

"Yeah."

"Once we get to the portal, just pucker up."

"That doesn't make any sense."

He wiped his chin, wadded up his napkin, and stuffed it into the empty bowl. "None of it makes sense—vampires, spells, talent-sucking, churches in dreams. All I ever wanted was to play guitar, sing, and get laid. Nobody ever said how complicated it was gonna get."

I tried to figure out what he was saying, but it was all starting to sound stupid. I got hit by a wave of hot shame, feeling flush and sweaty. What the hell was I doing? Why was I here? Did I really think this old dude was Elvis? I felt like I couldn't rely on my own judgment anymore, if I ever could. Thanks for making me second-guess myself, Carlos. You asshole.

And that heated, sweaty feeling got worse when I looked up at the TV screen over the cash register and saw both our pictures over the crawl. The sound was off, and I was too far away to read what it said, but I had a pretty good idea. Leaning on the counter right underneath the TV, Brenda seemed to be absorbed in working a crossword puzzle.

"We gotta go."

"Go? This is the first time I been out of that goddamn car in nine hours. Lemme finish my coffee."

I gestured to the TV.

"Shit!" he said.

Brenda raised her head and smiled at us, tucking her pencil behind her ear as she grabbed a pot and came toward us. "You boys need a refill?"

"Just the check."

She put the coffeepot down on an empty table and tore the check off her pad without turning around. The TV had switched to the weather. *She missed it*, I thought. *We're safe*. I handed her a twenty as she came up to the table. "Keep the change."

"Well, thank you." She tucked the bill in the pocket of her apron. She hadn't stopped smiling since she asked us if we wanted a refill. It was too wide to be genuine, and she seemed to be looking around the diner more than she had been. *Were those beads of sweat around her hairline? It wasn't hot.* "You boys drive safe," she said. She headed back to the register, got a cloth from somewhere and began wiping down the counter, looking up at us surreptitiously.

"She knows," I said. "Let's go."

"She does not. I have to piss."

"She does too. You can piss later. Let's get the hell out of here."

He rolled his eyes at me, but he slid out of the booth anyway. I hustled him toward the door, strong-arming him away from the restrooms. "Thanks again," I said with a wave as we passed the register.

"Night," she said with that same hyper-wide grin. Just before I pushed the glass door open, I saw her reflection as she pulled her phone out of the pocket of her apron and put it to her ear.

"Get in the fuckin' car," I said.

*

The moon looked fuller than it had earlier, but maybe I hadn't been paying attention. Maybe I could just see it better since we got off I-70 to avoid being spotted. These back mountain roads were confusing in the dark with all the switchbacks and stuff. I had to let him piss, so I pulled off by the riverside and tried to get my bearings. I thought we were still going west, but I wasn't sure. *I should turn on the GPS*, I thought, *just for a second*. I looked out the windshield and saw his surprisingly long, skinny old man dick in the headlights.

I rolled down the window. "Nobody wants to see that," I said. "Why didn't you piss on your side of the car?"

"Are you crazy? There's at least a ten-foot drop-off on that side. Why'd you have to pull off so close to the goddamn river? Are you even sure we're on a road? It's not paved."

Yeah, that had me worried, too. "Will you hurry up?"

"I got an enlarged prostate," he said. "It takes me a while."

The noise of the rushing river beside us melded with the sigh of the wind through the trees, but I didn't find it calming. The stench of peanut butter and bananas in the car made deep breaths impossible, and I needed to piss too. Damn coffee. I got out of the car and joined him.

He was pissing vigorously now, his eyes closed as he breathed out sounds of relief. He looked over when I whipped mine out. "Wanna swordfight?" he said with a grin.

"Um, not really."

Leaning over, he took a long look at my pecker. "Nice cock."

"I thought Elvis was straight."

He shrugged. "Just 'cause I don't wanna suck it don't mean I can't appreciate it. Learn to take a compliment, why don'tcha? Jeez." He finished, zipped up, and went back to the car.

I looked at the mountainside beyond the river, mulling over the fact that the King of rock and roll had not only been checking out my package but approved of it. I couldn't help but smile as it filled out a little in my hand. *Perv*, I thought. But as I scrutinized the mountain across the river, my smile faded. About halfway down, I saw flashing red and blue lights speeding along in a straight line, and not just one set. Five. And if I remembered right, the bridge was only a couple miles back.

"Turn off the headlights!" I yelled, but he didn't. He had the door open, getting something out of the backseat. "Turn off the goddamn headlights!" I zipped up before I totally finished shaking off, urine dampening my shorts. "Fuck!!" I screamed, lunging for my door.

As I got in and slammed it shut, he brandished the guitar in front of me. "HAH! *Here's* your fuckin' orcs!"

The strings glowed a faint blue.

He was off, teetering on the edge of the drop as he danced around trying to find a way down, holding the guitar high in the air and whooping. I tore open the door, not thinking about taking my keys. Or turning off the headlights. Or even shutting the engine off. All I wanted to do was shut him the fuck up. "Will you quiet down?! The fuckin' cops are coming."

"Screw the cops! I'm goin' home!" He moved quicker than I'd ever seen him, going first in one direction, then the other. The strings grew brighter on the left, so he ran that way, almost hitting a tree. He moved like someone half my age as he scrambled down the drop diagonally going left, gravel and sand raising a cloud in the moonlight.

I beat cheeks to keep up with him but even so, he stayed a good ten or fifteen feet in front of me, the now-bright blue strings the beacon I had to follow as I stumbled over roots, branches, and patches of loose rocks. I scraped my arms and shoulders and fell on my ass more times than I could count. The sound of the rushing water grew closer and closer until he finally stopped at a marshy shore.

"There it is," he said with tears in his voice. "The portal."

All I saw was the midnight postcard shot of a rushing river. The light reflected off the white water, shimmering and sparkling as brightly as the strings on the guitar, which now looked so blue they could burn you at a touch. But that's all I saw outside of the lights from the cop cars coming down the mountain and getting closer. "Where? I don't see jack shit."

"Not yet you don't, son. I ain't made it work." He cradled the guitar, using his left hand to finger the frets while he bent his head over and strummed tentatively with his right. The soft notes sounded strangled and aborted in the night air, but he kept at it until they were clearer and more confident. I swear he seemed to get younger the more he played.

Finally, he straightened up, faced the river, and hit a succession of three chords. No explanation for me, like I didn't exist. Like I didn't even fuckin' drive him to his goddamn portal. The police car lights came around the mountain again, lower and closer.

Nothing.

"FUCK!" he screamed into the night air. His voice was strong, and he was definitely looking younger. His grey hair was now black. He tried a different combination of notes, but his fingers slipped off the frets and he almost dropped the guitar into the muck.

"What's supposed to happen?" I yelled over to him.

"The church ..." He planted his feet solid and tried again, the riff ringing out strong and true. As the sound echoed and faded into river babble, I felt a deep rumbling beneath my feet. The ground wasn't shaking, but it wasn't still either. "YES!!" he hollered. "Goddammit, I'm goin' to glory at last!" He hit it again, the music floating out over the river.

I looked off and saw the cop lights again. They were almost down the mountain now. But as I turned back to the river, a long line bisected the surface of the water, stretching from one bank to the other. He kept chording, and the line got wider.

It was the peak of a roof.

Holy shit, I thought. *It's happening.* But what rose was not like any church I was used to seeing. No spires, no stained glass, no carvings of angels. It was a plain, white clapboard building. The windows were panes of ordinary glass—okay, not ordinary because it just rose out of a fuckin' river—but you get the idea. It gleamed brilliant white, illuminating the night. A sign on the roof of the porch said "First Assembly of God," and "You Are Welcome" was hand-lettered on the crosspiece of the door frame.

He stopped chording and walked over to me. The old guy was gone. This was goddamn Elvis Presley coming my way wearing jeans and a leather jacket, holding a guitar and swaggering like a badass motherfucker, even if he was wearing fluffy bedroom slippers and a Simpson's PJ top. His dark hair fell casually over his forehead, and his cheeks almost glowed with health as he smiled at me. Behind him, a church stood in the middle of the goddamn river, water pouring off the roof and dripping from the eaves.

"Thankyavurrymush," he said as he extended his hand. "Ain't that what you wanted to hear?"

I was crying, but I didn't know why. I didn't know what to say. Until I did. "Elvis is going into the building, right?"

He grinned so hard it almost hurt. "Somethin' like that." We shook hands, but before I had a chance to do anything else, he pulled me close and kissed me. But it wasn't a kiss. It was like the whole river rushed into me, lifetimes of experiences, a knowledge so profound I could spend my life studying it and only understand a part. It flooded every cell of my body, and who I had been was washed away. Carlos. Arbor Rose. The old man. The cop cars crossing the bridge toward us. None of it was real anymore. It was all Elvis, his guitar, and the dripping church.

He broke the kiss and handed me the guitar. "You keep this. I just gave you that new life you were lookin' for. It's the least I can do, but you got to know this shit comes with a price. He's gonna come for you. He'll smell it, no matter what you do. Just be careful who you invite inside." He shook my hand again. "Thanks, pardner."

Before I could say anything, he turned and walked away, stepping from the muddy bank of the river onto the wooden porch of the white church. He looked back, waved once, and then he disappeared through the door. The building hung there a moment, as solid as the guitar in my hand, then it shimmered and vanished.

Sirens filled the mountain air, blue and red lights bouncing off the clean surface of the water. I heard tires screeching, men yelling, and dogs barking as they trampled through the underbrush. I just sat down in the muck and held the guitar, playing chords I didn't know I knew. Every time I looked at the water, I saw an ocean of essence. Talent. But as peaceful as I felt, a sharp pinprick of a voice inside my head made itself heard over the din of the approaching cops.

Ah, it said. *So, that's where it went.*

***

ABOUT THE AUTHORS

Kathryn Collins

Kathryn Collins's poems and essays have appeared in the Rumpus, *Flyaway*, *Burner*, and *Bank Heavy Press*. She recently received her MA in Professional Fiction Writing from the University of Denver, and currently works as a librarian. After a long period as an expat in Germany, Israel, and Australia, she has returned home to the Rocky Mountains of Colorado where she writes about science fiction, fantasy, and politics and the places where the three meet. You can read her ongoing editorial series at https://vocal.media/authors/haybitch-abersnatchy

Bill Davidson

Bill Davidson is a Scottish writer of horror and fantasy. Although fairly new to short story writing, his work can be found in a number of publications from the UK and US, such as Flame Tree Publishing's *Endless Apocalypse Short Stories*; Dark Lane Books, "Storyteller," "Under the Bed," "Emerging Worlds"; Metamorphose, "Enchanted Conversation"; Tigershark Publishing and *Storgy Magazine*. Find him on billdavidsonwriting.com or @bill_davidson57

Keith Gouveia

Keith Gouveia is an accomplished horror and dark fantasy writer and fierce advocate of independent and artisanal publishers. His recent releases are *Animal Behavior and Other Tales of Lycanthropy*, *The Screaming Field*, and *The Dead Speak in Riddles*. He is also editor of the horror anthologies, *Bits of the Dead*, *Skeletal Remains*, and *The Snuff Syndicate*. Keith was born and raised in Fall River, Massachusetts, but now lives in Orlando, Florida.

Mary-Jean Harris

Mary-Jean Harris writes fantasy and historical fiction, both novels and short stories. Some of her short stories have been published in anthologies and websites such as the *Tesseracts 18* and *20* anthologies, Polar Expressions Publishing, Allegory Ezine, and SciPhi Journal. Four of her short stories have also been honourable mentions in the Writers of the Future contest. Mary-Jean is currently a student at University of Victoria in Canada studying theoretical physics and has a Master's degree from the Perimeter Institute in Waterloo. In her undergraduate, she also studied philosophy at Carleton University. Mary-Jean enjoys learning about ancient philosophy and loves to travel. Her novel, *Aizai the Forgotten*, is the first in the series The Soul Wanderers. To learn more, visit www.thesoulwanderers.blogspot.ca/ You can also find her on Facebook at https://www.facebook.com/SoulWanderers/

Brit Jones

Brit Jones has spent the last thirty-five years of his life pursuing an ultimately fruitless musical career. Recently he turned his hand to writing fiction and has had short fiction published in both the 2015 and 2016 *Onyx Neon Horror Shorts Anthologies* and in *Helix Literary Magazine*. In addition, he finished a novel over a year ago but doesn't yet have the confidence to try and get it published. Brit lives in Austin, Texas with his family.

George Karram

George Karram, a first-time author, is a sixty-one-year-old father of two perfect children. Currently he is pursuing his MSW at Rutgers University, and has been clean, sober, and abstinent from gambling for twelve years—one day at a time.

Matt Kolbet

Matt Kolbet has taught in England and the United States. He currently lives in Oregon. His most recently published work is from *The Last Line, The Hungry Chimera, Gravel, Foliate Oak*, and *McSweeney's*. He's had stories in anthologies by Laurel Highlands Press and Inwood Indiana. His second novel, *Lunar Year*, was published by Champlain Avenue Press.

Valerie Lioudis

Valerie Lioudis is an author who writes both novels and short stories in several genres, but her main focus is horror. The New Jersey native penned *The Many Afterlives of John Robert Thompson*, her debut solo novel, in 2017. Along with her husband, Kristopher, she had already published book one in the Aftershock Zombie Series in 2014. She loves the art of writing a short story and has been published in eight anthologies, most notably *Undead Worlds*. The Reanimated Writers, a group of indie zombie fiction authors, created a best-selling anthology that featured twenty-two undead worlds. Valerie spearheaded the project, along with several other endeavors including the Reanimated Rumble with this online community. To find out more about Valerie and her work you can visit her website AftershockZombieSeries.com or connect with her on Facebook @AuthorValerieLioudis or Twitter @AuthorVLioudis. She hangs out in The Reanimated Writers Facebook Group, and will talk to just about anyone, so join and say hello! If you are looking for her books, they are available on Amazon. If you type Valerie Lioudis, you will find her. She is the only one!

Shaun Meeks

Shaun Meeks is the author of the Dillon the Monster Dick series (*The Gate at Lake Drive* and *Earthbound and Down*), as well as *Shutdown, Down on the Farm*, and *Maymon*. He has published over fifty short stories, the most recent appearing in *Zippered Flesh 3, The Best of the Horror Zine, Dark Moon Digest, Rogue Nation, All That Remain, Monsters Among Us, Insidious Assassins, Fresh Fear*, and *Zombies Gone Wild*. His short stories have been collected in *Dark Reaches, Brother's Ilk* (with James Meeks), *At the Gates of Madness*, and the upcoming *Salt on the Wounds*. This year Shaun is set to release the third novel in the Dillon the Monster Dick series (*Altered Gate*), as well several short stories set to appear in various magazines and anthologies. He is currently working on the forth novel in the Dillon series, two standalone novels (*Gone Crazy ... Be Back Soon*, and *The Desolate*), as well as a collection of southern horror (*Blood on the Ground: Six Shots of Southern Discomfort*). Shaun currently lives in Toronto, Ontario, with his partner, Mina, and their micro-yeti, Lily, where they are always planning the next adventure. To find out more or to contact Shaun, please visit www.shaunmeeks.com, www.facebook.com/shaunmeeks, or www.twitter.com/ShaunMeeks

Charlie Palmer

Charlie Palmer has always lived in his own world (population: one), seeing bogeymen under the bed and shadows that linger in the corner of his vision. In 2013, after twenty-seven bone-numbing years of crunching numbers in the finance sector, he faced a health crisis and made the decision (crazy/prudent/delirious—remains to be seen) to leap off the conveyer belt and pursue his bucket list.

Top of this list sits a lifetime ambition to be a published writer. He is the author of several short stories and one novel, *The Frail Deeds of Good Men*, which is currently sitting with a publisher. Novel number two is in the works.

For him, writing is a cathartic experience. Nothing gives him greater satisfaction than the moment a page of scribbles comes together and sings, breathing life into his sometimes funny, sometimes disturbing, but always heartfelt dreams. Except maybe a decent curry. Curry makes him happy.

When not traveling the world following Formula One, trying new foods, and making new friends, you can find him in Colchester (England's oldest recorded town) with his wife, two teenage boys, and a Labrador cruelly described by some as obese.

You can contact him on twitter on @charliejpalmer.

Sergio Palumbo

Sergio Palumbo is an Italian public servant who graduated from law school working in the public real estate branch. He is also a co-editor, together with Michele Dutcher, of the new steampunk anthology, *Steam-powered Dream Engines*, published in March 2018 by Rogue Planet Press, an imprint of British Horrified Press. The first historical/horror screenplay written by him, titled *"Tophet - An Ancient Evil,"* completed in 2018, won an Honorable Mention Award at the 2018 International Horror Hotel Award script competition held in Richfield, Ohio. He has published a fantasy roleplaying illustrated manual, *WarBlades.* Some of his works and short stories have been published in *Aphelion Webzine, Weirdyear, Quantum Muse, AntipodeanSF, Schlock!, SQ Mag,* and in print inside thirty-five American horror/sci-fi/fantasy/steampunk anthologies, fifty-eight British horror/sci-fi anthologies, two Canadian urban fantasy/horror anthologies, and two Australian sci-fi anthologies by various publishers, with twenty-four more to follow in 2018/2019. He is also a scale modeler who likes mostly science fiction and real space models. Some of his little dioramas have been shown in some Italian (scale model) magazines like *Soldatini International, Model Time, Tutto Soldatini,* and online sites such as Starship Modeler, MechaModelComp, and others. Some sci-fi/fantasy/horror short stories by him in Italian have been published on Alpha Aleph, Alpha Aleph Extra, Algenib, Oltre il Futuro, Nugae 2.0, SogniHorror, La Zona Morta, edizioni Lo Scudo, Antologia Robot ITA 0.1, Antologia Il Segreto dell'Universo, Antologia E-Heroes, etc.

All of Sergio's short stories are initially edited by Michele Dutcher, a/k/a Bottomdweller, who lives in a carriage house in Old Louisville, Kentucky, with her border collie, Daisy Dukes. She has a BS degree in elementary education from Indiana University with minors in theology and sociology and has been writing science fiction stories for about a decade.

Seth Peterson

Seth Peterson has been writing for about three years. He was first published in his alma mater's literary magazine, University of South Florida's *Thread*, in 2015 for the poems "Sleeping Fits" and "Beware the Bacon." That same year he also published the short story "Dave and the Devil in Arizona" in the University of Houston's *Glass Mountain* literary magazine. When he's not writing, Seth enjoys watching movies. In fact, he's even involved in the local film scene, writing horror films for Wicked Window Productions (You can check them out on Facebook here: https://www.facebook.com/WickedWindow/) . His most recent contribution to them was his script "The Itch" used in their 2017 horror anthology *Wickedtober*. Seth also does freelance editing for The Hoth, an SEO company based out of St. Petersburg. His social media empire is limited to just Facebook, which you can find here: https://www.facebook.com/seth.peterson.501. Hitchcock's The Birds has given Seth a natural fear of Twitter and his absent camera dexterity has kept him off Snapchat and Instagram. He looks to remedy both problems in the future. Publication in Left Hand Publishers' *Terrors Unimagined* anthology represents Seth's first paid submission acceptance. He looks to continue writing, get paid for it, and maybe one day write that novel sitting in the back of his mind.

Charlotte Platt

Charlotte Platt is a young professional who writes horror and urban fantasy. Charlotte spent her teens on the Orkney Islands and studied for her profession in Glasgow before moving up to the north Highlands for her current job. She has taken inspiration from a wide variety of sources including haunted military buildings, sceptical horses and the creeping woods that line the Thurso River. She lives off sarcasm and tea and can often be found walking near cliffs and rivers, looking for sea glass. Charlotte was shortlisted for the Write to End Violence Against Women Award 2017, placed second in the British Fantasy Society Short Story Competition 2017, and has had short stories published in *Unfading Daydream, Dissonance Magazine, Econoclash Review*, and *Twilight Madhouse Volume 3*. Outside of writing, she enjoys music, dark comedy, and pugs, and can be reached on Twitter at @Chazzaroo.

Clark Roberts

Clark Roberts writes mostly short stories in the genres of horror and fantasy. His fiction has appeared in over twenty publications including *Dark Recesses Press, Anotherealm, Nocturnal Ooze, Alienskin,* and *Peaks and Valleys.* He is not a *New York Times* bestselling author, and for now, he's okay with that. He spent much of his teenage years reading the novels of Stephen King, Clive Barker, and Peter Straub. Mr. Roberts lives in Michigan with his wife and two children. Besides reading and writing, he enjoys spending time in the outdoors. He particularly enjoys fishing in the hours of dusk when trout streams whisper, and eyes open in the surrounding woods.

C.M. Saunders

C.M. Saunders is a freelance journalist and editor from Wales. His work has appeared in over sixty magazines, ezines and anthologies worldwide, including *Loaded, Maxim, Record Collector, Fortean Times, Fantastic Horror, Trigger Warning, Liquid Imagination, Crimson Streets* and the *Literary Hatchet.* His books have been both traditionally and independently published, the most recent being *Human Waste* and *X3,* his third collection of short fiction, both of which are available now on Deviant Dolls Publications.
Find out more on his website: https://cmsaunders.wordpress.com/
Visit his Facebook page: https://www.facebook.com/CMSaunders01/
Or follow him on Twitter: https://twitter.com/CMSaunders01/

Jay Seate

After Jay Seate read a few stories to his parents, they booted him out of the house. Undaunted, he continues to write everything from humor to the erotic to the macabre, and is especially keen on transcending genre pigeonholing. His tales span the gulf from Horror Novel Review's Best Short Fiction Award to *Chicken Soup for the Soul.* They may be told with hardcore realism or fantasy, bringing to life the most quirky of characters. Novels include *Valley of Tears, Tears for the Departed, And the Heavens Wept,* and *Paranormal Liaisons.* His story collections are *Carnival of Nightmares, Midway of Fear, Sex in Bloom,* and *A Baker's Dozen.* Links: www.troyseateauthor.webs.com and on amazon.com. Blog: www.supernaturalsnackbar.wordpress.com Facebook author page: J. T. Seate.

Book Publishing Credits:

- *Carnival of Nightmares* - Horror Collection - Mélange Books - September - 2010
- *Midway of Fear* - Horror Collection - Mélange Books - November 2011
- *Valley of Tears* - Novel - Mélange Books - February - 2012
- Tears for the Departed - Novel - Mélange Books - March - 2012
- *And the Heavens Wept* - Novel - Mélange Books - April - 2012
- *Paranormal Liaisons* - Novel - Books We Love - March - 2016
- *30 Multi-Author Anthologies* - including Chicken Soup for the Soul and more

Ailish Sinclair

Ailish Sinclair trained at one of the top dance and drama colleges in London and then ran her own ballet school for several years. Since then she has worked as a teacher, bookkeeper, website designer, special needs assistant, and for a short while as a housekeeper in a castle. She now lives beside a loch in Scotland with her husband and two children, where she writes many stories, both contemporary and historical, and eats a lot of cake. She blogs at http://ailishsinclair.com/ and can be found on Twitter: https://twitter.com/AilishSinclair, Instagram: http://instagram.com/ailishsinclair and Facebook: https://www.facebook.com/ailishsinclairauthor

Ann Stawski

In a pre-STEM world, where a girl was encouraged to pursue whichever degree she chose (not that STEM is bad or anything), Ann Stawski received her B.A. in English from Alverno College. She liked that so much she went on for her M.A. in English-Creative Writing at UW-Milwaukee, where her love for fiction writing was inspired and encouraged. However, as her career took off—ultimately landing her as a VP of marketing in a Fortune 500 company—her writing withered away. In a beautiful change of life, Ann escaped the corporate world and refocused on her fiction writing and freelance writing. Her freelance work appeared in *Alverno Magazine, Wastewater Plant Operator and Treatment Plant Operator* magazines, as well as on Cultivate Communications' blogs. She has two short stories published in the anthology, *It's About Time.* She is repped by The Purcell Agency for her young adult novels, and hopes to see a publisher's contract soon.

A Wisconsin native in Charlotte, North Carolina, Ann Stawski is a writer of young adult and contemporary fiction but also loves terror. A corporate marketer by day, she's also a freelance writer. Ann's a member of SCBWI, a founding member of the Write Brainers, loves to ski the Rockies, and has thirty-two sweet tooths.

Cedric Tan

Cedric Tan is a fictionist based in Manila, the Philippines. His love for fantasy and speculative writing comes alive in his short stories, which have been published in Ateneo de Manila University's Heights, Philippines Graphic, and Philippine Speculative Fiction Vol. 9. He was also fellow of the 13th IYAS National Writers Workshop.

In his spare time, he also writes for his sports blog Quill Zones, and continually searches for the best ramen in the country.

G. Ted Theewen

G. Ted Theewen lives on the Wisconsin/Illinois state line in a small town called Orangeville. When he's not writing fiction, he's making ice cream videos for his Youtube Channel, Ice Cream Every Day. Currently, he works from home as a customer service rep for a chain of grocery stores. Plus, he's the in-house ice cream maker for the local cafe, specializing in local flavors and ingredients. His work has appeared in Infernal Ink Magazine, as well as two of the clown horror series of anthologies *Floppy Shoes Apocalypse 1* and *2*, and the anthology of political horror, *Dread State*.

Philip Trippenbach & Blake Jessop

Philip Trippenbach is London-based journalist, writer, and social media expert. Blake Jessop is a widely published Canadian author of science fiction, fantasy, and horror stories. "Medium" is their maiden collaboration, but stay tuned: more are on the way. You can check out Philip's work at 30secSF.com, or follow Blake on Twitter @everydayjisei.

Gary Van Haas

Gary Van Haas is a graduate of UCLA School of Journalism, who has spent the last twenty years living in Greece while touring the world's most intriguing travel destinations such as Asia, Africa, and Americas, etc., at the same time researching their indigenous cultures, various customs, mythology and archaeological sites. He has been a feature news and travel writer for the *International Herald Tribune, Time, Newsweek, Conde Nast* and *Travel+Leisure Magazine*, and currently works as a novelist and screenwriter.

Gary is the author of *The Ikon*, a lively Greek island thriller set in Mykonos, Greece, and has recently completed another sequel thriller, in his "Garth Hanson" action-adventure series called *Malabar Run* set in popular Goa, India, and also has a new book completed called *In Search of Ancient Greece*, which is said to be one of the most comprehensive and compelling travel-historical works completed to date.

More recently, Gary has become involved in the film industry and has more than fourteen books-to-movies in development and preproduction with various movie production companies worldwide, including his latest $30 million film in production called *The Devil's Banker* about the Roberto Calvi murder and the Banco Ambrosiano Scandal, which involved The Vatican and Mafia.

Some of his other books are:

- *Latin Quarter* - about young Picasso's wild early years in Paris in 1902.
- *I Want My MTV!* - The unabridged true story about the beginnings of MTV!
- *Blood On The Border* - a tense police thriller about the DEA vs. drug cartel wars.

- *The Club* - about an unwitting poker player who can win a million dollars in cash or leave in a casket!

Timothy Vincent

Timothy Vincent (Tim Smith) is a published and award-winning author. His work has appeared in multiple genres and literary magazines. His previous creative writing publications include the novels *Prince of the Blue Castles* and *The Red House on the Hill* (Argus). His short stories have appeared in *3288 Review* (as Tim Smith) *Xchyler's Toll of Another Bell Anthology, The Bacon Review, Suspense Magazine,* and *The WriteRoom.* He is a former winner of the Terri Ann Armstrong Short Story Contest ("Star-Crossed,"), and a top twenty-five finalist in Glimmer Train's new writer contest in 2010. *Prince of the Blue Castles* was a finalist for the Killer Nashville Silver Falchion, Best Fiction/Literary Award and a Chanticleer Blue Ribbon Review. His latest novel, *Jack Out of the Box,* came out in January, 2018. A traveler of the world and learning, he holds a Ph.D. in Rhetoric and Composition, and an MFA from Fairfield University (summer 2018), where he teaches. He can be reached on Facebook (Timothy Vincent), or through his author's page at: timothyvincentauthor.com.

Rory Warwick

Rory Warwick is a British horror and science fiction writer who writes under the name R. W. Warwick. He lives in Tokyo with his wife who is a travel writer, and spends a considerable amount of his time writing his stories by hand on piles of notebooks, and exploring the Japanese countryside. When he is not writing, he enjoys mountain climbing, attempting to rekindle his relationship with the guitar, and looking for the next cyberpunk novel to fall into. Prior to moving to Japan, he worked for several years as an associate editor for US horror fiction quarterly magazine, *Dark Moon Digest.*
His writing credits include such horror and science fiction magazines as *Frostfire Worlds, Perihelion Science Fiction, Bewildering Stories,* and *Gathering Storm Magazine,* among others. His apocalyptic far future story "The Far Side of Eternity," received an honourable mention in the Writers of the Future contest and was subsequently published in a collection of science fiction short stories, *The Dial,* which is available on Amazon. He is currently working through the second draft of his

first full-length science fiction novel under the working title "Champion City," which he is happy to tweet about often. Rory's social media soapboxes include Twitter (@realRoryWarwick), and Facebook (@RWWarwick), on which he can be regularly contacted.

Jerry L. Wheeler

Jerry L. Wheeler is the editor of seven anthologies of gay erotica for Bold Strokes Books, Lethe Press, and other publishers. His collection of short fiction and essays, *Strawberries and Other Erotic Fruits*, was published by Lethe Press is 2012 and was one of his three appearances on the shortlist for the Lambda Literary Award. He lives and writes in Denver, Colorado, maintaining his review blog, "Out In Print: Queer Book Reviews" (https://outinprintblog.wordpress.com/) and his own editing business, Write And Shine (https://jerrywheelerblog.wordpress.com/).

Todd Zack

Todd Zack is a delivery driver, writer, and musician living in southwest Florida. His alternative rock band, Tape Recorder 3, composes soundtracks for independent films and documentary's. Todd's journalism and fiction pieces have appeared in *Thrasher Magazine, Red Fez, Crimson Streets, Jersey Devil Press* and *Ink Stains Anthology 2018*. He is an avid skateboarder and collector of vintage comic books. Mr. Zack lives with his wife and daughter in southwest Florida

Please Review Our Other Books

If you enjoyed this book, or any of our other books, please feel free to leave reviews. All of our books are available at all major online retailers, including Amazon and Barnes & Noble. You can also leave reviews at Goodreads.com.

Beautiful Lies, Painful Truths Vol. I
Amazon:
http://amzn.to/2reSyIe
Goodreads:
http://bit.ly/2BobVCi

Beautiful Lies, Painful Truths Vol. II
Amazon:
http://amzn.to/2ngBq0i
Goodreads:
http://bit.ly/2slkBpP

Realities Perceived
Amazon: http://amzn.to/2Dbe1ny
Goodreads: http://bit.ly/2nU9hvw

The Demon's Angel
By Maya Shah
Amazon: http://amzn.to/2EVjj7V
Goodreads: http://bit.ly/2son5E2

Drawing from the Well
By Rachel Bollinger
Amazon:
https://amzn.to/2th8WGE
Goodreads:
https://bit.ly/2M8h57h

A World Unimagined
Amazon:
https://amzn.to/2yvJ4vS
Goodreads:
https://bit.ly/2K7b6zj

***

Win A Free Kindle!

If you enjoyed any of our books, please register to review one of our books (and sign up for our e-newsletter). In our newsletter, we give you previews of upcoming releases, discounts, as well as free stuff for our fans! But if you review some of our books, you can also win a FREE Kindle. https://bit.ly/2Fc021g

***

MORE BOOKS FROM
LEFT HAND PUBLISHERS

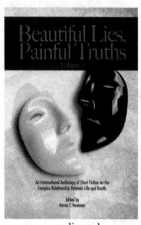

BEAUTIFUL LIES, PAINFUL TRUTHS VOL.I

There's an ironic beauty between humanity's love of Life and fear of Death. Life seemingly brings joy, happiness, hope, and love. Death can end sadness, illness, suffering, and pain. We asked writers to "Let the title and quote take your imagination, your story, wherever it wants to go."

Join them now as an international blend of authors, both fresh and seasoned, bring you an exceptional menu of speculative fiction, mystery, realism, horror, and the supernatural. If your palate varies from the macabre to the dramatic, *Beautiful Lies, Painful Truths* provides an assortment of tasty treasures that will chill, delight, and give you food for thought.

Reviews

★★★★★

"An incredibly amazing anthology.
Every author in this anthology should be commended for their work in this collection. Bringing in life and death into a collection of stories, all by different authors, and how their writing varies, but brings to life, this grand collection. I believe there was a lot of thought put into which authors would be contributing their work, and how this work will be displayed."

> **Amy Shannon,** Author. Writer. Poet. Storyteller. Blogger. Book Reviewer.
> **Author Blog:** http://bit.ly/2yLHuFZ
> **Facebook:** http://bit.ly/2ho273i
> **Review Blog:** http://bit.ly/2iPVV4x
> **Amazon Author** Page: http://amzn.to/2ynn2qM

***

"The quality of the stories read are amazing, with intricate plots in a short story form coming off as so perfect in their construction. The scope of the imagination of the writers just boggles the mind in the executions of stories that make you think. What might be considered 'good' isn't. What is seen as dark and painful is honestly the way it should be. Major kudos to these stories.

"Life is good and beautiful and death is dark and bad. Maybe not. This book presents twenty-four approaches with an amazing array of imagination in the depths of human drama, supernatural, humor, and unexpected twists. These stories will challenge everything you thought you knew–think again.

"*Beautiful Lies, Painful Truths* has stories guaranteed to challenge your view of life and death in mind boggling ways, taking you down unexpected paths of the serious, humorous, pathos, and, the twisted turns of fate. The qualities of the stories are good. The writers are commended. An excellent book. Kudos!"

Bruce Blanchard, Book Reviewer
http://bit.ly/2yLBq09

***

"It's an impressive read... It may be about death, but the mood isn't always dark. This anthology spans several genres including science fiction, horror, mystery and, even some humor. Well written and well edited, this book may be long, but it's hard to put down."

David Watson, Book Reviewer

REALITIES PERCEIVED

Nothing's more dangerous, or delightful, than invoking a cadre of talented authors to create short stories that defy our perceptions of reality. Do we create our own truth? Or does our view of it shape our world? Neither heroes nor heavens, victims nor villains, may grasp the true nature of our being.

From science fiction, to horror and the supernatural, to dramas about the fabric of our existence, this international fusion of artists will thrill you with an eclectic selection of tales that cross all genres. Sit back and be prepared to have your perception of reality both challenged and distorted.

Reviews

★★★★★

"... it kept me on the edge of my seat and I did not want to put it down even to eat or sleep. You have a great book here."

Lori Kibbey
Book Reviewer

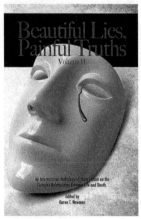

BEAUTIFUL LIES, PAINFUL TRUTHS VOL.II

Most believe that Life promises light, bliss, and wonder. Death scares most with its shadow of mortality, darkness, and destruction. But what if those may be, if not lies, just facets of the complicated entities that bookend our existence? Life does not mock Death, but feeds it. Death is not the cessation of Life, but an alteration of existence. What would you do if faced with either truth?

An international galley of authors brings us a second repast of tales featuring the complex relationship between Life, Death, and humanity. From the supernatural to the sublime, these writers, both novitiates and accomplished, serve up a banquet of speculative fiction across a wide spectrum of genres. Beautiful Lies, Painful Truths Volume II will continue to feed your craving for the fantastic.

Reviews

"You have to love an anthology that can give you well-written stories no matter what the genre is and it looks at important issues in addition to death such as love, religion, and redemption."
David Watson, Amazon Book Reviewer

"This collection is a recipe for a lost weekend as I found myself wanting to read 'just one more' until by nearly midnight I had finished all sixteen. I will recommend to my friends and fellow bibliophiles without reservation."
Natalia Corres
Book Reviewer, Twitter.com/Ncorres

"I read the first volume and was more than excited to read a new collection. Life and death is not just black and white, but all the in-betweens and as the title alludes, both are beautiful, but also full of lies and truths."
Amy Shannon, Author. Writer. Poet. Storyteller. Blogger. Book Reviewer.
Author Blog: http://bit.ly/2yLHuFZ
Review Blog: http://bit.ly/2iPVV4x
Amazon Author Page: http://amzn.to/2ynn2qM

THE DEMON'S ANGEL
By Maya Shah

Neha was excited to enter her sophomore year in high school. That was until the boy she went out with sprouted wings, and Lucas, the man who raised her since she was a baby, turned into a demon.

Neha is far from human. She is an angel, the natural enemy of demons. An angel raised by a demon has never been heard of before, which makes some angels see her as a threat. Neha not only has to prove that she does not know anything about demons, she has to prove that she is on the side of the angels. And she is. So she thinks.

This Young Adult supernatural thriller follows the tribulations of the teenaged Neha as she learns both the truth about her past and herself.

Reviews

★★★★★

"Intensely unique.
The character Neha is something very remarkable, she has depth and grows as a character, especially when she feels she has to prove herself. She thinks she's proving herself a good angel to the other angels, when in fact she's also proving it to herself. Neha is not your typical teenager, nor typical angel."

> **Amy Shannon**, Author. Writer. Poet. Storyteller.
> Blogger. Book Reviewer.
> Review Blog: http://bit.ly/2iPVV4x

***

"This flight of fancy with engrossing plot twists tempts anyone ever dumbfounded by a parental deception."

> **Wendy Landers,** Book Reviewer
> Author of Just Let Time Pass
> www.wendylanders.com

A WORLD UNIMAGINED

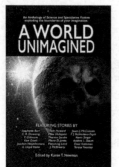

Beyond what is conceivable to what might be is a universe full of the unexpected and the unexplainable. From science fiction to science fantasy, the location of this realm of creation and the mind is...

A World Unimagined.

An international manifest of authors both new and experienced crew this voyage to the other side of the unbelievable with stories unique and though-provoking. This anthology of science fiction short stories transports us to the future, the past, and to cultures and civilizations undreamed of. Set your imaginations to stunned and your minds to light speed.

Reviews

"An eclectic menagerie of *X-Files* material. My favorite was the alien invasion of the Vietnam War's Hanoi Hilton."

Wendy Landers, Book Reviewer
Author of *Just Let Time Pass*
wendylanders.com

"Science Fiction is the great cosmos governed only by the power of What If. It requires minds seeing beyond our world of limitations and creating through imagination different species and stories boggling anything we ever thought. The stories here prove the writers included have done just that. They lay the backdrops of science and provide the fiction of imagination bringing the reader into other worlds and hopefully opening up their minds. The more you can imagine and wonder at, the better we all will.

... for the record, science fiction doesn't usually appeal to me. These stories do ... very nice. If these can turn me on, the book is definitely worth reading."

Bruce Blanchard, Book Reviewer
https://www.facebook.com/bruce.blanchard2

DRAWING FROM THE WELL

By Rachel Bollinger

A collection of parables, poems, and anecdotes to enhance your spiritual journey. Author, Rachel Bollinger walks you through her personal challenges and triumphs, referencing scripture and entertaining you as she walks closer to God.

Join her as she draws from her well of experience, faith, and victories on a journey of faith and discovery.

Reviews

We all journey through dark nights of the soul. In this lovely collection, Rachel shares some of her most challenging life experiences and how she coped and grew in grace through the unchanging Word of God. Rachel's memories, in story and verse, are honest, brave, and witty. I came away understanding that the grief I hold in my heart has a permitted place to live.

Susan V. Smith, Amazon Reviewer
https://amzn.to/2JuDfmz

Coming Soon from Left Hand Publishers:

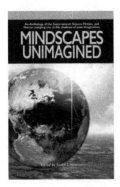

MINDSCAPES UNIMAGINED

Open the door to any genre and you will find places where the unimaginable and the unexplained collide with reality. These stories take you far past that point. From the unbelievable to the bizarre to the edge of real madness, you will travel to...

Mindscapes Unimagined

An international bevy of authors new and experienced weave tales both fantastic and exciting. This genre-bending collection of short stories blurs the line between what can be and what can be imagined. No monster, dimension, or mortal villain is off limits. When you are ready to risk sanity and sleep, start on the first page.